THE DUKE OF
TEMPLE STREET

The Duke of Temple Street
Copyright © 2025 Lynn Harrod

For information contact www.deerwoodpress.com

Book and Cover design by June Robina
Edited by William McCoy
Photos by Antonio Gravante and Choneschones

ISBN: 978-1-970506-01-3 (ePub edition)
ISBN: 978-1-970506-00-6 (Paperback edition)

First Edition: November 2025

WWW·DEERWOODPRESS·COM

THE DUKE OF TEMPLE STREET

a novel

LYNN HARROD

ALSO BY LYNN HARROD

Child of Imago

The Queen's Angel

Keepers of the Night Garden

Lucky Five

Of Gods and Devils and All In Between
Book One

For Terrance, my friend and mentor

1

Rules of Exchange

Where shall we begin? At what moment did I light the long fuse that wound its way to our end? The old man's office? No, we must go back further. The ice cream factory. The taco truck. The prison. The scrapyard. The desert airfield.

The tunnel. Of course.

Artists called it "golden hour," and so did he, for Los Angeles looked beautiful to Edgardo in its own ugly way. The gridlock of the 101 twinkled across the sunset like Christmas lights, a picturesque memory of December 2023. The towers of power in the Financial District loomed like silhouetted castles in the sky as a gentle rain began to fall. Street vendors in the labyrinth of Santee Alley beckoned, their knockoff treasures waiting to be discovered. In the heart of it all sat Union Station like the hub of the universe, with trains and buses and taxis bound for everywhere.

I always love driving through the city at dusk. The rush hour madness takes a breather, the sunset's golden aura looks surreal filtered through the dome of pollution, and the steady hum of my engine strikes me hypnotic as if magically timed with the rhythm of the landscape.

"El Pueblo de Nuestra Señora La Reina de Los Angeles de Porciuncula" roughly translates to "The Town of Our Lady the Queen of the Angels of the River's Small Portion." I'd always admired the full name of my beloved city and thought it shameful that we whittled it down to its bastardized abbreviation "L.A."

At a paltry 473 square miles, Los Angeles doesn't even crack the Top Ten list of biggest American cities, but if we ever seceded from the union, our economy would be the 19th largest in the world. With a quarter of a million active businesses, and the most minority-owned on the planet, L.A. has a net assessed valuation of $1.2 trillion. I study the figures daily, for I'm determined to take my cut.

No one knew Edgardo's love affair with the city or his obsession with its riches ripe for the taking. His older brother, Bram, saw him as a quiet family man. His children thought he was more interested in spreadsheets than family functions. Ex-wife Divinia assumed he preferred the controlled environments of boardrooms and offices. Sadly, he shared his poetic views with her only after their divorce was final.

As he drove his black Mercedes SLK through Downtown, his mind wandered to the journal he'd only occasionally updated, a chronicle that might never be seen. He hadn't yet decided if he'd ever entrust his memoirs – his confessions – to another soul. He simply recorded his life as a release, first detailed in his thoughts, then penned to paper, anything to quell the demons.

> *My name is Edgardo Rigo Duque. I'm 45 years old and have everything a man could want, though I still focus on the things I've lost and the goals just outside my reach. Call me a willing slave to endless ambition, a living cliché of the human condition.*
>
> *I'm starting this journal not to scribble down my life as a Filipino American, business owner, absent father, or abysmal husband, but to chronicle my secret parallel life as "The Duke." Men like me don't die in bed at a ripe old age. We stake our claims, swipe our fortunes, and fade into history. Unacceptable. I'll take my cut of history, too.*

The lights of the city flickered on as dusk turned to night, reflecting off the shimmering pavement, fresh from rain. Edgardo noticed each of them like thousands of fireflies awakening with the coming moon. They proved impossible to ignore as he continually noticed every minute change around him, striking a dull pain in his mind. Still, he beheld their beauty, the sight often starting his journal entries.

My first day in Los Angeles started 19 years ago at dusk on a night like tonight, with the sun disappearing behind Downtown's skyscrapers during a light rain. That's always been how I see Southern California, or "Low Cal" as my son puts it. The postcard views of sunny skies, crowded beaches, and miles of palm trees are for tourists. My hope is that these memoirs live long after my ashes are scattered across Mount Malabito, high atop the Philippine Islands. Someone needs to understand The Duke. Someone needs to put together what compelled me. If only Ozymandias had written a book before his empire crumbled to dust.

Edgardo often drifted into tangent memories, for he remembered literally everything. He had a hyperthymesic recall that granted him a genius-level I.Q. People referred to it as a photographic memory, but he could summon far more than visuals and could think ahead with equal clarity, almost as if he could foresee the near-future.

He'd just left a dinner meeting with his lawyer and was heading back to his office in the barrios of HiFi. Stopped at a red light, he stared at L.A.'s famous 2nd Street Tunnel awaiting him, its west entrance adorned with gleaming buttresses of glazed white tiles and a sparkling seasonal banner that read "Happy Holidays." The tunnel connected the high-rise heart of the city to one of its many clogged arteries, Temple Street, a four-mile thoroughfare that ran from Downtown through Little Tokyo and Historic Filipinotown – the locals called it "HiFi" – ending abruptly at the cement-lined Los Angeles River.

As he drove into the tunnel, Edgardo noticed a black Cadillac SUV behind him, its massive grille taking up a little too much space in his rearview mirror. At that hour, there was hardly any other traffic, which made the red Chevy Camaro in front of him also stand out.

The moment he turned his eyes to the classic muscle car, it screeched to a sudden stop, forcing him to slam the brakes in the middle of the tunnel, the SUV looming behind.

Of course, the tailgating Escalade pinned me in the second the Camaro stopped. I'd seen it coming, but hoped I was wrong. Things had been running smoothly for the past two years. A conflict now would be bad business. In hindsight, it was inevitable.

Edgardo reached under his dashboard and flipped a hidden kill switch, essentially bricking the engine, as four men emerged from the vehicles fore and aft, two from either direction. They wore gang colors, looked around to ensure no one else was coming down the tunnel, and approached his car, guns in hand. One of them, a young man from the Camaro, was beside his car in seconds. With no time to unlatch the pistol secured under his seat, Edgardo simply lowered his window and faced the scowling youth.

"Is there a problem?" Edgardo asked.

"Out of the car! Now, motherfucker!" The man stood short and stocky in a Raiders T-shirt, looked to be in his mid-20s, and spoke with a Filipino accent.

Edgardo opened the door and stepped out of his car, hands held at his shoulders. The Raider shoved him aside and sat behind the wheel, startled by the sight of two-dozen Post-It notes perfectly aligned across the dash, an odd task manager for any man, much less one with perfect recall. The Raider's partner, a thin boy barely seventeen, eyes partially covered by his shaggy black hair, frisked Edgardo and snatched his watch and wallet.

First question answered: They weren't out gunning for me. It was just a garden variety carjacking.

Edgardo scrutinized the gangsters' baggy clothing, guns, and tattoos peeking out from their sleeves. He recognized the distinct sun and stars from the Philippine flag, crudely burned into their forearms. He knew that tattoo well, just as he knew all the markings of the many criminal outfits of L.A.

Second question answered: They were with the Temple Street Boyz, a gang whose base of operations was a scrapyard by the river. The TSB was low down the pole, like rabid raccoons in a jungle full of tigers.

"What's the holdup?" the skinny younger man said to the Raider in Edgardo's car. He looked at their mark and at his two other comrades standing back at the SUV and Camaro. "You said this'd be easy, man."

"Shut the fuck up, Miguel," the Raider said, growing anxious as he struggled to turn over the engine. He winced when he realized he used his partner's name.

"Come on, Jorge, just start it up!"

Jorge Vega, wannabe alpha with the TSB. He was smart enough to know the security cameras were further apart that deep in the tunnel, providing blind spots, but not smart enough to unbrick my car. More importantly, he wasn't smart enough to realize who I was.

"What's going on?" Miguel said, looking down the tunnel. "Time's up, man! Let's get the fuck outta here!"

Miguel Hortiz, the baby of the gang, about the same age as my son, with the same desperate need to play the tough guy. In my business, I familiarized myself with every player, big and small, that might cross my path. I'd always figured it would be for business, not a robbery.

"Yo Jorge, let's bounce!" Miguel said, again nervously looking down the tunnel. He imagined a police cruiser appearing at any moment.

"I said shut the fuck up!" Jorge gritted his teeth every time his partner called him by name.

I couldn't let those amateurs open the trunk or take the car. There was too much at stake.

"What the fuck's up with your ride?" Jorge asked Edgardo. "It was running fine a minute ago."

The next minute played out in Edgardo's mind...

One: Fake out Jorge. End him.
Two: Use Miguel as a shield.
Three: Take out the remaining two at the front and rear.

Edgardo slid his thumb and forefinger over his belt and readied a small gold dagger hidden in the buckle. He tucked it in his palm, raised his arms, and walked back to Jorge at the car.

"It's tricky," Edgardo said as he knelt beside him. "You gotta wiggle the key halfway. I was going to take it to the dealer tomorrow, but being near Christmas they're booked solid..."

"That's right, you *was* gonna take it there, bitch."

"Here, let me show you how I do things..."

With frightening speed, Edgardo stabbed Jorge in the throat while covering his mouth, muffling his wild scream. He grabbed his gun from under the driver's seat, spun around, and pistol whipped Miguel while holding him upright as a human shield. He shot the Camaro driver twice, turned and shot the SUV driver as the gangster returned fire, hitting Miguel square in the chest.

Edgardo dropped Miguel's body to the road and stood alone in the tunnel. He'd just killed four men in seconds, his lone heartbeat pounding louder, echoing as he finished playing out the macabre minute in his mind.

It was just one possible outcome he'd imagined, and it was about to unfold.

"Here, let me show you how I do things..."

"Hold up!" Miguel called out in time as he sifted through Edgardo's wallet. The two other men at the Escalade and Camaro listened, confused. "Jorge, you know who this is? You're sittin' in The Duke's ride!"

"Bullshit," Jorge said in a hushed tone as those feared words "The Duke" landed hard in his mind. He immediately pulled his hands from the steering wheel as if it were burning hot and stared up at Edgardo with a sudden dread, feeling his heels teetering on the edge of a cliff. Though he now realized he'd chosen the wrong car to jack that evening, he couldn't have foreseen the bloody melee Edgardo had just been contemplating.

"Yeah, says right here," Miguel said, reading the driver's license in the wallet. "Edgardo Rigo Duque on Temple Street." He caught Edgardo's eyes with a sudden, sharp fear. "Oh, shit... I won't remember your address or nothin'... I mean..."

"You really think that's my address?" Edgardo asked. He subtly sheathed his gold dagger back into his belt buckle and offered a warm smile. "That's an old noodle shop, been closed for years."

Lynn Harrod

"Old noodle shop... right... I mean, 'course it is."

Jorge stepped out of the Mercedes, his tough guy facade gone. "This was my call. My bad."

"No harm done," Edgardo said. "Just business, right Jorge?"

"H-huh?"

"Jorge Vega?"

"Sure, yeah." Jorge felt unnerved that The Duke somehow knew his name. "No need to tell Calixto about this, right?"

"The way I see it, none of us were here. Keys in the ignition?"

Jorge sheepishly nodded. He waved his hand, gesturing to his men that the heist was a bust. Miguel returned the wallet to Edgardo.

"Thank you, Miguel," Edgardo said.

"What?"

"Miguel Hortiz, right?"

The teen's heart stopped for a second. "Man, we didn't know! I swear! We didn't know who you was!"

"You know now, Miguel Hortiz of the TSB, and you'll remember me, just as I'll remember you."

Miguel nodded and backed away as if the friendly man before him was The Devil himself. All four gangsters returned to their cars and drove off without another word. Edgardo stood his ground and watched them leave.

First Rule of Exchange: Avoid escalation unless necessary. When it is necessary, it's either all them or it's all me.

Edgardo looked down the dark tunnel and saw headlights in the distance. He sat in his car, cleaned his glasses with a cloth, and started his engine. Before shifting into Drive, he put on an earpiece and made a phone call.

Second Rule of Exchange: Always sweep away your footprints.

His assistant Felix answered the call. "Good evening, Amo."

"Good evening, Felix. I need you to wipe the cameras at the entrances of the 2nd Street tunnel."

"You got it," Felix said. "How far back?"

"Ten minutes will suffice."

"Thirty would be cleaner."

"Good man."

Edgardo hung up and drove down the length of the tunnel, blowing past a red light at the east end, turning left on Temple Street.

Third Rule of Exchange: Remember everyone and everything because the man you didn't notice, the detail you missed, those are what kill you.

2

Sanctuary

Mozart's Piano Concerto No. 21 floated down from speakers built into the ceiling of the lavish Mediterranean-style bedroom. As the music poured forth, the blackout curtains of the wall-length window parted, revealing a hilltop view of all Los Angeles. The early morning sun exposed the entire room, including the weary man in its center.

Edgardo woke up in his king-sized bed, nestled between layers of pastel silk satin and unbleached Egyptian cotton. Despite the soothing music in the air and the cool, soft fabric on his skin, he stared at the ceiling with sweat beading on his brow. He clinched his hands into tight fists to control the trembling he always awoke to. Averse to medicine and rehab, anything he felt outside of his control, he needed the distraction of his morning routine to settle his nerves and prepare him for the day.

After downing the tall glass of water waiting for him on the bedside table, he pushed himself into his home gym and lifted heavy dumbbells to another Mozart piece.

Piano Concerto No. 27 – Edgardo's favorite among the master's final works – could be heard throughout his exquisite home, each room wired to the built-in audio system. The intensity and tempo of music influences a workout, pumping up one's testosterone and adrenaline, but instead of the thumping beat of club dance, rock, or rap, he chose the gentle passages of the old world. Mozart, Monteverdi, Handel, Beethoven, Wagner, Vivaldi. Their beautiful masterpieces challenged him, as if their mild melodies tried to pull him down and tuck him warmly back into bed.

A loud, driving beat can fuel physical effort, offering easier gains. Unacceptable. Exercise is training, training is work, and for work to be effective, it should feel like an uphill climb through deep snow. Growth is a response to resistance. Each obstacle, each disadvantage, everything that stands in your way is a gift, an opportunity for greatness. The vines that see little sun, whose roots must reach further into a steep hillside, they are the vines that produce the richest, densest, most sought after wine.

After an hour of three sets of 12 repeated nine times, Edgardo replaced his weights and stood in front of his bathroom mirror, still catching his breath. He finished his shaving ritual of 14 downstrokes and eight upstrokes with two splashes of cold water across his face. Scrutinizing his reflection, he grimaced at the many scars on his lean, muscled torso and applied concealer down a vicious jagged line that wrapped around the base of his neck, the one old wound his suits, collared shirts, and vests couldn't completely cover. Bare-chested, he saw the black

Lynn Harrod

feathers tattooed atop his shoulders, merely the tips of the large Philippine eagle that spanned his upper back.

Belying his healthy physique, Edgardo reached into his medicine cabinet, past several bottles of prescription pills, for a silver flask of bourbon. He used the woodsy spirit to wash down three pills: one for depression, one for migraines, one for muscular pain. It only took a single swallow to get them all down, but he sneaked another quick swig before quickly tossing the flask to the bathroom rug as if it were sharp with electricity. He knew well that his morning flask had to leave his hands in a hurry or risk being emptied in seconds.

Returning to his bedroom, Edgardo stopped to admire the grand view his panoramic window offered. Alone on two private acres atop a hill above Highland Park, a former gangland neighborhood turned art community, the high-end residence served as his personal sanctuary. A short list of confidants knew he lived there, but only his brother Bram had ever stepped foot in the custom home, walked through its five bedrooms, long halls, four-car garage, gourmet kitchen, and sprawling back yard. Bram would get the chance again soon enough, and he'd be surprised by the extensive remodeling over the past ten years.

Edgardo stepped into his walk-in closet, nearly large enough to be the house's eighth room. Its racks were lined with dozens of tailored suits and dress shirts, all categorized for specific moments or stages of business. He sifted through the fine clothes, slid them aside, and pulled out a faded set of mechanic's coveralls, striped gray and blue.

Bloom and Plume Coffee stood on Temple Street within the southeastern wedge of Historic Filipinotown. The quaint, upscale coffeehouse occupied an old storefront and resembled a museum's gift shop, selling colorful clothing, artwork, and glassware besides fresh roasted brew and ten-dollar avocado toast.

Edgardo sat on the Bloom's sidewalk patio. He stood out in his old coveralls, surrounded by hipsters in trendy outfits typing on laptops or tapping on phones. Though his own high fashion hid beneath his faded facade, he was also writing, his tool of choice a simple pocket notebook bound in worn leather.

My morning Double Americano at the Bloom and Plume is the only time of the day where I'm truly at peace. For ten minutes, I forget everything – even The Duke – and simply observe the neighborhood.

He looked up from his journal and watched the world turn. A woman jogged across the street, passing a man loading a panel van, while a group of boys rode past on BMX bikes, popping wheelies down the sidewalk. Edgardo held up his phone and took a photo of the everyday scene before returning to his notepad.

Most days, the street scene resembles a symphony. I order 128 milligrams of caffeine and off I go. Other days, it looks like rats in a maze, so I add 120 milliliters of dark rum and slither away. I didn't know it then, but that morning landed squarely in "other days."

A young woman brought him his usual order, a pair of Americanos, slightly sweet, in 16 oz. to-go cups. The cheery Latina barista wore a green apron and red knit cap that held her long, curly hair in place. She'd introduced herself as Monica Torres nearly a year before. With her welcoming smile and morning small talk, she felt like the closest thing to a friend Edgardo had, someone outside of family who didn't work for him or want a piece of him. Of course, she knew nothing of Edgardo's secret life.

"Sorry for the wait, Eddie," Monica said. "I'm training someone. Holiday help."

"I saw. Poor girl's in over her head, doesn't know her way around an espresso machine."

"Neither did I at one time."

"With Mocha Master Monica, she'll be just fine." Edgardo smiled with the awkward humor, part of his public persona.

"Not many mochas right now. Pumpkin Spice is our top seller through Christmas. Folks can't get enough."

"Of course."

"I'd suggest you try one, but I know how devoted you are to your Americanos."

Calling him "devoted" was a nice way of pointing out his severe OCD – Obsessive-Compulsive Disorder – his ingrained need for daily rituals. She saw it in the way he always sat in the same chair, always faced north, always had a folded napkin to the left of his cup, perpendicular two inches to the edge of the table. But there was something new about him that morning.

"You got new glasses," Monica said. "So chic. Did Santa come early?"

"No, I treated myself," Edgardo said, thinking quickly. He usually wore his simple pair of no-name horn-rimmed eyeglasses on his way to work but had cracked a lens over the weekend. He'd hoped no one would notice his premium pair. "Too flashy?"

"They're a little much with that outfit," she said. "Cartier, right? Costs more than my scooter."

"Cartier? Me?" Edgardo laughed as he took off his glasses and looked at them as if for the first time. "I think they're 'Kartiarr,' some cheap knockoff. I got 'em in Santee Alley."

"Okay, that makes sense. I figured a mechanic in designer frames sounded crazy."

"My W2 agrees."

Monica laughed and returned to the espresso machine, where her new hire struggled with a backlog of orders for Pumpkin Spice lattes.

3

The Garage

Otto's Automotive was a four-bay full-service shop that stood at the north end of HiFi, a bustling business that contrasted the struggling inner-city neighborhood. A glittery wreath with red ribbons hung centered on the back wall above the oil pumps, the only trace of holiday decor on the property. A Jeepney sat on the corner of the lot, a pink-and-white vintage Jeep converted to service as a small food truck. "Max's Eats" offered authentic Filipino entrees and treats.

My businesses reside in Historic Filipinotown, one of five
Asian Pacific Islander boroughs in L.A. 24,000 citizens
live in this one-square-mile stretch running down the
spine of Little Tokyo.

Edgardo carried a clipboard to help him oversee the work in the bays, most of which came from long-time regulars who'd brought their cars and trucks to the old corner lot long before he took ownership.

I reopened the family garage after my stepfather, Otto Harrison, retired to the Bay Area with my mother, long before they later returned to Low Cal to be closer to their grandkids. For the comfort of his customers, both old and new, I kept his name on the sign, though I doubt he'd approve of the new customer base.

With two coffees in hand, Edgardo approached a service van pulling into Bay Two, a white "Waldo's Ice Cream" truck that visited them weekly. Two mechanics joined him to meet the incoming customer. Henry "Hank" Brighton, a stout White man in his mid-60's with a Santa Claus beard and mustache, took the clipboard from Edgardo as he always did, and glanced at the day's agenda. Candace "Candy" Claypool stood behind him, a young Irish-American woman adorned with crude Celtic tattoos, wearing coveralls and welder's googles. She examined the boxy vehicle, adorned with painted flowers and balloons, as it came to a stop.

"Truck's three hours late," Hank said. "This is becoming a regular thing, Ed."

"Yeah, I know. Have some coffee, Old Man."

"You know I need it."

"Don't we both."

Edgardo handed Hank one of the two steaming Americanos, another part of his morning routine. Hank took a sip without another thought.

Hank Brighton worked for my stepfather and had been with me since I took over the garage. On my short list of confidence, loyalty, and trust, Hank sits at the top. His cynicism is always refreshing and often helpful.

"We need to nip this in the bud," Hank said, sipping his coffee. "Trucks coming later and later, starting to feel like disrespect."

"It's fine, Hank," Edgardo said. "Maybe it'll be worth the wait."

"Sure, sure," Candy said, "and maybe it's actually full of ice cream."

Hank had found young Candy Claypool bruised and unconscious, on the edge of an overdose in his backyard shed. He took her in, raised her as his own, and taught her everything he knows about cars and our "side business," for better or worse. From what I know about Candy, wild horses couldn't pull her from that old man's side.

"What's that fool still doing in there?" she asked. "Probably getting lit."

"Take it easy, Candy," Hank said. "Where's your Christmas spirit? He's new."

"Says who?"

"Says Mr. Waldo himself."

"Sheeeet," Candy said. "Ten bucks says he's high as a kite."

Ricky Washington, the newly hired driver of the truck, a Black man in his thirties, stepped out with a pronounced limp. The nervous, skinny driver, with dreadlocks, dark sunglasses, and baggy street clothes, was clearly in over his head. He looked around to ensure he was in the right place.

Ricky Wash. Drove for Amazon, fired for assaulting a customer over a late delivery. I don't entirely blame him for choosing violence. That Doberman mangled his leg while its owner watched with a sadistic, racist grin.

"How can we help you, sir?" Hank asked.

Ricky ignored Hank and turned to Edgardo. With customers nearby, he carefully chose his words.

"I'm looking to get one of your premium tune-ups," Ricky said, trying to remember his instructions word-for-word.

"At this hour?" Edgardo said. "We're backed up. Not sure if we can take you right now."

"Come on, man! I was delayed! Shit happens, you know?"

"Shit happens here, too, amigo," Candy said, "but time is money. You screw up, it costs us, makes us look bad."

"Yo, who the fuck's talking to you?" Ricky said.

Edgardo gestured for Candy to leave them. She walked away, flipping off the driver as she headed into the next bay.

"Candy may be blunt," Edgardo said, "but she's right. Arriving this late is bad business. Unacceptable. Come back tomorrow."

Ricky Wash cursed to himself and lowered his head as if he were doomed. Edgardo pulled him aside, away from the other customers.

"Little advice?" Edgardo asked. "Don't stop to get high at your girl's house on the way. I smelled skunk weed and Emporio Armani Eau De Parfum on you the moment you walked up. I promise, you do not want to drop the ball with me."

"No, sir." Ricky realized his error but wallowed in his predicament. He didn't bother denying the accusation, eerily accurate right down to his girlfriend's fragrance. "Fuck, this is gonna cost me big."

"Relax." Edgardo succumbed to Ricky's plight and nodded at Hank to open the rear doors of the ice cream truck. "Ricky, right? You're new to Waldo's."

"Not new, exactly, but it's my first route."

"Well, Ricky, you're new to me, so I'm gonna cut you a break. Consider it an early Christmas gift. I'll take the cargo off your hands this time, but be on point from now on or the next delivery is on the house, and we both know Mr. Waldo wouldn't like that."

"No, sir. I mean... yes, sir."

"And show my people the same respect you show me. In this business, you get what you give."

"Yes, sir." Unlike the tunnel thieves, Ricky knew exactly who he was dealing with before arriving, something that made him more nervous with each mile closer to the garage. In their world, The Duke was feared almost as much as his boss, Mr. Waldo.

Hank entered the rear of the ice cream truck to find it stacked high with cases of "Tornado" candy bars. He tapped a quick count. "Forty cases, as ordered." He opened a case, revealing actual chocolate bars. After pulling out two handfuls of Tornados, he reached the real cargo: assault rifles and pistols encased in bubble wrap.

"Now what?" Ricky asked. "I mean, you do your thing with them, but what do I do?"

"There's a cheerful pink-and-white food truck parked on the corner," Edgardo said, pointing out the Jeepney. "Tell them you want a Halo-Halo." He turned to Hank. "Anything to add?"

"Palabok," the old man said.

"Halo-Halo and Palabok," Edgardo said to the unnerved driver. "Got that?"

"Ohh-kaay." Confused, Ricky pulled a pen from his jacket pocket and wrote the strange words on his palm. "Hello-Hello and... Pally Bock? What are these codes for?"

"They're codes for Filipino food, dumbass," Hank said.

Ricky finally understood. Edgardo took him by his shoulders and guided him out of the garage bay.

"Halo-Halo for me, Palabok for Hank," Edgardo said, handing him forty dollars. "Get yourself an Adobo Banh Mi and a Sarsi root beer. Trust me on this. Go have lunch while we sort through everything. It's in both our best interests that every gun and bullet is accounted for."

"I promise, Mr. Duke, it's all there. I would never skim on the side."

"I know you wouldn't. I have a good feeling about you, Ricky."

Relieved, Ricky Wash headed for the Jeepney outside. The cook, a young Filipino man with thick eyeglasses, saw the new customer and waved him over. Edgardo held up his phone and took a photo, something he often did after a conversation had ended.

Hank brought him a case of Tornado bars from Ricky's truck and pulled out a pistol. "Cleaned and oiled, ready to go. Serials have been filed, but I'll have Candy scrub 'em again to be sure. The girl works fast."

"She's certainly proven that," Edgardo said. "Let me know if the numbers line up. I'll be at the lounge."

"Wish I could lounge with you."

Edgardo looked at his old friend. It had been months since they spent any time together outside of work. "Let's do it. This weekend. Joey will whip up something special."

"Joey Gallo's famous 'Vacation In A Glass,' right?"

"That's what the big man calls it," Edgardo said with a laugh, "but Felix came up with the name." He handed Hank his clipboard, returning control of their side business.

"So, today's the day they turn your brother loose?" Hank asked.

"Tomorrow."

"I'll be counting the minutes. It'll be good to see Bram again."

"I hope you're right."

Hank frowned. "Don't go there, Ed. Can't you be happy to see someone for once?"

"You know I'm always happy to see you, Old Man."

The two friends shared a slightly uncomfortable laugh as Edgardo took off his coveralls and hung them on the wall, revealing his casual suit underneath.

"Honestly, I'm not so sure," Edgardo said. "Ten years inside can change a man."

"That kinda change ain't always bad. I'm walking, talking proof."

"No, Hank. You were an angel going into the war, and you were an angel coming out."

"If you say so."

Edgardo walked out of the bay to his awaiting Mercedes.

"Hey, what about your Halo-Halo?" Hank asked.

"I ordered it for Miss Candy. She's the one with the sweet tooth."

4

Corazon

Filipino-Americans were instrumental in establishing the first tiki lounges throughout America, starting with the famous L.A. watering hole "Don The Beachcomber" in 1934. Continuing the legacy, the Corazon Lounge stood as an upscale tropical bar, a sleek, modern HiFi institution, just a few blocks from Otto's Automotive on Temple Street.

Ang Corazon Tiki Lounge was opened by Divinia and me back in our salad days. I thought it might bring us closer. How naive I was. I often think I keep it open for her, for what we used to have. Even though our marriage didn't last, our dream would live on. There might be no room for sentiment in business, but at least it still turns a profit.

Lynn Harrod

Edgardo entered the bar, decorated with a dense nautical theme. The counter resembled the side of a tugboat. The "roof" of the counter comprised palm fronds and lanterns, and pillars were carved into totem poles. At that early hour, the lounge was closed, the throngs of patrons to come later in the evening.

Prepping for the evening was Joey "The Rose" Gallo, a 45-year-old Italian giant with slicked back hair, a goatee, and a permanent grimace. Joey's gentle name came from the large wine stain across the left side of his face, a sight he often attributed to his fierce days in the ring, tongue in cheek.

Joey The Rose was a professional boxer, paid to take one too many falls before they closed the books on him. I saved him from the wrath of the HK-9 when he decided to actually win for once. He's been my most trusted muscle ever since.

"Breakfast smoothie?" Joey asked. "Something I'm tinkering with. Vitamin C, Vitamin B12, scoop of hemp protein. I threw in a few juniper berries, you know, for a little Christmas flavor."

"Breakfast is no longer being served, Joey," Edgardo said, sitting at a table, checking his phone for new texts. "Wild Turkey, please."

Joey grabbed a glass and a bottle of Wild Turkey Kentucky straight bourbon whiskey, the same aged spirit that had sat on his boss's bathroom sink earlier, but stopped short of pouring. "Kinda early, ain't it?" he said in his deep, throaty voice.

"Joey, are we going to put on this sad theater every time I walk in?"

"Sun's out, barely past noon. A little early for bourbon, jus' sayin'. Can't blame me for lookin' out for you, Ed."

"Is this Ang Corazon Tiki Lounge or is it Jamba Juice?"

"It's your bar," Joey said, folding. "Wild Turkey, it is."

"Make it a double."

Joey knew what that meant.

"Ah, big meeting," the giant said as he poured a double shot of bourbon, neat. He brought it to Edgardo, setting it down on a napkin between his many yellow Post-It notes stuck across the table.

"Have I become boring?" Edgardo asked. "Predictable?"

"Boring, never. Predictable, yes. You always order a double whenever you got an important meet coming up."

"I'm overseeing an exchange, sure."

"Want me to tag along?"

"Unnecessary."

Edgardo sipped his bourbon, a contrast to his slamming it down earlier. He knew his facade was flimsy, that Joey was aware of his struggle, but still kept up his supposed casual enjoyment of liquor out of habit more than deception.

Joey returned to the bar and continued preparing for the evening, cutting fruit and arranging glassware.

"So, small-timers?" Joey asked. He knew he should have let it go, trusting his boss's instincts, but couldn't help himself.

"The Nines and the Wolves."

Joey tossed down his paring knife and looked at his boss and friend, incredulous. "Fuck that, I'm coming."

"No, Joey, you are not."

"The hell I'm not."

"Unacceptable."

"You're gonna sideline me while you financialize between those two tribes of maniacs? You can't be serious, Ed."

"I appreciate the concern, but I can handle it."

"With a belly full of bourbon?"

Edgardo put down his pen, perpendicular two inches to the edge of the table, and looked his friend in the eye. "I said I can handle it."

"I know you can handle things, but..." Joey shook his head in defeat, dropping the topic. "I tried."

"Keep trying, my friend. It's part of what makes you... you."

"What good that does," Joey muttered.

"Money in the back?"

"Three-hundred large, clean. When I picked it up, I had no idea it was from the fuckin' Nines. I shoulda known, seeing six pissed off Filipino runts pour out of a van."

"Everyone's a runt to you, Joey. And it was a simple pickup. No need to know who's who."

"I strongly disagree. With those vultures, you gotta watch your six."

"And my twelve."

They heard a knock-knock at the door, and Joey jogged to answer it. He let in a blonde delivery man with a dolly stacked high with boxes. The man was tall and built, but Joey still dwarfed him.

"You got the right place?" Joey asked, not recognizing him.

"I got booze," the man said. "You got customers. This is Corazon, right?"

Joey nodded for him to enter with his goods. He looked for a second man, but there was only the one.

"What have we today?" Edgardo asked as he continued to move notes about his table.

The blonde man looked at the invoice atop the boxes. "Five cases of merlot, five of chard, six cab, three kegs, three cases of cordials."

"I also requested glassware."

"Yep, got a couple of boxes of glasses and whatnot."

"Good man. New route?"

"Nah, I'm just covering for my brother," the man said.

"I thought Paul was an only child?" Edgardo asked.

"Well, brother-*in-law*, but he hates that last bit. Family is family, he says."

"Sounds like Paul," Joey said.

"Mr. 'Most Eligible Batchelor' finally married my sister. They're going to Maui for an extended honeymoon, so I'm working his route for a few weeks."

"This close to Christmas?" Edgardo asked.

"Boss said it's now or never. Vacation days don't roll over with the new year."

"Understandable."

"I told him he waited too long and... well, you know how he is." The delivery man noted Edgardo's flat tone and stare, his straightforward, almost "spectrum" way of speaking. "Paul and I are kin for a few days, and already I'm working for the guy."

"Brothers look out for each other," Edgardo said with a slight smile. "Where are you from?"

"I normally work in the valley, from Porter Ranch to Burbank. Today, you're my first stop on my first street."

"We're honored. Welcome to HiFi."

"I appreciate that Mr. Duque, Mr. Gallo."

"Hey, Brother-In-Law," Joey said in his bellowing voice. "Let's cut the chit-chat and unload the goods back here."

"No need to be rude, Joey." Edgardo stood and faced the blond man. "What's your name?"

"Brett." He set his dolly down and offered a handshake.

"Welcome to HiFi, Brett," Edgardo said, taking his hand. "My name is Edgardo Duque. You already met my bar manager."

"Joe, right?" Brett asked.

Lynn Harrod

"Joey," the big man said. He grew impatient at the sight of the stacked boxes still sitting by the door. "Come on, plenty of time to get to know each other while we load up."

Edgardo shrugged at Brett. "In this bar, what Joey says is law."

"I'll keep that in mind," Brett said.

As Joey guided Brett and his delivery to the back room, Edgardo raised his phone to take another photo, noting that Brett was the second "new" person to cross his path that day.

5

Divinia

Edgardo drove through the city, the urban neighborhoods and outer suburbs falling behind in his rearview mirror as he headed northeast into the desert. After forty-five minutes on the highway, the road cut through a desolate industrial landscape before reaching an endless expanse.

His usual choices of smooth jazz, classical music, or talk radio were on hold as he spoke through his sound system to a frustrated woman.

"I'm a little busy at the moment, Divinia," he said.

"You know I hate when you say that," Divinia Duque said. His ex-wife knew him well, heard his tone as more evasive than apologetic. "A little busy, indeed."

"You, of all people, should understand what it means to be a little busy."

Divinia spoke through a Bluetooth earpiece from within a television studio. Her half of the soundstage was outfitted with three walls of a country kitchen and adjoining rustic dining room, the space bustling as her crew prepared to shoot another episode of her new cooking show. She sat in a make-up chair while two women touched up her hair and eyes. Even before the layer of pancake makeup, the 40-year-old Filipina-American looked an easy 30, quite an achievement considering her long work hours and constant stress. She smoothed her apron over her pantsuit as she scrutinized her face in the mirror, cursing every wrinkle as if they'd be magnified tenfold by the cameras.

"'A little busy' sounds patronizing," Divinia said, "like you're making breakfast and don't want to burn the toast."

The contempt in her voice irritated him, as if his daily work was less important than her grand ambitions. "Okay, I'm a lotta busy, just like you over there, standing on the shoulders of Martha Stewart and Gordon Ramsey."

"How little you understand my world," she said. "Surely, you know why I'm calling?"

"Chris has already forgiven me. I told her I couldn't make it and she was fine. She said it was 'just another school award.' She's a bright girl, gets a new one each week."

"My God, you are so out of touch, Eddie. We're not talking about Christiana. This is about Carlo. You remember your son, right?"

"What about Carlo?"

"He has a sports awards ceremony at eight. I reminded you last night, asked if you'd be there, and you said 'Yes.' Stupid me, I thought yes meant yes."

Edgardo shut his eyes tight. His son's big night slipped from his radar.

My well-meaning ex-wife Divinia did tell me about Carlo's football ceremony the night before, but I was five inches into a bottle of Scotch when I got the text. Of course, I said yes. If she'd asked if unicorn meat was juicy, I would have said yes.

"His sports awards are only twice a year, Eddie," Divinia said.

"You don't think I know that?"

"I don't know, do you? You're the genius, not me. More important, are you going?"

Edgardo hated when she threw his unusual intellect in his face, as if he weren't allowed a single mistake. He often refused to admit he forgot family events, for it would further paint him as an ignorant, negligent father, something he feared might be true. "It wasn't in my day planner, if that's what you're asking."

"You can't find a way to fit your children into that precious day planner?"

"Carlo made it clear he doesn't want me there."

"And you buy that?" she asked, incredulous. "You really think an angry teenager doesn't want his father there to see him awarded MVP?"

"MVP?"

"If anything, it's his fantasy to show you what great things he can accomplish when you're not around."

"He can catch a ball and run it down a manicured field, and that's a great accomplishment for everyone to gather around? Should I pop champagne?" He instantly regretted his flippant remark.

"Unfuckinbelievable," she said, lowering her voice to keep the passing crew from overhearing. "It's a great accomplishment to *him*. That's all that matters."

"Agreed," Edgardo said with a sigh. He fumbled through the glove box for a stack of Post-Its, but left it be, keeping his hands on the wheel. Traveling at 80 mph down the highway, with not a minute to spare, he'd have to remember the event without the aid of his notes. While even the most trivial details were instantly cemented in his brain for life, important short-term events often escaped him. "You're right, Divinia. It slipped my mind. I know it's a big night for Carlo. I'll be there."

"That's all I wanted to hear, Eddie," she said. "That's what I wanted to hear five minutes ago."

"Now you heard it."

"What about Christmas?"

"Do you even have to ask?"

"Yes, Eddie. Yes, I do. You barely showed your face for ten minutes last year."

I understood her frustration. The year prior, I had a last-minute meet with the AFA – the Asian Family Assassins – on Christmas Eve. I brought several bags of wrapped presents for the kids, but had to duck out before dinner was served. I assumed my lavish gifts would quell their need for my presence, but I've since realized that all they wanted was my undivided attention, something I've failed to provide since they were out of diapers.

Of all the things a man can give his family, his time is more valuable than any trinket or trendy gizmo, for time is finite, the one thing an absent father can never get back. It's a lesson I should have learned from my own unresolved childhood.

"Can you call him now?" she asked. "Congratulate him about being MVP, even if he isn't *your* MVP, because you just don't give a shit."

"That's harsh, Divinia, even from you."

"Harsh is the only way I can reach you lately. Point is, our son needs you, even if he'd never admit it. It's like he's throwing footballs at you all day, all week, and all you need to do is catch one once in a while."

Edgardo's memory flashed back to an earlier time, when his marriage was still intact and his kids were too young to notice their father's increased absence. He recalled a picturesque day in Griffith Park. Divinia had set out a lavish picnic of croissant sandwiches, pasta salad, and pastries around thermal bottles of coffee and cocoa. Seven-year-old Chris – Christina Duque – built a house of playing cards on the park table. His eight-year-old son Carlo tossed a football with him, absent-mindedly throwing it at his sister's "castle." The boy stood speechless, frozen in fear, as his sister stifled tears. Edgardo pretended to be angry and tackled his son to the ground. His daughter piled on in laughter and fake rage. Divinia smiled at their silly horseplay.

It felt like a lifetime ago.

Chris was now a still-forgiving 16.

Carlo was now a bitter, distant 17.

"So, you're going to call him?" Divinia asked, jolting him back to the present and his defensive tone.

"I'm about to have a meeting."

"You're always about to have a meeting! Can't you cut into it?"

With anyone else, Edgardo would have total control, quick answers to sudden problems, but with his ex, he fell back to another poor, overly explained excuse. In that instance, it happened to be true.

"Divinia, if even one insignificant detail goes south at this meeting, there will be bloody murder. You'll have to dig up my body in the desert."

If only she knew how serious his words were.

If only she knew about The Duke.

"Yeah, I know, 'All Business, All The Time.' That's still your little mantra, isn't it?" She felt her makeup trail down her left cheek. "Shit, Eddie, you got me so worked up my eyeliner is runny from sweat!"

Edgardo's remorse dissolved. He'd had his fill of parental guilt and his ex-wife's holier-than-thou stance, deserved as it may have been.

"Don't you dare let them see you sweat!" he said. "Don't let them see a single hair out of place! The Gourmet Travel Network might kill your contract and you can wave bye-bye to Martha and Gordon!"

"No, GTN values me. They know I can be trusted to keep *my* obligations."

"Uh huh. Mother of The Year. Now that you I've told you I intend to keep my obligations, that I actually do give about a shit my kids, I have to go. I have business to tend to."

"Don't you dare let them see you sweat, Eddie! Whoever you're meeting with might decide to kill your contract and bury you in the desert!"

Divinia hung up, prompting Edgardo to shut off the stereo in frustration, punching it with the butt of his palm. He reached into the glove box again, sifting past the many stacks of Post-it notes, until he felt the silver flask beneath them. After staring at it for a moment, he shoved it back in and slammed the cover shut.

Divinia couldn't know how on-the-money our words were, our remarks of bloody murder and burying bodies in the desert. In my line of work, a drop of sweat gives the other man control. A brief expression of doubt or fear can bring everything crashing down like Christiana's house of cards.

Lynn Harrod

6

The Hangar

Halfway between the desert towns of Lancaster and Barstow, California, nearly two hours northeast of Edgardo's familiar L.A. streets, sat Anders Butler Airfield, nearly invisible on the horizon at dusk. The property comprised an 1,800-meter-long runway of cracked pavement and a simple 70-foot-wide hangar of weathered corrugated steel, all surrounded by rocks and shrubs disappearing with the fading daylight. The airfield's era of private service long behind it, Butler now housed storage for the Mojave Desert Air Quality Management District, though there was still room for the occasional light aircraft that flew under the radar, both literally and figuratively.

Edgardo drove up to the hangar and parked beside its west wall. The steel structure's massive door stood open, the only way in or out. A single-prop plane sat inside, while a luxury sedan and two motorcycles were parked out front. He knew the machines and their owners who were waiting for his arrival.

2023 Lexus LS-F Sport sedan. 2019 Harley Fat Boy 114. 2020 Harley Soft Tail. I knew exactly who to expect. A luxury car and two bikes meant between four and six men. Hopefully, they respected my rules against coming armed, but none of us are that naive.

After one last look at his array of Post-it notes across the dash, Edgardo stepped out of his car, opened the trunk, and removed a leather briefcase and large duffle bag. He spoke into a microphone hidden in his suit, tucked under his jacket collar.

"You with me, Carlo?" he asked, instantly realizing his error.

"What was that, Amo?" Felix said, his voice coming in clear through Edgardo's earpiece. "Carlo?"

As I readied myself for the meeting, the image of my family's salad days still flashed in my mind. I'd mistakenly called my assistant "Carlo" three times over the past six years, for I'd come to regard him fondly. It's not enough to have an immaculate memory. One must have mastery. Control. Perhaps I never would. Being a genius is as much a curse as a gift.

"I'm sorry, Felix. You hear me?"

"Perfectly. I'm in position."

"Good man. I just parked, going in now."

"Luck be with you, Amo."

"Luck be with us both." Edgardo checked his pulse, felt his heart racing. He looked up at the emerging starry sky, took a deep breath, and walked into the old hangar.

Upon entering, he spotted four anxious men standing in pairs on either side of the space, the small aircraft between them. They locked eyes with Edgardo as he headed toward a card table at the plane's nose.

At the plant's port side stood two White leather-clad bikers.

Cyrus "C.B." Bernard, a 55-year-old "Alpha" desert warrior, wore full leathers and aviator glasses over his weathered face. The crest of The Wolf Pack MC (motorcycle club) adorned the back of his jacket, a ferocious wolf's head engulfed in flames. With him was his "Beta," Timothy "Mace" Mason, the 30-year-old Sergeant At Arms of the gang, wearing an identical jacket or "cut."

C.B. stood perfectly still, a toothpick clinched in his teeth.

Mace paced in a circle, impatient, casually flipping a butterfly knife like a fidget toy.

Cyrus Bernard and Timothy Mason of The Wolf Pack MC. I'd worked with their Alpha "C.B." before, a smart and trustworthy man, but his Beta wolf and man-at-arms "Mace" was new to me, and new is always a red flag, an arrogant cub out to prove himself. I found it curious that C.B. would bring him to such a pivotal exchange.

Across from the bikers, two Filipino men with stone faces wore blazers over matching slacks and clashing Air Jordans. They stood at the plane's starboard side.

Rommel "Rom" Basilio was a seasoned 60. He smoked a Fortune cigarette and listened to jazz on earbuds, seemingly without a care. His young assistant, Nino Timbol, was a tender 35 and fully alert on behalf of his distracted boss. Like his counterpart, Mace, Nino also paced about in wait.

Rommel Basilio and Nino Timbol of the Mga Hari sa Kalle 9 gang – The 9 Street Kings – better known as HK-9 or simply "The Nines." We'd traded many times, but always between us, so that evening's business was unprecedented. Brokering for two rival gangs was always a tricky thing. Most nights, that hangar would be alive with gunfire.

Rom checked the time on his gold watch, pulled off his earbuds, and handed them to his assistant. Rom spoke with a formal Filipino accent that poorly hid his street roots. "Eight o'clock to the minute," he said to Edgardo. "So precise. How long were you waiting outside before you strolled in here? Honestly."

"Just arrived," Edgardo said. "Honestly. All hail Google Maps."

"Sorry for the obscene location. It was the One Percenters' ridiculous idea."

C.B. let that slight go. It took more than a simple jab to light the old roughneck's fuse. Instead, he responded in his usual thick, friendly Southern accent. "Better here than down in your territory. Lotta eyes in that city rit' now."

"And this desert," Rom said, "this airstrip, is it not your territory?"

"You bet your ass it is, but there ain't no bugs up in here."

"Oh, I know. My men did a sweep."

Mace flipped his butterfly knife shut, unable to contain his contempt. "Good on them," he said. "You Asian boys is always so thorough."

"Someone must be."

"What the fuck's that supposed to mean?"

Nino intervened, like a lawyer keeping balance, always trying to build a bridge. "Let's all calm down," he said in his forced tone of calm and reason. "I'm sure we can all..."

"I don't remember speakin' to you, Short Round!" Mace said, his smug grin daring Nino to punch back.

Edgardo ignored the pissing contest as he opened his briefcase and prepared his proposal, laying out a folder of paperwork beside a small laptop computer.

C.B. stood in front of his lieutenant and gestured for him to step back. Mace lowered his defenses but kept his blade in hand.

"Who supplied the plane?" Edgardo asked, starting business.

"We did," C.B. said. "I'm bettin' you wanna know the technicals."

"2015 Cessna 172 Skyhawk. Four seats. Single engine fixed-wing. Maximum speed is 163 knots or 187 miles per hour. Cruising speed tops out at 124 knots or 143 miles per hour."

The bikers looked dumbfounded.

"Is all that shit right?" Mace asked his Alpha.

C.B. nodded. "You know your planes."

"I also know it was stolen from Camarillo Airport a month ago," Edgardo said. "Investigation is still pending, no solid leads, but that doesn't concern us today."

"Right." C.B. was startled at both Edgardo's knowledge and flat tone. "Wanna ask me anything 'bout it? Anything 'bout what we're gonna do?"

"I know the plane and I know the plan. What I need you to tell me is if it's ready to fly and if you have a pilot for the job."

"It's good to go, and you're lookin' at the pilot."

"Of course," Rom said with a little laugh. "It's surely not your acolyte."

"What the fuck you sayin' now?" Mace asked with another flip of his butterfly knife.

"Business, Mace," C.B. said. "Remember?"

"Business, yeah. 'Bout that." Mace pointed his blade at Edgardo. "Why the hell we meetin' with this Flip? Supposed to be a simple transaction, right? You Asian boys want our guns and ammo. We want your money and dope. Simple. Why get your middle man involved?"

"I'm the one who asked for him," C.B. said, to the surprise of his lieutenant.

"Well, I don't know who 'him' is, and I don't know his other Flips, so fuck me for needin' clarification."

"Do you even know what a 'Flip' is?" Rom asked.

"A Flip is you, if you ain't been payin' attention," Mace said. "It's short for 'Filipino,' Einstein."

"It is not short for 'Filipino.' It means 'Fucking Little Island People.' Is that what you meant to call us? I just want to be clear."

Edgardo set down his file folder and walked up to Mace. "I'm sure you meant no offense. You just want introductions. Understandable." He offered a handshake. "You're Tim Mason a.k.a. 'Mace,' Sergeant At Arms of The Wolf Pack. He's Cyrus Bernard a.k.a. 'C.B.', your chief, or Alpha, as you call him. The men facing you are Rommel Basilio and Nino Timbol of Mga Hari sa Kalle 9."

"HK-9, we know that," Mace said, ignoring his host's extended hand. "Who the hell is *you* is what I'm wonderin'."

"My name is Edgardo Duque. I was asked to facilitate this exchange."

Mace finally shook hands with Edgardo, amused when he realized who this man was. "The Duke?" Mace said with a laugh. "You Asian boys really brought in The Duke for this deal?"

"I said I asked for him, Mace," C.B. said. "Don't you listen?"

"Sure, I listen, but I also read between the lines. I'm sure they pressured you to pick their boy here."

"I don't know how long you've been with the Wolves, Mace," Edgardo said, "but the last time your outfit met with The Nines, business ended with two men rushed to the ER. A lose-lose.

Unacceptable. I'm here to ensure that doesn't happen again. If you want money, I'm here. If you want a fight, I can go home and enjoy my dinner, Porterhouse steak and Yukon Gold potatoes."

C.B. again stood between his suspicious soldier and the rest of the room, shooting him a look to calm himself.

"This ain't the O.K. Corral, Mace," the old Alpha said.

"You actually wanted one of *them* to mediate this shit?"

"Yes, he does," Edgardo said. "And so do you, if you're smart." He returned to the table and brought up their deal on his laptop. "Forty cases of military-grade assault rifles and semi-automatic pistols in exchange for $350,000, plus a shipment of Damo. If we're in agreement, I can close the deal."

"Waldo's guns?" Rom asked. "Let's be clear."

"We bought 'em, didn't we?" Mace asked. "Last we hard, Waldo don't do direct business with The Nines, or don't you boys remember?"

"You have it backwards," Rom said. "We choose not to do business with him." He turned to Edgardo. "Scrubbed?"

"Twice," Edgardo said. "They arrived clean, but my people also processed every unit."

"Well, damn, I feel so much better now," Mace said with dripping sarcasm.

C.B. again gestured for his man to calm himself. "Tell me again about this 'Damo.' Pretty expensive for some bricks of weed."

Nino stepped forward, waited for all eyes to turn to him. "Our Damo is high-grade marijuana that's been cured for a year in cedar-lined rooms with Columbian coca leaves."

"Hold up now... cocaine weed?" Mace asked.

"It offers a potent, sustained experience. Highly addictive. Highly sought after. Highly valuable."

"We recommend that you... refrain from indulging," Rom said. "We don't want any junkies here. Save it for your network."

"Yeah, I bet you don't want us smokin' it," Mace said in a stern tone. "Bricks of oregano, for all we know."

"You got it all squared away?" C.B. asked.

Edgardo nodded.

"Sample?" Rom asked.

Edgardo opened his duffle bag and pulled out two guns encased in bubble wrap, a pair of unregistered and untraceable semi-auto weapons from Mr. Waldo's ice cream truck. Rom nodded to Nino to examine the hardware.

"How 'bout a sample over here?" C.B. asked.

Edgardo reached into the duffle bag and pulled out two stacks of hundred-dollar bills. He handed them to C.B. and Mace to examine.

"Fresh and clean," Edgardo said, "just like the weapons."

"Good enough," C.B. said. "We're in."

"As are we," Rom said, unwrapping his new gun.

"Hold up now, where's the rest?" Mace asked.

"We must first agree to terms," Edgardo said. "Territory lines. A one-year cease-fire. If we're all satisfied, I press a button, and the money is transferred, the weapons and narcotics are delivered."

"Nah," Mace said. "I don't like it."

"What's not to like?" his Alpha said.

"I wanna see it all. Two stacks of Bennies don't mean nothin'. What's stoppin' them from takin' our guns while we stand here like dumb shits?"

"We could wonder the same thing," Rom said. "Do you see a truck full of firearms here?"

"Last I checked, The Duke was one of you boys. He ain't no wolf."

"Don't let my race cloud your judgement," Edgardo said. "I'm not with the HK-9. Your chief asked for me. This is the third time you've been reminded."

Mace flung open his butterfly knife and raised it to Edgardo. It startled the biker that the well-dressed man didn't so much as flinch. "How 'bout you produce the entire lot rit' now before we say our good nights? Sound good?"

Nino stepped forward again, careful not to get too close to the irate man. "Mr. Mason, please, there's no need for this. We all want a fair trade."

Edgardo looked about the room, his hand resting on his belt buckle and the gold dagger hidden within. Time stood still as he assessed his predicament...

One: Disarm Mace. Kill him with a slash to the neck.
Two: Rush C.B. Kill him with a strike to the temple.
Three: Threaten Rom. Kill him if he tries to flee.
Four: Deal with Nino last. Snap his neck if needed.

Edgardo locked eyes with Mace as he approached with the butterfly knife. In a flash, he slapped the knife from Mace's hand and snaked it from the air. In one swift motion, he down-kicked Mace's leg, forcing him to his knees, and pressed the knife to the biker's throat. Rather than strike the killing blow he calculated, Edgardo paused, staring the man down.

In hindsight, ending them might have been the wiser choice, but in that moment, with money and territory on the line, I decided that these desperate fools would live. For now.

"If I die," Edgardo said in a commanding voice, "if anyone dies, the deal dies. Bad business. Unacceptable."

Shocked by Edgardo's unexpected pounce, Mace rose to his feet with the gold dagger still shoved against his neck. He stared at the stoic man in his fancy suit and blank expression, their faces inches apart. The biker clutched the blade to take back some control, blood trickling through his fingers.

"You think my knife is all we got?" Mace said with a grunt. "You don't think we brought heat? Ain't no way you're walkin' outta here till we get it all."

"We agreed!" Nino called out. "No guns!"

"Release him, Duque!" Rom said.

Edgardo extended his arms and released his grip on Mace. He flipped the butterfly knife shut and gently placed it on the floor next to the stack of cash Mace dropped during their brief scuffle, walking away to give him space.

With his bloody hand, Mace bent down and retrieved his blade.

Edgardo pointed at the cash as the biker reached for it...

BLAM!

The money ripped to shreds from a single, precision gunshot.

"That was ten grand," Edgardo noted. He pointed to the stack in C.B.'s hand.

BLAM!

C.B. lost his balance and tumbled to the floor as the cash in his hand was also destroyed by a dead-aim shot. He and Mace backed away. All four criminals looked around the hangar. They peered out at the dark desert where the unseen sniper must be.

"That was another ten grand," Edgardo said. "Consider it collateral damage for endangering the deal and wasting my time."

Rom readied the gun in his hand, but trigger locks rendered them useless. "These tangina guns are locked!"

"Of course. We agreed, no guns, but that wouldn't stop someone from bringing ammo, like the case of 9mm rounds and 5.56 NATO in your car."

Rom looked to Nino, both men confused.

"How did you know?" Nino asked.

"I didn't. But I do now."

Mace laughed at how Edgardo nailed them all to seize control of the room once again. "So, *this* is the fuckin' Duke I heard so much about! Goddamn, I ain't never seen shit like that! And I seen it all!"

Rom handed Nino his locked gun and gestured for another cigarette, returning to his poker face. "Enough of these fun and games. We're all a bunch of stubborn, demanding bastards, yes? Now that our peacock feathers have been spread, shall we get back to business?"

"Do we all agree with Rommel?" Edgardo asked.

Mace shrugged, begrudgingly deferring to his Alpha.

"Let's finalize this trade and get the hell outta here," C.B. said.

"Good man." Edgardo slid a paper from his file folder. "If we agree to the terms, you men sign this document and I release the goods – money, guns, drugs, keys to the trigger locks. If you can't see eye-to-eye, I can promise, I will walk out of here in one piece. I can't say the same for you."

C.B. eyed the shot stacks of cash. The threat was genuine. He brushed past Mace and approached the card table, the first to sign the agreement. Rom took the paper from him and added his signature.

"Signing for illegal shit," Mace muttered. "Fuckin' brilliant."

"Some of us honor our contracts," Rom said.

"That's right, some of us do," C.B. said. "Wolves never go back on their word." He handed the paper to Edgardo. "What's next?"

The gang leaders waited with bated breath as Edgardo typed new commands into his laptop. With a final confirmation beep, he shut the computer. "The money transfer is pending. Check your account in 60 minutes."

"No offense, but we'll be checking every 60 seconds," C.B. said.

"The weapons, money, and Damo sit in separate trucks five miles from here in opposite directions. Keys to the trigger locks will be in the front seat. I'll text coordinates in an hour. By then, I'll be home with my Porterhouse and potatoes." With no further protest, Edgardo gathered his things.

"What if it ain't all there?" Mace asked.

"It won't be. The money will be light the twenty-grand of confetti on the floor, plus my fee. To keep balance, the guns will be light one case. I have no interest in the Damo."

C.B. thought about the night's events and Edgardo's preparation. "You had us all figured out, didn't you, Duke?"

"Based on my experience with both parties, it wasn't much to figure out. Moving forward, it's all in our best interests that things go smoother next time."

Edgardo grabbed his briefcase and now-empty duffle bag and headed out of the hangar, into the dark desert. The sun had long abandoned the desolate airstrip.

"Tell me, Duque, how many men you got out there?" Rom asked, scrutinizing the moonlit horizon for snipers and guards.

"Enough." He turned and faced everyone, speaking in a direct tone. "Gentlemen, stand here and socialize for ten minutes. Get to know one another. *Ten minutes.* Then go home and know it was a pleasure doing business with you."

"Likewise," Mace said, still unsure about their situation.

Edgardo walked to his car at the side of the building, now barely seen with the rising moon. He threw his bags into the front seat, sat behind the wheel, and took a deep breath. He spoke to his assistant over his hidden mic.

"Felix, you still on?"

"Yes, Amo. What do you want me to do?"

"Wait until they're gone before you head back. Avoid the roads."

"I was never on them," Felix said.

"Good man. Cut across the desert to Palmdale. Give them ten minutes, then head out."

"What if they leave at nine minutes?"

Edgardo thought for a moment as he started his engine and drove away from the airfield.

"Kill Mace."

7

Dinner For One

Edgardo pulled into his driveway after his two-hour journey home from the desert, nearly double the time it would normally take. Just as he instructed Felix, he also took the "long way" home, taking impromptu detours and even doubling back in places in order to throw off any would-be followers. Though he didn't travel across unmarked desert like his assistant on his motorbike, Edgardo traced a zig-zag path across L.A. back to Highland Park.

> I took every highway, back road, dirt trail, and alley on the way home. It always felt like overkill, but the one night I don't tour the Earth after a deal, that would be the night of my undoing. It happened before, in another life.

After parking his Mercedes in the garage, he walked the perimeter of his property as he always did upon arriving home, entered through the kitchen, and secured the alarm.

The spartan kitchen's white and chrome surfaces held no aesthetic beyond a utilitarian, commercial feel, almost resembling a laboratory. The only decor was the oversized wooden spoon and fork mounted to the wall, Filipino symbols of food, comfort, and hospitality. They were a housewarming gift from his mother, one of the few things he cherished from her. Divinia had an identical pair on her dining room wall, her own mother also following tradition.

The rest of the well-appointed home was richly furnished in earth tones, lush plants, impressionist art, keepsakes, and framed family photos. Many pictures showed Edgardo with his brother, Abraham, who was older, bald, stocky.

They would be reunited soon enough.

Centered on one wall hung a *barong tagalog*, a white, cotton men's shirt, long-sleeved, embroidered with floral patterns. Though it resembled a simple laborer's shirt, art and culture had turned it into a formal garment throughout the Philippines, dating back to the island nation's Spanish Colonial days. But neither its simple beauty nor its cultural significance had placed it on Edgardo's wall, for beside it was a framed black-and-white photo of his family in their early days. His mother and biological father – the man dressed in that very barong – stood together in the Luzon countryside with two toddler boys, the young Duque brothers. Despite being mired in abject poverty, desperation, and fear, Edgardo viewed that chapter of his life as his age of innocence, one he often missed.

Hung next to the old photo was a more recent color family portrait, showing Edgardo and Divinia with their infant children, Carlo aged two and Christiana aged one. The four of them posed under a willow tree, smiling in a group embrace, as instructed by a professional photographer.

Edgardo leaned in, pressed his fingertips to his lips, and used them to kiss the faces of his children. As he kissed his daughter, he noticed a small gift-wrapped box on his coffee table, topped with a note from the girl: "Santa says eat your veggies, Tay! Love, Chris."

He opened the box to find pre-packed, vacuum-sealed ingredients for a nice dinner, just as she had promised – raw Porterhouse steak, Yukon gold potatoes, ancient grain rolls, and frozen mixed vegetables. Edgardo felt grateful that there was still one person in his life who genuinely cared about his well-being with more than mere words, whether they be from a place of concern or a seat of judgement. In a world where everyone wanted a piece of him, Chris loved him unconditionally, expecting only love in return.

Edgardo looked up as if to thank God for his good fortune, but spoke a monotone instruction to the ceiling. "Play Bach, Italian Concerto, F Major." Music faded in from the recessed speakers.

With one of the Masters blessing this house with his musical genius, it now felt like home, a sanctuary for rest, contemplation, and a good meal. Christiana would be proud. She worried about both my physical and mental health, fallout stress from witnessing her Lolo Otto's gradual decline. In a better world, an adolescent girl wouldn't have to see her mighty grandfather's fall or worry for her parents, but a better world can only be built from its ruins.

Edgardo took his daughter's care package into the kitchen and expertly prepared the food, discarding the rookie instructions. He pan-seared the steak with care, sliced the potatoes thin on a mandolin, and steamed the vegetables, upgrading the planned menu with his own homemade herbal butter. Moments later, with the kitchen shut down for the night, he set his perfect meal on the dining room table and paired it with a bottle of Napa merlot. As Bach played across the tiled ceiling, he poured a glass and took a sip to whet his pallet. The sip turned into a gulp, which turned to three swallows that emptied the glass.

He looked at the meat, potatoes, and greens, an arrangement fit for a magazine cover, but couldn't touch it. Another pour was needed.

BEEP BEEP

Edgardo's cell phone lit up.

Someone texted him a photo.

His stomach dropped out upon seeing a large trophy engraved with the words "Carlo Duque, Eagle Rock High School, Varsity Football, 2023 MVP."

Shit.

Carlo's sports awards ceremony, attended by proud friends, family, and teachers, was wrapping up while his father sat alone pampering himself. He grabbed his steak knife and hurled it across the room, nailing his own face in the color family portrait.

Another promise broken, another milestone missed. My sweet children were fading away to be replaced by bitter, distant young adults, and it was all my doing. Perhaps Divinia's rants and insults were wise and true, which would make my clever retorts foolish and ignorant. How I hated her for being right yet again, and how I hated myself for being blind to what should have mattered most.

He gulped down his wine, not even tasting it this time, and quickly poured another. As it went down his gullet, his phone rang, shattering the tranquility he so carefully curated. It wasn't Divinia as he'd feared, but his loyal man in the field.

"Hello, Felix," he said on the phone.

"It's done, Amo," Felix said, calling him "boss" in Tagalog, as he'd done for years. "All goods delivered. Transaction complete."

"How long did they stick around?"

"Ten minutes to the second. They left the hangar together. Apparently, they took your warning seriously."

"That means they imagined a platoon of sharpshooters crouched in the dunes," Edgardo said. "We can use that moving forward."

"Just as you planned."

"How was your exit?"

"Clean."

"Good man. Thank you again, Felix."

"My honor always, Amo."

Edgardo hung up and returned to his elegant meal, still untouched, now beside a half-bottle of merlot. It brought an old philosophical discussion to mind.

Is a partial glass half-empty or half-full? That's been debated by our greatest thinkers for centuries. A pessimist would say it's half-empty while an optimist would say it's half-full. Meanwhile, an unbiased, uninvested, or unemotional man would cite that it doesn't matter, for eight ounces is eight ounces, and perhaps we should just be content with that. Of course, this all speaks to things far more important than glasses or bottles, water or wine.

He considered the bottle for a moment before pouring yet another glass. His face showed no enjoyment, his eyes fixed in anticipation.

To me, the answer is simple. If a vessel is being filled, it is momentarily half-full. If it's being emptied, it's momentarily half-empty. Context in motion is everything, the root of abstract thought and problem-solving. Lately, my life, much like that bottle of merlot, is consistently half-empty, despite my ongoing efforts to fill it. I down alcohol every evening, but it feels like swallowing self-loathing and pity, a nightly bloodletting. Daylight can't come soon enough. May the dawn wash me anew. I'm entitled to ask for nothing more.

He reached into his briefcase sitting on the chair next to him and pulled out a Post-it note. He wrote a simple reminder but held it to his face like the most important point of business that day...

"CALL CARLO."

Edgardo rose to his feet and carried the note into the living room, to a wall already covered with dozens of yellow paper reminders. He pressed the note against the wall and stepped away, the little paper quickly lost in the sea of things to do.

Returning to his dinner, he picked up his fork, only to put it down for another two pours of merlot.

Bourbon and gin soon followed.

Edgardo woke up on his couch, dismayed to feel his suit still wrapped around his body. The designer outfit was now disheveled, drenched in sweat, and stained with meat drippings, butter, and merlot. On the coffee table beside him sat the wine and spirit bottles, all long empty, along with his spent flask. He sat up and felt food tumble from his sport coat, most of it having been pressed to his clothing rather than digesting in his stomach.

My nightly release of a fine meal and drink was spiraling, more drink than food. It was meant to be a respite from the day's events, but it started to feel like a slow poisoning of the mind. Unacceptable... but inevitable.

He peeled off his damp coat, shirt, and pants, allowing them to fall where they may as he trudged down the hall, through his bedroom, straight into his bathroom. He stared at his nearly naked body in the mirror, looking past his many scars and tattoos, to focus on his weary, defeated face.

I projected a 60 Percent chance that I'd die in the hangar at Anders Butler Airfield with either The Nines or The Wolves burying my remains in the desert. Even with Felix trained on me out in the dark, it was foolish to facilitate that exchange alone, a decision based on assumptions and hubris. Perhaps I should have brought Joey as he demanded, but I couldn't risk my friend's life. Not again.

Sunbeams pierced through the floral pattern of the bathroom window's curtain, burning his sore eyes. He looked about the mirror's frame, covered with dozens of yellow Post-It notes, each brighter than they'd ever been.

The only thing stopping me from self-destructing were my tasks, those many yellow squares keeping me busy. "All business all the time" was not just a mantra of ambition and success, as Divinia believed. So long as I had work to do, goals to chase, I couldn't allow myself to fall all the way to the bottom. Those little notes didn't merely help me organize, they forced me to focus, to live another day.

The small flask of bourbon that greeted him every morning lay on the shag carpet where he'd tossed it a day before. Rather than take a swig or two as he often did, he turned away from it, for the sight of it brought the boozy, oaken taste to his mouth, which made him double over and retch after a night of overindulging on an empty stomach. Instead, he returned it to its spot in the medicine cabinet next to his trio of pill bottles. Feeling light-headed from the visual trigger, he leaned forward, palmed the mirror, and read the two yellow square notes inches from his face...

"SPEAK WITH DIVINIA."

"PICK UP BRAM."

He recalled the note he stuck on the living room wall...

"CALL CARLO."

All at once, Edgardo's family obligations came rushing back. He needed to rebuild the sagging bridge to his son, regain his ex-wife's confidence, and check in on his young daughter. Being a family man meant ongoing maintenance, even if Divinia had full custody.

Most pressing at the moment was the release of his older brother, Abraham, fresh from a 10-year stretch in Lancaster State

Prison, an ominous property not far from the desolate airfield that nearly cost Edgardo his life the night before.

Looking at my notes, I felt like two men pulled me in different directions. For Edgardo Duque, the day was overwhelming. He was filled with doubt, anticipating failure. There was simply too much to juggle, and something, maybe everything, was destined to fail. It was different for The Duke. For him, it was just another day of business. All tasks needed to be completed by nightfall. End of discussion.

One of those men was wrong. The problem was that I never knew which man to turn to.

8

Hero of the Dish

Divinia Duque wore an apron of blue and teal trimmed with white lace, colors and textures chosen for their pleasant, down-home feel. She mixed raw pork in a large Pyrex bowl by hand, her diamond ring and French manicured nails coated in the meat's juices. The simple country kitchen was a well-crafted facsimile within Soundstage "D" at Royal Studios in Burbank, California, a facility leased by the Gourmet Travel Network.

Wrist-deep in the mixture, she addressed the camera centered on the kitchen's invisible fourth wall, her cheerful persona optically perfect.

"Some people let the pork rest in soy sauce," Divinia said to her TV audience with a wide smile. "For me, the flavor is too powerful. I want to taste the meat more than its marinade. Back in Quezon Provence, my mother simply used vinegar and garlic, and that's what we use in the restaurant."

She spotted a reporter and her photographer to the camera's left, blended in with the crew. Of all the eyes on her, theirs were the only ones watching in wait and judgement.

Journalist Laura Grisham of *Food and Wine*, dressed in a silk blouse and slacks, grinned at Divinia's step-by-step tutorial, impressed by her ease on camera. Professional shooter David Garrett, draped with a loaded utility vest, was too busy prepping his gear to notice the production, though in Divinia's mind, he, too, scrutinized her every movement.

"The marinade should be simple," she said as she wrapped the bowl with plastic wrap. "I know many of you want to add the bay leaves and onions now, but save them for the simmer. Add chiles if you like it spicy, but go easy. Pork is a mild meat and can easily be overpowered. You want to keep it the hero of the dish."

Twelve minutes later, during a lighting change, the show's director suggested a break. Divinia took the opportunity to sit down with Laura, if only to get her out of the building sooner. She led the journalist and her photographer to the fake dining room next to the fake kitchen. To her surprise, they'd already set up for the interview.

With Divinia sitting at the head of the family-style table, her make-up fresh and perfect, her blouse pressed and clean, Laura introduced her guest.

"Divinia Iglesia Duque is one of the hottest chefs in L.A.," Laura said to the camera in her trademark beaming voice. "Her bistro 'Uminom' just received its first Michelin star with a menu of both authentic and fusion Filipino cuisine. We're with her on the set of 'Masserip Divinia,' set to debut on the Gourmet Travel Network.

"Masarap," Divinia said with a smile, correcting the journalist.

Laura nodded to her and gestured to David for another take. "We're with her on the set of 'Masarap Divinia,' set to debut on the Gourmet Travel Network on Christmas Day. 'Masarap' means 'delicious'?

"That's right."

"It's on your menus, too. I'd been to Uminom several times before. I confess, I had to look it up. Great name for your show."

"Thank you," Divinia said. "It was my daughter's idea."

"Speaking of menus, you're offering a special Christmas dinner?"

"It's called 'Noche Buena,' a plate of hamon, kare-kare, caldereta, lechon, and a dessert. We're looking at leche flan or puto bumbong. My mother always made bibingka, so I might surprise a few guests."

Laura ignored her traditional holiday offerings as she looked through her notes. "Your first Michelin star. How does that honor change your day-to-day operation?"

Divinia took a moment to compose her response, a long pause she hoped would be edited out of the interview. With Laura Grisham, a woman known for her investigative teeth, one never knew.

"It is an honor," Divinia said, "but it doesn't change a thing. The most important customer is the one being served right now, whether she's a Michelin inspector or any customer exploring a new menu. At Uminom, we aim for perfection with every plate. It's our goal to provide everyone with an authentic Filipino meal, plus a few surprise twists. I find it easier to focus on the experience than trying to guess who's a food critic and who's not."

The two women shared a laugh, during which Divinia spotted Edgardo entering the studio. Seeing her busy with the interview, he kept his distance, waiting quietly nearby.

"And your new show, 'Masarap Divinia,'" Laura said. "Does it tie into that mission statement?"

"Absolutely. Many of the recipes on the show come directly from our restaurant's kitchen, and many of those come from my mother."

"Before you opened Uminom, you owned another hot spot, 'Ang Corazon Lounge.' How does the quiet Corazon compare with the throngs of foodies lined up at Uminom?"

"For one thing, Corazon is not a restaurant," Divinia said. "We only serve appetizers there, siopao and lumpia, things like that. I ran Corazon with my husband. He's since taken over and breathed new life into it."

"What made you return to your Philippine roots with Uminom after leaving Corazon?" Laura asked. "To go from a kitschy tiki bar to an upscale Filipino bistro? Quite a shift."

It started to feel like a chess match.

"Actually, tiki lounges are very much a Filipino thing," Divinia said, trying to hide her defensiveness. "All the classic tiki joints were started by men like my father. He ran the old 'Tiki Ono Koa' by the airport for twenty years. Call them kitschy if you like, but they're part of our history in America."

"Your husband still runs Corazon? Edwardo Duque?"

"Edgardo," Divinia said. "Yes, and he does a fine job. He embraces the community."

"The community being HiFi? Historic Filipinotown?"

"Yes. All the businesses on Temple Street know him. He's become somewhat of an institution there."

"And you're still partners?"

It was definitely a chess match.

Laura was hunting for a stinger.

"We've taken different paths in our careers," Divinia said, "but yes, still partners. We've always shared a common vision."

"Even though you divorced in 2014?" Laura asked flatly. "*Cuisine Magazine* did a brutal cover story on it."

There it was.

Divinia sensed the journalist's bait. She grinned and rose from her chair. "Thanks for coming, Laura, but I have to prepare for the next segment."

"Can we arrange a follow-up?"

"I'd love to," Divinia lied. "Call my manager. She'll work it out. Thank you Laura, David."

Divinia shook Laura's hand, nodded to her photographer, and gestured to the studio exit, a red light flashing above. In no hurry to leave, Laura pointed to a few points of the set for David to shoot on their way out. As they took their photos, Edgardo raised his phone and took some photos of his own. He followed his ex to her makeup chair, ensuring that the journalist and crew were out of earshot before addressing her.

"Good morning, Divinia," he said.

"Good morning, Mr. 'I'll Be There.'"

"Yes, I came to apologize for..."

"It's not me you own any apology to."

His head still ringing from his massive hangover, Edgardo sensed her anger. He treaded lightly. "You're the first I owe. I made you a promise, and unfortunately I couldn't sufficiently meet it."

"You broke your promise," she said. "That's the wording you're desperately searching for."

"Business took longer than I expected. I'll speak with Carlo."

"Good, because he has questions about Tito Bram. He's looking forward to seeing him again."

"I can bring Bram by the house after I pick him up."

"No, you most certainly can't," she said. "I haven't changed my mind."

"I understand."

"Though I'm sure Carlo was hoping to see Bram last night more than you."

Edgardo silenced himself, not wanting to start a fight. "If you wanted to wound me, Divinia, you succeeded."

"It's the truth, Eddie. And as much as I want Carlo to stay away from your thug brother, I can't stomach breaking his heart further."

"A little dramatic, don't you think?"

"Again, it's the truth, Eddie."

Edgardo looked to the exit but paused for a last word. "Congratulations on your new show. I've told everyone about it."

"I'm sure it'll help bolster business at Corazon."

Ouch.

"If you think I'm going to plaster your face on the walls of the bar to take advantage of your success, you're wrong. The bar is just fine."

"You heard that bitch puta," Divinia said. "It's a 'kitschy' tiki bar. Do what you want, I won't put up a fuss. Believe it or not, I actually want to see the bar thrive without me."

"I believe you. Tell Carlo I'll see him later. And thank you."

"Thank you? For what?"

"For being there for him when I wasn't. The boy deserves at least one dependable parent."

Edgardo headed for the exit. Though he walked with posture and a stone face, in his mind, he shuffled across the floor with his head hung low, a pathetic man who forgot his duty as a father.

As he left, Divinia felt a pang of regret well up in her throat. Through the reflection of her makeup mirror, she watched him leave after his attempt to mend fences, weak as it may have been.

"I'll tell him," she said to herself. "Better that way."

9

The Machine

The drive from Royal Studios to Lancaster State Prison was normally an hour and a quarter with good traffic. Edgardo made it in 49 minutes, gunning his engine past every car on Highway 14 as he returned to the desert. The desolate towns and their surrounding expanse were usually places of business for him, often dangerous scenarios, and he braced himself whenever he had to drive out there. He felt the same that day, even if no danger was to be found.

The desert always made me anxious. I'd had many meetings there, and so far I'd been lucky to make it home each time. Then there's this place. Even just visiting, prisons fill me with a deep dread.

Edgardo entered the massive property and parked his car in a lot designated "Release Area." The heavily guarded main entrance stood a short distance away, though it was the simple "exit" door he watched, built into a tall chain-link fence that allowed delivery trucks into a receiving bay.

California State Prison, Los Angeles County, Lancaster. With a staff of nearly 1,600 and an annual budget of over $100 million, the fortress doubled as a money machine. Locking up men like my brother was highly profitable.

He spied armed guards in towers, cameras on poles, and endless coils of razor wire atop every surface. Unseen by most, he knew there were also thermal sensors, scotopic cameras, and various biometric security measures at every door and gate. The complex containment system proved both morbid and fascinating.

Lancaster State Prison sits on 262 acres. Sounds like room to stretch your legs but incarceration burst at 217 Percent. Nearly 5,000 men were sardined within its steel-reinforced concrete walls at one point, my brother among them.

The metal door opened. A man stepped out and walked toward the parking lot, his stone expression bringing a smile to Edgardo's face.

Abraham "Bram" Duque, 50, bald and lean, wearing a vest over a white dress shirt, jeans, and leather boots, walked a straight line to Edgardo's car, alone in the Release Area lot.

Many of The Demonyo's enemies lived there. Bram likely had to fight each day just to see the next, ongoing for ten years. 3,285 fights. I have no doubt that my brother won them all.

* * *

Twenty minutes earlier, Bram sat on a wooden bench within a cinderblock room lined with shelves of folded clothes as he removed his pale gray prison uniform. His muscled body was covered in tattoos and scars, much like his younger brother, including a large black Philippine eagle spanning his upper back. It was the feared symbol of "The Demonyo," their old gang in San Francisco.

Prison Guard Wallace stood at the open doorway, a man of 35 with a 60-year-old comb-over and pot belly. He glanced down the hall as his departing guest put on his civilian clothes, 10 years out of style. Wallace – that was the only name Bram knew him by – bit into an egg salad sandwich wrapped in a napkin. The contrast startled Bram. A momentous day for one man, his first taste of freedom in a decade, was nothing more than a working lunch for another.

"I gotta admit," Wallace said, his mouth full of egg salad, "a small part of me will miss you, Bram. I'm used to seeing your piercing scowl at the end of the block at each night's count, not to mention I won a lot of money betting on your ass every day. Ten years, right?"

Across his 19 years as a prison guard, Wallace regularly supplemented his salary with gambling, betting entire paychecks on football games, days at the horse track, and the occasional fights between cons. The money from the fights proved so good that "occasional" no longer satisfied the correctional faculty. Prisoners with known beef, often belonging to rival gangs, were arranged to share the yard at opportune times, evening shifts when the warden and supervising officers had left for the day. The fiercest prisoners were taken to "The Alley," a narrow passage between buildings C and D, for private bouts witnessed only by guards who'd put down significant cash, advanced paychecks, or car keys.

"Ten years," Wallace said again. "Goddamn, that's a lot of nights, a lot of fights."

"No more fighting." Bram slid on his jeans. He was surprised that the prison washed them and that they still fit, though his face never showed it.

"Yeah, gotcha," Wallace said. "A fresh start, right? New year around the corner, time for a new life. Time to retire those fists of fury!"

"No more fighting."

"Hey, I hear ya, I hear ya. You did what you had to do in here, but out there, you can be any kind of man you wanna be, and you're gonna take advantage of that freedom. I respect that."

Bram ignored him as he put on his vest and tossed his uniform in a laundry bin. Seeing it mixed in with so many others, he knew it would be washed by day's end and assigned to another man of similar size, a literal example of Wash-Rinse-Repeat. It made him feel disposable, expendable, and that's exactly what he was within those stone walls. He hoped that feeling would dissolve the moment he left the building.

"I've always wondered," Wallace said, still chewing his egg salad sandwich. "How's it feel? About to walk out a free man after being cooped up for so long?"

Bram didn't feel like composing a verbal essay on his innermost thoughts, especially not for the likes of Wallace. He

Lynn Harrod

remained silent as he shoved his feet into his boots and the remains of his possessions into a small duffel bag.

"You don't have to answer, of course, but I imagine it's like holding in your piss all day until you finally find a tree."

Bram laughed.

The man has no clue.

"I find it curious, you know?" Wallace continued. "I envy that feeling of everlasting release. I mean, every time I clock out and head home, I feel like I can breathe again after suffocating in this shithole for eight hours. Is it something like that?"

"Something like that."

"I'll bet. Well, you ain't out quite yet, Bram. Three more papers to stamp before you're back out in the wild."

Bram stood from his bench, his civilian outfit complete. "Lead the way."

Prison Guard Wallace took Bram down the hall to a door labeled "Documentation" within sight of the release gate. He unlocked the door but remained in the hall, gesturing for Bram to go in alone. Bram eyed the release gate and hesitated to enter the final room.

"You're not coming in?" Bram asked.

"I'm not the one who needs to get processed," Wallace said. "Just head in, sign and stamp the papers, and away with you. Send us a postcard once in a while to remember you by."

Bram knowingly turned and looked Wallace in the eye, the first time in years.

"Take a good look at my face, Wallace."

"Okay, I'm looking," the guard said with a laugh.

"Consider this your first and last postcard. No small part of me will miss you at all."

Wallace laughed again, the first to break the stare. "I understand. I guess this is where we say goodbye."

Bram opened the door and entered the room. Upon hearing Wallace lock the door behind him, his suspicions were confirmed as three convicts emerged from behind a row of bookshelves, steel pipes in hand. They were led by Victor Acuña, a towering, musclebound Mexican.

"'Ang Makina,' right?" Victor said. "'The Machine?' Last day inside. Last day to send a message to The Demonyo."

"The Demonyo is four-hundred miles from here," Bram said. "We don't have to do this. I'm not with them no more, not for ten years."

"So you say. Still, the message will come across."

"It won't be the message you want. Have you learned nothing?" The three men were unmoved by the warning. "You're right. It is the last day. Your last chance. Once I walk out the gate, Ang Makina will be dead to the world, and you'll have to find some other fool to obsess over."

Bram dropped his duffel bag.

The three men rushed him, pipes raised.

Two minutes later, Wallace finished his egg salad sandwich and heard a fist pound on the door. "You boys work fast." He unlocked and opened it, stunned to see Bram step out into the hall, duffel bag over his shoulder.

"All three papers have been stamped," Bram said. "If you got any more, I'll stamp them all."

Bram took the napkin from the shocked guard and wiped the blood from his hands, pocketing it without taking his eyes from the man.

"I guess I was bound to lose a bet," Wallace said, his face blank.

"*This* is where we say goodbye," Bram said. "If I ever see you again, Wallace, here or anywhere, you'll finally know that feeling of everlasting release."

* * *

Edgardo stepped out of his car to get a good look at his brother, dressed in the same clothes he wore when he turned himself in a decade before. He wiped away tears and cleared his throat as the two men stood staring at each other.

"Hello Bata," Bram said, always calling his younger brother "child" or "boy" in Tagalog.

"Hello Kuya," Edgardo said, referring to Bram as "brother."

"Diyos, I hope you're real. I expect to wake up in my bunk at any moment."

"Trust me, Bram. So long as I live, you're never going back in there again."

10

Freedom

The brothers drove down the desert highway back to Los Angeles. At first, they shared tense silence, and Edgardo wasn't sure if they could reconnect their bond after so long apart. Bram stared out the window, his brother allowing him all the time he needed to be lost in thought.

"It's a strange feeling," Bram finally said, "being out in the open desert. So much space."

"That prison has always been filled beyond capacity. Not sure how you endured."

"It's bigger than it looks."

"Like Pinoy Point?"

"Yes," Bram said with a smile. "Like Pinoy Point." They shared a laugh, as if to finally release their pent-up feelings together. "Shet! I'd forgotten about Pinoy Point! Our little sanctuary."

Edgardo was instantly transported back to their childhood home in the Philippines, recalling every detail. "Best clubhouse an eight-year-old could wish for. From the outside, it looked like it could barely hold us two. The kids from school were always surprised at how much bigger it was inside."

"We had twelve boys in there on any given day. Took me weeks to dig into that hillside."

"Kept us cool in the summer."

With a reluctant smile, Bram joined his little brother in their nostalgia. "I should build a clubhouse for Carlo and Christiana, or are they too big for that now?"

"Nah, Chris would love it. She'd spend all her time reading in there. Carlo would love it, too, but he wouldn't dare show it."

"Ah, Mr. Tough Guy."

"Like his Tito Bram."

"Of course. Every boy needs a real man to look up to."

Edgardo smiled at the little jab. "You know how else Carlo's like you? He's the Big Man On Campus, the star jock of his school. MVP, Varsity, gave him a giant trophy. He dreams of joining the 49ers."

"That's my Mahal Caloy," Bram said. "The brown Joe Montana."

"The boy works very hard. They both do. They're better than we ever were at that age, Kuya."

"Then you and Div have done your jobs."

Bram saw the emotion welling on his brother's face and changed the subject by admiring his car. He gripped the leather seat, tapped the touchscreen, and listened to the purring engine. "Such a fine machine. Looks like taking over Tatay's garage was the right move."

"You think oil changes and tune-ups bought this?"

"Bata, please tell me you've cut ties to The Demonyo."

Edgardo had a ready response, but silenced himself, not wanting to rain on what should have been a joyous afternoon. It was futile, as his older brother could clearly sense that he was holding back.

"No more Demonyo, right?" Bram asked.

"I left them in San Francisco."

"So, why the face?"

"What face?"

"You never could lie to me, Eddie."

Edgardo was hesitant to update his brother on his new life, the unexpected, twisty evolution of his career.

"Eddie? Talk to me."

"I have a plan," Edgardo said. "I'm going to become a cottage industry like Divinia, open a chain of tiki bars."

Bram's face lit up. "Ang Corazon Lounge in every city! Of course! Like Starbucks, but with siopaos and piña coladas!"

"You laugh, but the plan's got legs."

"No, no, I don't doubt you. I'm sure it has the legs of a centipede! Rum punch in a coconut shell? With a little umbrella and a hibiscus blossom sticking out? Who doesn't love that?"

"Felix calls it a 'vacation in a glass.'"

"Well, Felix is right, whoever that is. Recipe books, bottled drinks, Hawaiian shirts, tiki mugs, Corazon cologne..."

"Look at you, full of ideas," Edgardo said. His brother's enthusiasm was contagious. "But I was thinking more of a resort."

"Perpekto, Bata! It's the American dream!"

"Yeah, well, every American dream requires American capital."

Bram's playful smile faded as he sensed the new tone. "I see. Something more than oil changes and tune-ups can provide. You gonna fill me in?"

"Carlo's already got college football scouts calling. He's fierce like his mother. He can't wait to tell his Tito Bram all about it. And Christiana is a little computer wizard..."

"Eddie..." Bram caught the sudden shift. "Are you gonna fill me in? The business, I mean. Catch me up on ten years?" Despite Bram's affectionate laugh, Edgardo kept his eyes on the road. "You ain't slingin' weed and glass on the street corner, right? I mean, those days gotta be over."

"No more street corners," Edgardo said.

Not put at ease, Bram waited for his brother to continue his thought, a tense pause that Edgardo sensed.

"You'll need a drink first. It's... a lot."

"Okay, we drink," Bram said. "Then you tell me everything."

11

The Cousins

Galvez Salvage and Scrap occupied 18 acres of industrial land two miles southeast of Historic Filipinotown, sitting against the paved Los Angeles River within the shadow of Highway 101 passing overhead. The urban wasteland stored stacks of dead sedans, rows of rusted appliances, sunken furniture, and derelict construction machines. Between them, a corrugated steel warehouse offered a junk disposal drop-off and a recycling center, both of which existed mostly as fronts for the owner's real income.

The scrapyard served as the domain of the Temple Street Boyz – known by most as the TSB – their initials spray-painted on the warehouse wall in 20-foot letters. The gang boasted 35 members involved in small business extortion, illegal gambling, and side-street drugs. Unlike the HK-9, the old-money, suit-and-tie mob comprising Rommel Basilio's Filipino family, the TSB were a motley pan-Asian crew run by two Filipino cousins.

On that late morning, while the cousins met in the warehouse, Jorge Vega and Miguel Hortiz waited for them outside in an unusual lounge. They sat on ripped, discarded leather couches arranged like a living room set in the mud of the junk lot, Jorge's red Camaro parked nearby. They were still dazed from their unnerving confrontation with The Duke in the 2nd Street Tunnel and now waited to discuss that night's events with their bosses.

Jorge and Miguel shared a joint, a sliver of marijuana rolled and wrapped by the younger man moments earlier. Both men were nervous, scared, but young Miguel made no attempt to hide it.

"He don't like the Honda," Miguel said, shaking his head. "I fuckin' know it."

"Shit yeah, he does," Jorge said. "It's a sweet ride. That's why he's still in there checkin' it out now."

"Nah, man, it's bagito shit. He probably gets wheels like that all the time. So what's he really wanna meet us for?"

"Gotta keep a cool head, Miguel..."

"That ain't no kinda answer! What's he wanna meet about?"

"Does it matter?" Jorge said, frustrated with his comrade's transparent fear. He took the joint from him. "If the man says we meet here, we meet here."

"Hell yeah, it matters! Calixto don't meet guys to give 'em candy and popcorn, you know what I'm sayin'? Tell me straight, are we gonna get got? For fuckin' with The Duke?"

"Shit, it ain't like that."

"Yeah? And how do you know what it be like?"

"Forget that!" Jorge said. "The cousins will be here in a minute. You let me do all the talkin', understand?"

"Hey, no problem there." Miguel wouldn't dare speak for fear of trembling as if he were having a seizure.

Jorge heard two sets of footsteps approaching, first echoing in the warehouse, then clumping in the mud. He passed the joint back to Miguel and sat bolt upright as the two cousins emerged from the shadow of the structure.

Calixto Cervantes, a short, bald man, his body covered with muscles and tattoos exposed by his white tank top, walked toward the two young gangsters. Calixto turned 40 a month prior, and in a world where most of his peers had died, walked away, or were locked up by 25, he was considered a veteran, a general among street soldiers. He walked ahead of his younger cousin, Gabriel "Yoy Yoy" Aquino, a stocky man in head-to-toe denim topping dark leather boots.

As he often did, Calixto started their meeting in Tagalog.

"Jorge and Miguel!" he said in his Spanish-accent Filipino, arms outstretched. "My two favorites! Merry Christmas!"

Jorge smiled at the seemingly kind words. Miguel still appeared shook, as if a bullet would pierce his skull at any moment.

"Merry Christmas, Calixto," Jorge said in his rough Tagalog. "How's it goin'? You start the chop on that Honda yet? Or maybe you wanna keep it. Maybe it's too good to part out. She's a sweet ride, yeah?"

Calixto sat on a sofa opposite Jorge and Miguel's couch. If not for the mud and machine noise of the recycling center, it seemed like a casual get-together in a parlor.

Yoy Yoy remained silent as he stood behind his cousin.

"Sweet paint job, maybe," Calixto said, "but we'll get to the Honda in a minute. Yoy Yoy says you boys had a run-in with Duque."

"That's right," Jorge said. "As always, your cousin knows everything. Nothing happens in this city don't catch his attention."

"Something like this, even the sleepy old men on the bus stop benches caught it." Calixto laughed, impressed. "I mean, fuck, you actually tried to jack Duque's ride?"

"Yeah," Jorge said with his own forced laugh. "But we figured out fast who he was, so we backed off."

Calixto gestured for the joint. Jorge quickly took it from Miguel and passed it to his boss.

"What kind of ride?" Calixto asked, continuing their Tagalog.

"The Duke's?"

"Yeah, what was it?"

"Umm... Benz. SLK. Special Edition something."

"Nice. What color?"

"Black. Real cherry, you know?"

"Very nice. I can see why you tried to score it."

"Yeah, but like I said, Calixto, once we knew who he was, we backed off right away."

Jorge and Miguel looked at each other, unsure. Calixto took a slow draw from the joint, exhaled in thought.

"So, 'bout that Honda," Jorge said.

"Yeah, about that. I told you to boost a premium ride, and you come back with some college boy's day-glow Civic. That rice rocket is covered with cheap Pep Boys plastic shit."

"But... Kalaw took Civics all the time..."

"Kalaw ain't here, is he?" Calixto took a moment to calm himself. "Last I checked, my brother's dead and gone. But none of that shit matters 'cause any Benz is gonna be a bigger fish than any Civic, right?"

"Calixto, man," Miguel said to his partner's dismay, spitting out his words in broken Filipino. "We thought... we didn't think... we figured you didn't want us to mess with..."

"Shut up," Jorge said, staring fire at the teenager. "What Miguelito means is we didn't want to fuck up any business between you two. I mean, he is The Duke."

Calixto winced at hearing "The Duke." He nodded, took another puff of the joint, and returned it to Jorge. As the boss exhaled, his smile fell away, and he switched back to English, their native-tongue pleasantries over.

"Let me tell you about business between us two," Calixto said in a stern tone. "Every dollar we earn anywhere in the city, Duque gets his cut. Every street we take, every brick of weed we score, Duque gets his cut. We earn a quarter, he gets a nickel. Some say things are better this way, peace between territories and shit. Others miss the days when you'd deal direct, man to man, with no fuckin' 'Duke' snippin' a corner off every buck."

Jorge carefully chose his next words. "So you're sayin' the next time we bump into him, he's fair game? I just wanna understand."

Calixto leaned forward. "I'm sayin' the next time you bump into him will be today. I'm sayin' I want that black cherry Mercedes SLK 'Special Edition something' and anything else you find. To be clear, I'm sayin' I wouldn't even mind if The Duke retired from sittin' in on our deals, if it comes to it."

"For reals?"

"It don't get more real. Tell me you understand that."

Jorge hid his fear even as eyes widened. "Yeah, you got it, Calixto. Now we know." He nudged his partner. "Right?"

Miguel nodded, looking down at the mud.

Without another word, Calixto rose to his feet, took the joint from Jorge for one last puff, and walked back to the warehouse.

Yoy Yoy took his cousin's place on the sofa across from the young gangsters, who sat relieved to still be alive while also overwhelmed at their new assignment.

"What about you, Yoy Yoy?" Jorge asked. "What do you think?"

"I don't think, I work," Yoy Yoy said, his monotone voice sending a chill through the two thieves. "I listen. Now you listen."

"Sure, always."

"My cousin wants me to shadow you, watch you make shit right. So take the lead, Jorge."

Jorge flashed his fake smile. "Yoy Yoy, it ain't that easy. The problem is the fucker's a ghost. No one knows where he..."

"I know where," Miguel said.

Jorge sat stunned.

It pained Miguel to continue. "I mean... I think I do."

"Where?" Yoy Yoy asked.

"He's got a plush crib up on a hill in Highland Park. Ain't nothing around it. Pretty sure it's his."

"The Duke's sanctuary," Yoy Yoy said with a grin. "Okay, there we go. Progress."

Yoy Yoy stood, walked to Jorge's Camaro, and climbed into the backseat. Hesitant, Jorge joined him, sitting behind the wheel. Miguel took the front passenger seat.

As Jorge started the engine, he heard the frightening, distinct sound of Yoy Yoy loading a pistol in the backseat and braced for his end. A moment later, still alive, he realized he and Miguel truly did get a second chance.

A last chance.

Miguel looked out the window, tried to hide the sudden regret on his face. "What now?"

"Highland Park," Yoy Yoy said, as if it were obvious. "We stake it out, go in after dark, go in heavy."

"Heavy?" Miguel asked. "What for?"

"Retirement."

12

A Brief Dream

The reunited Duque brothers were back on the streets of Los Angeles after nearly two gridlocked hours on Interstate 5 to Highway 110 and finally to Beaudry Avenue, along the southeast edge of Historic Filipinotown. Bram hadn't seen his brother's adopted community since 2012, a year after it was recognized as a cultural neighborhood of significance. Back then, small blue signage on lampposts, like the one they'd just driven past at the corner of Beverly and Belmont, were the only evidence of HiFi's official status. Before that, only alley murals and a handful of restaurants and shops amidst shuttered storefronts shared the district's heritage. But on that sunny, smoggy day – the first day of the rest of Abraham Duque's life – the neighborhood looked more alive, more cared for, more loved.

Lynn Harrod

After leaving San Francisco, Bram still had loose ends with The Demonyo. He lived in L.A. for a couple of years before taking the fall for me and moving to the guarded walls of Lancaster. Before that, he'd rented a rathole in Lincoln Heights, just a bed, a toilet, and a hot plate. I remember every inch of that slum as I remember every detail of every day. The roaches, the peeling paint, the creaking of the pipes, the sounds of domestic violence behind paper-thin walls.

Only 10 minutes from Hifi, Bram lived close enough that he spent nearly every day with me and my family. How they adored their big, strong, crass Tito Bram. Christiana saw him as a superhero. Even Divinia loved him, though she would never admit it now. As for Carlo, I don't blame him for looking up to his uncle even as he looked down on me.

"This place sure has changed, Bata," Bram said, unaccustomed to seeing fresh paint and neon signs on the 75-year-old buildings. "It was the fuckin' hood when I lived here. We used to call it 'Far East L.A.' But now... did we just pass a Starbucks?"

"You want to go to Bloom and Plume," Edgardo said, referring to his daily coffee house. "That's where locals get real coffee. They do it right, treat you like family. Don't you dare walk into Charbucks."

"Charbucks?" Bram laughed.

"That's what they do to their beans. They blowtorch them, whip them into milkshakes, and serve them with all the care and customer service of a McDonald's."

"Pakshet! My little brother has become a fuckin' coffee hipster snob! Can I get you a Cuban cigar to go with your espresso?"

"Only in the mornings, Kuya," Edgardo said. "By noon, I'm onto the harder stuff."

"Speaking of which, where are we going for our 'you'll need a drink first' talk?"

"Corazon, unless the tough ex-con prefers something less stuffy, as you might say."

"No, stuffy is good," Bram said with a laugh. "Classy is good. After being behind cinderblocks for ten years, I'm dying for sophistication, pinkies up, and dark lounges. Besides, Corazon was my place to be any night of the week, remember? Even a fuckin' punyeta like me felt like a million bucks sittin' in there. No better spot in L.A."

"The free drinks surely helped."

"Is it my fault I knew the owners?" Bram said, grinning wide. "Maybe take the ball-busting down a notch, I've barely been out a couple of hours."

Edgardo laughed. "Sorry, old habit."

"I fuckin' love Corazon. You know that, and you should be proud, building a little piece of paradise in the shit. You and Div still partners?"

Edgardo tried to hide the pangs of regret swirling inside. "She left Corazon to me, wanted to start fresh. You know the feeling."

Bram knew there was far more to that delayed response but let it go, not wanting to swat back at his brother's light jabs. "Good for her. She was always the bright one."

"Agreed. That's why she divorced me."

"Someone had to say it," Bram said. "Brother, when you let a woman like her get away, I wondered if maybe you weren't no genius after all."

"Me, too."

As they turned onto Temple Street, Bram looked out the window at the storefronts, many of which were still boarded up with graffiti-tagged plywood. The district may have been riding the crest of a modern renaissance, but it still had its lingering scars and warts. Still, the sight of the empty shops stirred something within him.

"I see a lot of opportunity for us, Bata," Bram said. "Every night inside, I thought only of getting out, leaving our old days behind. Every night at Lights Out, laying in my bunk, I always imagined how it would be."

"And when those lights went out, what did your imagination come up with in the dark?"

"You really wanna know?"

"More than anything, Kuya."

Bram thought back to those lonely nights in his cell, at the visions that filled his head as he drifted to sleep. "I imagined walking out of that impiyerno and into your arms. I'd get in your fancy car, buckle my seatbelt, and never look back. I imagined proud brothers driving through the city without a care, no cops on us, no asesino hunting us. To be rid of that dirty world, that's what freedom meant to me."

Edgardo felt his years of regret pounding at his heart, the image of his big brother locked in a 7x10 room with only a wafer of a window offering a view of the open desert.

"I imagined us building a legitimate business together," Bram continued, "something Nanay and Tatay would be proud of. I imagined walking into Corazon again, hugging the kids, getting a kiss on the cheek from Div, hard at work as she prepared the bar for another busy evening. I saw myself walking up to your house, seeing the life you built with your big brain while I was inside, a garden away from the jungle of shit we've been through. Now that I'm out, it's like a living dream, not having to worry about a gun in my face or a boss to kneel to, hustling a few grand a day, struggling to keep us alive. No threats, no fear, no fighting. Just a family reunion around the corner from Christmas that's been a long time coming. That's always been my dream, Bata."

Edgardo remained silent, not wanting to dash his brother's hopes. He peered dead ahead, his hands gripping the steering wheel as if clutching his facade of calm composure. "It sounds like a wonderful dream."

He would dismantle that dream soon enough.

13

Strawberry Wine

As Bram walked past the lounge's heavy double doors, their frames etched with palm fronds, flowers, and tropical birds, he immediately felt at home. The gentle breeze of the central climate system cooled his skin while the fragrance of freshly cut citrus filled the air. Dim recessed lighting made the room fade into view as his eyes adjusted from the morning sunlight outside. It proved a fitting entrance, for Ang Corazon Tiki Lounge was more than a bar to Bram. It was a multi-sensory experience akin to the perfection sought in Michelin-star restaurants, an obsession with detail that sprung from Divinia Duque's grand design.

Edgardo could see the contentment, the peace, on his brother's weathered face and felt grateful for the moment of bliss, short-lived as it would prove to be.

*The last time Bram was in Corazon, Divinia and I were
celebrating the bar's third anniversary. The kids were in
Second and Third Grade. We had just moved into a two-
story house in the Hollywood Hills. It seemed like the
perfect life. They were my world. The Duke didn't exist
back then.*

Corazon had just opened for the day, as evident from the
groups of patrons sitting in booths in the main room and on
sunken sofas in the adjacent lounge. Philippine jazz played on a
stereo sitting behind bottles of rum. Louis Reyes's "Get My Drift"
was the selection as the brothers took seats at the bar, a pleasant
surprise to Joey The Rose as he brought out a flat of glassware
from the kitchen.

"There goes the neighborhood!" Joey said. "The Duque Boys,
together again!"

Bram laughed at the big man's bellowing greeting. He stood
from his seat to meet the bartender's offer of a handshake, as if
they were old friends.

"You must be The Rose," Bram said. He nodded to the man's
wine stain birthmark.

"Just 'Joey.' How'd you guess? I suppose a six-foot-two Italian is
rare on this street."

"My brother speaks highly of you. That's even more rare."

"Ed said something nice about me? Somebody get me a tissue!"

Though they'd just met, the two two men shared a deep and
heartfelt laugh. Within a minute, the chemistry between them
was palpable, and it pleased Edgardo to see two people he loved
connect with one another, a feeling he'd long missed since
starting his parallel life.

"Bottle of Baguio," Edgardo said to Joey. "Three glasses,
please."

"Goddamn, straight to business, eh?"

"We'll all laugh and dine together another day. Right now, Bram and I have a lot to catch up on."

"You got it, Ed."

Joey turned toward a wine rack built into the wall. He grabbed a bottle and readied three small dessert wine glasses. Edgardo reached across the bar counter and took them from him, handing the nested glasses to his brother.

"Is Felix in?" Edgardo asked.

"Waiting for you."

"Good man."

To Bram's confusion, Edgardo led him back outside. Joey followed them to the door.

"Since we're talkin' business," Joey said, "how'd it go last night?"

"The deal was done."

"So, the start of a beautiful friendship?"

"Just a deal, Joey. Baby steps. Remember?"

"Hey, I'm just glad you made it back in one piece." Joey returned to the bar as the brothers stepped out into the sunlight.

Upon that ominous gratitude, Edgardo led Bram next door, bottle and glasses in hand. He fished for keys in his jacket pocket and unlocked the door to a noodle shop, one that looked abandoned. Like its neighboring storefronts, its windows were covered in plywood and tarps, with cobwebs suggesting there hadn't been a customer in years.

"You own this place, too?" Bram asked.

"Kuya, I own half the block."

"Pakshet."

As the brothers entered the old noodle shop, Edgardo turned the two deadbolts behind him. Despite the empty shelves, the glass door papered over, and the tables and chairs covered with sheets, the air conditioner pumped strong as if new. It didn't kick up any dust for the defunct restaurant had been cleaned regularly, always kept in a state of "arrested decay," as Felix had put it.

"What did that red-faced higante mean?" Bram asked. "He said he was glad you made it back in one piece?"

"Joey always talks like that," Edgardo said in a dismissive tone.

Bram looked up at the sun-faded menus still affixed to the walls, a third of their letters missing. "I suppose an order of pancit is out of the question?"

"This was a *Japanese* noodle shop," Edgardo said. "Tonkatsu ramen was the order of the day, but not this day."

"Not for a lot of days, from the looks of it."

Edgardo prepared a table and three chairs. He gestured for Bram to join him as he poured three glasses of the bright red wine.

"Baguio strawberry wine?" Bram said. "What you have to say must be serious, Bata."

"It's a lot, and it's been a while since we talked."

Edgardo's words stung his brother.

"I'm sorry I refused visitors while I was inside. I didn't want anyone to see me in a cage. Even you. Especially you."

"Wouldn't have been my first time."

"County lockup is different from prison. One is a nuisance, the other is shame."

"I didn't see it that way," Edgardo said, "but I respected your wishes."

"I appreciated it, and I appreciated the packages. The commissary never made adobo."

"If they did, would you dare eat it? State prison adobo?"

Bram laughed at the ridiculous notion. "I might've. I mean, I don't see any noodles in this noodle shop."

"Not for nine years now. I may knock down that wall, expand the bar."

Bram heard someone enter from an unseen rear door. He stood on alert, but followed his brother's calm as a young Filipino man emerged from the back room.

Felix Ramirez, 35 years old, tall and trim in a white Polo shirt over jeans, brought a long carrying case and a large red envelope into the dining area. From his expression, he clearly didn't expect company and would normally be on guard, but like Bram, he took his cue from Edgardo's composed demeanor.

Six years prior, Felix worked as a top fence, using his formidable hacking skills to source and transport illegal goods both rare and valuable. He smuggled imports through Los Angeles Port Authority with Bakal Diaz as his muscle until his warehouses were raided. Though he was vigilant and discreet, always carefully vetting his wealthy clients – including me – a surprise raid at the crack of dawn ruined him when he was most vulnerable. Bad luck. But he'd set up an impressive alibi that protected us both, one that I helped cover. It would've been easier for Felix to throw me to the pigs, but he kept us clean. I got Fish to get him off on a minor offense. Felix has been with me ever since.

I haven't yet introduced Fish. I'll get to him shortly.

"Felix, this is my brother," Edgardo said.

"Abraham?" Felix asked, setting the case on the floor beside their table.

"My mother calls me Abraham. The screws at Lancaster call me Abraham. You call me 'Bram.'"

"Bram it is," Felix said. "I've heard great things about you."

"And he's heard nothing about you," Edgardo said. "Please don't feel offended."

"Not at all, Amo. My worst fear is that someone's heard of me."

Edgardo pulled out the third chair for Felix and slid a glass of wine to him, as if *three* brothers were reunited.

"Amo?" Bram said. The formal word was Tagalog for "boss." "You work for my brother?"

"Six years. And now I work for you. Welcome to HiFi."

"HiFi?" Bram asked with a laugh. "Like a stereo?"

"Historic Filipinotown."

Bram nodded and smiled at the nickname. He stood and raised his glass in a toast. "To HiFi!"

The three men drank Philippine strawberry wine together and sat at the table. Bram eyed the long carrying case.

"What's in there?" Bram asked the young man. "A sniper rifle or a trombone?"

"I play piano," Felix said with a smile.

"Pakshet, I think I do need a drink."

Bram slammed his wine, and Edgardo poured him another inch. As he downed his second drink, Felix slapped the large red envelope onto the table. Edgardo opened it and pulled out five 8x10 photographs, fresh from the printer. Bram didn't see them and didn't ask, allowing his hosts to reveal their importance, if they chose.

Edgardo scrutinized the photos and turned to his brother. "What do you know about HiFi, Bram? I'm sure you heard things inside."

Bram poured a third finger of wine and thought about the question for a moment, sipping the fruity spirit. "I heard three gangs run these streets. Educate me."

"Which three gangs?" Felix asked.

"I heard about 'Mga Hari sa Kalle 9.' Big Filipino outfit from what I hear. Big money."

"HK-9. Tip-top of the food chain. Rommel Basilio is the original 'One' of The Nine, and still boss. Lots of power and influence, we're talking political pockets. FBI tracks their every move, or tries to, anyway."

"I know Rom," Bram said. "Even on the boat from Manila, 20 years ago, he always saw himself as Fortune 500."

"That's Rom alright," Edgardo said. "I'm surprised you remember him."

"You don't gotta be a genius to remember that punyeta. He may come across as a serious businessman, but to me, he's just a puta Tondo hood rat with a rotten temper, I don't care how much his suit costs."

"Agreed. Who else, Kuya?"

"I also heard a lot about the Temple Street Boyz. Old gang. Small-time punks. Still in business?"

"TSB," Felix said. "Nickle-and-dime, pushing on street corners, mostly herb and cola."

"Just say 'weed' and 'coke,' Mr. Felix. We're all grown-ups here. No need for the latest hip labels."

"Right." Felix sought to tread lightly until he fully gained the ex-con's trust. Abraham Duque was an underworld legend, after all, once considered the deadliest man of the Bay Area's worst gang, The Demonyo. "TSB's grown a lot bigger since Calixto Cervantes took over for his brother, Kalaw. Cops brush against them from time to time."

"Pakshet," Bram said with a little laugh. "Little Calixto was stuck in Kalaw's shadow for so long, he probably pissed himself hard-on and jumped at his shot to run the yard when his brother passed. I'm surprised cops still care about that shit chongke they try to unload."

"Lately, they've unloaded quite a lot," Edgardo said. "A majority of the street marijuana in this neighborhood runs through them."

Bram glanced at his empty wineglass but turned away, knowing what too much Baguio can do to him. "I also heard about the Mexicans moving in. The 13 Loverboys or some shit. Don't know much about them."

"LB-13," Felix said. "Two-hundred strong. They're all about flexing, though rumor has it they're planning something big."

"So why are we talking about all this basura? Is one of them leaning on Corazon? Or the garage? You paying for protection?"

"Not exactly." Edgardo looked at his brother as he poured everyone another round. "Kuya... we do business with all of them."

Bram picked up his glass but only held it in front of him, lost in thought as he took in the alarming update. None of it should have come as a shock, but his dream of a legitimate life blinded him to Edgardo's reality. His jovial face fell away as he turned to his little brother.

"What kind of fuckin' business are we talking about, Eddie?" He braced himself for the response.

"Laundering, mostly, and transport."

"Transport what?" Bram asked with a forced laugh. The news was still sinking in. "Herb and cola?"

"Whatever needs moving. Guns. Trucks. There's also the AFA, the Koreans, The Panginoon back home..."

"Putang ina mo!" Bram shouted, slamming his full glass to the table, spilling wine across the red envelope. "And here I thought you left San Francisco to go straight!"

Going straight was news to Felix.

"That was the plan," Edgardo said, side-eyeing his assistant. "And I was straight... for a couple of years."

"But then what? Back in the shit?"

"We had debts to pay."

"You mean I had debts," Bram said, trying to hide his shame. "You bought them, didn't you, Eddie?"

"Bram..."

"And now you're hustling all over again, trying to make things right, just to end up inside like me? Is that what I'm hearing?"

"It's not like that, Kuya. We supply, that's all."

"Cops don't see it that way!"

"We remain invisible," Felix said. "Rumors. Ghosts."

Incredulous, Bram turned to the young man. "We just met, Mr. Felix, so forgive me when I say you sound like a fuckin' mokong."

"Easy, Bram," Edgardo said. "He's right. The cops don't know we exist. And I trust Felix like family. He's been instrumental as my left hand."

"Who's been your right hand?"

Edgardo was hesitant to answer. "Hank."

"You pulled that sweet old man into your operation?"

"*Our* operation."

"What would Nanay think?"

"I need people I can trust. You know Hank would kill for our family."

"Hank Brighton can't kill no one," Bram said. "The man is a living saint. What you mean is he'd *die* for our family."

Bram felt overwhelmed. He stood and paced the room, and in that tense moment, Edgardo had no idea what his older brother would say next. If he threw up his hands and walked away forever, there would be nothing anyone could do to stop him.

"He knows what he got into," Edgardo said. "He's helped keep us off the radar again and again."

"And again and again and again? He's your fence, ain't he? Any more 'family' on the payroll? Nanay? Div and the kids?"

"Divinia's in the dark, and you know I'd never get Chris and Carlo involved..."

"Do I really know that?" Bram asked. "Do your people know what happened to me? What happened in San Francisco? In Quezon City? Who else is tied to you?"

Edgardo and Felix looked at each other, unsure. Edgardo nodded to his assistant.

"We also have an arrangement," Felix said, "with Mr. Waldo..."

"Putang ina mo!"

"How many times are you going to say that?" Edgardo asked.

"A lot, it seems! Mr. Waldo is a lowlife négro gun runner with no loyalty!"

"There's also a new outfit," Felix said. "They're outside the city. The Wolf Pack MC."

Bram knew that name, heard it spoken many times in prison, always at the end of a horrific story. The "motorcycle club," new to Los Angeles, was almost as notorious as The Nines, the TSB, or the LB-13. "The Wolves?" He turned to his brother with a glaring stare. "Nazi basura! Since when do we trust a fuckin' biker gang? And since when do they trust anyone not wearing their colors?"

"They trust money," Felix said, "and they're gaining ground north of L.A."

"Shut the fuck up!" Bram shouted at the young man. "I'm talking to my brother!" He turned back to Edgardo, who sat stone-faced. "Shaking hands with other pinoy is one thing, Eddie, but now Mr. Waldo? And wannabe Hells Angels? They'll fuck you into the ground the second they get the chance!"

"But they won't take that chance," Edgardo said. "We have mutual interests, that's what I'm trying to convey. And no matter what happens, we always stay ten steps ahead."

Bram looked at the floor as he caught his breath. "How do you stay ahead of a bunch of reckless, leather-jacket meth-heads? You can't play chess with doped up fools."

"We're ahead of the DEA, ahead of LOCC, and you're concerned with small-time bikers?"

"Lock?" Bram asked. "Who or what is 'Lock'?"

"City task force," Felix said. "Los Angeles Organized Crime Crackdown."

"LOCC." Bram's head was ready to explode. He kicked over his chair and circled the room, tempted to smash his fist into a glass display case. The idyllic life he'd fantasized about now seemed a million miles away. "Whatever they're called, the Locks are the least of our worries! Feds got rules! Gun runners and biker gangs don't!"

"Sit down, Bram," Edgardo said, rising to his feet to meet his brother's eyes.

"This ain't no time for sitting..."

"I said SIT." Edgardo instantly regretted his firm tone, akin to commanding an unruly dog. He rarely used that angry voice, certainly not with his older brother. It prompted Felix to stand as well, as if a brawl was about to spark.

Edgardo hated bringing them all to that point of fury, confusion, and mistrust, and silently swore never to do it again. With his wife and children estranged, and his parents' health failing, these two men might soon be all he had left in the world.

"I mean no disrespect," he said to them both. "Sit with me, Kuya." He poured Bram another finger of wine and gestured for everyone to return to their seats.

Bram calmed himself, uprighted his chair, and sat at the table. He picked up his wine but merely held it in indecision.

"Bram, I didn't bring you here to shit on everything I've built. I need you."

"You? Need me?" Bram pushed out a laugh through an agonized expression. "You're a genius, Eddie, the smartest man I've ever met. Everyone knows that. Since when did you ever need an idyota like me?"

"You're anything but an idiot, Brother, and I've always needed you."

"Bushet..."

"And I need you now... as my Head of Security. My plans for Corazon are real. I meant everything I said about going straight. I just need money and time."

"Money and time..."

"You said you also dreamed of going straight when you got out, but the fact is we can only leave The Life together. That's always how it's been. You have to trust me."

Bram looked at the swallow of wine still in his hand. He downed it in one gulp, pushed the glass across the table to signal he's had enough, and pondered his brother's plea. The wide eyes staring at him left their mark. "I'm sorry I yelled. I also mean no disrespect."

"I don't blame you, Kuya. Ten years is a lot to take in."

"You've always been the smart one, Eddie. Of course, I trust you, and I trust your 'left hand' here, if you say so. It's fuckin' everyone else I'm worried about."

"Again, that's where you come in."

"As for 'money and time,' haven't you figured out by now there's never enough of either?" Bram sighed as the two men sitting across from him awaited his blessing. He realized that their plans truly did pivot on his involvement. They desperately needed a third man, someone whose loyalty was unquestioned, unbreakable. "Tell me about yesterday's job, the one Joey The Rose was talkin' about."

"Good man." Though Edgardo's stoic face didn't betray his anxiety and doubt, he subtly breathed a sigh of relief upon his brother's acceptance and willingness to help. "Felix will fill you in. Afterward, we'll go see Fish."

"I've wanted to meet that little man for a long time." Bram had finally calmed himself.

"Believe me, he also wants to meet you. You're the heart of every story I've told him."

"Lucky me."

As Felix detailed their delicate deal at the airfield, Edgardo picked up the red envelope and walked to a hole in the papered window. He pulled out the five photos and examined them closely in a beam of sunlight.

14

Stakeout

Jorge's red Camaro was parked a quarter-mile down from Edgardo's home atop an isolated hill in Highland Park. The classic muscle car was too distinguishable to be parked any closer. Jorge sat at the wheel. He kept one eye on the house ahead and the other on his rear-view mirror, on Yoy Yoy in the backseat. They shared a joint as they waited for their young comrade to return from his reconnaissance.

"You sure this is the place?" Yoy Yoy asked as he puffed the joint. "It's been almost three hours. Maybe nobody lives here."

"It don't look like an abandoned house to me," Jorge said, unsure.

"Who the fuck said abandoned?" Yoy Yoy always spoke slow and calm, even as he grew more agitated. "Just saying maybe this ain't the house you boys thought. Maybe The Duke don't live here. Maybe nobody does."

"Miguel will let us know."

"So where the hell is he? If this really is The Duke's house, maybe Miguel got made? Maybe he's been fuckin' dead the past half-hour?"

"He'll come back. You just gotta have faith."

"I got faith in my cousin," Yoy Yoy said, "but faith in Miguelito, that's another thing."

As if his ears were burning from the doubt, Miguel returned from the house. He had cut across an adjacent field, crossed the street, and sat in the front passenger seat. Upon seeing the questioning looks, he shook his head.

"Nothing?" Jorge asked.

"I looked in all the windows," Miguel said. "No one's home."

"What about the Benz?"

"There's a window into the garage from the back. Nothing."

"Shit."

"He'll be back by sunset," the teen said. "I swear."

"How the hell do you know?" Yoy Yoy asked as he passed the joint back to Jorge. "How'd you even know about this place?"

"I... I just know shit, alright?" Miguel didn't want to reveal his source and started to regret saying anything. "I just keep my eyes and ears open."

"That don't tell me shit."

"Miguel spotted his ride in town," Jorge lied, saving the boy from Yoy Yoy's interrogation. "He tailed him here and watched him a while."

"That's it?" Yoy Yoy asked.

"Yeah, that's it," Miguel said, going with his partner's story. "Just eyes and ears, man."

"My boy knows what's up," Jorge said.

"He sure-as-shit does." Yoy Yoy took the joint back for another puff. "It's like he admires the fuckin' guy."

Jorge didn't want Yoy Yoy to question his partner, which would mean questioning him. "You heard Calixto. We just need to sit and wait."

Yoy Yoy reached into the front seat, into Jorge's jacket pocket, and pulled out his pistol.

"What the hell, man?" Jorge asked.

Yoy Yoy opened the chamber and confirmed that the weapon was loaded. "Just wanna make sure you're ready for the Retirement Party."

"We were ready before we left the yard." Jorge turned to his young partner across from him. "Ain't that right?"

"Ready," Miguel said, though he couldn't shake his feeling of guilt. "So, we really doing this?"

Yoy Yoy took another drag from the joint and held it up for his men to see. "Either this shit is stirring up my brain and makin' me paranoid, or you two are fuckin' terrible actors." He handed the smoke to Miguel, who simply passed it to Jorge. "I guess we'll see soon enough."

15

The Law Office of Milo Fisher

In the heart of HiFi, a few blocks from the central intersection of West Temple and North Alvarado, stood a two-story camel brown structure. Tall palm trees lined the sidewalk, graffiti tags covered the curb and trash cans, and a billboard for Victoria Mexican Lager stood on the roof. With stucco walls, arched balconies, and Spanish tile, the small office building looked like a typical California apartment building that had been converted for commercial use. Three businesses shared the space.

On the north side, the "Ooh-La-La" nail salon offered "real frech manacures," hand-written just as crudely as it was misspelled on a square of poster board. The only thing "real" about the service was the fact that the owner had backpacked through Paris in her youth, had her nails done once in a little shop on the Champs-Élysées, and therefore felt qualified to call her own French manicures authentic.

On the south side of the building, "Parker Discount Printing" boasted of "500 business cards for $5.99," annotated with a tiny asterisk leading to the small-print disclaimer of "standard quality." The discounted cards of this bait-and-switch deal were as thin as tissue paper and were almost never chosen to be used in any professional setting. Instead, customers who came in for the deal ended up choosing "premium quality," a costly upgrade which provided the actual standard 16-point thickness.

Between the two storefronts stood a steel security door that led to a flight of stairs, ending at The Law Office of Milo Fisher on the second floor. The cluttered office was adorned with framed accolades and education hung on cheap wood paneling, Walmart chairs, and IKEA bookshelves, with stacks of files atop it all. A small Christmas tree sat on a particle-wood desk that took up the windowed corner, and behind it sat the sole lawyer of the practice, a small man with a large presence.

Milo "Fish" Fisher was a dwarf with a mop of curly black hair dangling over his deep-set eyes, chiseled face, and five-o-clock shadow. At 4'5", Fish needed his workspace arranged for his short stature and limited reach. His considerable workload would normally be assigned to a team of attorney and paralegals, particularly his off-the-books legwork for Edgardo.

Milo Fisher used to be a partner with Whitney, Cain, and Brown, with corporate clients in Hollywood and high office. "Fish" enjoyed a plush life of golf, luxury cars, and cocktails with his wealthy clients, and took more than his share of cocaine and kickbacks, pop stars and starlets. The brief ride came to a sudden end when Councilwoman Hightower used his wild nights to leverage him. But that's a story for another day.

After being buzzed in at the sidewalk, Edgardo and Bram walked past the reinforced security door, headed upstairs, and entered the small office. Fish was busy typing as if racing the clock. He hardly glanced at the brothers as he gestured for them to sit in the two chairs in front of his desk. Bram had to remove stacks of folders before they could take their seats.

"Good afternoon, Fish," Edgardo said. "This is my..."

"One second, Ed," Fish said, nailing his email. He typed so blindingly fast, Bram wondered if he was just writing gibberish for show, but Edgardo knew better. His long-time lawyer didn't need to showboat, for his results spoke for themselves.

Bram spotted a coffee machine in the corner. He rose to pour himself a cup and held out the carafe, offering a cup for his brother. Edgardo subtly mouthed "no."

"That's coffee's old," Fish said, still fixed on his work, "but you're welcome to it if you need a little pick-me-up."

Bram tilted the carafe only for a cold black syrup to ooze forth, a surface of fussy gray mold floating on top. Revolted, he quietly set the carafe back on its base. "Pakshet."

"Blume and Plume," Fish said without eye contact. "Six blocks down. That's where the real coffee is."

"Didn't I tell you?" Edgardo said with a grin.

"I think I'll wait." Bram returned to his seat.

Ending his email with a flourish of his fingers, the lawyer straightened his tie and turned to the brothers. "Alright, you have my complete attention. What's on your mind?"

"What happened to Yolanda?" Edgardo asked, nodding to a vacant desk behind them, piled high with files.

"Yolanda didn't work out, I'm sad to report."

"Of course not. Sorry to hear that. I actually liked this one."

"Well, that girl you actually liked walked out the door without warning, so now I'm rushing to catch up on her mountain of work. That's what happens when you take a nineteen-year-old with zero experience under your wing."

"But boy, was she hot," Edgardo said with a teasing raise of his eyebrow.

"Sizzling," Fish said flatly.

Bram laughed at their quick back-and-forth, a natural repartee honed over the years. He wasn't used to seeing his all-business younger brother so relaxed and jokey with someone. Affectionate teasing was never in his DNA.

"Fish, you need to forget aspiring actresses and models," Edgardo said, "and stop telling them you're a TV producer."

"I was a co-producer, Ed. I produced two pilots."

"Which produced nothing."

"Which produced two pilots."

"Do yourself a favor," Edgardo said. "Hire an ugly, ignorant, sweet old lady you can flirt with while she runs your office like a slave."

"What's your mother's number?"

"I said a *sweet* old lady."

Bram clasped his hands and laughed at the notion.

"I've met your mother, Ed. She'd be real sweet to me, I can promise you."

"Be careful, Fish," Edgardo said. "She's his mother, too."

Fish swiveled his chair toward Bram and held out his hand. "Then you must be Abraham Duque, the scary big brother everyone's been buzzing about. Milo Fisher."

Bram leaned forward and took his hand in a firm shake. "Bram."

Fish promptly slathered his hands with sanitizer and offered the pump bottle to his guests. Edgardo took a squirt, but Bram politely shook his head.

"No doubt, you're here to follow up on the deal at the airfield?" the lawyer asked.

"Felix says it was clean. I want to know how clean."

"Allow me to confirm Mr. Felix's optimism." Fish dug through the files on his desk, opened a folder, and skimmed its contents. "By the way, remind that young man that he still owes me fifty bucks."

"Don't worry, he's no fool."

"He bet against my Dodgers, didn't he?" Fish flipped through the pages in the file until he found what he was looking for. "That being said, Mr. Felix is right. Money was transferred and accepted, so your bikers were happy. The trucks were taken, GPS placed them at known properties of both outfits, so your brethren were happy."

"The HK-9 are not my brethren," Edgardo said.

"I'm sorry, Ed, I meant to say your fellow Filipino criminals based here in HiFi, those guys are happy... or were..."

"Unacceptable," Edgardo said with a grunt, interrupting his friend's forthcoming news. "Make no mistake, Fish, those men don't see me as a brother any more than they'd see you."

"Uh huh. Doubt that. But let's move on to an interesting development." Fish searched for another file and looked through it for a moment. "Okay, here we go..."

"You know I don't like 'interesting developments,' Fish."

"Well, you certainly won't be doing cartwheels for this one. Early this morning, cops raided a house in Silverlake, arrested some Nines, confiscated a lot of the shiny new guns from your deal. Please tell me Miss Candy scrubbed them well."

"She certainly did," Edgardo said, "as did Waldo before her, but I fail to see how this is interesting news to me. Once product leaves my hands, I wash them of it."

"Fair enough." Fish side-glanced Bram as if to ask his client for permission to continue in front of his newly released brother.

Edgardo nodded to them both. "I already filled Bram in. I keep no secrets from my brother."

"Not no more, anyway," Bram said.

Awkward.

Fish cleared his throat. "Well, for one, if I were President of the HK-9... or High Chief or Supreme Leader or whatever... I'd be thinking someone had set me up. I mean, they get a fresh shipment of weapons only to be raided hours later? Smells funny. If you were Rommel Basilio, what would you think?"

"If I were Rom," Edgardo said, "I'd think the Wolf Pack MC sold me out."

"A bunch of meathead bikers?" Fish asked. "Come on, Ed. Rom is even more narcissistic than you. He thinks they're beneath him, too high or too stupid to sell him out. Nah, he'd think it was The Duke, packaging a perfect deal between two notorious gangs just to sell it to the feds, tossing them to the mud while keeping your hands clean, as you say. We both know that's not true, but as I recall, HK-9 doesn't see you as brethren any more than they see me, remember?"

Edgardo conceded, looking at his curious and confused brother. He couldn't deny Fish's logic. "You at least got me covered during the deal?'

"Airtight alibis are an art form, my friend, and you're talking to the Leonardo DaVinci of alibis. When those ruffians met in that hangar in the desert, you were sitting prim and proper at The 1642 Bar with me, sipping a couple of Cosmos. I even got video."

"Good man."

"Video?" Bram asked, shocked. "How the hell'd you pull that off?"

"Big Brother," Fish said, "I got enough doctored video to place Ed on the deck of the Titanic."

"Pakshet, you really are good."

"That's what it says on my business card."

Edgardo reached into his jacket's inner pocket and pulled out the red envelope Felix had given him. He handed it to Fish, who slid out the five photos.

"And who are these lovelies?" Fish asked, scrutinizing the photos.

"You tell me."

"On it."

Satisfied, Edgardo stood and headed for the door. His brother followed him, still unsure of their situation.

"Anything I can do for Brother Bram?" Fish asked. "Surely, a free man fresh from the cooler needs... something?"

"Just wish me luck," Bram said.

"Then luck you shall have. Welcome to HiFi!"

Bram started to appreciate that odd greeting.

* * *

Edgardo drove his brother south down Temple Street, then north up the 110. Silent on the city streets, Bram's curiosity overcame him on the winding freeway.

"You trust that little lawyer?" he asked.

"Fish? More than most."

"Where'd you dig him up?"

"Long story," Edgardo said, "but washed-up lawyers, even brilliant ones, end up in the same place as disgraced doctors and convicted hackers: working for guys like us."

Bram looked out the window at the changing landscape. The towering skyscrapers, bustling traffic, and inner-city decay soon gave way to quiet, tree-lined suburbia. "Where we going, Bata?"

"My place. Highland Park. I'm just dropping you off. Make yourself at home, get some rest."

"What about Carlo and Christiana?"

"I'm bringing them over to see you. Divinia isn't ready yet."

"So, no 'Welcome to HiFi' from my sister-in-law?"

"She'll come around, Kuya. Baby steps."

16

Katulong

After five hours of sitting in Jorge's car, Yoy Yoy fell asleep in the backseat, leaving Jorge and Miguel to continue their stakeout. As the sun dipped behind the top of the hill, neither of the unnerved gangsters knew exactly what was expected of them, and neither wanted to ask for clarification. All they knew was that a confrontation with The Duke was inevitable.

"Sun's almost down," Jorge said. "Be ready."

"We sure we doin' this?" Miguel asked. "I mean, he let us go in the tunnel. He wasn't even mad or nothin'. He was cool."

"It was four-on-one. No shit, he let us go. Probably pissed himself."

"The Duke? I don't think so, man. I heard he can fight, like he can take on ten guys and shit."

"Yoy Yoy's right," Jorge said. "You do admire this fuckin' guy."

"I'm jus' sayin' he can handle shit is all."

"You're thinkin' of his brother. He's supposed to be a monster off the chain, used to be top enforcer for The Demonyo up in The Bay."

"Shet, I think I heard of him. Anthony or Arturo or something."

"Don't sweat it. They got that fucker locked up..."

Before Jorge could finish his thought, a black Mercedes crested the hilltop street as if emerging from the sunset, pulling into The Duke's driveway.

"It's Go Time." Jorge reached into the backseat and nudged his boss's leg.

"When he get here?" Yoy Yoy asked, groggy.

"He's just pullin' up now."

Yoy Yoy fully woke up fast. "Let's move."

"We for sure 'bout this?" Miguel asked one last time.

"Move!"

The three Temple Street Boyz stepped out of the Camaro and crossed the street. They crouched across a field of tall weeds and quietly hopped the fence at the rear of Edgardo's property. Before landing in the backyard, they saw a bald man step out of The Duke's car.

A moment later, hidden behind the storage shed, they heard the car drive away.

Bram entered the well-appointed home alone. Even while standing in near darkness, he felt overwhelmed by its opulence. A motion sensor triggered soft lights built into the ceiling tiles and classical music over the house speakers. Mozart's *Piano Sonata No. 8 in A Minor* welcomed the exhausted man into what looked like a Mediterranean country villa. He smiled at the luxury, but paused upon seeing his brother's family photos on the walls, all centered around their father's barong tagalog in its Plexiglas frame. The cold, all-business genius could be sentimental after all.

Entering the kitchen, Bram tossed his duffle bag on the dining room table and rummaged through the fridge. He peeled open a foil-wrapped plate. Disgusted by the leftovers, he pulled out his cell phone and called his brother.

"Everything alright?" Edgardo asked on the other end of the line.

"Nice place, Bata. Very GQ. But do you really eat this shit?"

Edgardo laughed. "Ah, you've found the refrigerator. Probably made a beeline for it."

"Fuck it," Bram said into the phone. "I'm cooking for you."

"No need. I'm bringing home a couple of pizzas for you and the kids."

"I didn't do ten years just to come out for fuckin' pizza-pizza."

Edgardo could hear him taking everything out of the fridge and cupboards and slamming them to the counter. "Careful, that's Italian tile!"

"This is a kitchen," Bram said. "If your precious tile can't take a few pots and pans, you wasted your money."

"The pizza is coming from Casa Bianca, if that makes you feel any..."

"You got two pounds of pork belly," Bram said, surveying the bounty he pulled from the fridge. "There's some roots, some half-decent spices, a sack of rice. No soy sauce, though, which makes me wonder if we're really related."

"Don't cook, Bram."

"You might as well ask a bird not to fly. Tell me, when's the last time Carlo and Christiana had real food?"

"Their mother is a Michelin-star chef."

Holding the phone with his shoulder, Bram unwrapped a large cut of beef, grabbed some onions and garlic from a nearby basket, and scanned the cupboards. "And their father reheats tin-foil TV dinners. Maybe they eat filet mignon with Div, but I'm guessing they get Lunchables over here."

"Pakyu ka!" Edgardo said with a laugh.

"How about something simple? Adobo and steamed rice?" Bram placed the meat in a large Zip-Loc bag and filled it with vinegar and herbs. "No bay leaves. You sure you ain't adopted?"

"I mean it, Kuya," Edgardo said while driving across the city. "Don't trouble yourself."

"Too late. I'm already troubled."

"Agreed."

"And I was cooking for your runt ass years before you met Div and started going out to fancy..."

A faint sound cut the silence.

Someone was rummaging through the garage.

"You heard that?"

"No," Edgardo said, concerned. "What did you..."

"Got a guest? Bram asked in a lowered voice.

"Just you."

"Maid? Cats? A dog?"

"No."

"I'll call you back."

"Wait, Bram..."

Bram hung up, wiped the three-inch paring knife clean of garlic, and hid the blade up his long sleeve, keeping it in place under his watchband. A small concealed weapon, instantly ready at any moment, was one of the first lessons he taught his bookish brother long ago. He grimaced at his paranoia, but his instincts couldn't be denied.

Upon hearing the phone cut, my first thought was to whip a U-turn back home, but I didn't want to further distress my brother, who was already alarmed about the drastic turns in my life. I also couldn't disappoint my children again, not after missing their last three milestones. With each lost opportunity, I felt Carlo's bitter anguish rising and Christiana's loving bond fading. At that moment, I pictured them sitting by the front door, awaiting their Tito Bram, eager for some semblance of the family union we once had, a desperate hope we shared.

I kept the wheel steady and continued to Divinia's. I told myself that the odds of a home invasion were slim, and concluded there likely wasn't cause for concern. None of my underworld contacts – friends or foes – had managed to trace my path back home, though some tried. I'd always been careful about being tailed, especially on that day, welcoming my brother back to the world.

Edgardo convinced himself that things were fine, that Bram could handle himself in any situation, and that he'd be back home for family pizza and adobo soon enough.

If only his need to gain favor with his family hadn't clouded his normally impeccable judgement.

Bram entered the dark garage with the paring knife hidden under his wrist. He felt for the light switch, flipped it on, and was greeted by the disturbing sight of three TSB gangsters staring back at him. His brother's life was more complicated than he'd been led to believe.

Yoy Yoy Aquino stood ten feet away in front, his pistol pointed at Bram's head. Jorge Vega and Miguel Hortiz flanked Bram, just five feet away.

"Hello, Mr. Duke," Yoy Yoy said. "I heard so much about you. It's good to finally put a face to the name."

"That ain't him," Jorge said.

"You sure?" Yoy Yoy looked to Miguel, who nodded in agreement. "Then who's this?"

"I dunno," Miguel said, confused.

"You dumb-asses sure we got the right fuckin' house?"

"Where's the SLK?" Jorge said in a demanding tone, his mind fixed on completing Calixto's task.

"SLK?" Bram asked, as if he knew nothing about cars. He slowly raised his hands above his head.

"The black Benz!"

"Black... what Benz?"

"The one that's normally parked right where we're fuckin' standing! Where is it?"

"More to the point," Yoy Yoy said, forgetting about the car for the moment, "where the fuck is The Duke and who the fuck are you?"

Bram sized up the three gangsters, realizing they didn't recognize him. He clinched his eyes shut and acted terrified. "My name is..." he said with a stutter. "My name is Rodrigo... please... don't hurt me."

Yoy Yoy nodded to Jorge to frisk the bald man. He patted his shirt, vest, pants, and nodded to his boss, failing to find the hidden paring knife held high above "Rodrigo's" head.

"Listen carefully, Rodrigo," Yoy Yoy said. "Whether or not we hurt you depends on what you tell us. So again, where's The Duke? Where's the car?"

"I... I don't know. I just watch the house while he's away... water the plants... feed the cat..."

"You're Duque's fuckin' katulong," Yoy Yoy said, thinking the man was a simple house servant.

"Yes. He brought me over from Manila last year."

"We saw him drop you off. When's he coming back?"

"I don't know. I swear."

"Fuck, Katulong, looks like you're not much use to us alive." Yoy Yoy lowered his gun and again nodded to Jorge, who raised his own gun to Bram's head.

"Hold up!" Miguel said. "Wait a second..."

"Count to three, Jorge."

"Hold up, man!"

"Twenty-thousand!" Bram shouted, his voice quivering.

The gangsters looked at each other, curious, unsure. Jorge lowered his gun.

"He's got emergency money stashed away," Bram continued. "Twenty-thousand. That's all I know! Don't kill me, please!"

"Take us to it and we'll see," Yoy Yoy said.

"It's in the backyard. Please... don't tell him I told you."

"Oh, you don't got to worry about that, Katulong."

Jorge shoved his gun into Bram's face and nudged him back into the house.

* * *

Divinia Duque lived with her two children in a two-story Colonial house high in the Hollywood Hills, in the affluent neighborhood of Beechwood Canyon. The famous Hollywood sign could be seen in the distance, just a mile up the road.

Edgardo parked in the brick-lined driveway, the car's black paint and trim a contrast to the colorful flowerbeds lining the property. He walked up the front steps but paused upon reaching the door, taking a deep breath to gather himself before pressing the doorbell.

Divinia opened the door, revealing an interior straight from a spread in *Better Homes and Gardens*. Without a glance, she gestured for him to come in.

"Are they ready?" Edgardo asked.

"Is anyone really ready to see the infamous Tito Bram?" she said.

"Ten years softened him, Divinia. He's not the man you remember." Edgardo craned his neck and shouted up the stairwell. "Carlo! Chris! Let's go!"

"Whatever you say, Eddie. You going to see Reyna and Otto?"

"Tomorrow night. Dinner. You coming?"

"I have plans."

"This close to Christmas?" Edgardo dreaded his ex-wife's response. "She will not be pleased. She's probably already setting the table."

"Your mother is never pleased, Eddie. I could cure cancer and she wouldn't be pleased."

Edgardo's two teenage children came downstairs.

Carlo Duque, 17 near 18, marched down toward his father, his athletic build dressed in a fitted T-shirt and cargo shorts, a scowl fixed on his face.

Christiana "Chris" Duque was barely 16, her large, round eyeglasses over her pleasant face. She wore floral print overalls and dressy boots. The girl smiled wide and held a homemade bouquet of LEGO flowers.

Chris hugged her father while looking over his shoulder, out the window to his car.

Carlo kept his hands in his pockets.

"Where's Tito Bram?" Chris asked.

"He's waiting at my house. Let's go. Time is burning."

"I wanna show you something first," Carlo said as he walked into the living room. He opened a cabinet and proudly produced his golden MVP trophy, the same one from the photo on Edgardo's phone the night before. A little football player cradled a ball on top.

"Very nice," Edgardo said. "I saw it on my phone last night."

"Yeah, well, I wanted you to see it for real, up close. This is what winning looks like."

"MVP. Good man. Your mother said you worked hard for this."

"All season, every day."

"You earned it, boy."

"Hell yeah, I did."

"It should be on the mantle for everyone to see," Edgardo said. "Why keep it in a cabinet?"

"Why do you care?"

"Carlo!" Chris said.

Edgardo didn't know how to respond, afraid that anything he said would further fuel his son's anger.

"Your father called me, Carlo," Divinia said, choosing to help diffuse the scene. "He was on his way, but he had last-minute urgent business."

"All business, all the time," Carlo said with a snort. That pathetic phrase, which had long been burned into him, was meant to emphasize a strong work ethic but only served as a sad excuse for his father's continual absence. To the boy, it meant "I don't care enough to be there."

Edgardo picked up the trophy and read his son's name across the base plaque. He caught his own lost expression reflected back at him in the curved brass, his loss of control, and remembered the brewing scene he left back at his home. It made him wonder if perhaps tonight was a bad time to take his kids to Highland Park, though he conceded he didn't have much choice.

"I'm sorry, Carlo," he said to his son. "You're angry with me, I get it. But Tito just got out, and he's dying to see you."

"Then let's go," the boy said. "For Tito."

Carlo grabbed his football trophy from Edgardo and shoved it back into the cabinet, as if the thing itself was worthless to him next to the look of shock and dismay on his father's face. The man had no involvement in the teenager's success, no influence or support or pride, and that was the real trophy. He put on his letterman jacket and stood ready to go.

Edgardo had many things to say to his hurt, rebellious son, but was halted by someone at the door...

KNOCK KNOCK KNOCK

"I thought you told Peter and Jesse you were busy tonight?" Divinia asked her son.

"I did. They both had plans anyway..."

KNOCK KNOCK KNOCK KNOCK KNOCK

Divinia turned to Edgardo. He pressed his ear to the door.

"Police officers!" a man's deep voice called from the porch. "Mr. Duque! Open the door! We have a warrant for your arrest!"

Divinia walked up to her ex-husband and leaned in close to whisper in his face. "Eddie... what did you do?"

17

Out of Respect

At gunpoint, Bram as "Rodrigo" led the three Temple Street Boyz through Edgardo's immaculate home. He felt their breath and footsteps taint his brother's sanctuary, and while the gangsters' audacity angered him, their knowledge of this place concerned him, for he feared they were all on a path to ruin. History was repeating itself. It made him feel small and helpless, a feeling he'd have to shelve for now.

He took the three men through the living room, the kitchen, and the dining room. Only Yoy Yoy followed as he continued past the French doors that opened to the backyard, an inviting outdoor space just as exquisite as the home's interior. Lush landscaping framed a lap pool and its adjoining hot tub. A river-rock path bisected a long grassy lawn, ending at a redwood storage shed.

Yoy Yoy stood on the back porch, his pistol raised to Bram's back, and took in the charming backyard. "Where to now, Katulong?"

Through the glass French doors, Bram saw Miguel and Jorge still inside, wandering the house, looking for valuables.

"Talk," Yoy Yoy said, pressing his gun to the back of Bram's neck.

"He buries it in the flower bed by the shed. Please, it's yours if you leave me and my brother alone."

Shit.

"Sooo, that's who you are?" Yoy Yoy said. "The Duke's brother?"

Jorge slid open the glass doors and joined his boss. Miguel remained inside.

"I'm gonna need help moving a heavy stone," Bram said. "Someone used to manual labor."

"Manual labor," Yoy Yoy laughed. "That ain't me, Katulong, not for a long fuckin' time." He looked to Jorge, who looked to Miguel inside, of course.

"Miguelito!" Jorge shouted. "Get your skinny runt ass out here!"

"Start digging," Yoy Yoy said. "Brother." He saw the confusion on Jorge's face. "Homeboy's his brother."

"Nah, man. Duke's only got one brother, and he's locked up."

"Not no more, he ain't." Yoy Yoy stared at Bram and quickly pieced together what little he knew about Edgardo Duque. "Rodrigo my ass, you're Abraham! You ain't as much trouble as I'd figured, brother. The crazy stories I'd heard about you, I shoulda known it was all bushet."

His cover now blown, Bram turned to the invaders, dropping his timid act. "Everything you heard about me is true, ginoo." He stared down Yoy Yoy, who still held his gun at ready.

"Ooh, scary," Yoy Yoy said. "Maybe you is a bad man after all?" He shoved Bram onto the back lawn.

"You're here to kill him," Bram said, his tone now flat, direct. "You're here to take the money, the car, and you're gonna kill him."

The TSB boss laughed. "Don't forget the house! Lotta prime shit in there. But you dig up that cash, might buy you some time, assuming you weren't fuckin' lyin' about that, too."

Miguel stepped out of the house and joined them on the lawn.

Bram now saw all three men around him. "Out of respect, I wanted you all outside."

"How is us being out here showing us respect?" Yoy Yoy said with a laugh. "Explain that to me."

"Respect for my brother. I didn't want to get blood all over his house."

In a flash, Bram revealed the paring knife...

He slashed Yoy Yoy's gun hand, disarming him... rushed Jorge, slashed him twice across the throat... plunged the blade deep into his chest, slicing it upward... turned and hurled the knife into Yoy Yoy's neck.

Miguel collapsed, terrified by the carnage dispatched with lightning speed.

Bram walked to Yoy Yoy's bleeding body... yanked the knife out of his jugular... and viciously cut his throat.

He picked up the gangster's gun and pointed it at Miguel flailing on the ground, staring into him like a fiery demon.

"Pl... please... don't hurt me..." Miguel said.

"There, now that's a helluva lot more convincing than my performance." With two men dead behind him, Bram took his time with the last one.

"No performance!" Miguel's body shook on the edge of a convulsion. "We just... we just wanted... the car... the money..."

"Pakshet! You came here to kill my brother. And me. The car, the cash, it was just gravy to you boys."

"Yes!" The young gangster gave up trying to lie his way out of his predicament. "I mean, no! I was against it... I didn't want to hurt The Duke! I swear to God!"

"Who signed off on it?"

"Calixto!" Saying his boss's name aloud made him nauseous. "Calixto sent us! But we didn't know you got out! I swear!"

"Calixto Cervantes," Bram muttered to himself, knowing the name well. "That fuckin' rat buwisit."

"Please, I got nothin' against The Duke! I was sucked into this shit! I didn't want to do nothin' to him! He spared our lives! Please believe me!"

Bram looked into Miguel's eyes and recognized his fear, felt the pressure of his gang. He couldn't bring himself to end the boy's life, for he'd stood in his shoes years ago. Back then, he would have instantly pulled the trigger, simply following orders, but a decade of prison and the lingering hope for a life free from violence had taken hold. Abraham Duque, former enforcer for The Demonyo, now had traces of mercy pecking at his soul. He heard the boy's pleas, and they froze his hand.

"Miguel, right?" Bram asked, hiding his hesitation. The boy nodded. "Miguel what?"

"Miguel Hortiz!"

"Who drove you here, Miguel Hortiz?"

"Jorge!" Miguel pointed to his dead partner a few feet away.

Bram knelt beside Jorge's body and fished his car keys from his pants pocket. He tossed them to Miguel's feet. "Listen carefully, Miguel Hortiz. You go back to that shithole junkyard and you tell Calixto the TSB ain't gettin' a dollar or a dime or speck of dust from my family. Tell him everything you saw tonight. Describe every moment, every detail, every drop of blood."

"I will! I... I promise!"

Bram eyes were aflame as he spoke with the dooming voice of Ang Makina. "Tell him Abraham Duque is alive and out of the joint. Tell him the only reason he's still alive is because I allow it. Can you remember all that?"

"Y-yes!" Miguel clinched his teeth to keep them from clattering. He sat in on the damp grass, his head fuzzy, ready to pass out, unsure if this monster of man would keep his word.

"Good. Don't make me regret cuttin' you loose."

"I'll never forget! Thank you!"

"You also live because I allow it. Now go, before I change my mind." Bram felt pangs of guilt for instilling paralyzing fear in the boy, clearly in over his head. In some ways, he reminded him of his misguided nephew.

"Wh.. what about... them?"

"There is no 'them'," Bram said. "Not no more."

"I mean... what are you..."

"I'm keeping your friends. They belong to me now."

Bram lowered his knife and pointed to the back fence. Miguel stumbled to his feet and clumsily scrambled over it. The moment he landed among the tall weeds of the field on the other side, he sprinted back to Jorge's car as if the Grim Reaper himself was chasing him.

18

Accomplice to Murder

Standing at her front door, Edgardo looked at his ex-wife with a stern expression of control that masked his overwhelming feeling that his life was about to burn to the ground.

"Duque!" a police officer yelled from the other side of the door. "We have a warrant!"

Edgardo glanced at his kids before turning to Divinia. "Let them in. I won't resist."

"Eddie, tell me what's going on before I open that door," she said, horrified at what she didn't know.

"They're about to kick it down. Just open the door and let them take me. It'll be okay."

With Carlo and Chris standing back, paralyzed with fear, their mother unlocked the door and swung it open, revealing two uniformed officers on the porch...

Officer James Robinson, a Black man in his late 50s, stood in the doorway, taking in the sight of the frightened family. The tall, calm officer had an apologetic look on his face, as if he could relate to the Duques' confusion and dismay. His partner, Officer Paul Vernon, a young White blonde with only a few years on the force, saw the scene differently. Half of Robinson's age in terms of years, experience, and wisdom, Officer Vernon didn't see a family about to be ripped apart, rather just another rich, self-entitled prick to haul in.

Officer Robinson did all the talking.

"Thank you for your cooperation," he said.

"You won't get any trouble from us," Edgardo said, shooting a look at his family. "No resistance."

"That's good, because this is never easy."

They nodded to the woman of the house, walked past her... past Edgardo... and grabbed Carlo.

They turned the teenager around and handcuffed his wrists behind him.

"Carlo Duque, you're under arrest," Officer Vernon said, tightening the cuffs a little too much, pinching into the boy's skin.

"What is this?" Divinia asked. "You want... Carlo?"

Carlo stood in shock, stooped slightly because of the cuffs. Like his father had promised, he didn't resist the police.

"Eddie, do something!" she shouted. "This has to be some kind of mistake!"

"What are you charging him with?" Edgardo asked, trying to piece things together.

"Come to the station and make a statement," Officer Robinson said. "We'll disclose the charges there."

"Carlo??" Divinia said to her son as he was taken outside.

"I didn't do nothin'!" the boy said.

"Tell the truth!"

"I was just drivin', Nay! I swear! I didn't know nothin'!"

The two cops took Carlo down the front steps, down the river rock path to the driveway where their police cruiser was waiting, its motor running. Edgardo hurriedly followed, choosing to speak with the elder officer.

"I'm his father!"

"I'm sorry, sir. I can't disclose anything until he's in custody."

"He looks like he's well in custody to me."

"You'll have to come to the station."

"Unacceptable," Edgardo said. "I'm not asking for names or any other confidential information. I just want to know what my son is being accused of!"

Officer Robinson slowed down. He relinquished their suspect to his partner, gesturing for him to continue to the car, and pulled Edgardo aside for a word.

"Aiding and abetting," he said, keeping his voice low. "Accomplice to murder."

"I didn't do nothin'!" Carlo said, having heard the charge.

"So you're just taking him away?" Edgardo asked. "What about his rights?"

"My partner will go over the boy's Miranda rights in the car. He'll be well versed with them by the time we get to the station, I promise."

"Unacceptable!" Edgardo rushed to the police cruiser and stood between Officer Vernon and the vehicle. He could see his ex-wife and daughter on the porch in the distance, crying in an embrace. The sight shattered his heart.

Officer Vernon simply glared at Edgardo, who knew there was nothing more he could do at the moment. He had no choice but to let them proceed without incident, as he'd promised.

"Carlo gets good grades," Edgardo told the cops. "He has friends who love and respect him. He was awarded MVP of his football team last night for Crissakes! Accomplice to murder? Unacceptable! He's my son!"

"Mr. Duque," Officer Robinson said in his deep, calm voice. "The situation may be unacceptable, I get it. Believe me, I do. But every criminal, every suspect, is someone's son."

On the porch, Chris turned to her mother in the open doorway.

"I... I didn't think it was true," the girl said.

"You knew about this?" Divinia said, her mind scattered. She'd thought her preteen daughter shared everything with her, especially with family matters.

"He bragged about hanging out with gangsters, but he laughed like it was all a joke. I thought he was messing with me."

"What gangsters? What did he do?"

"They were at a party. Lots of drinking. They drove somewhere to... to scare someone. It sounded bad but..."

"Why didn't you think to come to me with this?" Divinia asked. "You didn't think I'd..."

"Because you're always angry!" the girl said in a sudden outburst. Her mother couldn't remember the last time her shy daughter raised her voice. "You and Carlo and Tatay, you're always mad at each other! Any little thing sets you off! Maybe I should've said something, but I didn't!"

"Oh, Chris..."

"If I told you about every stupid little thing Carlo did, it would just break us apart more! Is that what you want?"

Christiana broke down in tears. Divinia gently placed her arms around her, and the girl held her tight, crying into her chest. They crumbled together, not knowing if this was a minor thing that could be resolved quickly, or if this was forever the end of their family as they knew it.

Divinia looked out at the driveway, at Edgardo still pleading with the cops as they entered their cruiser and shifted into

Reverse. For the first time, she saw her ex-husband, the genius who always had control, slouched before the officers, powerless as he watched his son being driven away.

He returned to the house, trudging the curved river rock path back to the porch. By the time he reached the front door, his ex-wife and daughter had already retreated to the living room. The young girl sat on the couch with her head down between her bent knees. Divinia sat on a chair beside her, trying to contain herself.

"We need to bail him out, Eddie," Divinia said, quashing any blame or resentment she felt toward her ex-husband for the moment. "We need to arrange it tonight."

"We can't," Edgardo said with a sigh, having spoken further with Robinson. "They're going to process and hold him until his hearing. Ten o'clock tomorrow morning."

"I don't understand. We can't post bail before then?"

"That's what the man said."

"Something's not right, Eddie."

"I'll get my lawyer on it."

"That's all you can say..."

"That's all I can do!"

Looking into each other's eyes, both of their emotional dams, their fronts of strength and control, had finally burst. All their anguish poured forth through what seemed to be a crisis without beginning or end. Their upstanding son behind bars, even for a single night, seemed unthinkable.

"Your lawyer?" Divinia asked. "That shady Mr. Fisher?" She quickly calmed herself, ashamed of questioning the man. She remembered the many times Milo Fisher had helped their family, their businesses. He'd arranged meetings with universities for her children, expedited licenses and permits for Corazon, even negotiated early talks with the Gourmet Travel Network. She owed Fish for everything they had, even as she suspected that he occasionally skirted the law for them. "I'm sorry, Eddie. I know Fisher will do whatever it takes for Carlo."

Edgardo appreciated how she took a breath, a moment to reassess. She was intelligent and rational and just got caught up in the emotions of the ordeal. For a moment, he remembered why he fell in love with her so many years ago, and he blamed himself for "letting her get away" as Bram put it.

"Fish will do whatever it takes for all of us, Divinia. I'm essentially his only client, which means we're his only client."

"Yes, I know."

"If anyone can get Carlo out of this mess, it's him."

"You're right. Getting him out, keeping him safe, that's all that matters." Divinia composed herself more for her grieving daughter than her helpless ex-husband. She turned to Christiana, still sullen on the couch, her head between her knees. "Chris, is there anything else you can tell us? He said he was just driving?"

Chris nodded, rose to her feet, and threw her arms around her mother again. With Edgardo watching helplessly across the room, she buried her sobs in her mother's shoulder.

Edgardo wasn't sure what to say, a feeling he wasn't used to. "I can stay if..."

"Go tend to your brother," Divinia said. She'd had enough of her husband's secrets for now.

"Bram can take care of himself tonight."

"It's his first night out. Go look after Abraham before the cops haul him away, too. I'm sure he has something to do with this."

"That's not fair, Divinia, and it's not true..."

"True or not! Just go!"

Divinia led Chris upstairs. Edgardo reached between the stairs' posts and grabbed his daughter's arm. "I will fix this, Christiana. I swear to you, I will bring your brother home. Until he's back in this house with you and your mother, nothing else matters to me."

Chris nodded. She believed her father.

Divinia gave him a look of hope. It's what she needed to hear, even if she didn't completely believe it.

As the women headed up, Edgardo eyed his ex-wife's wet bar in the corner of the living room, their ornate bottles beckoning him, before walking out the front door.

19

Guard Dog

After 30 minutes on the road, driving up and down the steep streets of Echo Park and Silverlake, Edgardo returned to his hilltop home. His exhaustion, both mental and physical, subsided at the sounds and smells of food cooking. He stepped out of his garage and entered his kitchen.

Bram whipped around and stared at him, paring knife in hand.

"So, you were serious?" Edgardo said.

"Serious?" Bram hoped his highly observant brother hadn't picked up on his paranoia, his waiting for more assailants, waiting for the front door to be rammed down. He realized Edgardo was commenting on the dinner in progress, the nostalgic smell of steamed rice and braised pork. "You know I'm always serious about food, Eddie."

"I can see. You were busy while I was gone."

"Yes... I was busy."

Edgardo lifted the lid of a pot simmering on the stove, unsure of how to break the news that his son – Bram's sole nephew – had been taken into custody for charges unknown. He smelled the adobo and noticed Bram returning the paring knife to the butcher block, even though there was no need for such a blade at the moment.

"No pizza-pizza?" Bram asked. "All the better. I made plenty."

"It smells amazing, Kuya, but I'm afraid it's just going to be us tonight."

"The kids ain't coming?" Bram felt both disappointed and relieved, mostly the latter. "Div won't let them see me?"

"No, it's nothing like that. Divinia's fine with it. She actually wants them to see you again. But the kids..."

Bram sensed his brother's unease. "The kids are what?"

"Carlo's been arrested." Edgardo felt his chest tighten upon saying the words. "They took him a half-hour ago."

"Arrested?" Bram was shocked, even as his little brother calmly perused his wine rack and readied two glasses. "For what?"

"Not sure, but the cops are talking murder."

"Pakshet! Carlo? The boy's no killer!"

"Accomplice."

Edgardo didn't know what else to tell him, for it happened so suddenly, and he didn't know much. For a man who anticipated and prepared for every scenario, the feeling of being powerless in the dark was unnerving. "Whatever happened, Carlo was the driver."

Bram threw his towel to the counter. "Then let's go get him!"

"The hearing is tomorrow morning. We can't touch him until then. Again, I'm not sure why."

"Something ain't right, Eddie."

"That's what Divinia said."

"Div's right," Bram said. He couldn't bear the lost gaze in Edgardo's eyes. "I always worry when you aren't sure about something."

"Me, too, Kuya." Edgardo selected a bottle of wine, a four-year-old Cabernet Sauvignon, and poured two glasses. "I called Fish. Maybe he can get Carlo out early or, at the very least, maybe a private cell."

"I don't even want to think about him mixed in with the basura."

Edgardo opened the rice cooker and paddled two scoops into his bowl, another two for Bram. "For tonight, we need to stay positive. This meal helps, the one bright spot of the day. Thank you, Abraham."

Bram knew his brother only used his full name when he felt lost and alone, frightened, a throwback to their early childhood when Edgardo was a stuttering little boy diagnosed with mild neurodevelopmental disorders. "Eddie, there's no need to thank me..."

"Don't be modest," Edgardo said, interrupting his brother's confession. "Everything looks perfect." He set the rice and wine on the table.

Bram lowered his head and walked to the glass French doors that led to the backyard. "Puchanggala..." he muttered with a sigh.

"What is it?"

"Don't thank me, Bata. I hate to add more bad news, but that's what I got. Maybe we should eat first..."

Edgardo knew his brother's "tells," his head bowed low, breathing hard through his nose, and now he stood in an awkward spot to block the back door. Edgardo peered out the window above the sink. Upon seeing the carnage in his backyard, he stormed outside, shoving past his brother.

Stepping out onto his back deck, much to his brother's dismay, Edgardo saw the bloody bodies of Jorge Vega and Yoy Yoy Aquino lying on the grassy lawn. Bram joined him, and Edgardo turned in a fury.

"Your first day out?" he said. "What the fuck happened?"

"They came to kill you. And me."

Edgardo kneeled over the bodies, barely able to get the words out. "This one is Jorge Vega, one of the punks I told you about. Tried to carjack me."

"Him?" Bram said, incredulous. "Punyeta sticks a gun in your face, you let him loose, and this is how he repays you?"

"And you had to kill him?"

"You're pissed at me? You said yourself, you were seconds away from taking them out in the tunnel! How is this any different?"

"I could have covered it in the tunnel! No one would know I was there! I'm a ghost on the streets! But this is my house, Abraham! If the feds ever come here... there's DNA everywhere!"

Bram flew into a rage, feeling that his brother was being short-sighted. "What the fuck was I supposed to do? Talk my way out of a gun to my forehead? Use my charm? I ain't the diplomat deal maker you are! I don't talk, I act! I ain't The Duke of Whatever!"

"No, you certainly aren't," Edgardo said, breathless. He looked at his brother as if he'd lost his mind. "You're the loyal guard dog, just released from his cage. Maybe Divinia's right. Maybe I should keep the kids away from their thug Tito Bram."

"Tumahimik ka!" Bram felt crushed by his brother's words. He'd endured harsh judgment all his life, but never from Edgardo. "Don't say that, Bata. Don't you fuckin' say that to me. Not now."

"You have any idea the world of shit you've dropped us into? Forget the feds, TSB is gonna figure out what happened sooner or later."

"Sooner." Bram's voice trailed as the word fell out.

"What's that supposed to mean?" Edgardo asked with dread.

"I let one of them go." The words tumbled clumsily out of Bram's mouth. His brother sat on the grass, barely able to breathe from the news.

"You... let one go..."

"Just the one."

"You let one go..."

"Eddie, he wasn't part of it. He was just a kid in over his head."

Edgardo finally exploded. "So you let him scamper off? Back to Calixto Cervantes?"

"That's right! I let him off as a warning to Calixto and those Temple Street gagos! Ain't that better than *three* bodies lying here?" To Bram's despair, Edgardo looked overwhelmed, his normal air of control gone. "Eddie, listen to me. If they declare war, we deal with it together, like we did back home. Just get your men on this..."

"I don't have any men!" Edgardo screamed in a choked exhale, a quiver of desperation in his voice.

Bram felt confused. His brother was The Duke. In prison, he'd heard of the legend long before realizing the name or discovering it was his little brother. "What's *that* supposed to mean?"

"You don't get it, Bram. I have Hank, I have Felix, I have my warehouse and my business connections, and that's it. 'The Duke' is just an empty reputation, respect and fear with nothing to back it up. If any army comes after me, comes after my family, what do I have to fight them with?"

"You have a loyal guard dog," Bram said, "just released from his cage."

Edgardo turned away and wept into his palms, a sight Bram hadn't seen since they left their beloved Philippine fields behind as children. He sat beside him on the grass and placed his arm around his shoulders.

"You're the smartest man I know, Bata. Not just smart, you're better than me in every way. I don't say that enough, and I'm lucky you're my brother because you'll figure out this mess. I know you will, and I'll help you."

Keeping his head down, Edgardo turned and sobbed in his older brother's arms. His mind a whirling storm, Bram hugged him tight and shared his tears, ready to destroy anyone who dared to return to that house.

20

Fancy Cage

Otto's Automotive had a busy morning, as always, a mix of old regulars with new word-of-mouth customers. HiFi and its surrounding boroughs were full of tire shops, transmission shops, brakes and suspension, body and paint, tune-ups, window repair, stereo installation, and quickie oil changes, but Otto's stood out as a true full-service facility. It was one of the few one-stop-shops within a five-mile radius, and the only one within 30 miles whose rates wouldn't break an average household, something Hank Brighton had always been proud of. Cost of parts may have risen over the years, but their labor fees hadn't increased since the days when the garage's namesake, Otto Harrison – Eddie's stepfather – ran the business with Hank as his Lead Technician.

"Over here, Eddie!" Hank called out from Bay One. He'd spotted Edgardo walk into the adjacent bay wearing his casual suit, not bothering with his usual subterfuge of stained mechanic's coveralls. He also brought no coffee, another deviation from routine that concerned Hank, but he knew why.

The old man quickly pulled his friend aside and handed him the red envelope. "Fish brought this by last night, says he's done with it. I'm guessing that's why you're here."

"Did he tell you about Carlo?" Edgardo asked.

"Everything. I'm so sorry, Eddie."

Edgardo peeked inside at the photos, now paper-clipped to documents. Fish did his job well. "You take a look?"

"I did. Christ, I recognize two of them."

"I thought you might."

"So, what do we do?" Hank asked. "With that many foxes circling, the logical thing to do is lock up the henhouse."

"Unacceptable. We continue, business as usual."

"You sure about this?"

"No, but image is important."

"Never let 'em know how much you know, right?"

Edgardo nodded. "We just need to stay alert."

"I'll keep an eye out. Anything else?"

"No trucks for the time being."

"But we got two coming in now..."

"No trucks, Hank," Edgardo repeated in a firm tone. "None until I say."

"You got it. I'll tell them to piss off until further notice."

"Good man."

"What if they raise a ruckus?" Hank asked.

"Offer an extra 20 Percent for next time if they so much as raise an eyebrow."

Hank spotted Bram standing in the distance, near the Jeepney food truck. "I see my boy's free at last. You keeping him out there?"

"Until I figure out the situation."

"What kind of situation are we talking about, Eddie?"

"The kind where I can't risk anyone piecing together that you two are close."

"Well, tell that big gorilla we all missed him," Hank said. "Tell him welcome back to the world."

"You'll get your chance soon enough, Old Man." Edgardo folded the envelope and placed it in his inner jacket pocket.

Hank glanced at his girl in the back corner of the shop. "Candy's already working on modifications to your home security, gonna have that place sealed up like Fort Dixon."

"Tell her to hold off. A new house may be the best move."

"Damn, it's that kind of situation?"

"We'll see." Edgardo stepped out of the garage, back to his awaiting brother.

"Gonna go take care of Young Master Carlo now?" Hank asked as his friend left.

"Gonna go try."

* * *

The Metropolitan Detention Center was a modern, towering white complex in Downtown Los Angeles, a federal prison with hundreds of narrow windows, one for each inmate. With its sleek inset glass and curved walls, it resembled a corporate office building from afar, a design that helped it blend in with the surrounding cityscape. Such aesthetics were a far cry from the network of chain-link fences and coiled razor wire of Lancaster.

Edgardo paced near the public entrance as he spoke to Felix on the phone.

"The system didn't pick up anything?" he asked.

"Nothing on the cameras," Felix said.

"Motion sensors? Thermals?"

"Nothing."

"You take a good look around?"

Felix Ramirez stood 24 miles north at the entrance of an isolated warehouse in the foothills. His dirt bike, outfitted with saddlebags and off-road tires, leaned against a tree nearby.

"Walked the property twice," Felix said to his boss on the other end of the line. "Checked all the doors inside and out. I'm positive no one's been here, Amo."

"Do me a favor and run a quick inventory."

"Sure, but what's the rush? You know something I don't?"

Edgardo looked around him, satisfied he was just outside the view of the prison entrance's security cameras. "Maybe something, maybe nothing, but it feels like dark forces are out to get us lately. For years, we've run a tight operation. Suddenly, the sky's falling. Waldo's trucks showing up late, two run-ins with the TSB, Carlo gets picked up for a bullshit charge..."

"And your brother was released."

"What about my brother?"

"Like you said, maybe something, maybe nothing, but the timing makes me wonder. Maybe dark forces are out to get Bram, and we're the collateral damage."

"I hope we're both wrong," Edgardo said. "I have a feeling we'll know shortly."

"I'll get on that inventory and report back in two hours."

"Good man."

"My honor always, Amo."

Edgardo hung up and looked at the imposing building looming over him. He felt his feet frozen in place as a disturbing thought occurred to him.

He called Felix again.

"Yes, Amo?"

"Forget the inventory, Felix. Lock up and get out of there."

"You sure? Why the change of plans?"

"Just a funny feeling."

"What feeling?"

"Like I'm about to be blindsided."

* * *

The Visitation Room just beyond the prison lobby comprised white and tan cinderblock walls lined with steel railings. Divided glass partitions were positioned in a row every six feet, with two chairs for each and cameras mounted above.

Bram and Fish sat at the third partition, waiting for Carlo to emerge from the other side. Bram wore the same clothes from the day before, while Fish wore a custom suit and dress shoes, mens size six.

"This place is something else," Fish said. "Looks like the Beverly Hilton next to other lockups I've visited."

"A fancy cage is still a cage," Bram said, "especially to a scared kid. Don't let the paintings in the lobby fool you."

"Who's Ed talking to out there?"

"His boy, Felix."

"Well, he needs to hang up on Mr. Felix and get in here now. It's a small miracle I managed to sweet talk us ten minutes with Carlo. And when they say time's up, believe me, that time's up."

"Have faith. Eddie knows what's going on."

"Really?" Fish said. "Then that makes one of us, Brother Bram, because I'm winging it here. Everything is off about this."

"Like what?"

"Carlo's a minor, but they take him to Metro? He drove around with some kids months ago. Now there's this sudden urgency? Booked an immediate hearing?"

"You talked to Carlo?"

"Just a 60-second phone call, yet another strange detail." Fish looked up at a wall clock: 8:57 a.m. "It's almost nine. What's so important that Ed can't make a call after we sort this out?"

"TSB's gunnin' for him," Bram said.

Fish felt a shiver of nerves run through him as the gravity of the news sunk in. He knew that anyone "gunning" for Ed would surely be out for them as well. "TSB? You sound so sure."

Bram could still see the bodies of Jorge and Yoy Yoy bleeding out on his brother's back lawn. "Pretty fuckin' sure."

To Fish's relief, Edgardo entered and joined them, standing behind their chairs. He arrived in time to see his son being brought to the window in orange coveralls, his hands cuffed in front of him, the cuffs chained to his ankles. The precaution felt like overkill for a clean-cut teenager with no criminal record.

Seeing my boy in shackles, trapped behind stone walls with murderers, rapists, and thieves, it sapped my strength and resolve. I could never let Carlo see it on my face, but I felt helpless and small. For the first time in my adult life, I was an impostor, a fool who'd only believed he was smart but was actually just another victim lost in the system. As time slowed to a crawl, I knew I'd find our aggressor sooner than my son would regain his freedom.

Carlo sat in a chair opposite his family, the glass partition reflecting the overhead lights into his eyes.

"Tay!" Carlo said. "Tito Bram!"

Bram leaned forward and pressed his palms to the glass. "My Mahal Caloy. Goddamn, last I saw you face-to-face, you were still a little runt. Now I hear you're the big football star, big trophy, even made MVP. We're all so proud of you."

"Suddenly, none of that don't mean shit no more," the boy said. "When they lettin' me outta here?"

"Fish is working on it," Edgardo said.

"You'll be out soon, kiddo," Fish said. "I promise."

Carlo paused, tried to contain his emotions. "Thank you, Mr. Fisher."

"Fish is the best," his father said. "He'll fix this. It's what he does. But right now, you need to tell us everything."

"It was stupid, Tay. I didn't know what they were doing. I still don't really know..."

"It's okay, Carlo," Fish said. "Take a breath and run us through it, point by point."

"It was back in June, late at night," Carlo said. He took a moment to recall the fuzzy memory which became clearer with each word. "I met two pinoy at a party. They bragged they were HK-9. I thought they were bullshittin' me."

"What made you think that?"

"I mean, they were younger than me and the party was tame. Nice house in a nice neighborhood. Top-20 music on the radio. A case of Coors Light and a bottle of Jack between twenty jocks. None of that sounds gangster to me. And I only had one beer, I swear."

"I believe you, boy," Edgardo said.

"I didn't even finish it. Tasted like warm piss."

"Those guys you met," Fish said, "they asked you to drive them somewhere?"

"Yeah, 'cause they didn't have their licenses yet. Real gangsters wouldn't care about that either, right? So I drove them to a house in Alhambra. Midnight. Quiet street. One guy gets out of the car. 'Raymundo,' I think. He told me to keep the engine running."

"This doesn't sound good," Bram said.

"Raymundo runs behind the house. I heard a loud bang, like a gunshot. He runs back laughing, says he lit an M-80 under his buddy's window to scare him. I bet it worked 'cause it sure as hell scared me."

"That was it?" Edgardo asked, confused. "A firecracker?"

"Maybe," Fish said. "Maybe not. What happened after that?"

"I took them to get chili dogs, left them at Tommy's on Beverly at 2AM. Honest, it felt like just a stupid prank. I mean, they weren't drunk or nervous or nothin'."

"Did you see them after that night?"

"No, never."

Fish had more questions, but a uniformed guard walked up behind Carlo and gestured for him to stand. With a frightened glance back at his family, he was led away from the window.

"Tay? Tito?" The teen's voice trembled as he muttered over his shoulder. "Mr. Fisher?"

Edgardo was furious.

Bram was confused.

Fish stood up and slammed his palm to the glass. "Hey! I was granted ten minutes with my client!"

"They told me five," the guard said as he opened a door back into the bowels of the prison. "Take it up with the C.A."

"Who?"

"Corrections Administrator. Marvin Ellis."

"Unacceptable!" Edgardo yelled. "We're talking to you! Right now!"

"Now you hold on a minute!" Fish yelled to the guard as he nudged the boy through the doorway. "This violates Right to

Counsel! Carlo hasn't finished briefing me on the charges! No one has!"

"It's gonna be okay, son!" Edgardo called out.

Without another word, the guard followed the handcuffed boy through the open door and shut it behind them. The deadbolt echoed across the room like a tone of doom.

The brothers looked at each other, distraught, as if it might be the last time anyone would see Carlo again.

"I didn't want to say his in front of the boy," Fish said, "but they denied bail."

"What did they ask for?" Edgardo said. "I gave you a goddamn blank check!"

"They processed him right away, but threw out the California Bail Schedule. It didn't matter that we were willing to pay the moon and stars, I was told in precise legal terms to fuck off. This case is miles off the books, Ed."

"Did you call Judge Collins?"

"Vacation."

"What about Judge Abernathy?"

"Heart surgery."

"Pakshet!" Bram said.

Their tense exchange was cut short by the sound of a turning doorknob as Corrections Administrator Marvin Ellis, a short, fat, middle-aged man in a shirt and tie, entered from a side door. With half his body in the doorway, he called to the men.

"Mr. Duque?" Ellis said. "Edwardo Duque?"

"If you're here to help my son, I'm Edgardo Duque."

"Edgardo, my apologies. Come with me, please."

Bram and Fish rose to their feet, but Ellis shook his head at them. "Just Mr. Duque, gentlemen."

"Unacceptable. My family comes with me."

"I'm sorry, Mr. Duque, but I can only bring one, and that one must be you."

"Putang ina mo!" Bram said, his eyes aflame. "That's my nephew you've got locked up like an animal!"

Edgardo gestured for his brother to calm down. "Rage will only make things worse."

"Ed's got this, Brother Bram," Fish said, hiding his apprehension. He leaned in and whispered into his client's ear. "Ed, I don't know what the hell is going on. Like I said, this is way off the books. They're breaking a dozen incarceration laws just to keep us in the dark."

"Agreed, but it looks like they're about to shed some light."

"Tell me everything later, Ed. *Everything.* Put that mighty hyperthymesic memory to work."

Ellis looked at the men with sympathy. "You gents might want to grab some lunch. It may be awhile."

Edgardo looked back at his brother and lawyer. "It's okay. You guys take off. I'll dig into this."

"Good luck, Bata," Bram said. "Better that you walk into that impiyerno than us."

Unsure, Bram and Fish headed for the exit while Edgardo followed Ellis through the side door, into the unknown.

21

Blindside

Edgardo followed Administrator Ellis down a long tan-and-white striped hallway, massive pendant lights hanging high above, to a lone door at the far end. To Edgardo's surprise, Ellis gestured for him to enter alone.

"You're not coming? You're the Corrections Administrator, right? The man who denied my son bail?"

"That wasn't my call," Ellis said, "and neither is this. They want to speak with you in private."

"And who is 'they'?" Edgardo asked.

"When you find out, you can tell me."

Edgardo looked at the door with an uneasy feeling. As he always did, he ran a number of possible scenarios before turning the knob. Unable to predict who or what was waiting for him, he composed himself and opened the door.

I told Felix dark forces were conspiring against us, that I felt like I was about to be blindsided. I didn't know how right I was. Even though I could feel the heat coming from behind that door, it still ended up burning me.

He entered a long, windowless conference room, lit by large white globes hung high above. A meeting table ran down the center, flanked by 12 chairs on each of its long sides, nearly occupying the entire space. He shut the door and remained standing at one end of the table as two men entered through a door at the other end.

Edgardo had always prided himself on seeing a situation ten moves ahead, unfolding every scenario from every angle within his sharp mind. That day, however, the only thing he felt coming was a thunderstrike, and so it was that The Duke of Temple Street stood stunned in the large, silent room as two men entered from the opposite door.

Cyrus Bernard and Tim Mason of The Wolf Pack MC, not seen since the desert airfield, shut and locked the door behind them. The veteran Alpha and his hothead Sergeant-At-Arms were dirty and sunburned, dressed in their boots, bandanas, and road leathers. They sat in chairs at the far end of the long table.

The last two fools I expected to see in the maw of the Metropolitan Detention Center were C.B. and Mace. My first thought was that the police raids had been more successful than I'd realized. They'd surely cut a deal with the feds, turned confidential informants, and were brought in to place me at the hangar.

But then they spoke...

"Good morning, Mr. Duque," Mace said, his loose cannon persona gone.

"Have a seat," C.B. said without a trace of his southern accent. "Might as well get comfortable because this is as hospitable as it's gonna get."

Their calm, professional manner and tone of control told Edgardo everything in an instant, giving him a fresh set of scenarios to calculate. He still played the role of a disoriented, questioning victim, if only to disarm them and learn what he could.

"Comfort is impossible right now," he said, still on his feet, "and hospitality is hard to imagine, especially from a pair of CIs... but you're not CIs, are you?"

"Before we start," C.B. said, "know that everything disclosed here is confidential and stays between us three. You have my word."

"And what's that worth? The word of a fake gangster?"

"It's worth a shit-ton more than the word of a real gangster, don't you agree?"

"Not many words I hear are worth much lately," Edgardo said.

"Fair enough."

"Ellis says he knows nothing about this. The man runs this facility, yet he's kept in the dark. I find that curious."

"It's above his pay grade," Mace said. "He's never even met us."

"For his safety, and the safety of his family," C.B. said, "the less the man knows, the better. Only ghosts and nomads are cut out for this work."

Edgardo kept pecking. "Ellis is classified SF-85, standard security clearance for a prison administrator. This means you two are SF-86 or maybe even SF-87."

"Mr. Ellis is actually an SF-85P-S, as of a month ago. I know details matter to you." C.B. was surprised by Edgardo's familiarity with national security clearance levels. "But he plays no role in this. Again, please take a seat. We're gonna be here for a bit."

Edgardo sat in the end chair opposite his hosts on the other end of the room. "You're definitely not informants. FBI? CIA? Or just good ol' LAPD?"

"DEA-LA," C.B. said. "LOCC, to be precise. Familiar with us?"

"Los Angeles Organized Crime Crackdown," Edgardo said. "Yes, I'm certainly familiar with you."

"No, you certainly ain't," Mace said. "Not really. Otherwise, you wouldn't have had that What-The-Fuck expression splashed across your face just now when we walked in. That was quite a Kodak moment."

"So, you're poker players," Edgardo said, "and you caught my tell?"

"We are indeed poker players," C.B. said. "We're professional, highly trained, veteran poker players who've raked in hundreds of millions in blood money over the years. But our strategy has always eluded you, Mr. Duque, because our goal isn't to win. No cash purse or gold bracelets for us. Our goal is that everyone else at the table loses."

"And who else is at the table?"

"HK-9," Mace said. "TSB, LB-13, AFA, Mr. Waldo. Even The Demonyo and The Panginoon, all players you're quite familiar with."

"Don't forget The Wolf Pack MC," Edgardo said. "How would they feel if I walked into their desert clubhouse and told them two of their brothers are rats?"

Mace looked at his Alpha, unsure if he should continue. C.B. nodded. It was all out between them now. "The Wolf Pack would be fine with it... because there is no Wolf Pack."

"Bullshit," Edgardo said. "I know the dates and times of every job you've done, every truck boosted, every plane jacked, every back alley rumble. The Wolves are a hundred strong. There's no way you're all feds."

"Everyone believes we're a hundred," C.B. said. "We're actually six doing the work of a hundred. Reputation is everything, as you well know, and if you were fooled, Mr. Duque, you can rest assured everyone else is fooled, too."

Edgardo felt floored by the revelation, though he hid it well. "And how do I fit in? Am I to be Number Seven?"

"To continue our poker analogy, as we play against L.A.'s biggest gangs... you're our pocket Ace."

C.B. pulled a manila folder from his satchel and slid it down the table to Edgardo. He opened it and found a stack of 8x10 photos...

Edgardo in his garage next a Mr. Waldo's ice cream truck...
Entering the hangar at Anders Butler Airfield...
With Joey The Rose at Corazon Lounge...
In his car with Bram at Lancaster State Prison...
In front of Divinia's house, the night Carlo was arrested...

Mace revealed a bound stack of cash, destroyed at the hangar deal. "By the way, that was a neat trick with the money. At first, we thought you had the god of sharpshooters out in the desert."

"Didn't I?"

I thought of my loyal assistant, always watching my back out in the moonlit dunes. Felix's marksmanship was simply unmatched. To this day, I have yet to meet another man with more precision with a firearm. Still, I had no desire to accidentally harm anyone in that hangar if it could be avoided... and the Wolves knew it.

"Whether or not you had a man out there," Mace said, "you hedged your bets. We found traces of potassium nitrate, charcoal, and sulphur between the bills. Pretty clever, sticking firecrackers in the stacks."

"They were more than just the usual safe-and-sane variety," Edgardo said, "but my compliments for spotting them."

"Out of curiosity, did you even have a sniper camped out in the dark?"

"Maybe. Maybe not." Edgardo remained vague, looking to protect Felix. If they hadn't yet made him, so be it. He wanted to keep his man invisible. "You figured out my ruse. How about we get to your ask?"

"It's more of a tit-for-tat," C.B. said. "Young Carlo is staring at a Murder Accomplice charge. Victim was Kevin Polish, son of retired police chief Albert Polish." He opened another folder and slid a photo down the table. Edgardo saw a blond teenage boy, dead from a headshot.

"Forget the fact that your son is 17," Mace said. "Cop killers are tried as adults in this town."

"You know as well as I that he had nothing to do to with it."

"Of course we know," C.B. said, "and we can push his hearing left or right, it depends on if we can strike a deal."

"Your photos show that I own a garage and a bar, and that I was in that hangar brokering your deal, with only two guns and two stacks of cash present. You can't prove I know anything more about that night because there was no audio recorded. The Nines did a sweep for mics. Knowing them, they also likely wanded you when you arrived."

C.B. looked defeated as Edgardo dismantled their sting. "That they did."

Lynn Harrod

"And Carlo? He's a kid with a clean record. I'll fight it and I'll win. Doesn't sound like you have much to squeeze me with."

Mace stood and walked the length of the room to Edgardo, taking a seat beside him. "Those guns may have been run through Mr. Waldo, but they were Uncle Sam's guns. Our guns. You facilitated the sale of federal firearms to the HK-9. We also have intel on past deals with the Mexicans, the Koreans..."

"My educated guess is that your intel is shit," Edgardo said. "Circumstantial at best. Otherwise, I'd be sitting in a cell, forced to comply. It wouldn't be 'Good Morning Mr. Duque' in a conference room. I'd be just another poor sap under your thumb. Deals are only made with men who still have options."

"It's true, we'd rather you work with us willingly," C.B. said with a sigh. "You're more valuable to us as an active CI on the street with your reputation and resources intact, but we're not naive rookies. We figured 'willingly' was a long shot."

Mace took the surveillance photos from Edgardo and laid them out on the table. "Take another look, Mr. Duque. As you can see, we've been monitoring you for quite a long time, and we're going to keep monitoring. Your life will become our favorite reality show marathon."

"Help me understand," Edgardo said, dismissing the photos. "Why reveal yourselves to me?"

"As I mentioned, we're no rookies," C.B. said. "I've been working deep cover for thirty years, tracked guys like you a hundred times, and I've come up with three scenarios. If the crook is dumb, you tell him you're a cop and he'll do whatever you want. If the crook is smart, you keep your cover, make him think you're an outlaw. However, if the crook is *very* smart... as you are... you reveal yourself, work a deal where you both benefit. Deals are your specialty, right? Besides, we both know you'd have made us eventually."

Edgardo feigned a laugh at their strategy. "I'm flattered, I suppose, but what stops me from walking out of here and blowing your cover with every gang in Southern California?"

"You won't, because it would be just as easy for us to spread the word that you're our CI."

Edgardo looked at the agents, the incriminating photos, and considered the situation, seemingly at an impasse.

"We have eyes everywhere," C.B. said. "We're watching you 24-7, open holidays, we never close. Wherever you go, there we are. I assure you, we will eventually get something solid on you, to 'squeeze' you into working for us."

In business and in life, you occasionally miss something, get stuck, get pinned in the corner. To be truly prepared is to always have one more move. Your opponents are so busy crowing, they never see it coming.

Edgardo looked at their photos again, his face centered in each one. "So much manpower just to keep tabs on me."

"Oh, you're worth it, Mr. Duque."

"The problem with having 'eyes everywhere' is that they become easy to spot."

Edgardo reached into his jacket pocket and revealed his large red envelope. He pulled out the five photos, each with a document and Post-It note. One at a time, he slid them down the table to C.B.

The cook at the Jeepney food truck...
Blonde delivery man at the Corazon Lounge...
Barista trainee at the coffee house...
Photographer at Divinia's interview...
Woman jogging across from the coffee house...

Lynn Harrod

"What am I looking at?" C.B. asked with an unconvincing scoff. "A day in the life?"

"Special Agent Mick Angelino," Edgardo said, pointing to the cook. "Worked the food truck outside my garage. No self-respecting pinoy chef would dare offer soggy lumpia."

"I see."

"Agent John Slauson delivered wine to my bar. The man didn't know merlot from pinot, and his cover story about my usual man, Paul, was full of holes. Agent Flora Diaz made my weak, watery Double Americano at the Bloom and Plume. Special Agent Randall Sled took pictures at my wife's studio. I found it curious to see a professional use autofocus."

"I would, too."

"Agent Lori Lanham jogged down Temple Street. After passing my coffee shop three times in a forty minutes, she might as well have worn her badge."

C.B. and Mace looked at each other, speechless, their entire team made in a single day.

"I believe when you say that you two aren't rookies," Edgardo said, "but the rest of your team certainly are."

"Lanham is," C.B. said with a sigh, realizing his covert efforts turned out to be pointless. "It's her first year in the field. I told her to change outfits, wear different wigs..."

"It wouldn't have mattered."

"No, I suppose not. You would have remembered the cadence of her stride, the scent of her deodorant, or some other insignificant detail, am I right?"

"There's no such thing as insignificant details," Edgardo said. "Not to me. The point is, gentlemen, your operation was quite an invasion of privacy, one that my lawyer would love to take apart. Did I miss anyone?"

"You certainly do your homework," C.B. said, his tone again assertive, in control. "That's what makes you 'The Duke.' That's why we need you, and it's why you're now forcing our hand."

C.B. nodded to his Lieutenant as if they had one last move to make. Edgardo saw Mace's expression stretch into a wide grin.

I was wrong to see these fake Wolves as fools. They remained focused, unmoved, even after I blew up their team. They knew just what to do when I countered their blindside, their backup plan locked and loaded.

"We have pictures, you have pictures," Mace said as he returned to his seat beside C.B. "Everybody has pictures, and they say a picture is worth a thousand words, but *video* is worth a million pictures." He reached into his briefcase and pulled out a tablet computer. With a few taps on the screen, he summoned a video and slid the device down the table.

To his surprise, Edgardo watched a live video feed of his storage building in the foothills. A team of agents brute-forced their way in and explored its interior. The feed came from one of their body cams as they uncovered cases of Tornado candy bars and other seemingly ordinary goods.

Shit.

Edgardo's stone face betrayed a look of dismay.

"That is your building, Mr. Duque?" Mace asked knowingly. "It's owned by Pinot Point LLC, which is owned by Quezon Corp, which supplies your bar. Lotta hoops to go through. But it is yours, right?"

"I own several buildings."

"Including this one?"

Edgardo nodded.

"You're right, Mr. Duque," C.B. said. "You and your lawyer probably can weather everything we throw at you, and you're right that our intel is circumstantial. You cover your tracks well. We can't really tie you to the gangs, and we probably can't tie you to anything in this building up in the hills... but we can certainly confiscate it."

Mace savored the mounting defeat in Edgardo's eyes. "Can't wait to see what's in those boxes. We imagine there's more than just chocolate bars and bottles of merlot... I mean, pinot. No, we're thinking there's gotta be a fortune in contraband in there, not to mention that safe. Our boys have been looking forward to cracking that baby open."

"We can take everything," C.B. said with the tone of a hammer slamming down, "or we can work out a deal."

Edgardo looked deflated. "Tell me about your deal."

The Wolves looked at each other.

We got him.

"Simple. Business moves forward as usual. You keep contact with the gangs, arrange meetings with them, tell us when and where, then we swoop in and cancel Christmas. We'll time the raids, so it's not too obvious, and you get to keep your warehouse."

"And if I refuse?"

"Then the only Christmas that's cancelled is yours. We confiscate it all and you lose everything you've worked hard for all these years. Your network falls apart, no one returns your calls, and you lose far more than money."

"Consider it a compliment," Mace said. "You impressed us at the hangar. We knew right then you were our guy."

That hangar deal wasn't for the benefit of The Nines or
The Wolves. It was a job interview. The position was
Confidential Informant, and I was the lead candidate.
C.B. and Mace had pegged me as a Person of Interest,
and my actions that evening confirmed their intention of
keeping me on retainer. How I hate being deceived.

Edgardo shut his eyes and took inventory of his foothills warehouse as the agents waited to close the deal. He opened his eyes and glared at them in defiance. "I know nothing about the contents of that building," he said in a flat tone. "Haven't used it in years."

"Really?" Mace asked. "We spotted a young Asian fella out there earlier today, just before we walked in here. Might have been Filipino. He took off on a real nice dirt bike." He checked his notes. "Kawasaki KLX-110R. One of yours?"

"I know nothing about the contents of that building. Haven't used it in years."

"Final answer?" Mace shut his file folders and shoved them back into his briefcase. "I ask 'cause you're all out of lifelines."

"I know nothing about the contents of that building. Haven't used it in years."

C.B. threw his hands in the air. "Then I guess we're barking up the wrong tree. We thought this was your stuff. Someone else must have broken in over the years and used it without your knowledge. I feel silly now. We'll just take it all and figure out who it belongs to."

Edgardo seemed wounded, having just made an enormous sacrifice to stay out of their pocket.

"I'll admit, Mr. Duque, that building was our last move, but since its contents clearly aren't connected to you, we've got nothing. Dammit all. Luckily, you still have your auto repair shop and your bar... but *someone* will lose the untold fortune sitting in that warehouse."

"I know nothing about..."

"Yeah, yeah," Mace said, "you don't know shit and you're sticking to that. As dumb as that decision may be, I can respect it." He made a call on his cell, spoke to one of the agents on the scene. "Take it down. All of it."

Edgardo watched the live video on the tablet as the agents carted away all the boxes in his storage building. Two of them started drilling into the safe.

He remained silent, barely able to look the agents in the eyes.

They gathered their things and headed for the exit behind them.

"Sorry we wrangled a legitimate businessman into this," C.B. said. "Despite everything we've discussed, know that we support you and your community." He took a moment to listen to the sounds of the drill against the safe, to relish it. "We'll leave the iPad."

"What about my son?" Edgardo asked. "Now that I'm no longer any value to you?"

"Ah yes. That. I think the court will realize there's been a serious clerical error. A mix-up of case files. Carlo Duque was part of a juvenile prank involving a firecracker. The cold-blooded murder of a police chief's son? That occurred across town and on an entirely different night."

"You sons of bitches," Edgardo said through clinched teeth. "You never had anything on him! You used my son, a child! Put him through hell... all for a long-shot bluff?"

"We're playing pro high-stakes poker, remember? Last I checked, bluffing's part of the game."

"Stay as long as you like," Mace said. "Give the iPad to Ellis on your way out."

The Wolves walked through their door and locked it behind them, leaving Edgardo alone in the conference room with the tablet. He remained at the table for another 95 minutes and watched the long, thorough looting of his warehouse.

22

Small Price to Pay

In the moonlit foothills above Sylmar, California, 27 miles north of HiFi, Edgardo and Bram drove to the entrance of The Duke's warehouse, a large, gray, nondescript building partially set into a hillside. After witnessing it being ransacked by a dozen agents, followed by five more carting away its contents, Edgardo expected to find nothing inside.

He shut off the headlights, throwing them into disorienting darkness, but kept the engine running as he observed the narrow, winding road in his mirrors and the dense trees to his left for any movement. Below them, the city's ocean of lights stretched to the unseen horizon. Though he was sure they were alone, Edgardo had his flashlight and pistol ready before he cut the engine. He didn't need to remind Bram to follow suit.

They stepped out of the car and shined their lights around. The silence felt unnerving. He tapped the top of his car three times, signaling his assistant to come out of hiding.

Felix approached from around a corner of the structure, his dirt bike parked nearby.

"You've been made," Edgardo said.

"I figured. My apologies, Amo."

"We were all nailed, Felix, but I appreciate you coming back here."

"Most wouldn't," Bram said, impressed with the young man's loyalty. "You truly are my brother's right hand, Mr. Felix."

Moments like that night were where Felix's talents shined. You want a man like him in your corner, for damage control was his specialty. I was glad that my brother, always fiercely protective of me, could be there to see how much I'd come to rely on Felix.

"I made a few calls before I drove up," Felix said, "then I droned the area for miles."

"What calls?" Bram asked.

"Felix knows people contracted with city security," Edgardo said. "We pay them well."

"They've likely heard about the raid," Felix said. "I gave them all a bonus this month."

"Acceptable."

Bram nodded, as he finally realized how Felix could wipe almost any security camera in Los Angeles with accuracy to the minute. He personally hacked private surveillance wherever he could, but had insiders handle municipal equipment. Every base was covered.

"The drone's radius?" Edgardo asked.

"Four."

"You searched the hills eight miles all around?" Bram asked, piecing together the math.

"Yes. Trust me, I wouldn't have returned here if I thought it was too risky, and I certainly wouldn't have called you with the all-clear."

"Acceptable." Edgardo placed a hand on the young man's shoulder. "That being said, whatever alias you've been using..."

"Already burnt," Felix said, "and I'm going to sunset the bike as soon as we're done here."

"Good man." Edgardo looked at the dark forest surrounding his property. "Sweep come up with anything?"

"Three cameras in the trees," Felix said with a sigh. "They're powered by a central solar panel. Been there about a week, maybe ten days."

"How do you know?" Bram asked, incredulous.

"The dust on the panel, the moisture in the cameras' housing, and the moss overlapping the mounting brackets, about half a centimeter."

"Pakshet," Bram said. "You continue to amaze me, Mr. Felix."

"I was trained by the best."

"Did you kill 'em?"

"No. I could have killed one unit, but more than that would likely bring folks up here."

"So, how did you handle them?" Edgardo asked.

"I fed them all 24-hour loops." Felix looked up at the overcast sky. "The clouds don't quite match, but it's close enough to give us a day, maybe two."

"Good man. Let's look at what we're working with."

The three men walked up to the warehouse door. Felix readied a ring of keys to unlock it, but Bram noticed it was ajar. Dented. He swung it open. "Battering ram did this."

"Agreed," Edgardo said as he examined the dent, noting its depth and diameter. "Standard police ram, 35 pounds of alloy steel swung squarely against the locks, just enough force to crack the two deadbolts. They could've blown the door wide open, but they wanted to send a message."

"What message?" Bram asked.

"They wanted me to see that the bare minimum force was necessary to take me down." Edgardo turned to his assistant. "Possible they compromised our cameras inside?"

"Doubt it," Felix said. "It might've tipped us off, plus the alarm was cut before they entered."

"Good enough."

Edgardo held his breath and led his brethren into the building.

Upon entering the dark warehouse, Felix threw a switch on the power box by the door, flooding the vast room with overhead light. After a moment to adjust their eyes, they were greeted by dozens of rows of empty shelves.

The agents took everything. The once-dense warehouse now stood as a pillaged disgrace. At the far end of the room, the safe's door hung open, its lock destroyed, all contents gone. It served as yet another "message."

"Sorry, Bata," Bram said. "Even when you make all the right moves, you can still lose."

"Be sure to engrave that on my headstone." Edgardo walked around his ransacked warehouse. He peered up at the corners and the air vents high above, pointing them out to Felix. "Grab a ladder and sweep the vents. You'll probably find nothing but spiders and dead rats, but check them anyway."

Lynn Harrod

"At once, Amo," Felix said.

Over the next ten minutes, Edgardo and his brother looked through the few remaining crates and cases while Felix checked the vents for hidden surveillance. Both the containers and the vents turned up empty, as expected, like the rest of the building.

"How much did we lose?" Edgardo asked his assistant when they regrouped.

"Just north of a quarter-million."

"Puchanggala," Bram said, breathless.

"Acceptable," Edgardo said, to his brother's surprise. "Small price to pay for Carlo's release." He thought of his son, soon to be back home with his mother and sister, and realized he would have taken that financial hit a hundredfold for the boy.

It was at that moment that the distraught Bram noticed a keen look on his brother's usually stone face.

C.B. and Mace thought we were playing a game of poker and were convinced that they'd landed a Royal Flush. They were wrong. We were playing chess, grandmasters sitting together across a long conference table.

Edgardo revealed a small remote on his keychain and handed it to his brother. Confused, Bram pushed its single button.

If they knew we were playing chess, they might have realized that sometimes you must sacrifice a Knight in order to protect the King.

Upon the click of the remote, a wall-sized hidden door opened before them. The lights in the room beyond flickered to life.

"Puchanggala," Bram said, again breathless, this time with eyes wide. "You've got to be shitting me."

Edgardo and his men entered the hidden room, three times as large as the front room, filled floor-to-ceiling with crates, boxes, and exotic cars.

"How's this possible?" Bram asked. "The inside is bigger than the outside?"

"Like Pinoy Point," Edgardo said with a slight grin.

Bram looked at the bounty surrounding them as he connected their childhood clubhouse to the hidden room. "You built it into the hillside."

"Kept us cool in the summer." Edgardo turned to Felix. "Did you wipe the prison cameras?"

"I didn't know which one, so I wiped the entire first floor."

"The 117 minutes I was there?"

"Two hours was cleaner."

"Good man."

On the far wall sat an untouched safe, much larger than the first. Edgardo turned its dial and opened it, revealing tall stacks of cash, more money than Bram had ever imagined.

"How much do we still have?" Edgardo asked.

"Liquid and otherwise, just north of $22 million."

"Tangina," Bram muttered to himself, finally figuring out the subterfuge, the way Edgardo played the Wolves even in their moment of victory. "Why not tell me?"

Edgardo smiled. "I like to hear you say 'puchanggala.'"

"The brain power between you two... it's clear I have a lot to learn. So, what now, Bata?"

"We move our goods. Felix has five new spots picked out, all secure, remote, and vetted. With LOCC on our heads, it makes sense to spread it across the city."

"No, I mean... what now?"

Edgardo understood the longing in his brother's eyes. "Now, we welcome Carlo home. He's been eager to spend quality time with his Tito Bram again."

Bram smiled. "Finally, something I can wrap my head around."

The three men walked out of the room. The wall-sized door slowly closed and locked behind them. The lights shut off and the secondary alarm secured the premises as they stepped out into the night and headed down the hill.

23

Magnolia Street

Less than 24 hours after Abraham Duque's hectic first day as a free man, and after a much-needed night of sleep, he and his brother put on slacks and pressed dress shirts and headed to a suburb of Eagle Rock, a quiet little town between Los Angeles and Pasadena that boasted a large Filipino community. Edgardo drove past manicured lawns and picturesque homes, and with each block, Bram grew more nervous, something Edgardo rarely saw.

My brother Bram is a force of nature. Many regard him as a walking Hell-on-Earth, but even a monster of a man can still succumb to tangled nerves. He'd only been free for a day – one hell of a day – and was still adjusting to the demands of my new life. Our new life. I would have pitied him, but I know my Kuya is stronger than I'd ever been.

"I'm not sure I'm ready for this," Bram said, staring into space. He clutched a black plastic bag. "I mean, I just got out."

"Abraham Duque is scared? After what we went through yesterday?"

"Yesterday is gone. Today is now. And I didn't say I was scared. I'm just not sure the time is right."

"There's no better time than now," Edgardo said. "You always told me that."

"Then I was always a fool, and you were a fool to listen." Bram checked the time on the dashboard. Each passing minute landed with a thud in his mind. "What about the bodies?"

"They stay locked in the shed until I figure out the plan."

"In fuckin' mattress bags?" Bram asked. "Will they contain the smell?"

"They'll do the job well enough..."

"Until you figure out the plan."

Edgardo understood his brother's unease but knew it had more to do with what was coming that night than what had occurred the night before. "Take a breath, Kuya. I'll get Felix to move them when the time comes. Acceptable?"

"I trust Mr. Felix." Bram shut his eyes and took a deep breath, as Edgardo told him. "When?"

"I need time to think, to decide when and where. You trust me as well?"

"Of course."

"Then let's focus on this evening. We both know that's what's really got you on edge."

"Tangina..."

"Kuya, it may start off bloody, but by the time it's over, we'll have conquered the night."

Bram looked out the window and turned to look behind them. "You sure they're meeting us there? I ain't goin' in without backup."

"Relax. No one goes in until we go in together. I have it all timed."

"At least you got this plan figured out." Bram gripped the black plastic bag tightly as he continued to stare out the window. "Okay, maybe I am a little scared."

* * *

Divinia and her children stepped out of her house together, the Hollywood Sign shining down on them eight blocks up the hill. She wore a pants suit and heels while Carlo donned a San Francisco 49ers jersey and Christiana endured a black floral dress, the kind of outfit she wore only on special nights.

"You want us to make you a plate?" Chris asked her mother.

"No thanks, Love. The producers are taking me to Providence for dinner."

"Providence. Ooh la la." The girl was familiar with the famous fine dining spot, having seen it featured on TV and in her mother's foodie magazines many times.

"We'll make her a plate, anyway," Carlo said to his sister. "I'll eat it if she doesn't, no problem."

"Prison food didn't suit you?" Chris asked with a grin.

"Shaddap."

"We will make you a plate, Nay. I'll Photoshop you eating it later if I have to."

"So you can text it to her?" Divinia asked, incredulous. "Is this what it's come to?"

"It makes her happy. What do you have against Lola?"

Divinia scoffed at the question. "Oh, I don't know, her desperate need to always be the center of attention? Her judgmental remarks? Her ignorance? The lack of decorum?"

"I meant her food," Chris said flatly.

"Too salty."

"Yes, you are."

As they walked down the steep steps to their driveway, a man watched from the shadows across the street. He sat in his car within the thick undergrowth of an ancient oak.

"What do your producers want to meet about at night?" Chris asked her mother. "It's either really good news or really bad news."

"Why do you say that?" Divinia asked, curious about her daughter's assessment.

"Nanay, they're taking you out to Providence."

Carlo was oblivious, texting his friends on his cell as he approached the driveway.

Divinia took a moment before replying. "They want to retool the show with burgers and barbecue, not sisig and bistek. Clearly, they don't think highly of my audience."

"Clearly, you need new producers!" Chris said. "Mr. Fisher was a TV producer once. He loves HiFi. He'll support your vision for the show."

"Fish is a good man, I suppose, but he works for your father."

Chris shrugged as if to say, "so what?" Divinia let it go with a dismissive wave and gestured for them to leave.

The family separated at the driveway, getting into two cars parked side-by-side: Divinia in a red Lexus sedan, the teens in a white Volkswagen Beetle, Chris at the wheel. Divinia started her engine. Before backing out of the driveway, she rolled down her window for a last word with her kids. They rolled down theirs.

"Text me when you're about to leave," she said. "Text me again when you get home."

"We're going to Eagle Rock, Nay," Carlo said, "not Compton."

Chris backed out of the driveway first and headed east, followed by her mother, who drove west.

The shadowed man across the street also started his engine.

He shifted into Drive and followed the teens' white Beetle.

* * *

On Magnolia Street in Eagle Rock, the sun set over the quiet cul-de-sac of Craftsman homes. The Duque Brothers sat on the hood of Edgardo's Mercedes, enjoying the peaceful suburb. They would soon discover it to be the quiet before the storm in more ways than one.

Bram smoked a cigarillo – his third – as he peered at the quaint two-story house at the end of the street. "So, this is where the old man chose to relocate?"

"Not what you expected?" Edgardo said.

"Not at all. I pictured something more rustic, out in the sticks, not picket fences and perfect lawns."

"Enough waiting." Edgardo plucked the cigarillo from his brother's hand and snuffed it under his shoe. "I say we head in."

"What happened to having it all timed? We wait for our backup!"

"Diyos, I wish you wouldn't call them that. You make it sound like we're on a job."

Christiana's Beetle pulled up and parked behind them. The sight of the cute, white car brought some relief to Bram.

"You feel better now, Kuya?" Edgardo asked.

"Not at all."

"Before we go in, remember... they don't know."

"They don't know about Carlo gettin' busted?"

"They don't know anything. Nanay especially."

Bram nodded.

That night would be more tense that he'd thought.

Chris and Carlo stepped out of their car. With wide smiles, they rushed their Tito Bram for a group hug, something they all waited years for. Edgardo kept his distance, allowing them their tender moment.

Bram gripped Carlo's upper arm. "Goddamn, boy! You packed on some muscle! 100 Percent prime baka!"

"Just like you, Tito."

"Your father says you work very hard every day. I respect that. Hard work is more important than smarts, even though you got both. Always remember that." He turned to his niece. "And you, batang babae, wearing a long, pretty dress? Where are your denim overalls?"

"I have this one dress for special occasions," Chris said.

"So, seeing your decrepit old uncle is a special occasion?"

Chris laughed. Carlo merely smiled.

"Always, Tito," she said.

"Speaking of smarts, I hear you're the brightest brat in school. Is that true?"

"Almost the smartest," Carlo said. "It's neck-and-neck between her and Jenny Passante."

"Naw, you make ol' Jenny think it's close, keep her off guard, but then you swoop past her when she ain't expectin' it, leave her in the dust. That's what your father did."

"I'm taking AP classes," Chris said. "Gonna finish school a year early. Carlo and I will graduate together."

"Yay for us," Carlo said in a bored tone.

"You hear that, Eddie?" Bram said. "Finishing school early? The boy may take after his uncle, but our little girl certainly takes after her old man."

"I thought getting out early meant she takes after you?" Edgardo said. The teens laughed. Bram did not. "Sorry, I couldn't resist. Come on people, let's stop stalling. Take another deep breath, Kuya."

"Any deeper and I might pass out."

Christiana took her nervous Tito Bram by the hand and the four of them headed toward the house at the end of the cul-de-sac.

* * *

Reyna Duque Harrison heard the door chime as she rinsed a large pot of rice in her kitchen sink. She set the pot in the cooker, wiped her hands on a towel, straightened her apron, and went to open the front door.

Bram hadn't seen his mother in over a decade, and though she was now 72 years old, she looked the same as the day he turned himself in to the authorities a decade before. She had short, dyed black hair, thick eye makeup, and pearls over a lace gown topped with a floral apron.

"Lola Reyna!" Christiana said.

"Hello Lola," her brother said.

Lola Reyna hugged her grandchildren with a big smile, not offering an inch of it to her sons just behind them.

My nanay, Reyna Duque Harrison, was a far better grandparent to my children than she has ever been a mother to me and Bram, or at least she usually was.

She's a seemingly loving woman whose charm masks the most extreme case of narcissistic personality disorder I've ever witnessed or read. Her generosity and warm affection were tempered with passive-aggressive judgement and thick doses of guilt, her mood turning on a dime the second she didn't feel like the star of the show.

Bram reached to join the group embrace, but Edgardo stopped him with a stern look. He gestured to the black plastic bag in hand. Bram held it up, but Lola Reyna acted as if she didn't see them.

Lola Reyna craved compliments, always needed to feel she was Number One. Anything less, the claws came out. Carlo was once brutally lacerated by those claws when he boasted about his football team's undefeated season for a minute too long.

Christiana had yet to feel her Lola's wrath as she always showered her with fountains of praise and love. She was always a smart kid, always able to figure people out. I often wondered if she had her suspicions about me.

"No hugs from my sons?" Lola Reyna finally said, coldly.

Edgardo and Bram gave her one-armed hugs and pecks on the cheek. In contrast to his older brother's anxious expression, Edgardo held a neutral, rested face, an affront to his demanding mother.

"Just leave if you don't want to be here, Doy," she said, calling Edgardo by his childhood nickname. "I can see your tired eyes. No one is forcing you to stay."

"I'm not going anywhere, Nay."

"Sure, eat first, then run."

"Of course."

I managed a tolerable relationship with my mother after learning early in life to hide my intellect from her and to never discuss my achievements. They would only enrage her, and she wouldn't care to hear them, anyway, for no one else was allowed happiness or success. When I was around her, she had the stage and I sat in the nosebleeds. Acceptable, as it had to be.

Bram reached into the bag and pulled out a long, flat gold box. He awkwardly handed it to his mother.

"Is this supposed to impress me, Bam Bam?" she asked, using his old nickname. "I hope it's not food."

"It's chocolate, Nay," Bram said in a faint, trailing voice. He'd been careful to choose something she wouldn't have prepared herself.

"Candy," she said with a scoff. "Save it for your girlfriends on the street."

"You're my Number One girl, Nay."

"Uh huh."

My beast of a brother turned into a timid little boy around our nanay, which worked for her just fine. She preferred streams of adulation but would settle for confrontation, guilt, and misery, anything that grabbed the spotlight.

"You know I don't like chocolate." She read the elegant lettering on the gold box. "Valerie Confections?"

"Eddie says they're the best," Bram said. "They make stuff for movie stars."

"Well, the kids can eat it. I have to watch my blood sugar."

"I bought it for you," Bram said in a faint, trailing voice.

"Thank you anyway, Bam Bam."

"Smells good in here," Edgardo said, placating his mother as he always did.

"It should," Lola Reyna said. "I've been cooking all day, since six this morning." She looked out through the open front door for a moment before shutting it. "Where's Divinia?"

"She had plans."

"Of course she did. The smell of real Filipino cooking might send her into shock."

"She's at a work meeting."

"At night?" Lola Reyna said. "And you believe her? She's probably cheating on you."

"We're divorced, Nay, remember?"

"Exactly. Divorced so she can be with all the men she wants."

Divinia never stood a chance with my mother. Being an educated, successful, and famous businesswoman, she was everything my mother wanted to be. In her burning envy, Lola Reyna considered Divinia a blight on her personal world. She felt small next to my ex-wife and expressed it with hate and contempt. If I'm painting my mother as a heartless, jealous monster, it's because that's precisely what she was and will forever be. But she's family, and I wouldn't deny my children a relationship with their Lola.

Lola Reyna took Carlo and Chris into the living room where her husband was posted in front of the TV, a drifting snore rising from his weathered face.

"Your Lolo is glued to his recliner, watching the news. Let's wake the old man up!" She leaned down and yelled in his ear. "Otto! They're here!"

Otto Harrison was a White man pushing 70. His thick gray beard and long mustache laid over his plaid button-up shirt. His baggy jeans had stains and rips in the knees, and his right hand permanently gripped an old glass Gatorade bottle filled with ice water, one of several always on standby in the fridge. Edgardo used to fetch them for him when he came home from working all day at his garage.

"Are those my kids?" Otto said with a snort as he woke from a partial slumber. "They can't be. They're too big!"

My stepfather, Otto Harrison, met my mother when his ship was stationed at U.S. Subic Bay Naval Station in the Philippines. Bram and I were two twigs running barefoot in the fields, and our father had been in the ground less than a year, when the Bluejackets disembarked and fell in love with our women en masse.

Otto told me he and his shipmates were proud members of the "Filipino Mafia," a group of American sailors who loved and actively supported our people, many of them even learning to speak Tagalog. He also told me that the Navy had an "Eleven Percent Club" at the time, so named because that was how many American sailors returned home from the Philippines single. After meeting Reyna, Otto had no chance of joining that club.

Lynn Harrod

Otto adjusted his hearing aide, a smooth, casual gesture Edgardo noted. The old man surely hid it from him over the years until he reached a point where humility no longer mattered.

"What's up, Lolo?" Chris asked.

"You bring your football this time?"

"Shit, sorry..." Carlo said.

"Carlo!" Lola Reyna said from the kitchen. "You sound like your uncle!"

The old man reached under the couch and revealed a neon green Nerf football. "Well, shit, lucky I still got mine!"

"Otto!"

Lolo Otto was an old roughneck from the San Joaquin Valley, where he grew up working on big commercial farms until he graduated to Master Mechanic in the military. Carlo and Chris loved their lolo. He treated them like his prince and princess, and my mother like his queen. I'm glad someone did.

Edgardo and Bram knelt and hugged their stepfather in his chair.

"Tatay," Edgardo said. "It's good to see you still kicking."

"You look good, Tay," Bram said.

"Do I?" the old man said with a laugh. "This looks good to you?"

"Hell yeah. You look like you could still kick some ass."

"If they keep their ass real still, maybe."

Otto slowly rose to his feet and took a long look at his older stepson, overjoyed to see him again after so long apart. "It's real good to have you back, Big Boy. I can't say that enough."

"That means you got work for me."

"I was thinking of painting the garage, yes." Otto embraced his sons and grandchildren in a big group hug. As everyone backed away, he singled out Carlo. "And you, young man. Your Lola and I heard what happened to you, kiddo."

Carlo felt nervous. He looked back at his father and uncle.

"It was a mistake, Lolo..."

"MVP? Winning touchdown? You take after your grandfather! And that is no mistake! Remember that!"

Edgardo shared his stepfather's pride until...

"You were there, Lolo," the boy said, confused. "You held up my trophy for everyone to see, remember?"

Otto took a moment to recollect.

Bram looked concerned.

"Of course, kiddo!" Otto said. "And I see you're wearing the watch!"

Carlo pulled up the sleeve of his letterman jacket to reveal his silver watch.

"I picked that out special for you," the old man said.

"He wears it all the time, Lolo," Christiana said, "even in the shower and when he goes to bed..."

"And how would you know?" her brother asked, his brow turned down.

"Easy, boy," Edgardo said.

"Hey, nothing wrong with wearing your Timex all night.," Otto said. "Takes a lickin' and keeps on tickin'. Tough. Just like your dad."

Carlo looked at his father. "Yeah, I know."

"Wait a minute, now. I got something burning a hole in my pocket..." Otto pulled two Twenties from his pants pocket and gave one to each of his grandkids. They smiled wide. "Save those for a rainy day."

"Lotta rainy days lately," the boy said.

Reyna emerged from the kitchen and slapped her husband's shoulder. "Otto, you spoil them!"

"And you don't?" He turned to his grandkids. "Hey, I've been making progress with the game! I'll show you. Go set it up."

Carlo and Chris ran into the next room, where Carlo set up a video game on a wall-mounted TV.

Otto turned to his frustrated wife, leaned in close, and spoke in a lowered voice. "Yes Reyna, I do spoil them, and I'm gonna keep spoiling them while I still can. The day's coming when twenty bucks, a video game, and a football toss from an old man don't mean nothing no more. Let me have this."

"Diyos, don't be so dramatic," Lola Reyna said as she returned to her bubbling pots in the kitchen.

Otto stretched with a mild groan, put on his best happy face, and joined his grandchildren in the parlor.

With the brothers alone for the moment, Bram pulled Edgardo aside. "How long's Tay been like this?"

"Past couple of years," Edgardo said. "He gets emotional, loses time, forgets things he did in the morning. I've taken him to lunch at Uminom many times, but this last time, he was surprised to see Divinia come out of the kitchen."

"Pakshet."

"A few times, he got out of bed and just wandered off. Took us hours to find him."

"Poor Tatay."

"It happens to the best of us, Kuya."

24

Chardonnay

The yellow-orange sunset beamed through the bamboo blinds of the Corazon Lounge's front windows, creating stripes of warm light across Joey The Rose and his row of barstool regulars. The busy evening filled both the main front room and the adjoining lounge with white-collar office workers, trendy hipsters, and college foodies, all clustered together in red leather booths and tropical-print sofas. They enjoyed sweet signature tiki drinks in unique, quirky mugs resembling Polynesian totem gods, completing the kitschy-cool experience from the walls to the furniture to the ambient music.

Divinia Duque entered alone in her pantsuit and heels. She stood at the open door for a moment, basking in nostalgic awe, taking in the exquisite lounge that she'd lovingly designed and co-managed with her ex-husband. Though Corazon had hardly changed since her time there, and her memories of those nights remained vivid, it felt still like a lifetime ago.

Joey noticed her through the crowd. She seemed hesitant to take another step. "Hey lady! You come to drink? Or you just taking in the atmosphere?"

"Do you speak to all your patrons this way?" she asked.

"Just the sexy ones." He picked out a bottle of Chardonnay from the wall rack behind him.

"Mr. Gallo, you silver-tongued devil." Divinia smirked at the giant bartender as she approached the bar.

"Mr. Gallo? Last time I heard that, I was sitting in the principal's office. Friends call me 'Joey.'"

"That still includes me?" Divinia forgot how much she liked him. In distancing herself from Edgardo and rebooting her life, she left so many others behind, people she once considered family. "I mean, you still consider me a friend?"

"Well, it never hurts to butter up the boss or his wife."

"I'm not your boss anymore, or his wife, remember?"

"Yeah, yeah, I know. I woulda never called you sexy out loud if you were still with Ed."

Divinia laughed and took a seat at the bar. Joey uncorked the Chardonnay and poured her a quarter-glass. She picked up the bottle and admired its label, a pen-and-ink drawing of a castle estate. "Chateau Montelena. You remembered."

"It's my job to know what people want." Joey set a plate of cheese in front of her, a small, crusty wheel of brie cut into slices. "You taught me that, Div."

"I apparently taught you well. These pair perfectly."

Joey tended to patrons down the bar while Divinia sipped her oaky white wine full of round citrus, stone fruit, and tropical notes. The brie's creamy texture and tart flavor balanced well with the wine. When she first met the gruff, no-nonsense former boxer years before, she never imagined he'd develop such a fine palate, or at least, a divine attention to others' tastes.

"Join me?" she said to Joey when he returned.

"Why not?" Joey set another wine glass on the bar and allowed Divinia to pour him a share. He swirled the wine, viewed it against the light from a wall-mounted, glowing glass turtle, and took a sip. "Yep. It's wine, alright."

"If you ever get tired of slinging Mai Tais, Joey, there's always a place for you at Uminom."

"You trying to poach me away?"

"It is working?"

"Nah," Joey said. "I ain't exactly Michelin-star quality."

"Neither am I, sometimes," Divinia said with a sigh.

"Yeah right. Your worst day is others' best."

"Stop it, Joey."

"You know I brag about you and Uminom all the time? Every night, I've told everybody who's ever sat here to drop what they're doing and head over for the best meal of their lives."

"Oh, I know," Divinia said with a smile. "I've heard many times that 'the big bartender at Corazon sent us.' You're better than my agent, may as well hand out business cards at this point."

Joey laughed. "So, what's it like running the first Filipino joint in the world to get a star?"

"*Second* Filipino joint."

Joey looked confused. "But in your interview with *Food and Wine*..."

"I wasn't about to correct know-it-all Laura Grisham," Divinia said, recalling that dreadful interview. "She spoke about Corazon as if it were a cheap novelty pop-up, so I let her publish her poor research. No, I was at Morihiro in Atwater Village when I got my first star, before Uminom was even a dream, but the first Filipino restaurant to get a Michelin star was actually Kasama in Chicago."

"They better than you?"

"Different," Divinia said. "I mostly use my mother's traditional rustic recipes. They embrace fusion. Their mushroom adobo is a work of art. Maitake shrooms, scallops, mussels." She poured them both another quarter-glass. "Back to my offer. Uminom's bar would be yours, complete creative control. What do you say?"

"Tempting." Joey shook his head. "But Ed would be lost without me."

"The man's already a lost soul. Still, I admire your loyalty." She gave up her recruitment effort and changed the subject, looking at the wine bottle again. "2020 vintage. You are good."

"I have my moments."

"I mean it, Joey. Clean glassware, nice cheese pairing, excellent vintage, and it's perfectly chilled."

"My chards are set to 52 degrees. I learned that from Ed. He says it brings out that woodsy taste and highlights the fruit. Never thought I'd understand this stuff, but he's educated me. He's a stickler for perfection, like you."

"And who do you think educated him? Fish?"

"Is that a fact?" Joey laughed. "Someone knew something The Great Edgardo Duque didn't?"

"You think he was sipping flights of chard with Bram back in The Bay?"

Joey laughed at the image, considering the fact that the brothers had been night-running with The Demonyo at the time, a chapter in their lives that Divinia knew little about. She knew Bram had belonged to a gang, but she didn't know that he served as their infamous enforcer for years, and she knew nothing of Edgardo's brief involvement that ultimately led to Bram's 10-year prison sentence.

Across the lounge, Felix served patrons on a wide U-shaped sofa. They thanked and handsomely tipped "Hector" – his latest alias – as he set down a platter of pork shumai and talong bola bola before gathering their empty glasses and returning them to the bar. He was taken aback upon seeing his boss's ex-wife sipping wine at Stool 12, an unnerving sight he thought he'd never see.

To Felix's relief, she didn't seem to know him.

"The place looks better than when I left it," Divinia said to Joey. "Eddie must have hired a pro."

"Nope," Joey said. "This is all Ed, with some input from me, of course."

"I see the trees are no more. Where's your Christmas spirit?"

"Christmas is still a couple of weeks away. But you'll be pleased to know they go up tomorrow."

"Maybe I'll come back and see for myself," she said.

"Maybe I'll have another bottle of Chateau Montelena waiting for you."

Divinia gestured for Joey to join her in another glass. This time, he served himself. "Just a finger's worth," he said, pouring an inch of wine. He raised his glass in a toast. "To seeing old friends at Corazon."

"Tahanan ng aking puso," Divinia said.

"You gotta help me out. My Filipino is rusty, by which I mean rusted solid."

"Where I left my heart."

"Keep it here, Div," Joey said. "It'll always be safe on my watch, yours and Ed's."

To her surprise, she suddenly missed her ex-husband, if only for their many nights together in the lounge. "Eddie's still at his mother's?" she asked, dodging her welling emotions.

"Yep. Along with everybody else. He said you couldn't make it 'cause you had big Hollywood plans?"

She laughed, exhausted. "I had a cocktail with my producers, but that's over. Now my plans are to drink wine here with you."

"It went that bad, huh?" Joey gathered glasses and cleaned them in perfect little rows in the sink.

"Could've been worse." Divinia wanted to forget that horrible dinner meeting, where her producers pressured her to feature more American fare over authentic island dishes. "You ever met my mother-in-law?"

"Reyna? Haven't had the privilege."

"I assure you, Joey, you're lucky to be underprivileged."

"That seems to be the consensus."

25

Always The Smart Child

Lola Reyna's kitchen was the only part of her house with any kind of Philippine decor, most prominent of which were an oversized wooden fork and spoon mounted to the wall, a framed print of Leonardo da Vinci's The Last Supper, and two six-inch Sta. Niño Catholic statues atop the refrigerator. A wall calendar featured photos of the Rice Terraces of the Philippine Cordilleras. Small, round rattan baskets hung above it all.

Reyna worked several pots on her stovetop while her two sons sat on barstools at a nearby counter. She spoke to them in her native language as she always did whenever it was just the three of them.

"I hope you haven't eaten, boy," she said in Tagalog.

"You talking to me or Eddie?" Bram asked in Tagalog.

"You're both boys, aren't you?"

From his barstool, Edgardo looked out at the living room, at Lolo Otto on the couch with his hands on an Xbox controller while sandwiched between his grandchildren. He showed them his progress on *Red Dead Redemption 2,* an immersive Old West video game. It was originally a birthday gift for Carlo, but the boy favored sports titles like *Madden NFL 20,* leaving the outlaw life for his grandfather to explore. As Otto and his digital gang robbed a train, Chris and Carlo chattered on about science fairs and football playoffs. Edgardo could tell the old man loved every second of their time together, as if it all served as a secondhand childhood.

Watching my kids with Otto, my mind wandered to a past Christmas in that house when Christina and Carlo were six and seven, sitting at the base of a tall Christmas tree beside their jolly grandfather. My mother entered with two cups of coffee, clearly perturbed at the children's attention on her husband rather than her. She handed a cup to Divinia by the fireplace and sat beside her to exchange recipes, if only to boast of her cooking knowledge. Even within that balanced dysfunction, it's hard to imagine a time when those two women were still on speaking terms.

Within his vivid memory, Edgardo saw himself enter the room wearing a Santa Claus hat and coat, a silly, sentimental act that seemed inconceivable today. He carried a pillowcase full of presents, and the children ran to him in pure, innocent glee. They harbored no stress of a family breaking apart, no pressure of college around the corner, no fear of cops or crooks beating down their door. They were still kids. Their parents were still the moon and sun in their shared universe. The dolls and action figures in their bedrooms were their friends. The colorfully wrapped gifts in that pillowcase felt life-changing. How Edgardo missed that simple, happy time in their shared life.

He remembered that Santa hadn't come alone that night long ago. His grizzled, stocky elf, "Sweet Abraham" – complete with a green pointy hat and glittery vest – hauled tall stacks of boxes and bags, nearly all of them for the youngsters.

CLANG

The sharp sound of a pot lid hitting the tile floor swept the memory away, and Edgardo was ripped back to the present. Lola Reyna placed the lid in the sink and stirred a large pot. She spoke to her sons in a stern tone, without eye contact.

"You still like women?" she asked Bram in Tagalog.

"What?" Bram asked.

"You need to forget about those big sweaty négros in prison. Think about finding a good woman."

"Nanay!" Edgardo said.

She ignored her younger son. "I know what they do in those prisons, Bam Bam. Don't tell me you used only your hand for ten years. I'm not stupid."

"Nanay! That's enough!"

"Quiet, Doy!"

"It wasn't like that, Nay," Bram said.

"Of course it was. That's why you never wanted me to visit. You didn't want me to see you with your many lovers. You were ashamed."

"Your imagination is running away!"

"Okay, you keep your secrets," Lola Reyna said. "Just find a good Filipina now that you're out here. Give me some grandchildren before I die. That's all I ask."

Bram swallowed his frustration, his anger, and walked up behind his mother at the stove. Despite feeling unheard, as he'd always felt growing up, he hugged her from behind. "I missed you, Nay."

"Uh huh. That's why you told them not to allow your mother to visit. That's why I was banned from your prison."

"I didn't allow anyone to visit."

"You let your brother visit," she said, pointing to Edgardo with a wooden spoon.

"No, I didn't."

"You were ashamed of me, admit it."

"I was ashamed of myself," Bram said. "I didn't want you or anyone else to see me in that place."

"Why not? You chose to go there. You chose to be bakla."

"Putang ina!" Bram said. "That's not why I turned myself in!"

"Then why?" Lola Reyna asked. She didn't know Edgardo's role in his prison sentence. "Tell me, Bam Bam, why did you go in there on your own?"

"Would it have been better if I'd ran and let the cops find me? Drag me in there?"

"Let's all calm down," Edgardo said.

"Yes!" Reyna yelled, ignoring her younger son. "Then everyone would know you'd rather be with your family! With your mother!"

"Nanay, 'everyone' doesn't care!" Bram said. "Nobody cares when you're inside!"

"You're saying I didn't care?"

"I'm talking about all the people not in this house!" Bram slumped back on his barstool and looked away, trying to hide his building tears. "You don't know what it was like."

"And I don't want to know! You made your decision, Bam Bam. I don't understand it, and I don't care. I know you needed to humiliate your mother. You had your reasons, so you must live with them. Be a man for once!"

Bram was cut to the bone by his mother's cruel words. Edgardo placed a sympathetic arm around his brother, which attracted his mother's wrath like a lightning rod.

"And what of you?" she barked at Edgardo. "Mister Power Businessman! You didn't get him out?"

"There was nothing I could do, Nay."

"Says the man with the 166 I.Q. That's right, I remember! Best of your class. Graduated college at nineteen. Because of me! Because I supported you! And there was nothing you could have done for him? You let him rot in there with his boyfriends behind bars? You let them laugh at me for raising a man who became their whore?"

Bram slammed his fist to the counter, busting a tile. The sharp crack grabbed everyone's attention, including Otto and the grandkids in the next room. They'd long become numb to the arguments in Tagalog, barely hearing them, but sat bolt upright at Bram's rage.

Otto put down his controller and leaned in close to his grandchildren. "Don't mind them. You know how they can get."

"Why's Lola so mad?" Chris asked.

"Because she missed your uncle. Because she was worried about him every day he was away."

"Funny way of showing it," Carlo muttered.

"Easy now, boy."

"What are they saying, exactly?" Chris asked.

Otto Harrison, having served as a naval officer in the Philippines for two years, had become familiar with Tagalog and knew every stinging barb his harsh wife had been hurling in the kitchen. "Never you mind that. Watch me kill the O'Driscoll Gang."

In the kitchen, Lola Reyna stared at her hulking, fuming older son, now on his feet, looking down at her. His angry eyes fed her constant need for attention, and she chose to further fan the flames.

"There is it," Reyna said in Tagalog. "There's the anger that got you in trouble in the first place. Always angry for no reason! I'd hoped you'd have it under control by now, but I still see it in your face. You say you left the gang life, but did it leave you? No. I don't think so."

Bram stormed out of the kitchen. Reyna returned to her pots as if nothing happened. Edgardo wanted to follow him, but remained with his mother.

"Nanay, he turned himself in to protect me," Edgardo said in Tagalog.

"Protect you? From what?"

"I have a family. I have a business, a home, and it's all because of his sacrifice."

"No, you're a good boy, always the smart child." He remembered what he told Christiana earlier, word for word, and feared that he'd been raising his children in the same cruel, imbalanced way she'd raised hers. "You would have been fine, Doy."

"He doesn't deserve your guilt trip."

"Guilt trip? What did I say? Forgive me for speaking the truth! You two, always defending each other!"

"And we always will," Edgardo said flatly.

"Sure, sure, always against me."

"Will you ever learn, Nanay?"

Edgardo felt Bram's anger and frustration, felt unheard as he so often did, but he also pitied his mother, her narcissism and contempt deeply ingrained. He gave up trying to reach her, stood from his barstool, and followed his brother into the next room.

26

A Wolf Comes Calling

Dusk at Galvez Salvage and Scrap enshrouded the tall stacks of cars and junk in a backlit glow, a city of trash against a sky of rich color emanating from a sunset filtered through dense pollution. Calixto stared at the fading light from the makeshift living room set of sofas and tables in the mud between his warehouses. He looked down at his phone as several members of the TSB surrounded him, including his First Kapitan...

Bakal Diaz was 35 but looked 55 with his leathery, lined face, receding hairline, and dead expression. His shoulder-length black hair rested atop his white T-shirt, which topped his baggy jeans and military boots.

"Nothing yet," Calixto said. "Pakshet. Your men swing by my cousin's place?"

"Twice," Bakal said. He always spoke fast, his words often slurring together. "Yoy Yoy ain't been there, and Jorge's woman ain't seen him either."

"What about Miguel?"

"Ghost."

"Curious."

"I've been all over the cop channel," Bakal said. "Nothing about any of them."

"Stay on it," Calixto said. "If they ain't here, if they ain't anywhere, it means they're locked up or they're runnin'."

"Or worse."

"We ain't goin' there just yet."

The men heard a faint rumbling over the relative quiet of their riverside scrapyard. It grew louder, cutting through the background noise of the city, and soon it was apparent that a motorcycle had entered the property.

"Is that our man?" Bakal asked, his question rushing out as "that'r'mun?"

Before his boss could respond, the gangsters turned to see Mace of The Wolf Pack MC pull up on his black-and-chrome Harley. He wore a matte black half-shell helmet and a muscle shirt under his "cut," his leather vest adorned with the Wolf Pack's crest across its back. A small red cooler sat strapped to the back of his bike, barely big enough for a six-pack, standing out as the only touch of color to the man.

Mace stopped his massive cruiser a few feet behind Calixto's couch – uncomfortably loud and close – and shut off the motor, returning the yard to its city-outskirt calm. As Mace rose from his bike and untied the cooler, Bakal could see a sawed-off shotgun resting in a steel sheath within the machine's wraparound exhaust. Mace noticed the many eyes glued to his weapon.

"It sure is loaded if that's what you all's wonderin'," Mace said in his faux Southern accent, "but it stays put if'n you do." He brought the compact cooler to Calixto, set it on the coffee table before him, and plopped onto the opposite sofa, arms outstretched as if he owned the place.

"Amoy dumi siya," Bakal said with a frown in his country-slang Tagalog. He stepped away in disgust, preferring to view the scene from a distance.

"Hindi naliligo ang lalaki," Calixto said with a laugh. His men smiled at the insults.

Mace knew enough Tagalog to understand them, though he didn't dare reveal it.

He smells like shit.

The man never bathes.

"English, please," Mace said. "We're all Americans, ain't we?"

"Hello Mr. Mason," Calixto said in his sharpest English as if to mock the man. "My associate simply noted that you're late."

"Hey, I'm here, you're here. That's rit' on time in my book. I mean, this ain't no job interview, is it?"

"It's bad manners."

"We're meeting in a junkyard, boys. Forgive me if I forgot my tuxedo and salad fork and arrived five past the hour." Mace looked around at the structures, the towers of cars, stacks of appliances, the mountain of miscellaneous scrap. "You know, for a dump, this place is actually kind of nice, like the Beverly Hills of shitholes."

"That sounds like a back-handed compliment," Calixto said. "You think it's a good idea to start like that?"

"Count to three, brother," Mace said. "It's a good location, jus' sayin'. A real fixer-upper. Lotsa potential."

"Agreed. A lot of potential business to be done here."

"I hear you. Believe me, I do. Now, how about you unwrap the Christmas present I brought you?"

Calixto grinned at his guest, amused. He opened the cooler and pulled out three bricks of "damo," the cocaine-infused marijuana the bikers bought from the HK-9. He set them on the coffee table.

"What's that smell?" Calixto asked.

"I dunno. The smell of money? Meaning your money handed to me, of course."

Calixto sniffed the bricks and dropped his proper English. "This don't smell like no weed I ever known."

"And here I thought you Asian boys knew all about it," Mace said. "It's that damo shit, straight from your islands. Luzon, I think? It's weed that..."

"I know what damo is, Mr. Mason."

"Nah, you don't, 'Mr. Cervantes.' This here's diff'rent. It's patented magic weed, fused wit' cocaine. A real gourmet blend. Careful when you smoke it. It could hook yo' ass for life."

Calixto flung open a butterfly knife and randomly chose a brick by stabbing and slicing it open. He pulled out a pinch of herb and held it to his nose. "I smoked a lot worse."

"So you say. Then you got a stronger constitution than most. One of my guys can't get nuff' of the stuff. We mighta lost him for good."

"My condolences," Calixto said. "Good men are hard to find."

"He was a good man. He just liked a good smoke a bit too much, if you know what I'm sayin'."

"Luzon, you said?" Calixto revealed a small metal box full of rolling papers and crafted a joint with the damo between his fingers. "Who'd you get it from? The Nines? The Demonyo? Maybe The Panginoon?"

"Ah, a magician never reveals his secrets, amigo."

"Doesn't matter. I like it already, and do you know why, Mr. Mason? Because you brought it directly to me. For once, Duque didn't have his greedy hand in any of this."

Mace simply nodded, choosing not to bring up The Duke's involvement.

"That said, we discussed one brick to start," Calixto said. "I see three here. I ain't buying three or even one till I know it's for real."

"The extra two are on the house. We wanna start out as good buddies, am I right?"

"Free shit ain't never free. What do you Wolves want?"

"Information," Mace said. "At the very least, speculation."

Calixto grinned at his guest as he lit the joint. "Information about what, exactly?"

"Not what, but who. The Duke, or 'Duque,' as you call him. What do you know about the man?"

"What do you care?"

"We're the new kids in town and we got business wit' him comin' up," Mace said. "I jus' wanna know what kinda man I'm dealin' wit'."

"He's not a man to be fucked with."

"So I hear. I mean 'sides that."

Calixto took a couple of puffs of his joint. He held the smoke in his mouth for a moment, like a cigar, and slowly let it seep into him. His eyes widened as the herb kicked in.

"How is it?" Mace asked. "Does it pass muster?"

"Fuuuck," Calixto said with a gasp as he continued to hold in the smoke. "Now that is different."

"Diff'rent good?"

"Different, very good, Mr. Mason. I don't know about magic, but it's worthy."

"No more of this 'Mr. Mason' malarky. I ain't no lord or magistrate. 'Mace' is jus' fine."

"Calixto."

"Now ain't it good to get acquainted?"

Bakal returned with a six-pack of San Miguel Beer and set it on the coffee table in front of Mace. The biker pulled off a bottle and curiously read the label before popping it open with one of his rings.

"Well shit, I ain't never had no Filipino beer before. Didn't even know it existed."

"And I never done business with no tangina puti kano before."

Fucking White American, as Mace understood.

"Ain't we a pair?" he asked, taking a swig of his beer. "So, tell me, Cal, whatcha got on The Duke?"

"What I got is three men on him now. I'm waiting to hear back." Calixto passed the joint over his head to Bakal behind him. Bakal took a puff and quietly reeled from the unique sensation.

"The sun's goin' to bed," Mace said. "How long's it been since you heard anything?"

"Gonna hear from them soon. When I know, you'll know."

Mace laughed. "That long, huh? No sir, The Duke is definitely not a man to be fucked wit'." He chugged his beer and tossed the empty bottle to the mud, opening another in the same sweeping motion. "Tell you what, since you're still waitin' to hear from your boys, I'll start by tellin' you my shit."

"I don't have the patience to hear something I already know," Calixto said, "so make it good, understand?"

"Understood. Okay, so I hear rumor that The Duke lost all his shit to the feds, got cleaned out over the weekend. Does that line up with what you heard?"

Calixto took the joint back from Bakal and held it in thought. "I don't believe it for a moment."

"Well, never you mind, it is jus' a rumor, anyways. Now that it's clear you like my product, how's 'bout my money?"

Calixto drew another pull from the joint, finishing his thought. He nodded to Bakal. "Pay him for three bricks."

"Two was free, remember?"

"Generous, but I also remember that we ain't no fuckin' charity case."

Bakal counted money in a plastic shopping bag and tossed it onto the coffee table. Mace opened it and pulled out six stacks of cash.

"Nice," the biker said. "This suits me well an' good. Now, 'bout The Duke..."

"I said when I know, you'll know. Good night. Mace."

Calixto waited for his guest to mount his motorcycle and leave. Instead, the man looked at the gangsters around him and leaned back on the sofa as if he owned it.

"I think I'll stick around until you do," he said. "If that's okay wit' you. Cal."

27

Charles

Further into the evening at the Corazon Lounge, Divinia and Joey continued to enjoy each other's company at the bar. Their bottle of Chardonnay sat empty as they moved on to a pair of Fog Cutters, a tiki standard made with rum, brandy, gin, lemon juice, and cream sherry. Joey made them knowing the classic drink was among her favorites.

"Are you drunk enough that I can ask you some personal questions?" Divinia asked.

"You see how big I am, right?" Joey asked. "Takes more than a few fingers of chard and a Fog to loosen these lips."

"Here I go anyway. What do you know about Carlo? About what happened to him the other night?"

Joey didn't immediately respond. He glanced at Felix beside him behind the bar, restocking glassware. "What about him?"

"He was arrested for some drive-by shooting. What did Eddie tell you about it?"

"Not much. The cops fucked up, as usual, pardon my French."

"I speak French, too, fucker," she said, "and I know Eddie talks to you about everyone and everything. That's how Joey The Rose knows so much. Now tell me..."

"The kid pranked someone, the wrong someone from what I heard. Some judge's son. Dumb-ass cops mixed it up with a random shooting. That's it." Joey deliberately got it wrong, citing the murder victim as the pranked teen. He played dumb enough to hopefully end the conversation.

"You sure that's it?" She watched his face and body language, looking for his tell. "Just a prank?"

"Look, Div, what do you want me to say? Carlo's a good kid. Everyone knows that. You really think he'd be mixed up in something stupid like a drive-by?"

"Of course not," she said, "but when the police were ready to break down my door, Eddie assumed they were there for *him*. He was ready to give himself up. Why?"

Joey took a long sip of his Fog Cutter as he thought of a response. Before he could think of some way to deflect the question, a well-dressed older man entered the lounge and looked their way.

C.B. stood at the door in a casual suit and shined dress shoes, a gold watch gleaming on his wrist. The outfit was a stark contrast to his worn Wolf Pack leathers. He sat on a barstool next to Divinia.

"Evening," Joey said to the man, relieved to have a distraction from the tense talk with Divinia.

"Good evening to you as well," C.B. said. "This place is nice."

"No place better, my friend. What's your poison?"

"Not sure, but I hear you guys make a mighty Rum Runner."

"You heard right," Joey said with pride. "Best in the city."

"How good can it be? Just rum with some bananas and berries, right?"

"Nah, ours is a mix of light and dark rum, banana liqueur, blackberry liqueur, orange juice, pineapple, and a touch of our famous in-house grenadine. It'll blow your hair back."

"What hair I have left," C.B. said with a smile as he ran his hand across his scalp. "Sold. I'll take two."

Joey prepared two Rum Runners in tulip glasses. C.B. turned to Divinia, sitting beside him. He eyed the empty Chardonnay bottle. "White wine? In a tiki bar?"

"I have simple tastes," she said.

"I respect that. Normally, a glass of Irish whiskey is my go-to, but I figure when in Rome..."

"You're saying you don't 'normally' order tiki drinks?"

"Only if they're the best, and this place is supposed to be top-notch."

"The absolute tip of the top."

Joey handed two Rum Runners to C.B. who promptly slid one to Divinia.

"What's this for?" she asked.

"Old Irish tradition. My first time in a bar, I always buy a drink for someone."

"For good luck?"

"It's kept me alive and out of trouble for thirty years now."

"So, you're superstitious?"

"When it comes to people." He offered a handshake. "I'm Charles."

"Divinia."

The two held hands for a moment before offering the slightest shake. Divinia's straight face betrayed a faint smile.

"Okay, full disclosure... I recognize you from TV. 'Masarap Divinia.' I've watched every episode."

"So, you're the one?" she said with a grin.

C.B. laughed and took a sip of his drink, making a face of delightful surprise.

"My producers and I, we're still ironing out bugs. Be honest, what do you think of the show so far?"

"So far, I've made your lechón on my backyard grill. Turned out perfect. You got that from Quezon?"

"It's from Cebu, but my family's originally from Quezon. You're familiar with the Philippines?"

"I visited Quezon City once on business," C.B. said. "Not what I expected."

"And what did you expect?"

"I expected to want to get the hell out of there the moment I stepped off the plane, but it turned out to be a nice place."

"I'm flattered that you didn't see my hometown as a dump or war zone, as many would say."

"Far from it," C.B. said. "A man could comfortably retire there."

"Retire from what?" She was fishing for personal details now.

"Security software. You're talking to the oldest hacker in the western hemisphere."

"Are you good?" she asked. "Could you hack me?"

"My darling, I'd love the opportunity to hack you."

Joey and Felix looked at each other, keeping an eye on "Charles" and Divinia and their awkward flirting.

28

Mild Trouble

Back at the Harrison residence on Magnolia Street in Eagle Rock, Edgardo entered his stepfather's study. Otto's large space had bookshelves lining the walls, an ornate desk with two leather chairs, and dozens of framed family photos. The old man came in behind his son and shut the door before sitting behind his grand desk.

Edgardo remained standing, silent. The photos of happier times grabbed him, particularly one of his middle-aged parents in front of an old Victorian home with their two adolescent sons and young daughter.

I often miss our old house in San Francisco. When Christiana was born, my parents moved to L.A. to be part of her upbringing. I was grateful for Carlo and Chris, but I now realize I was grateful for me.

"Forgive your mother's sharp tongue," Otto said. "She's glad Bram is out, I can tell you that. She just doesn't process it like us normal folks."

"I hardly consider myself normal," Edgardo said, "but I do forgive her, Tay. I try to give her a lot of slack. It still hurts."

"You know how she is, Eddie, missing a few filters. More than a few. Whatever fleeting thought crosses her mind comes barreling out of her mouth. She's just worried for you boys."

Otto reached into his desk drawer and pulled out a bottle of brandy. He poured himself a glass, readied a second glass, but paused. "I'm sorry, I forgot..."

"It's okay. I have it under control."

"You ain't bullshittin' an old bullshitter, are you?"

"Tay, I own a bar," Edgardo said. "If I fell off the wagon again, you'd know it. Everyone would know it."

"If you say you've got a handle on it, Eddie, I believe you. The thing about falling off the wagon is, it's easy to make people think you're just running alongside it, and you can hop on and off whenever you please. But I've been there, son. I know it can be a lie we tell ourselves."

"I'm okay, Tay. Scout's honor."

"Good man."

Edgardo always loved when his stepfather told him that, starting in his early childhood. It ended up being a phrase he'd also use whenever speaking with people he trusted.

Perhaps against his better judgement, Otto poured the second glass of brandy for his son. Edgardo picked it up and held it casually, as if to show it had no grip on him.

"So, how's my garage doing?" the old man asked.

"If you're referring to *my* garage," Edgardo said with a smile, "it's doing well. However, we recently lost the Triple-A account."

"Ouch. Who has it now?"

"Sunset Collision."

"Bradley," Otto said, recalling his old rival. "That fuckin vulture."

"But all the old regulars keep coming in. Half of them still think you run the place."

"Let them keep thinking that. Hell, give them my number if you need to."

Edgardo smiled. "That would be dishonest, Tay."

"I see. And 'The Duke' is never dishonest, right?" His son smirked at the notion. "So long as they get their cars back running good, I don't see no harm in letting them think I'm the one hunkered under their engines."

Otto had long known about The Duke, even if he was spared the increasingly grim details. It remained a secret they shared and kept from the others.

The two men took a moment to enjoy their drinks together, the silence a brief respite from the evening's manic confrontations.

"Good job with Carlo," Otto said. "He's becoming a strong young man."

"He takes after his mother, for better or worse."

"We gonna see her anytime soon?"

"Ask your wife."

"Ah, yes, that old pissing contest," Otto said with a sigh. "Don't worry about that none, your mother will come around."

"I wish I could say the same about Divinia."

"She'll come around, too, for her kids. Baby steps."

"Baby steps," Edgardo said. It was yet another phrase he'd taken from his stepfather. "If you say so, Tay."

"I do say so. Now drink up. I got a football game waiting."

* * *

Otto spent ten minutes throwing a foam football to his grandson before needing a moment to catch his breath. He tapped his left palm to his right fingertips in the universal "time out" gesture and collapsed to the grassy back lawn.

"The first five minutes are the worst five minutes," Carlo said. "Gotta play through it."

"What rotten fortune cookie did that come from?

"Coach says the body hates sudden changes. That's why you gotta warm up and cool down, and the first five minutes are the toughest."

"It's been fifteen!" Otto said with a laugh. "Don't worry, I got more in the tank, especially after I finally 'warm up'."

They tossed the ball to each other again, Carlo holding back against his grandfather.

"You gonna show me that golden arm of yours, kiddo?"

Carlo smirked, looking around the quarter-acre backyard. "In this rinky-dink space?"

"Good form can be spotted in any yard. I mean, you're not always hurling long bombs out on the field, right? Now drill one over."

"Lolo..."

"Come on, it's a Nerf ball, you won't hurt me."

Christiana stepped out from the house and readied her phone to take video of the two athletes.

"You're supposed to help Lola in the kitchen!" Carlo said.

"She said to come out here and get video of you two horsing around."

Otto laughed. "Well, now you gotta throw a good one, kiddo. It's gonna be all over the you-tubes and tick-tocks in the morning!"

* * *

Out on Magnolia Street, the TSB's red Camaro drove down the cul-de-sac, slowly passing the suburban homes like a shark searching for prey. It made a U-turn at the Harrison house, headed back down the street, and parked a good distance away.

The driver didn't need to knock on the door or otherwise invade the house. Knowing The Duke, he just needed to sit and wait.

* * *

From the small window above her kitchen sink, Lola Reyna looked out at her husband and grandchildren playing football. She turned to her two sons as they cut veggies for salad, the one dish she didn't take any pride in preparing.

"Now tell me about Carlo," she said firmly in Tagalog.

"What about him?" Edgardo asked, responding the same.

"The police still want him?"

Edgardo and Bram looked at each other, taken unaware.

My fragile mind had been slipping away. To be blindsided by my mother. She knows nothing about The Duke, and she mustn't know about Carlo, Christiana, and Divinia getting entangled in his world. No good could come of my mother also getting involved, something I certainly didn't have to tell Bram.

"Wait, what's this about Carlo?" Bram asked in Tagalog, in his best puzzled expression.

"Police?" Edgardo said.

"Don't cover up his crimes, Doy," Lola Reyna said. "I expect that kind of nonsense from your thick-headed brother."

"Pakshet," Bram muttered. "Does it ever stop?"

"Nanay, what are you talking about?"

"Carlo called your father while he was in jail," she said.

Bram glanced at his brother.

Shit.

"Your father was having one of his 'bad days,' didn't answer, so Carlo left a long message. He was crying, begging for your someone to come get him. So I know everything."

"What's 'everything'?" Edgardo asked.

"Something about a shooting. They think he did it. I know all about it. So tell me."

"If you know all about it, Nay, what else is there to tell? He's here, right?"

"Your father doesn't know. He has a weak heart, and he gets confused easily. I didn't want him to panic."

"So, what did you do?" Bram asked.

"I went down there to get him, but they said he was already released. They wouldn't tell me anything. I stood there in my house clothes at midnight, no makeup, looking like pangit na panakot and they treated me like a fool!"

Edgardo gave up his feigned ignorance. He looked out the back window before speaking. "The police picked him up by mistake. He and some idyotas played a stupid prank. The cops got it mixed up with another case. That's all."

Lola Reyna stared at her sons, waiting for more.

"That's all, Nay," Bram said.

"You knew?" she asked him. "When were you going to tell me?" She felt more offended at being left out of the loop than concerned about the boy's ordeal.

"It was a dumb mix-up, Nay," Edgardo said. "We didn't want you to panic, just like you didn't want Tay to panic. Ask Divinia if you don't believe me."

"So, she knew before me? Did everyone in the world know?"

"She's Carlo's mother," Edgardo said. "The cops came to her house. Of course, she knew."

"Does Analisa know? I bet you told her."

"I didn't think to bug her with something so trivial."

"Your sister deserves to know what happens with her nephew," Lola Reyna said, abruptly switching gears from being offended to supposedly being concerned, as she often did, whatever it took to keep the spotlight.

"Should I call Analisa now?" Edgardo asked. "Should I call everyone whenever one of my kids gets into some mild trouble?"

"I was at that jail!" Lola Reyna said. "It didn't look like mild trouble to me! Do you think I'm stupid?"

"It's over, Nanay!" Bram said, ready to pound the counter again. "Carlo is fine! He's here! It was a simple mistake. Don't make it worse."

"Me? Make it worse?" Lola Reyna looked at her sons as if they'd gone insane. "You think they make stupid mistakes like this with White kids? I don't think so. And you're so quick to forget about it! You let them run you over and you say nothing!"

Without another word, she turned her back on them, back to her cooking.

Edgardo hated the way his mother always sapped the energy from the room, sucked the joy out of the evening, all for her selfish need for undivided attention, good or bad. Like a mischievous child, if she couldn't have the showers of praise she craved, she'd settle for guilt, unease, and anger, so long as all eyes were on her. Though Edgardo knew she was mentally unbalanced, that nothing could quell her rant, he still succumbed to the instinct to comfort her, something she'd always counted on.

"Nanay…"

"Fine, forget it. Why tell me anything?" Her Tagalog became more pronounced, more formal, as her rage swelled. "Why tell me what's happening with your family? It's none of my business. You have your own life. Forget me."

"Nay…"

"Fix it yourself, Doy. Obviously, you don't need a buwisit like me, and do not dare tell your father. He can't handle it like I can, and he won't be able to keep your secrets."

She turned off the burners and started bringing pots to the dining room table. Edgardo knew what that meant. No serving dishes meant she didn't care, that she would likely escalate the scene at dinner. It frustrated him.

"You want to fix something?" he asked. "How about fixing your feud with Divinia?"

"What's to fix? The woman is jealous of my cooking, jealous that her awards and her TV show and her celebrities don't impress her children. Coming here for authentic food made with love, that's what they want. It's what they need."

"Not this again…"

"Calm down, Nay," Bram said.

"Real Filipinos don't watch her show because she turned her back on us. Only stupid White housewives do. Those are her friends now." Lola Reyna set two pots on the table and turned to her older son. "And I'll be calm when you settle down with a job and a wife. Give me some grandchildren before your pututoy dries up. You're not a child anymore, Bam Bam. Grow up!"

"Pakshet! I just got out!"

"Bram has a job, Nay," Edgardo said. He placed his hand on Bram's arm, as if to keep him from storming out of the room. "He works for me."

"Really?" she said, defiant. "What work?"

"He's my Head of Security."

"So, Bam is the bouncer for your bar? I feel so much better! You really know how to make your mother proud!"

"Tangina!" Bram said. "Maybe I should've stayed in prison!"

Lola Reyna grinned deviously, as if her son walked into her clever trap. "You see! There it is! The truth comes out! I raised you by myself in the Philippines and you have no gratitude! Puchanggala! You'd rather be locked up with your négros than taking care of your mother!"

"Ayoko na! You know nothing about..."

She interrupted his response by opening the glass door to the backyard and calling out to the others. "Dinner is on the table!" she said, switching back to English.

"Nanay..."

"Can we have a simple dinner without your drama?" she asked in Tagalog. "Not everything is about you, Bam Bam."

29

All The Truth You Got

At Ang Corazon, the evening crowd filled every seat, every corner of the main room and its adjoining lounge. Pleasant small talk became drunken nostalgia of past outings, airing out dirty laundry and outspoken complaints about coworkers and managers. Couples on first dates were on their third round of Mai Tais and Zombies, their secrets spilling out on the tables between them in loud fits of laughter.

"Charles" and Divinia also laughed aloud, engaged in deep conversation, still at the bar. Divinia seemed tipsy, taken by her well-spoken new friend.

Joey served them a fourth round of Rum Runners. He shot a concerned look at Divinia, who didn't seem to notice.

"Divinia, darling," C.B. said. "I have something to confess. I didn't just come here on a whim. I had a reason to walk through that door tonight."

"You mean, besides the famous Rum Runners?" she asked with a twinkle in her eye.

"I came here, to the middle of Filipinotown, intent on meeting a beautiful Filipina, right here, sitting at this bar."

"Oh... I see..."

"But she stood me up," he said sadly. "I never did feel comfortable with blind dates."

Embarrassed, Divinia's eyes widened.

"So the bad news is that I didn't get to meet the lady from the trending dating app."

"Sorry to hear that," she said. "I find it hard to believe that a distinguished gentleman like you would have trouble with women."

"You're very kind. The good news is that I still got to spend time with another beautiful Filipina, right here, sitting at this bar."

"Oh, really now..."

"Yeah. Cecilia. Met her here yesterday. Wonderful girl."

"Stop it!" Divinia laughed and slapped him on the arm. "Tell me the truth!"

"You first," C.B. said. "What's a world-famous chef doing all by herself, nursing a bottle of wine?"

"I'm hardly a world-famous anything... yet. And this isn't just any bar, it's my bar. Well, it was mine. In fact, I came up with the recipe for these Rum Runners, the appetizers, even the name 'Ang Corazon Lounge.'"

"That can't be all the truth you got."

"Okay, let's see... I opened this lounge with my ex. He actually owns it now."

"Why him?" C.B. asked. "Why not you?"

"He got the bar, I got the kids. That was the arrangement. I wanted to reboot my career."

"Ex-husband, huh? Sucks to be him. I can't imagine some lucky guy being foolish enough to let you go."

"I'll be sure to tell him that."

"So what's the verdict?" he asked. "Is it really better to have loved and lost than to have never loved at all?"

"Maybe you can tell me, Charles." Divinia stirred her drink and thought about the question. "I've asked myself that many times, and I'm still not sure how to answer it. We were happy once. We had children together. He was a good father."

"Was?"

"But when I talk to him now... he's like Jekyll and Hyde."

C.B. pulled the little pink umbrella from his drink and pointed it at her. "I know exactly what you mean."

"Now your turn, Charles. All the truth you got."

"The truth," he said, pausing in fake embarrassment. "I really was supposed to meet a Filipina here, someone I found on a silly app, and she really stood me up. She probably looked in the window, saw this gray old man sitting here, and turned tail. It happens to us all, even a 'distinguished gentleman' like me."

"I'm sorry, Charles." Divinia suddenly felt for her new friend and saw his jovial manner in a new light.

"I even brought her this..." Charles reached into his jacket and pulled out a small jade plant in a decorative two-inch pot wrapped tightly in cellophane. He held it up and turned it for her to see. "Supposed to be good luck. I don't know, maybe I'm just a hopeless romantic."

"No, it's true," she said. "To Filipinos, Jade Plants give you 'financial energy,' whatever that means. They also bring great friendship, great prosperity."

"That's what the guy at the flower shop said. She was supposed to display it at her house, some place everyone can see." Charles thought for a moment before placing the small wrapped plant on the bar in front of her. "It's now yours. May it bring you friendship and prosperity, not to mention that financial energy. We could all use a little of that."

Divinia picked up the little plant as Charles rose from his chair and straightened his jacket. He handed her his business card as if he'd had it palmed the entire time they were together. She held the plant and card in both hands.

"The plant is for luck," she said, "but what is the card for?"

"Security. That's what *I'm* almost world famous for. If you and your children ever need some, call me."

"I feel safer already." She spit out a tipsy little laugh.

Divinia smiled as Charles tossed a couple of Twenties on the bar and headed for the door, a little drunken wobble in his step. "Man, you don't really know how much you've put away until you finally stand for the first time."

"It happens to us all."

"Exactly."

As the well-dressed man left, Divinia's tipsy smile fell away. She turned to Joey. "Thank you for going easy on the rum."

"I figured you could use an edge with that silver fox," Joey said.

"You really can read people's minds." She glanced at the empty stool beside her. "He wasn't so bad, really."

"That's high praise coming from you."

Joey walked to the shelves behind him and returned the bottles of rum and grenadine. Felix put down his tray of glassware and spoke into Joey's ear in a low voice. "I'm heading over now."

"Call me if you need help," Joey whispered back as Felix took off his apron and hurried out. The big man approached Divinia and took her empty glasses. "Yeah, I suppose he was a charming enough fellow. You interested?"

"In Charles? Not at all." All traces of booze vanished from her tone. "But he seemed unusually interested in me."

"Give yourself some credit. The man has good taste."

"Mr. Gallo, you silver-tongued devil."

Divinia looked at the small jade plant now sitting on the bar, curious.

30

Two Minutes Late

Edgardo sat at one end of his parents' dining room table, his stepfather facing him at the opposite end. His mother sat in the middle with her grandchildren flanking her. Bram sat alone across from them. An empty chair stood between him and his brother, a spot meant for Divinia. Though it was clear to all that she wasn't coming – not that night or anytime in the immediate future – Reyna still made a place for her, if only to point out her absence.

The plates and silverware came from Lola Reyna's china cabinet, reserved for holiday gatherings and other special occasions. Their matching glass goblets never held anything harder than Martinelli's sparkling apple cider, but they still offered a sense of importance.

On the table, their feast comprised steamed rice, baked salmon, crispy pata (fried pork leg), lumpia (egg rolls), morcon (stuffed meat rolls), kaldereta (beef-vegetable stew), pancit (pan-fried noodles), and buko (coconut salad). Lola Reyna spent hours preparing the meal, and she wanted heaps of gratitude and praise for every minute at the hot stove.

She stood at the center of the table and held out her hands. Everyone followed suit, standing and holding hands with one another, forming a chain around the table.

Reyna led them in prayer, in Tagalog.

"Pagpalain Tayo, Panginoon, at ang mga kaloob na ito na aming tatanggapin sa iyong pag-ibig. Sa pamamagitan ni Cristo, Panginoon namin. Amen."

My mother spoke the same words at every meal, as if she were a pastor giving a sermon. "Bless us, O Lord, and these, Thy gifts, which we are about to receive from Thy bounty. Through Christ, our Lord. Amen."

Despite my agnostic view, I sometimes uttered those comforting words when I dined alone at home, if only to remember my simple upbringing. Not everything my mother said was toxic, even if she didn't heed the prayer's underlying meaning.

Everyone echoed "amen" and dug into their food. Reyna circled the table, serving everyone before even a crumb touched her plate.

"Another dinner, another night without your wife," she said to Edgardo in English as she finally sat down.

"She's not my wife anymore."

"Does she not eat anymore?"

"What kind of question is that?"

"I set a plate for her and she refuses it," Lola Reyna said in a calm, albeit annoyed, voice.

"She already had plans tonight."

"All those times she said 'What a lovely home' and 'I always love your cooking' were lies. She's too good for this house now? Too good to celebrate your brother's return?"

"They're business plans, Nanay," Edgardo said.

"Business plans," Reyna scoffed.

"She's been working hard night and day on her career, her new show, while still running the restaurant. The woman never sleeps."

"I watch her little show, talking about 'old country' food. What does she know about the old country? What she knows is that it isn't as good as a mother's home cooking."

"Her dishes come from her mother in Quezon," Edgardo said.

"She may have been born in Quezon, sure," Lola Reyna said, "but they moved up to a big house in Makati City. What kind of country cooking could they have there?"

"They lived in Cebu. She went to cooking school in Makati."

"Makati school?" Reyna laughed in defiance. "That's even worse!"

Edgardo's cell phone rang. He took a breath, stood from his chair, and excused himself, a relief from his mother's petty insults.

"Take it in my office," Otto said. He shot his wife a condemning look. "Take as long as you need, Eddie."

Edgardo entered his stepfather's study, checking the time every few seconds. He closed the door behind him and sat at the grand desk during his phone call. "Okay, I'm free to talk. Thank you for calling, Felix."

"My apologies for being late, Amo," Felix said on the other end of the line.

"No worries. Two minutes is not late in my book, considering what I've tasked you with. Everything alright?"

"I was about to ask you the same." He'd heard the stress in his boss's voice.

"I'm fine, just glad to be pulled away for a while. Is it all moved?"

"We'll be done soon," Felix said. "All the vehicles and most of the crates have already been relocated."

"You showed your face at Corazon?"

Felix spoke to his boss from the storage building in the foothills of Sylmar, from within the hidden room built into the hillside. It stood mostly empty now as a dozen workers loaded merchandise onto a caravan of trucks.

"I put in a few hours there before I returned to the warehouse," Felix said. "Decent crowd tonight."

"Good man."

Just as Edgardo loved to hear those words from his stepfather, so too did Felix when his boss used them, affirming his loyalty and hard work.

Good man.

Felix wanted nothing more than to appease his mentor and boss, to repay him for keeping him out of prison and for providing him with a fulfilling life with purpose beyond his past import smuggling. Joining The Duke's crew also gave Felix a sense of belonging, an honor above that which was shared among thieves, for he'd never felt a place in any family before. He'd never formally met Edgardo's family but considered them his distant relatives just the same.

"You said to call when we were in the last hour," he said.

"Yes, there's one more detail to take care of before you head out."

Edgardo opened the door of his stepfather's study and looked down the hall to ensure no one else was listening.

"What detail, Amo?" Felix asked.

"The Wolves think they've ruined us, but we must assume they're still watching. It stands to reason we'd tour the building to survey the damage they did."

"I see."

"*They* need to see, Felix. Are their tree cameras are still on loops?"

"They're secure, and so far, no one is here but us. I have lookouts stationed in all directions."

"You trust them?" Edgardo asked.

"I paid them a grand apiece, as you instructed, with the promise of more to come. I trust them that much."

"Good enough." Edgardo considered his next disturbing order, unsure. "You won't like this, Felix, but I need you to allow one camera to catch you walking the property, head down, miserable and pathetic. Is this acceptable?"

"Acceptable." Felix knew his boss would never knowingly force him to take any risk, that he could bow out at any time, but he would have surely jumped off a mountain for the man. Felix admired The Duke and wanted to protect him and his family. Even if Edgardo hadn't fully realized it, his assistant's loyalty was unbreakable. "Trust me, Amo, I can do miserable and pathetic. I'll turn off some lights, let them see me roaming the shadows."

"No," Edgardo said. "Leave the lights on. They already know what you look like."

Felix felt alarmed, not only for his own wellbeing, but for his boss's delicate plan. He looked around at the hired help as if any of them might be a mole. "Did they I.D. me?"

"I don't think so, not beyond your dead-end alias. Let one of their cameras spot you walking around in shame, do a quick wipe for prints, then get out of there."

"My honor always, Amo."

Edgardo hung up, satisfied with Felix's assessment. He'd come to trust the young man, perhaps more than he felt comfortable with, and felt a sweep of relief whenever he referred to him as "Amo," a holdover from his days serving The Panginoon.

"Good man," he said as he hung up the call.

Good man.

Felix would not let his boss down.

31

We All Got Friends

As night fell over the scrapyard, Mace downed another bottle of San Miguel beer, five empties at his feet. He remained on the sofa opposite Calixto, Bakal, and the other TSB, the gangsters still unsure about their guest.

"Let's be real," Mace said. "Am I wearin' out the welcome mat? I feel you all's starin' fire at me."

"You came for the deal," Calixto said. "You got your money. I'm wondering why you're still on my property. It strikes me as... unorthodox."

"Look at you and the big words! No offense, but any dirt on The Duke is worth more than the few stacks you coughed up. So that's part of the deal now."

"What we uncover about Duque is up to me to decide who knows and who don't."

"Yeah, but think of how it would cement our friendship!" Mace said. "Look, Cal, this ain't no pajama party. I'll leave your hacienda in a bit. I'd just like to be around when you hear something about our boy. I mean, if I had something to share, you know I would."

"Maybe you would," Calixto said. "Maybe you wouldn't. Or maybe you're working for him. I just wanna know if you're for real or not."

Several TSB caught the tension in their boss's voice. They moved in closer, gun in hand. A few surrounded the Wolf's bike.

Mace took in the numbers surrounding him and remembered his training, his years of research into these gangs. "Here I thought we was buddies. What kinda talk is that, Cal?"

"You sitting here drinking all my beer gave me time to think," Calixto said. "Normally, a new seller would trade his brick and say goodbye, but with you asking all kinds of questions about Duque, it got me curious. I mean, you said you're the 'new kids in town.' So now I guess I got questions of my own."

Mace didn't seem fazed at the looming threat, a poker face he'd spend years perfecting. "Hmm, alrighty then. I hate that it comes to this, but here's the part of our meeting where you really find out what's 'for real.'" He pulled a flashlight from his jacket pocket and shined the beam at several points around him.

Calixto followed the light and saw five Wolves standing apart at the perimeter of the scrapyard, rifles in hand. They had left their bikes near the entrance and spread across the property in the dark to flank the TSB. They'd be back on their hogs soon enough.

"You brought friends," Calixto said.

"I got friends, you got friends, hey, we all got friends. We're such a friendly fuckin' bunch."

"You really willing to destroy our friendship over Duque and a few bricks of Damo?"

"Are you?"

Calixto eyed the bikers surrounding them, not sure of their true numbers.

"These are just my bum rushers," Mace said. "I got me a dozen more men parked all around this shithole. If I die, so be it, but goddamn, Cal, you're gonna be so full of fuckin' holes if they don't see us shake hands like ol' buddies rit' now."

Calixto raised a fist, signaling his men to back down. They promptly lowered their guns.

Mace smiled and turned to Bakal. "Fetch me another drink, son. Something strong and brown."

Bakal looked to his boss, who simply nodded. Bakal walked away.

Mace shut off his flashlight and spun it on his palm. "I hope homeboy brings something better than that San Miguel piss this time. Tequila would be nice."

"Tequila it is."

Calixto swallowed the biker's blunt bravado.

For now.

32

Remember Me

During dinner, despite the many compliments before and during the meal, Lola Reyna continually fished for praise. She needed to hear how moist, delicious, and flavorful everything was with every other bite. Their glowing words were never enough, so she'd prompt them for more.

"It's not too salty?" she asked.

"No, Lola, it's perfect," Christiana said.

"It's not too spicy?"

"I love it spicy," Carlo said.

"Is it overcooked? Don't lie to me."

"Just right, as always," Edgardo said.

After dinner, Bram cleared the table while his mother served coffee with dessert. She set out the box of chocolates he'd given her along with homemade maruya (banana fritters) and store-bought leche flan (milk custard). Though Carlo wanted the flan, which came from the famous Chaaste Family Market, he knew to take one of his grandmother's maruya first. Lola Reyna still complained about not being appreciated for all her hard work, but the group effort to placate her kept things below a boil.

Evenings with my mother were always a delicate balance of dinner, dessert, and games, in that order. If we made it to the games without a full meltdown, we knew the rest of the night would be fine. She loved to choose and host the silly activity, usually "Bring Me," with her guests hanging on her every word. She'd even smile and laugh. For that brief time, we felt like a healthy, close-knit family.

With the plates and flatware upright in the dishwasher and the pots and pans soaking in the sink, Lola Reyna sat in a chair by the fireplace with a list in hand. Carlo, Chris, Bram, and Lolo Otto stood over her, waiting. Edgardo watched from across the room.

Lola Reyna read the first line of her list. "Bring me... a red pen or pencil."

Everyone searched the house in a mad scramble. Edgardo alone remained in the living room, sipping a cup of after-dinner coffee. He relished the sight of his family enjoying themselves like the old days.

After Nanay had her time to vent her venom and point fingers, condemning us for not cherishing her, she usually calmed down and became the loving grandmother, the celebrated hostess, if only for an evening.

"What's wrong, Doy?" Lola Reyna asked in a pleasant, concerned tone. "You're not going to play?"

"I'm supervising."

It was as if her earlier tirade of how grotesque Bram and Divinia and I are had never happened. That was my mother's pattern: harsh judgement followed by an expectation of things running smoothly.

"But you always win the game," she said.

"The kids can win this time. Besides, I have another phone call to make."

"Of course. 'All business all the time.' It never ends with you."

"Why does everyone throw that in my face like a curse?" Edgardo asked.

"You should wonder why it makes you feel that way," Reyna said.

Chris returned from the kitchen with a pencil covered in ketchup. "Red pencil!"

"What the fuck?" Carlo said in protest. "That doesn't count!"

"That's up to your lola," Edgardo said as he smiled and walked out the front door.

"It counts, Carlo," Reyna said. "Don't be a bad sport."

Outside, in the quiet of the driveway, Edgardo pulled his flask from his inner jacket pocket, his real reason for privacy. As he took a swig, he spotted the red Camaro a few houses down, blended in with other parked cars in the dark.

Lynn Harrod

The problem with the TSB was worse than I'd realized.
Finding my house was an affront, but coming to Nanay's
was an act of war. Unacceptable.

He walked to his car, opened the door, and reached under the driver's seat for his Glock 42 pistol. With gun in hand, he headed for the Camaro and saw one man inside, at the wheel. Upon recognizing the young gangster, he pocketed his gun before opening the passenger door and sitting in the front seat.

"Miguel Hortiz of the TSB," Edgardo said. "I thought I saw the last of you in the tunnel."

"Yeah, I thought so, too."

"You should feel blessed. My brother has never let an assassin go free."

"I ain't no assassin," Miguel said in a cold, firm tone.

"Regardless, you're either very brave or very stupid to confront me alone."

"I ain't confrontin' no one, and I had to come alone. You know my partners ain't of this world no more."

"Such prose. And why shouldn't you join them? You want revenge?"

"No!" Miguel's voice quaked with fear, but he pushed on. "I came to apologize again for the tunnel, and for going to your house. It wasn't right, and it wasn't what I wanted."

"And what did you want?" Edgardo asked.

"It was supposed to be just about the car. I didn't know Calixto wanted you done."

"Fortunately, my brother handled that. Perhaps I should bring him out here to finish the job. If not him, I guarantee you Calixto will. I'm surprised he hasn't yet."

"That's 'cause I ain't gone back to him yet. He don't know what went down."

"Calixto Cervantes may be a junkyard rat," Edgardo said, "but he's a smart rat. He will learn what happened, which means you're here to make amends before you trot back to him..."

"I ain't going back."

Edgardo stared at the young man who could barely look him in the eye. He tried to figure out his game.

"How'd you make me so fast when you came out here?" Miguel asked. "I ain't got no license plate or flashy paint."

"A 1987 Chevy Camaro RS, garnet red, dent in the front right fender, crack across the top of the windshield, Forgiato seven-spoke wheels. To me, your car is one of a kind. You might as well have come here in a parade float."

"It's Jorge's car, not mine."

"Well, your partner is no longer of this world no more, remember? His troubles are over. We're talking about you, Miguel Hortiz of the TSB. Your troubles are just beginning."

"Believe me, I know."

"The point is, wherever you go, I'll always see you, with your tactical black Ruger LCP, your ripped forest green Converse shoes, your gray baseball cap and black Paisley bandana around your neck. It's impossible to fool me."

"You're real smart," Miguel said, crouched in his seat, his voice cracking. "That scares people. You're as smart as everybody says."

"Smart enough."

"No, not enough." The boy sat upright as he gathered his nerve. "I've been fooling you for years, Edgardo Duque of Temple Street."

Edgardo felt surprised by the young man's sudden defiance.

"I'm the one who knew about your house in Highland Park, your Mercedes SLK, and your parents' house here in Eagle Rock. I know that your daughter Christiana has a Justin Bieber poster on her closet door, from his 2017 'Purpose' World Tour, right next to a photo of you and her fishing on the Santa Monica pier. Black Cod and Sea Bass."

"Who... where did you..."

"I know your son Carlo has an autographed photo of Eugene Amano of the Tennessee Titans on his desk, and that the day after he got it for his birthday he sprained his left ankle during his first junior varsity football game. I know your ex-wife Divinia keeps her mother's bamboo-covered cookbook on a stand in the kitchen pantry in front of a case of CoCo Rico Soda, and that you're the only one who drinks it. Even though she can't stand you, she still keeps that soda around for when you visit."

Edgardo froze in fear, a feeling he wasn't accustomed to.

Feeling empowered, Miguel turned toward him. "And I know more. A lot more."

Edgardo's momentary fear welled up into rage.

I'd never been nailed like that, not by any gang, not by the feds. The Duke had been a ghost, a rumor, for nearly ten years. Hearing him describe my family with impossible detail, all I could think was to kill him, to go to that damn junkyard and kill them all.

"A lot more?" Edgardo placed his gun on the dashboard, his finger teasing the trigger. He was ready to kill Miguel where he sat, for his family, but curiosity kept him at bay. "Of all the gangs of misfits in L.A., how the hell do the fucking Temple Street Boyz know so much about me?"

"They don't know shit 'bout you. I do."

"And how do you know all this?"

"Like I said, I've been fooling you for years."

Summoning all his courage, Miguel nervously removed the bandana from his neck and the cap from his head and suddenly spoke in a feminine voice, revealing he was actually a young woman.

"My real name is Maria Hortiz," she said in her natural voice. "Do you remember me now?"

Edgardo sat speechless. He took his hand off his gun as the familiar face and her history came flooding back to him.

"Of course you do," Maria said. "You're The Duke. You remember everyone and everything."

Edgardo could only stare at the nervous, vulnerable teenager beside him.

Maria Hortiz was Christiana's friend. They were in the same Girl Scout Troop in Atwater Village, same string section in Junior Orchestra, same science team. She used to come to Divinia's house every day. She was like family... until she disappeared. Now, here she sat, a fledgling foot soldier of the TSB. What cruel fate led her to this?

Maria wiped away a single tear. "Please say you remember me, Mr. Duque."

"I remember."

How could I have been so blind? Stuck in the shadows of the dark forces surrounding me, my fragile mind had been slipping away. If someone from my past, someone dear to my daughter, could hide from me in plain sight, who else did I fail to see?

* * *

Lola Reyna sat in her spot by the fireplace, continuing her game of Bring Me. She read the next item off her list. "Bring me... a dandelion."

Otto, Bram, and Carlo raced to the backyard, shoving each other on the way. Christiana paused and turned to the front door.

"You're not going to wrestle them in the backyard?" Lola Reyna asked.

Chris grinned. "There's a lot more yards out front."

* * *

Edgardo sat speechless after the teen's big reveal. He pocketed his gun and bowed his head in silent apology, speaking calmly to Maria like an old friend. "In the tunnel, when you stopped Jorge, told everyone who I was..."

"It wasn't because I was afraid of you," Maria said. "I mean, I kinda was, but... for real, none of us knew whose car we was boosting until you stepped out. When I saw you, I just... I just didn't want them to take your car is all. I swear, Mr. Duque."

Maria had always called me "Mr. Duque," starting from the day we met on the front lawn of my family's home when she and Christiana were in the first grade. I had only met her mother once, but it told me enough that Maria's courtesy didn't come from good parenting. The respect she showed me and Divinia came from her heart.

"Why not tell me who you were right away?" he asked in a comforting voice. "Why play this game with me?"

I usually see every scenario from every angle, but I realized how badly I got the tunnel robbery all wrong, as did Maria. She thought she'd simply saved me from a carjacking, but she had no way of knowing what would have happened had she not intervened. I felt ashamed for considering killing those youths, and for considering killing "Miguel" just moments before in the front seat of that Camaro.

"It wasn't no game, Mr. Duque," she said, still in her natural voice. "It's just... the way you singled me out in the tunnel. I thought you recognized me but that maybe you didn't give a shit. Chris always talked about how you see through people, how you have them pegged right away. I'd just pointed a gun at you, tried to jack your ride. Later that night, I figured maybe you didn't see me after all."

"I confess, I didn't," Edgardo said. "I'm sorry, Maria."

"It's 'Miguel' now." He switched back to his masculine gangster voice, a convincing and startling contrast to the gentle voice he used a moment ago. He donned the bandana and cap again to complete the persona.

"Of course," Edgardo said, nodding. "I may see Maria, but I'll regard you as Miguel." He looked out the windshield at his parents' home down the street. It brought his brother to mind, which brought back the home invasion. "You said you're the one who knew where I lived? You told them?"

"I told them." The color drained from Miguel's face as he confessed. "Calixto was real pissed off, more than usual. He ranted about wanting some kind of payback. I gave up your house 'cause I figured if we boosted your SLK for him, maybe he'd back off, leave you alone. A little revenge to calm him down, you know? I didn't think he was set on taking you out, I swear."

"No need to swear to me, Miguel, I believe you. Calixto can be hard to read, even for me." Edgardo scrutinized the boy's outfit, the bandana that hid his lack of an Adam's apple, the cap that covered the gentle arch of his brow, making him appear more masculine. "Do Chris and Carlo know?"

"Nobody knows 'cept you now," the boy said. "But ain't that how it is? Sooner or later, The Duke knows everything, right?"

"Only because you shared yourself with me. It's like you said, I wasn't smart enough to see you, but I promise, I see you now."

Miguel made a slight smile, his first genuine expression in years. "It's actually kind of a relief that somebody in this world sees me, I mean all of me."

Edgardo looked out through the windows. At that time of night, no one was around. "What happened to you? How'd you end up running with the TSB?"

Miguel felt uncomfortable revisiting his past, but was compelled to press on. "My parents were poison, especially after my pops lost his job at the tire shop. He'd been there 20 years, worked his way up to Supervisor, but the shop was sold to a big company, and the first thing they did was get rid of anyone making above minimum. My pop was no angel, but he didn't deserve that. He was always a worker, you know? Mom said guys like him need hard work to keep from getting in trouble. When they took that from him, he got abusive, angry all the time. He couldn't find a job, not enough to keep up with the bills, so he started selling for Calixto, around Dodger Stadium."

"He worked Elysian Park?" Edgardo was familiar with the low-level dealer. "Arturo Hortiz was your father?"

"'Fraid so."

"So, your dad brought you into the gang?"

"No way." Miguel shook his head, fighting back a tear. "He'd have never wanted his little girl mixed up with that shit. No, my pops had a heart attack, right in the middle of a deal. Assholes fuckin' took his bag, like a week's worth of product. They left him in an alley at 2AM. EMTs said he died an hour later."

"I'm so sorry, Miguel." Edgardo placed his hand on the boy's shoulder.

"Don't be. I'm not. He sold at all hours, hardly slept, like was just waiting for someone to put him out of his misery. After we buried him, Calixto kept harassing my mom for the money he felt he was owed from that stolen bag. He claimed my pops was selling on the side, which was bullshit. It scared my mom bad, seeing gangsters hanging 'round the house. She started drinkin' again. That's when I decided to finally come out, in a way. I went to the scrapyard as his 'son' to work off the debt."

"How'd your mother handle that?" Edgardo asked.

"She didn't. She checked out, left the house for groceries one day and never came home. I guess I never did, either."

"Which brings us to tonight," Edgardo said with a sigh. He assumed the TSB would soon reach out to him, but he certainly didn't expect such a revelation. He looked at the young man sitting beside him with sympathy, knowing now that his visit was no spy mission. "How'd you find me here?"

"I followed Chris and Carlo."

"Why?"

"Calixto don't know about Jorge and Yoy Yoy yet," Miguel said in a hurried tone, "but like you said, he'll find out soon enough. By then, I'll be outta here, maybe go up north. I just wanted to set things right with you before I hit the freeway."

"That's your plan?" Edgardo asked, incredulous. "To run? Calixto Cervantes may seem small-time, squatting in his junkyard kingdom, but he's connected across California, Nevada, and Arizona. He will find you eventually."

"No need to warn me, Mr. Duque. I actually came to warn you. He knew where we was going. When he figures out what happened, he's gonna go to war, I know it. I mean, he hated you already, and now that I see he wanted to take you out... he jus' needed an excuse to rally the troops and make a move."

"Thank you for the heads-up."

"Thank you for not killing me, I guess." Miguel's joke didn't land. He saw the concern on Edgardo's face. "Look, Mr. Duque, I'll be in the clear 'cause Calixto will think I'm dead, right? He'll think me and Jorge and Yoy Yoy all bought it together."

"No, I'm afraid he won't think that." Edgardo's tone held a trace of apology. "Since he sent you to my home, he'll look to me if you three vanish, so I have to get creative with the bodies."

"What does that mean?" Miguel suddenly felt scared.

"It means I have to ensure he finds Jorge and Yoy Yoy, framed in a way that leads him down another trail. It's my only play. When that happens, when he discovers your friends..."

"Ain't never been my friends."

Edgardo gestured for Miguel to collect himself. "When he discovers your associates, he won't see you lying beside them. He'll assume you're a traitor, and he'll hunt you down."

The teen could barely breathe.

"I'm sorry, Miguel."

"Maybe he'll find me, maybe he won't. I mean, I'm gonna be so gone, like a fuckin' ghost..." The young gangster banged his palms on the steering wheel, overwhelmed. He glanced at the time on the dashboard clock and started the engine. "Take care of Chris, alright? I gotta put in some miles while it's still dark."

Edgardo grabbed the key in the ignition and shut off the engine. Something had occurred to him, the way his enemy thought, how he made decisions.

"What is it, Mr. Duque?"

Edgardo kept his hand on the key as a crude plan and conclusion formed in his mind. "You can't leave."

"Like hell I can't!"

"Calixto has textbook Completion Bias. Every chip on his shoulders must be knocked down. He can't help himself, and he'll hunt you for as long as you run."

"I'll take that chance..."

"Listen to me, Miguel. Even if he doesn't find you, you'll never experience any semblance of a normal life. You'll be forced to live off the grid, a vagrant until the day you die. Do you understand?"

"Yes, but..." Miguel felt as if he might implode. "If I can't run, what can I do?"

Edgardo pulled out his phone and made a call.

"Felix... Is everything moved?... I need you to bring the Beemer to my mother's house... Yes, right now... I'll explain later... Good man."

"Who you talking to?"

Edgardo hung up and turned to Miguel with a sense of urgency. "You're taking my car to Calixto, as planned."

"No fuckin' way! He's gonna know!"

"No, he won't. You've proven yourself a talented actor, able to adapt. I just need you to put on that act a little longer."

"You can't make me do this, Mr. Duque! It's suicide going back to him!"

"It's risky, yes," Edgardo said, "but not suicide, not if you remember everything I'm about to tell you."

* * *

Bram ran back into the house, returning from the backyard with a dandelion. Carlo tried to muscle it from him, but his uncle shoved him to the sofa as he delicately handed the weed to his mother. She blew into it, sending spores across the living room, as Otto entered with his own dandelion, ten seconds too late.

"Bam Bam," she said. "Don't be so rough with the boy."

"Bam Bam?" Carlo said with a laugh.

"If he can take getting sacked by a defensive line," Bram said, "he can take getting pushed onto a cushy couch."

"I don't know about that," Carlo said, smiling. "You hit a lot harder... Tito 'Bam Bam.'"

"Remember when we used to call you 'Boy Boy'? You wanna bring that back?"

"Where's Christiana?" Otto asked.

"Front yard," Reyna said.

"Nerd girl thought she could outsmart us," Carlo said.

Bram took his spent dandelion from his mother and held it high like a trophy kill. "Well, she's in for a big surprise!"

Christiana's strategy was sound, that two dozen front yards likely held more dandelions than a single backyard. However, her quest for the pretty weed halted when she spotted her father sitting in a red Camaro with a young man. Forgetting the silly game, she crouched behind the bushes by her grandparents' porch and watched them from afar. After talking for ten minutes, they emerged from the car and walked down the middle of the street back to the house. She wished she could hear their conversation.

"Is it true what they say?" Miguel asked.

"I don't know," Edgardo said. "What do they say?"

"That you can fight ten men."

"Nonsense." Edgardo laughed at the notion as he handed the boy the keys to his car. "You're thinking of my brother. Remember him?"

"How can I forget?" The image of the menacing enforcer haunted him.

"He's the Totoong Lakan, not me." Edgardo smirked at the boy. "I can only handle five."

They shared a laugh as they reached the Mercedes. Miguel opened the driver's door and sat behind the wheel. Their eyes widened when they saw Chris emerge from the shadows of her grandparents' front yard. Edgardo's mind spun as she walked toward them.

"Christiana?" he asked.

"Who's this?" Chris asked. "Why's he taking your car?"

Before Edgardo could concoct a cover story, Miguel bowed his head slightly and offered his own. "I'm your dad's Executive Assistant. I'm gonna take care of his car."

In the dark, with the boy's head down and his male voice perfect, Chris didn't recognize Miguel as her childhood friend Maria. Edgardo had no choice but to go with his story.

"Chris, this is Miguel. 'Executive Assistant' is our little joke. He's taking my car to detail it."

"Right now?" she asked. "It's like nine o'clock at night."

"I was running errands for him all day," Miguel said, daring to speak. "This is the only time I got."

"It's a surprise for your Tito Bram," Edgardo said, thinking fast. "I'm giving him the car." Chris smiled at the idea. "So not a word to anyone, babae. You know this house can't keep secrets."

Edgardo nodded to Miguel to proceed. The boy started the car as Chris walked up to his open door.

"You work for my dad?" she asked. "I didn't know he had an assistant."

"You know how busy I can get," her father said.

"Why not ask me?"

"I have bigger plans for you, young lady."

Miguel simply nodded to her, keeping his head down over the steering wheel.

"Then I guess I'll be seeing you around," she said to the boy. "I'm Chris."

"Oh, he knows all about you," Edgardo said.

"He does?"

"Mr. Duque talks about you guys all the time," Miguel said.

"Well, that's a pleasant surprise."

Miguel nodded again, shifted the car into gear, and drove the Mercedes down the street. Edgardo put his arm around his daughter and took her back into the house.

When we returned to my parents' home for another cup of coffee and another round of Bring Me, I looked down the street one last time before shutting the front door. The taillights of my car disappeared three blocks south as it rounded the corner, and I'd hoped that was the first and last time my daughter would encounter "Miguel."

At the least, I hoped she'd never piece together the boy's complete identity or the real reason for his late visit that night. If Carlo took after his mother, her strength and persistence, then Christiana certainly took after me with her uncanny observation and deduction. I had to be careful, for she'd only need an inch of thread to pull apart the tapestry of my life.

Despite his concern, his careful assessments and measures, Edgardo didn't know that Christiana had long suspected her father of routinely breaking the law.

Two years prior, Fish gave her one of his laptops for school use, a gift for both her 14th birthday and her Freshman year of high school. He'd planned on wiping and discarding the computer for security purposes anyway. Why not give it a second life with her? She needed it for class, and Algebra and World History posed no risk to their operation.

Fish erased the device's storage and restored it to factory settings, and Chris assumed she'd been given a brand new laptop until it crashed a few months later. She reinstalled the operating system and ran a recovery program to retrieve her deleted schoolwork.

The deep dive also recovered some of Fish's old spreadsheets.

Chris eagerly combed through them, expecting to find remnants of the lawyer's former life as a television producer. Perhaps she'd find pop singers and movie stars. Instead, she saw her father's finances, dozens of rows of people – first name only – being paid small fortunes under the table. The vague job descriptions and tall figures didn't fit an auto shop or cocktail bar.

"Francisco" received $15,000 from Edgardo for "Arrangement."
"Roberto" received $20,000 for "Delivery."
"Thomas" received $45,000 for "Agreement."

The many invoices were equally puzzling.

"George" paid her father $25,000 for "Confidence."
"Marco" paid him $50,000 for "Consultation."
"Chang" paid him $100,000 for "Storage."

One of the files contained personal correspondence, saved texts threads from clients. It revealed more of the same, business transactions with deliberately hazy details. They often ended with "Thank you Mr. Duque."

One client ended his text with a odd message for her father...

"It's an honor working with The Duke."

Chris took to the internet.

Edgardo's symbolic tapestry soon lay in tatters on the girl's bedroom floor.

33

Gotcha

Divinia entered her dark home, continuing a phone conversation on her Bluetooth earpiece.

"Turkey and stuffing?... I know it's a Christmas thing, but that's not what we ate growing up... yes, I know, but..."

She carried the wrapped jade plant from Charles as she turned on the lights, taking a quick look around. Her children were still out, hopefully on their way home. She walked into the kitchen and set the little potted plant on the counter.

"We planned on lechón and pancit malabon... everything's already prepped... of course I know how to roast a turkey but... okay, let me see what comes close... no, I'll be ready... I can handle any surprise they throw at me."

Divinia hung up, frustrated. She opened the pantry door, revealing a bamboo-covered cookbook spread across a stand. Behind it sat a six-pack of CoCo Rico Cola, a coconut-flavored soda only her ex-husband enjoyed. Though their marriage had ended, she still bought the drink for him whenever she went shopping. She assumed it was more out of habit than any form of affection.

She took the book to the counter and skimmed through its recipes, but kept glancing at the plant beside it, wondering where to put the traditional good luck charm. Unable to focus on her new task of creating a traditional American holiday dinner episode that still somehow reflected Filipino culture, she unwrapped the plant, took it to the living room, and set it on the fireplace mantle. She needed all the luck she could get.

Outside, three houses down the street, two LOCC agents sat at consoles in an unmarked van outfitted with surveillance equipment. The exterior of the windowless van resembled an old former U-Haul, while its interior looked like a mobile television studio.

C.B. entered the van through the rear doors, still in his designer suit and polished shoes, fresh from his "date" with Divinia Duque at the Corazon Lounge. He sat beside his agents.

"I gotta say, boss," one of them said, "you sounded real smooth tonight, a bonafide player."

"I can still be charming when I need to be," C.B. said.

"Never woulda thought."

"Uh huh. Anything so far?"

The agent handed him a pair of headphones. He listened closely.

Divinia's voice came in clear.

"We planned on lechón and pancit malabon... everything's already prepped... of course I know how to roast a turkey but... okay, let me see what comes close..."

"Gotcha," C.B. said.

"I'll be ready... I can handle any surprise they throw at me."

34

Good News

At a quarter past ten o'clock at night, the only lights at Galvez Salvage and Scrap were the single floodlight mounted atop the large warehouse and the fire pit in the middle of the outdoor living room set, the worn sofas and loveseats scooted across the mud, away from the flames. The fire lit Calixto's face from below, making him look like a storyteller about to unfold a devilish tale. He sat with a drink in hand, an ornate square bottle on the coffee table, and two of his men flanking him.

One of them was Bakal, standing nearby as always, never allowing himself a moment to relax. Though he'd recently been made a kapitan – an underboss – he still felt like a foot soldier, preferring to silently stand and observe. As such, he was the first to spot a pair of headlights approaching down the winding dirt road. He brought it to his boss's attention and soon everyone saw a shiny black Mercedes SLK pulling up to their central campfire, Miguel Hortiz alone at the wheel.

Miguel shut off the engine, took a breath, and tried to remember the cover story Edgardo went over in detail.

He stepped out of the vehicle, his arms outstretched, a wide smile across his face. He spoke in Tagalog, adding to his forced enthusiasm. "Calixto! Check it out! The Duke's Benz, washed and waxed for you! I told you we'd do it! Good news is that he never even saw us! We was like fuckin' ninjas!"

"He wasn't home?" Calixto asked, also in Tagalog.

"Nah, we had the place to ourselves. I mean, we was locked and loaded if he showed his face, but he never did."

"I see." Calixto sized up his young sundalo with an amused expression. "My compliments. I'm happy to finally see this car I've heard so much about."

"I thought you might be."

"Where's Jorge and my cousin?"

"That's even better news." Miguel hoped his face matched his confident tone.

"Please, tell me. I have a feeling this is going to be good."

Calixto gestured for Miguel to sit with him on the long couch by the fire. He poured him a clear drink from the elegant square bottle. Miguel found his boss's calm, welcoming manner curious, unnerving.

"Not a fan of tequila?" Calixto asked, noticing the boy's torn expression.

"Hell yeah, I'm a fan," Miguel said, realizing his poker face had fallen for a moment. "I mean... I jus' didn't know you was. I drink mezcal shit, you know, but this looks kinda fancy."

Calixto held up the bottle, the firelight dancing across it. "Tequila Herradura Ultra Añejo. I've gotten a taste for it. A man gets sick of beer after a while."

"I'm with you. Hey, did you know Filipinos invented tequila?"

"I didn't know that." Calixto turned to Bakal as if he were genuinely curious. "Did you know that?"

"Nope," Bakal said, monotone.

"Tell us, Miguel, how did Filipinos invent tequila?"

Miguel smelled that something was wrong but had to keep up his facade. "Yeah, so lambanog was brought to Mexico like 500 years ago, right? Coconut wine from Manila..."

"We all know what lambanog is, boy."

"Yeah, but I mean, they ain't got no coconuts in Mexico, so they used agave instead, and that became tequila."

"And the rest is history," Calixto said. He held up his glass and the two men took a sip together. "I had a feeling you were smarter than you look, Miguel."

Miguel laughed.

No one else did.

"Please, go on," Calixto said, pouring two more glasses. "You were about to tell me 'even better news.'"

"Right! So we was turning over The Duke's house, found all kinds of shit to bring you. Like, a lot of shit. Information."

"Information?"

"Yoy Yoy told me to take the car while they went out to some warehouse."

"What warehouse?"

"I dunno," Miguel said, stalling for a moment, trying desperately to recall the cover story. "He said he found out about The Duke's stash. Fuckin' gold mine. He and Jorge went to go check it out." He took a sip of tequila, hoping it would make him appear at ease despite his pounding heart. "You ain't heard from them?"

Calixto rose to his feet and loomed over Miguel. The friendly small talk over, he switched back to English, his words slow and pointed. "Yoy Yoy and Jorge ain't been around all day."

"All day?" Miguel paused, feigned confusion. "Pakshet..."

"Pakshet is right. I been callin' and textin' for hours. None of you got back to me. You gonna tell me what the fuck happened?"

"I can't speak for them, but I had shit to take care of. Got the car ready for you. Had to check in with my peeps. You know how it is." His boss looked unconvinced. "Man, all I was told was to take the car here late after dark so no cops would be on my ass. I figured Yoy Yoy and Jorge woulda told you the rest. They ain't been here?"

"No, they ain't been here," Calixto said, mocking Miguel's tone. "They ain't been here, ain't been picking up their phones, ain't been at home. So I ask again, what the fuck happened?"

"This is news to me!" Miguel felt terrified, but did his best to hide his fear behind confusion, just as Edgardo had coached him. "I swear, Calixto, I don't know shit. I mean, we went to The Duke's place, nobody was home, we tossed every room and Yoy Yoy found everything."

"Everything meaning what?"

"Whoa, let's slow down... I sense hostility, man." Edgardo had also coached the boy to show concern but not fear.

"That's frustration you sense," Calixto said. "Hostility comes later. So, 'everything' meaning what?"

"He found the keys to the car, the address to the stash, a list of hot items, all that shit. I was just supposed to take the car to you and they was gonna meet me here. That was the plan."

"Fuck the plan. Where'd they go?"

"Like I said, The Duke's warehouse. That's all they told me."

Calixto scooted uncomfortably close to Miguel on the sofa, their pant legs touching. He seemed unsure, which Miguel felt was better than smelling his bullshit outright.

"You don't know where it is?" Calixto asked. "This warehouse?"

"They don't tell me shit. You know that."

"Well, that needs to change, doesn't it? We need to put you in the know, brother. It's high time we tell you anything and everything."

"Hold up, do *you* know where it is?" Deflecting the question with his own was more of Edgardo's coaching. "'Cause if you do, I'll go check it out first thing, at the crack of dawn."

"This disturbs me, Miguel. You say you don't know, and I say I don't know. You want me to believe that no one knows where my cousin went?"

"I know," a voice said from the dark behind them. To the boy's shock and dismay, it was one of those meth-head biker gagos from The Wolf Pack. "Up in the foothills," Mace said.

"Where, exactly?" Calixto asked.

"Sylmar."

"Who the fuck is this guy?" Miguel asked in Tagalog.

"English, please, when we have company," Calixto said. "This is Mr. Mason. His men have also been watchin' Duque."

"We heard something 'bout a warehouse," Mace said, "even got a rough location. Never been up there. I'm also curious 'bout your lost brothers."

Calixto leaned toward Miguel, pressing their foreheads together. "You said you're up for checking it out, Miguelito?"

"You got it, man. Just gimme the address. I'll head up there at sunrise, report back anything I see."

"Let's go see now," Calixto said. "I call shotgun."

Miguel's nerves twitched as his boss stood, his eyes fixed on him. "We're leaving?" the boy asked.

"How about you drive, Miguelito, since you're now in the know." Calixto turned to his two men. "Bakal, you're with us. Roberto, you stay in case my cousin shows up, which I'm guessing won't happen."

"We're goin' right now?" Miguel asked. "I mean, it's eleven o'clock, gonna be close to midnight by the time we get up there."

"Right now is always the right time," Calixto said. "I got nothin' more important goin' on. Do you?"

Miguel felt cornered, all eyes on him.

This wasn't the plan.

"Sure, whatever you say, man. Let's go."

"That's the spirit!" Calixto gazed at his prized SLK. "Sadly, my new Mercedes only seats two."

"I'll follow you boys," Mace said.

"No, we'll take my Caddie. You'll like it, much smoother than your old beast."

"I like a rough ride."

"I'm sure you do, but I insist."

Mace took a moment to consider. He suddenly felt just as cornered as the boy. "Hell, Cal, if you insist, I'm in."

"Him, too?" Miguel said to his boss. "Yo, he ain't with us."

"We all have an interest in my cousin and Jorge and Duque and this mysterious warehouse in the hills. So yeah, him too. Don't be rude, Miguel. The man's our guest."

Calixto walked to a nearby black Cadillac sedan and sat in the front passenger seat. Bakal and Mace sat in the backseat.

Still glued to the couch, Miguel heard deafening roars seemingly all around him, the rumbling of motorcycles as five Wolves came down the main trail and lined up behind the

Cadillac. They'd figured out the plan and returned to their bikes moments before.

Calixto looked around at the bikers who now outnumbered him. He looked at Mace in the backseat through the rearview mirror. "They're tagging along? And here I thought you were a lone wolf?"

"Ain't we all lone wolves?" Mace said. "It's a party, Cal, and we're *all* your guests."

"They weren't invited."

"Shit, you think my guys ever RSVP for anything?"

Calixto considered the unwanted escort for a moment before sending a quick text to his men. "Who am I to ruin a party?"

"That's the spirit!" Mace said, mockingly repeating what Calixto had told the boy. "Let's get this train a-going. The open road is calling!"

Scared out of his mind, Miguel peeled his sweaty back from the couch. He walked to the sedan, sat behind the wheel, and started the engine. On the edge of his seat with his suspicious boss beside him, he drove the Cadillac out of the scrapyard and into the night, with the convoy of bikers close behind.

35

Two Blue Dots

Midnight in the foothills of Sylmar, California can feel unnerving, with its winding dirt roads rising north above Los Angeles, far enough from the light pollution to offer an eerie, silent darkness. Edgardo's recently ransacked warehouse sat against a hillside almost completely obscured within its shadow. The hidden cameras in the surrounding trees, installed weeks ago by undercover LOCC agents wearing Wolf Pack leather, still monitored the property from all angles.

Miguel drove the TSB's black sedan up the long dirt road to the metal building. His insides felt hollow, his stomach twisted and wrung as he shared the tense silence with two serious, suspicious men. A few hours earlier, the boy had been set on fleeing Southern California and imagined himself on the endless highway, the red Camaro cruising across the Arizona desert heading to New Mexico. Instead, he gripped the steering wheel of the gang's

Cadillac with white knuckles as he carefully navigated the narrow, steep, twisting road that felt as if it were climbing to the moon. He had imagined being alone and free out in the dark desert, hip-hop low on the stereo, rum and Coke in the cupholder, as he left everything behind – the scrapyard, The Duke, and his dead brethren. How harrowing it then felt for the teen to glance to his side and see Calixto Cervantes fixed dead ahead, to look in the rear-view mirror and see the TSB's new unang kapitan, Bakal Diaz, and that wild biker Mace sitting in the backseat, and to hear the deafening rumble of motorcycles following close behind.

With each corner, Miguel expected an ambush from a rival gang, a SWAT team, the trailing bikers, or the ice-cold men with him in the car. The boy kept driving because he had no choice but maintained his act of calm compliance because he trusted Edgardo's plan. He consoled himself with the notion that The Duke surely wouldn't throw him into a suicide mission, not someone with such a long history with his family. Surely, he'd planned for such a deviation.

Upon seeing the warehouse, he breathed a sigh of both relief and dread. The long, unnerving drive had come to an end, but perhaps so would his life. It all depended on what happened next.

Shifting into Park, Miguel heard the Wolf Pack's motorcycles slowing to an idle as he shut off his engine. The bikers also killed their motors, but kept their headlamps on, casting the only light upon the derelict structure. They stayed back as the men in the sedan stepped out of the car and faced the warehouse's lone open doorway.

"Thank you for driving, Miguel," Calixto said. "You were quite gentle with the road. My sciatica and frayed nerves appreciate it."

"You got it, Calixto." Miguel grew to fear his boss's moments of calm praise, particularly when he revealed his weaknesses, for it usually preceded a sudden turn in mood. "Jorge always says I drive like his old lola."

Calixto ignored the boy's jest as he turned to look his guest in the eyes. "And thank you for guiding us here, Mr. Mason. Such precise directions."

"I'm nothing, if not precise."

Mace's cool attitude covered for his grave error. He realized that the foothill trails were an endless, intimidating labyrinth in the dark, and he'd just expertly guided the boy turn-by-turn, all based on a destination he was supposedly unsure about. He should have feigned confusion at some point, taken them on a couple of wrong turns, in order to keep up his facade.

He chose to quickly change the topic.

"Enough of the 'mister' shit," the biker said. "We been together all day, longest friendship I had in years. Call me 'Mace.' M-A-C-E. My fuckin' parole officer calls me 'Mr. Mason.'" Calixto smiled, nodded. Miguel and Bakal were unmoved. "And don't thank me just yet. We're up here chasing a rumor I caught wind of, remember? We don't know for sure if this is the spot."

"We're about to find out... Mace."

Bakal walked to the building's entry, its steel security door bashed open. He stood at the threshold and peered into the dark interior, waiting for word from Calixto.

Rather than join him, Calixto opened the trunk of the car. Miguel's heart raced. He expected him to pull out a shotgun, but was surprised to see him holding a tablet computer. Calixto tapped the tablet, the glow of the screen ominously lighting his face much like the fire pit in the scrapyard.

"Oh, this is definitely the spot," he said.

Mace felt unease about the tablet. He had a good idea what was on it. "Didn't take you for a computer geek, Cal. What you lookin' at?"

Calixto held up the tablet, revealing a peculiar graphic...

Two blue dots inside a large gray square.

Unlike the teen, who was genuinely at a loss, Mace immediately knew what he was looking at but had to play dumb. He shrugged his shoulders as if annoyed and confused. "Do I get points if I guess right? Come on, Cal, what is this?"

"I give my men everything they need," Calixto said. "Money, guns, vests... and phones. I love modern technology. It lets me keep track of them." He pointed to the tablet screen and spoke like a grade-school teacher. "This is a map. It's hard to tell because it's zoomed in tight."

"Okay, so?"

"See here? The big gray square is this warehouse. The little blue dots are my cousin and Jorge."

Mace tried to hide his mounting dread.

Miguel felt it, too, his feet rooted to the ground. "What about me? Did you look me up on that thing?"

"Of course," Calixto said. "I tried to, at least. Don't worry, Miguel. We'll get to you later."

"My bad, man," Miguel said, quickly thinking. "Phone died a while ago. Ain't had a chance to plug it in. This shit happens to me all the time. I guess I don't love technology like you do."

Mace tried to manage the piling tension. "Let it go, kid. He said he'd get to you later. Let the grown-ups talk." He turned to Calixto with eyes of convincing rage. "Right now, let's get back to you. Why ain't you shared these blue dots wit' us sooner? If you didn't need me to navigate, you coulda saved me and mine the trip."

"Until an hour ago," Calixto said, "around the time you were sippin' your last tequila by the fire, tellin' us 'rumors' about this place... there wasn't no blue dots."

Mace turned to look back at his fellow Wolves, waiting a good distance away, out of earshot. The five members of the infamous

Wolf Pack MC – the entirety of their outfit – sat on their steel hogs as they watched Mace and the others at the warehouse.

Two of them led the pack...

William "Ratch" Rawlings was 40, tall, and heavily built. He wore full leathers mostly covered by a long brown beard. His distinct voice coupled with his white ear buds contrasted his rough appearance. "What the hell is going on?" he muttered.

Killian "Killa" Stone was 35, a short, stocky man whose leather vest exposed the huge tattoos across his arms and chest. He answered in a low, grizzled voice. "You're the one with ears on. Can't you make out what they're saying?"

"No. Camera mics are barely picking them up. I'm mostly getting wind in the trees."

"Shit, we gotta move in, Ratch."

"Not yet. We're gonna wait and observe until there's signs of a conflict."

"Wait?" Killa looked at his comrade as if his brain had short-circuited. "If shit goes down, Mace gets it while we sit and watch? Fuck that! Orders become null and void if one of us is in harm's way."

"We're all in harm's way, Killian, all the time. Mace knows that, and he knows they won't touch him with us here."

"Bullshit. We're not dealing with the best and brightest over there. You never know what these doped up morons will pull next."

"Don't underestimate Cervantes," Ratch said. "He's a player. He thinks ahead."

"Even more reason to move in."

"We have our orders. We get any closer, it might rattle Cervantes. We let Mace lead this."

"This don't make no sense," Killa said. "Why'd Mace wanna tag along at all? We already got this place covered."

"He wants any and all intel on Duque."

"We cleaned out Duque. He's a fuckin' dead end now."

"C.B. doesn't think so. More important, Mace doesn't think so, and he's point man on this, so we sit tight."

Back at the warehouse, Mace turned away from his distant brethren. He could only stare blankly as Calixto laid everything out, still tapping at his tablet.

"No signs of Yoy Yoy or Jorge all day and all night," Calixto said to Mace, "until you spoke up by the fire and... BLOOP... the dots on the map pop up. Curious..."

Mace kept up his defiant act. "I'm so glad you find that curious. Yeah, put me down for 'curious' too, because I ask again, why the fuck are me and my men out here if you already knew 'bout this place?"

"I wanted to see if your perfectly timed rumors lined up. Seems like they do."

"Ain't it good to know things."

"That's just it, Mace. I got new questions now, but I still don't know shit yet."

"New questions, huh? Wanna consult with my five men just behind me?"

Calixto shook his head. "I'd rather consult with my twenty men just behind them."

Mace realized what Calixto's quick text at the scrapyard was for.

Reinforcements.

He looked back at his brothers, in part to hide the fear on his face. Sure enough, three SUVs pulled up behind the Wolves. His pulse skipped a beat as two dozen TSB emerged, outnumbering the bikers five-to-one.

Mace turned back to Calixto. "No need to bother any of them 'cause I think I might know somethin' after all."

"Please, tell me what you might know."

Mace went all-in, cranking up his attitude. "What I think is that this here's a goddamn set-up! I think I heard 'bout a warehouse and suddenly your two boys conveniently pop up on your little gizmo there! What's your fuckin' game?"

"I was about to ask you that."

The tense exchange was cut by a sharp creek of metal as Bakal pulled open the bent, battered door. "Someone bashed it down," he said.

"Then what are we waiting for?" Calixto tossed his tablet atop the Cadillac's hood and joined Bakal. Miguel entered behind them.

Mace glanced up at the hidden tree cameras, as if for the last time, before going in.

Using the flashlights on their phones, the four men stepped into the dark, empty warehouse. Their beams soon passed over a grisly sight...

The bodies of Gabriel "Yoy Yoy" Aquino and Jorge Vega laid on the floor in the center of the room, riddled with gunshots, giving the impression of a shootout that ended badly.

"Pakshet!" Miguel said. Though he'd seen them killed by Bram the night before, his paralyzing fear sold the idea that he was now seeing their corpses for the first time. "What the fuck!"

"Looks like The Duke beat you boys to 'em," Mace said, hiding his own apprehension behind his braggadocio act.

In an eerie contrast to his guests, Calixto looked merely disappointed at the sight of his bloody fallen men. He knelt beside Yoy Yoy's body for a moment of silence.

"Pasensya na pinsan," he whispered. "Hindi pa ito tapos."

Both Mace and Miguel understood the Tagalog.

"I'm sorry, cousin. This isn't over."

Calixto rose to his feet and nodded to Bakal who promptly knelt down and checked the dead men's pockets, pulling out their cell phones.

Miguel felt uneasy.

"They got pretty good charge," Bakal said as he logged into the phones. "Both of 'em. You were right, Calixto."

"Right 'bout what?" Mace asked.

Bakal stood and pointed his gun at Mace. The biker was shocked, scared, but expertly kept his stone expression and angry tone, something they drilled into him at the DEA training facility in Quantico, Virginia, years before he joined LOCC.

"I told you I give my men phones," Calixto said, "but I ain't paying for no 'iPhone 3000 Pro' fancy bushet. I give 'em small, old ass phones which got small, old ass batteries, and they drain like a motherfucker. So why ain't these dead like Miguel's was? Ain't even low. Come on, Mace, you're a smart man. Put two and two together for me."

"You're talkin' jibber-jabber, amigo," Mace said, acting more offended than intimidated. "I don't know nothin' 'bout phones or phone batteries, and I can't rightly make no sense of it all with a fuckin' pistol to my face."

"Then let me make some sense. This whole shitshow was staged. My men were killed someplace else. Their phones was shut off while they was moved here for us to locate. They were *meant* to be found, Mr. Mason. Ain't that obvious?"

"Shit, you put it that way..." The sworn undercover agent in Mace wanted to figure out what the hell was going on, but the notorious biker in him had to stay in control to keep him alive. "Good work, Sherlock, you're onto somethin'. So now you're lookin' at me? What about little Miguelito here? Wasn't he joyridin' with them?"

"Now you're getting it." Calixto turned to the boy. "So now we get to you, Miguelito, as promised. You said your phone died, but before it did, I tracked you in Eagle Rock a few hours ago, around nine."

"I told you, man," Miguel said, thinking on the spot. "I was prepping the car for you."

"On Magnolia Street? In the middle of a cluster of White family houses, pink flamingos, and picket fences? Now ain't the time for fantasy stories, boy. Don't make me stick a gun at you, too."

"Calixto, man..."

"Was you working with The Wolf Pack? Did they do this? Don't be afraid of Mr. Mason here. You can tell me." Calixto knew, whether it be Mace or Miguel, that one of them was going to throw the other under the bus.

"Fuck that!" Mace said. "I jus' met this fuckin' kid tonight!"

"Quiet!" Bakal barked as he pressed his gun's barrel to the biker's cheek.

"Big man with the big gun." Mace glared at Bakal as if daring him to pull the trigger. "You really gonna shoot me before we figure this shit out?" He defiantly walked away from the pistol and up to Calixto's face, a convincing act. "We got business 'tween us! Money! A lot of money! Why the fuck would I off your boys? Open your eyes, Cal! Can't you see it was The Duke? Ain't that obvious?" Mace didn't want to shove their potential CI in the crosshairs, but had no choice at the moment.

Calixto considered the biker's logic as he stared at Miguel. The young gangster's mind was a flurry. Calixto had him dead-to-rights.

"This shit's embarrassing, man," Miguel said, thinking fast. "Okay, truth. I was at this girl's house. I wanted to show off the SLK before I took it to the yard. I cleaned it up first, waxed it, made it shine like glass. You saw it."

"A girl?" Calixto asked, amused.

"Been tryin' to get with her for a while. When Yoy Yoy gave me the keys to that sweet ride, told me to lie low until after dark, I figured I got the Duke's car for a few hours, might as well flex. Might even get my dick wet, right? I pulled up with the windows down, bass bumpin', told her I was a straight-up gangbanger."

Calixto laughed. "Did it work?"

Miguel feigned disappointment. "Naw, man. She's a good girl, clean, straight A's, ain't down with gangster shit. I felt like a fuckin' dumbass. It's why I didn't say nothin', you know? Hard to tell your boys how you struck out."

Calixto thought for a moment, looked through Miguel as if reading his mind. Satisfied, he turned to Mace, still at gunpoint.

"Lookin' at me again?" Mace said. "We can't talk civilized with a gun at my head."

"Were you also at a good girl's house in Eagle Rock?" Calixto asked.

"I was with you, amigo, drinkin' piss beer and fancy tequila, or don't you remember none of that?"

"What about the rest of your pack? The ones who weren't lurking 'round the yard?"

"Most of my brothers was at a bar all day." Mace spoke with certainty. "We call it church. Knowin' them, they're probably still there, all fucked up by now. We close that place down every night."

"Church," Calixto said, thinking. "Regulars."

"We pack the house, practically own the joint."

"And what's the name of the joint?"

Mace thought for a moment. "The Wagon Wheel, out in Palmdale. Real classy joint. Hardly any bloodstains on the floor."

Calixto nodded to Bakal. He lowered his gun and pulled out his phone to look up something.

"What's he doin'?" Mace asked Calixto.

"Lookin' up The Wagon Wheel in Palmdale. We love real classy joints out in the desert."

Mace held his breath as Bakal found the bar online and made a call. A tired male voice answered. "Wagon Wheel."

Bakal handed the phone to Calixto.

In his surveillance van parked a few houses down from Divinia's home in the Hollywood Hills, C.B. sat in a swivel chair at a multimedia console beside two of his plainclothes agents, men who were not part of the biker gang front. While they monitored the Duque residence, he logged audio files from his remote microphone, the small device literally planted in the family's living room.

Christiana tutored a student, a boy whose football scholarship depended upon his upcoming math exam. Carlo spoke to a friend on the phone, telling him about getting arrested and how his brief stint in the detention center had affected him. Divinia argued with her agent, upset about the direction her show was heading.

After several hours of continuous recording, there was no word about the notorious fixer known as The Duke or even the family's father and ex-husband, Edgardo Duque.

They don't know, C.B. realized.

His revelation was interrupted when a cell phone rang, one of eighteen lined up on a console. They each had a label representing a fake location: "Gary's Custom Motorcycles," "St. Nelia Church," "Flora's Country Diner," "Dale's Automotive," "SoCal Bail Bonds," "Hammond Imports," "Seville Trucking," all places The Wolf Pack MC supposedly frequented.

C.B. identified the ringing phone: "Wagon Wheel."

His agents knew what that meant.

"Shit, he got made," one of them said with dread.

"Maybe not," C.B. said. "Don't count Mason out yet."

"GPS places him in Sylmar," the other agent said.

Shit.

C.B. gestured for his men to remain silent as he pressed a button on the console. The ambient sound effect of a bustling bar filled the van. He took a breath and answered the phone with a sigh and the worn voice of an overwhelmed bartender. "Wagon Wheel."

"Wagon Wheel Bar in Palmdale?"

"None other." C.B. didn't recognize the calm male voice on the other end, but the slight Filipino accent was a clue.

"I'm looking for a friend of mine," Calixto Cervantes said. "Big biker guy, probably getting piss drunk by now. Just wanna know if he's still there so I can pick his ass up."

"A lot of bikers in here."

"That's good to know. If his friends are still around, it'll save me driving way out there. How many bikers?"

"A lot," C.B. said. "Place has been swarming with them since noon. 'Wolf Brothers' or something like that. They take over every other day. Gotta be fifty, sixty of 'em."

"Sixty, huh?" Calixto thought for a moment, did some quick math.

"All I know is the county says I got official capacity for 45, and they blow that up whenever they're here."

"How do you manage?" Calixto laughed.

"Who says I do?" C.B. offered his own forced laugh.

"I hear you. What's your name?"

"Chuck."

"Chuck, you've been very helpful," Calixto said. "I think my friend has all the help he'll need."

"What's his name?" C.B. asked, hoping Calixto wouldn't drop the actual name of one of his agents, the same men who'd escorted the gangster through the foothills...

Cyrus Bernard ("C.B.")
Elijah Winston ("Winter")
Benjamin Prendergrast ("Preacher")
Daniel Silver ("Dice")
William Rawlings ("Ratch")
Killian Stone ("Killa")
Timothy Mason ("Mace")

Hearing an agent's birth name would have meant someone's cover was blown, which would mean they were all burned. "I know some of these jokers," C.B. said. "I can try to find him for you."

Calixto looked at the speechless biker standing before him at gunpoint. "Do you know... Mason?" he asked over the phone.

"Mace?" C.B. replied. "Yeah, I know him alright, biggest loudmouth of the bunch. The man owes me five hundred."

"That sounds like Mason."

"But he ain't here, ain't been here for a few days. I'm kinda glad, to be honest, even if he is skipping out on his tab... no offense."

"None taken," Calixto said. "He owes me, too."

"Anyone else?"

"No. Thank you so much, Chuck."

Calixto hung up.

C.B. exhaled in relief and shut off the sound effect, throwing the van into a tense silence.

"What's the status?" one of his agents asked.

"We still in business?" the other agent asked. "Or are we made?"

"Mace has more training and experience than the rest of you put together," C.B. said. "He has the situation under control."

"We sure about that, boss?"

"No. We are not."

* * *

Inside The Duke's dark, ransacked warehouse, Calixto handed the phone to Bakal, nodding for him to put away his gun.

"Gentlemen, forgive my paranoia," Calixto said, seemingly satisfied with the phone call. "You understand how the timing of all this made me stop and think."

"No sweat, Calixto," Miguel said. "I get it."

"Mr. Mason... Mace... I hope we can continue to do business. That damo you got your hands on is fire."

"Ain't we a pair," Mace said, still keeping his eyes on Bakal.

The four men stepped out of the warehouse. Bakal waved his hand in the air, signaling the two-dozen backup TSB to depart, leaving only the five Wolves on their bikes.

"So what are you thinkin' now?" Mace asked.

"Duque is behind this," Calixto said.

"Shit, now why didn't I think of that?" Mace said with dripping sarcasm. "Finally, Cal, we're on the same page."

"Forgive me for not trusting you, Mr. Mason. We just met, and I trust no one."

"Same, brother."

"You ain't mad that I was off the grid for a while?" Miguel asked.

"I can forgive your fuck-up, Miguelito. We all do stupid shit when we're horny and hard, right?"

"Right. Thank you for gettin' it, man."

"Just tell me the girl's name."

Miguel stood silent, at a loss, not sure how to respond after Calixto had pinpointed his exact location with ease. Afraid of being caught in a lie, he quickly replied, "Christiana."

"Christiana," Calixto said, as if committing the name to memory. "Sounds like a lovely, good girl. I hope it works out."

"I wish. Pretty sure it's a dead end."

"We'll see." The gang leader turned to Mace. "Can you give my boy a ride? Bakal and I aren't returning to the city just yet."

"Done," Mace said. "So long as we're good now."

"It appears that way."

Calixto nodded to Bakal. Without another word, they got in the Cadillac, Bakal behind the wheel. They drove away, past the awaiting Wolves, leaving Miguel and Mace alone in front of the warehouse.

Up in the treeline above the warehouse, Felix and Joey crouched in tall weeds, having just watched the entire scene unfold below. Felix worked a small camcorder tethered to a parabolic microphone and headset, recording every moment.

"Those TSB fuckers came quick," Joey said. "Probably raced here the moment those phones went live."

"That was expected," Felix said, "though the bikers weren't."

"I thought Ed shook those goons?"

"Apparently not."

"You heard everything?" Joey asked.

"Got a little dicey when they were inside, but I picked up most of it. Amo needs to see this right away."

"What are they sayin' now?"

Felix continued to watch, listen, record. "Nothing good."

* * *

With the TSB gone, the five Wolves started their bikes and joined their sergeant-at-arms by the building. Miguel's anxiety didn't subside as he was now surrounded by another gang, their rumbling engines deafening. It felt like one monster handing him to another.

Why would Calixto leave him with the bikers?

"Now that Little Lord Calixto is gone," Mace said, his men flanking him, "you and me got a business arrangement to work out."

"What business?"

"I didn't buy your story for a second, kid. I don't think Cal did neither, not a 100 Percent. The way I see it, we're both lucky to be alive."

"You don't believe me?" Miguel asked, nervous.

"A wanna-be gangster runt visits a sweet, wholesome girl in an upper-class neighborhood at night? Sounds like a shitty after-school movie."

"What the hell do you want?"

Mace walked to Ratch's bike, reached into his saddlebag, and pulled out something small and shiny. He returned to Miguel and held up Ratch's badge.

Miguel's eyes widened in fear. "Calixto was right... pakshet..."

"Look into my eyes, kid," Mace said. "I don't give a fuck about you or Cervantes or the TSB's junkyard empire, and I certainly don't care about Straight-A Christiana Duque hanging out at her grandma's house. I'm out for The Duke."

36

Sparring Partners

The early morning sun made the sheer curtains glow, casting a warm, diffused light into Edgardo's bedroom. Chopin faded in from the ceiling – *Nocturne No. 20 in C Sharp Minor* – so gradual as to not interrupt his circadian sleep cycle. The climate control maintained a perfect 76 degrees. The linens were crisp yet soft, fresh from a wash. Despite the many pleasantries, Edgardo hadn't slept well.

I once read an article in Forbes about how Fortune 500 CEOs get a solid eight hours each night despite the constant pressure and mountains of responsibility on their shoulders. They made their decisions for the day and left them at the office, not to revisit them until returning the following morning. How I envied that skill, the ability to partition one's mind, to place certain thoughts on hold, allowing others your full attention. My mind doesn't work that way. I feel like I'm facing 20 chess boards at any given moment, trying to stay ten moves ahead with each one. It's exhausting. The strategizing doesn't end simply because I turn off the lights. My mind never truly sleeps. It's a weakness, and it shall one day be my downfall.

In his early days of family, academia, and business, Edgardo viewed his life as a never-ending game of chess with each person a piece, each moment a move. That analogy served him well even as he later ventured into petty theft and cybercrime with Bram. The game became more complicated once he started associating with other criminals; outlaws, gangs, mob families. Suddenly, the pieces were often unpredictable. Even when factoring a man's greed, ambition, and history, Edgardo could still be surprised by a reckless move or an impulsive decision with seemingly no logic or motive. Having fools and cowards as partners landed you behind bars more than any brilliant detective or dogged task force.

That night, in my few moments of deep sleep, I dreamt of Miguel Hortiz and Calixto Cervantes, a pawn moving against a rook in the late-night shadows of my foothill warehouse. Like an actual chess game, the pairing was a bold, risky move, one that could end up with my pawn thrown back into the box. Unlike a simple game, I'd forever feel responsible for the young man's life should he never be heard from again, no matter how I might justify it. I only hoped that Calixto was as smart as I'd assumed, for you can't outwit the witless.

Overwhelmed and fatigued, he put on his glasses and retreated to his Chopin, his perfect room temperature, his morning workout, and his cup of coffee. The mundane, repetitive acts – rituals slaved to his OCD – reset his thoughts and readied him for the day. He groaned as the sound of rock music emanating from elsewhere in the house reminded him that this was no ordinary day, and that such simple, controlled mornings were behind him now.

Routine kept me focused, kept business in motion. Most importantly, it kept me from falling off the wagon again. Bram's way of life flew against that. Tranquility was never in his DNA, for Abraham Duque was a blunt instrument that struck first and assessed the situation later. I had to quickly come to terms with my need for routine versus my love for my reckless, well-meaning brother.

Edgardo walked across his house to his kitchen where a countertop stereo blasted AC/DC's "Shoot To Thrill" while Bram worked the stove. He danced, twirled, and smoked a cigar as he cooked with the flair of a teppanyaki chef.

He tossed an egg into the air and caught it perfectly on the edge of a cleaver above a frying pan, allowing its contents to fall onto the bubbling butter. He chopped tomatoes, diced onions, and pulled a loaf of bread from the oven, all with the glee of a newly freed man cooking the first meal of his choosing.

"Sit, Bata," Bram said. "There's good stuff on the table."

"Good morning, Kuya."

"Yes, good morning, now sit."

Edgardo entered the dining room to find a large breakfast already waiting for him. Arranged in a thoughtful place setting was Kape at Pandesal (black coffee and sweet bread), fried rice, sunny-side-up eggs, and grilled tomatoes. Bram brought in a bowl of sliced bananas tossed with melon and grapes.

"With all this food," Edgardo said, "what are you still cooking for?"

"Seconds and thirds, brother."

Edgardo sat down to his rich meal. "Impressive, but I normally skip breakfast."

"Batugan! No wonder you're such a grumpy runt. You leave the house with an empty stomach?"

Edgardo glanced at his wet bar in the corner. His usual bottle of Wild Turkey beckoned, but he ignored it today. He failed to notice his brother tracking his eyes.

"Coffee, at least?" Bram asked. "I can save the rest for the kids."

"I get coffee on the way to the garage."

"You can ignore my efforts if you wish. I'll weep in private later."

Edgardo smirked and relented, picking at the morning feast. Bram joined him with his own plate. AC/DC continued to blare, the screeching vocals cutting into his ears.

"Can we at least take a break from the Monsters of Rock?" Edgardo asked.

"It's your house, Bata." Bram sighed and tapped his phone – a gift from his brother – shutting off the countertop stereo. Chopin filled the room again from overhead speakers. "I've been cooking for cons every sunrise and sunset all these years. Let me cook breakfast for my little Edgardito just this once."

"I doubt it will be just this once."

"You should be so lucky."

The brothers ate together as if their ten years apart never happened. Edgardo took a bite and nodded his approval.

"Thank you, Kuya. This is more than I'm accustomed to."

"What a sad statement," Bram said. "Even inside, I had a full breakfast each day. Most of the time, I made it myself."

"Did your passion for food start in Lancaster?"

"Don't insult me. Our three squares in the joint were pre-packaged basura. I may have doctored it up, but it was mostly heat-and-serve processed shit."

"So, Nanay taught you?" Edgardo asked.

Bram held up his ring and pinky fingers. "One little piggy went to college. The other little piggy stayed home."

"To care for pamilya." Edgardo treaded lightly as he ate his breakfast. "Regrets?"

"Nope. So long as you went on to a better life, I was happy to rot and die in that impiyerno."

"Bram..."

"I mean it. God kissed your forehead, not mine. He gave you that brilliant mind, and I wouldn't have it any other way. Hell, I wouldn't even know what to do with a 160-whatever I.Q. My only regret is that you returned to the streets."

"I had debts to pay."

"You mean *I* had debts, Bata. The Demonyo never forgets. But you had a family, and I could have settled my obligations myself. I still intend to."

"No need," Edgardo said. "Those debts are paid in full. Rest easy. The Demonyo has let us go."

Bram felt relief, but also the weight of his shame. The foolish decisions of his youth, the fires he sparked in the Bay Area, all doused by his little brother. "Even now, you're still looking out for me."

"We look out for each other, from our first day to our last, remember? That was our vow over the ocean."

Bram nodded, remembering how he'd made that promise with his nine-year-old brother back in their island days, back when they left for America. He shook his head, his mouth full of eggs and rice. "Yet you still work with a heater in your coat and a knife in your belt, your head filled with Temple Street gagos, Rom's sundalos, and Waldo's trucks full of guns. And what do you get from it? You come home to an empty house while your family lounges in the hills and your children forget your face. Forgive me if I'm uneasy, Bata."

"Harsh, even from you," Edgardo said. "You're starting to sound like Nanay."

"What's the saying? Even a broken clock is right twice a day?"

Edgardo took his brother's slings, silenced himself, and enjoyed his breakfast, his first meal made with love in years.

* * *

Chopin had moved on to *Piano Sonata No.2 in B flat minor, Op.35* by the time the brothers finished breakfast, changed into sweatpants, and moved on to the workout room. They spent 25 minutes on cardio, followed by 45 minutes on free weights, during which Bram offered advice with nearly every rep of every exercise. Edgardo continually assured him he didn't need help, but the brotherly advice kept coming.

> *Growing up, Bram insisted that I not limit my education to matters of the mind. As far as he was concerned, my mental prowess needed no further tempering, but my body, my reflexes, they needed constant sharpening. He compared me to a swordsman who maintained his scabbard and hilt while ignoring his blade. It was through him that I first began my strict training regimen, and from that I added my physical being to my*

Lynn Harrod

daily discipline. After a decade without his coaching, I'd
become complacent, or so he'd have me believe.

"Breathe out during the exertion," Bram said, looking down at Edgardo on bench press.

"Isn't that what I'm doing?" Edgardo asked between reps.

"Yes, but do it in one controlled exhale, not a bunch of quick puffs."

"Disagree."

Edgardo felt slightly annoyed by the unsolicited advice, but realized he was pressing more weight than he ever had. Bram always had a way of pushing him further.

"Don't extend your arms fully," Bram said. "Always keep control, going up and coming down."

"I know how to lift a barbell," Edgardo said with a grunt.

"It's not just a matter of the lift. The return is just as important, maybe more."

"Disagree."

Bram's frustration approached a boil. "Disagree, disagree, you want to stay flexible, Bata. What happens if three more men come for you while I'm praying for your soul at church?"

"Pray for *them*," Edgardo said, puffing as he pressed the barbell upward. "I can handle myself in a fight."

Bram grabbed the barbell from Edgardo and shoved it in its cradle. "Ayoko na! Let's see you handle it!"

"Kuya, calm yourself..."

Bram bounded to a wall of Philippine weapons and took down two Kali practice sticks, foam-covered rods two feet long.

"Kuya..."

"Tumahimik ka! Face me!" He tossed one stick to his younger brother and nodded to the center of the room, a 15-foot circle drawn on a padded floor. "Single-stick spar. Show me what you remember."

"We're not kids anymore, horsing around in the fields behind Lola's house in Quezon."

"No, we're not. We're preparing to face your enemies."

"Kuya..."

"Manahimik ka! We're done when you strike me five times."

Edgardo relented and matched his brother's crouched stance. He took a wide overhead swing at Bram, landing a hit to his shoulder, but in those few seconds, Bram nailed him four times in with blinding speed before stepping back to the edge of the circle.

"Rusty, but not hopeless," Bram said.

"Pakshet!" Edgardo backed away, stunned, disoriented. Even though the sticks were padded, they still stung. "I think my way out of fights! I only attack when I have to!"

"And one day you will have to! That's why we train!"

The brothers circled each other like predators. Both men were highly skilled, but Edgardo was clearly outclassed as Bram struck another four hits before he could position a defense.

"Bram!"

"Holding the baston behind your shoulder gives you power, but having it at ready in front of you allows for defense, for quick jabs."

"Ayoko na!"

"Again!"

Bram advanced on his brother. Edgardo followed the advice, expertly attacking Bram but still not landing a hit. Bram spun around and swatted him another five strikes in a hailstorm.

"I forgot how much these fuckers hurt!" Edgardo said, reeling back.

"Again! Forward stance!"

Edgardo's pain, anger, and frustration welled into his fists. He swung down and across, striking Bram's forearm. Bram stepped back, lunged forward, and landed five more strikes in seconds. Edgardo wasn't used to being dominated in combat.

"You're holding the baston at the end," Bram said. "It gives you reach but kills your speed. Hold it one fist down. Move the wrist. Strike three times and step back."

"This is pointless..."

"Do it!"

Edgardo adjusted his grip as told, and they circled again. He managed three hits to his brother's torso, rushed in to grapple him, and they fell to the floor. After rolling in an entangled struggle, Bram slammed him hard to the wall.

"What's wrong with you?" Edgardo asked, his face inches from his brother's.

Bram released his grip, if only to grab hold of his swelling emotions. "You chose this life, Bata! You need to be prepared! The men out there won't just bat you around!"

Edgardo dropped his Kali stick and laid flat on his back in surrender as he realized why his brother had become so adamant.

Bram wasn't trying to control or correct him.

He was afraid.

"Don't worry, Kuya," Edgardo said, staring at the ceiling, trying to catch his breath. "I can take care of myself. I see everyone and everything coming."

Bram held out a hand to help his brother off the padded floor. "Normally, I'd agree, but the last couple of days say different."

"No disrespect, but I survived ten years while you were inside."

"One lucky first year plus the nine lives of a tangina cat." Bram took a moment to breathe, to calm himself. He stood and returned his fighting stick back to the wall rack. "Forgive my temper, Bata. Blame the remnants of 'Ang Makina.' He's still part of me."

"Despite your aggressive manner, you're right. I must be better prepared. I also love reliving our days in the fields, but what good is Kali against guns and knives?"

"Kali. Arnis. Eskrima. They teach discipline and form, things you use in any fight."

Edgardo nodded. "But I'm not in danger. Not anymore. You're here now, Kuya."

"I won't always be. Men like me don't die in bed of old age."

Edgardo heard the familiar words, something he wrote in his journal long ago. He rose to his feet and placed his stick on the wall. "I got my five strikes, Kuya."

"You did."

"Now, I must get to the garage. We'll pick this up later, I promise." He held out his hand. Bram clutched it and brought Edgardo close for a one-arm hug.

"As your new Head of Security, I will insist on it."

Lynn Harrod

37

Bacon and Pancakes

Hank Brighton's house was a modest, single-story Burbank home built at the end of World War II. Each room was dressed in well lived-in country decor, all serving as a 1,500-square-foot shrine for the late Marceline Brighton, a tall redhead who used to smile with her entire being. Framed photos on bookshelves depicted their many travels across North America. They considered themselves "child-free" for the first 12 years of their marriage, but started using the term "childless" after multiple failed attempts at starting a family.

Hank's wife Marci was a sweetheart, up to the morning she died of breast cancer. She'd always been kind to me and Bram. I still have the green wool blanket she made for me.

Hank flipped pancakes on a griddle while tending to over-easy eggs in a pan. Plating the food, he set a tall stack of pancakes on the table along with the eggs, a platter of bacon, a tiny pitcher of warn maple syrup, and a cracked coffee cup that now held daisies from his backyard.

After years of widowers' group counseling, Hank eventually accepted that he'd grow old alone in that stagnant house. That was before he found Candace Claypool seven years ago, at the delicate age of fifteen. Homeless and hooked on stolen prescription opioids, she overdosed in his backyard shed like a feral child facing the end. Instead of calling the cops or chasing her away like so many others had, he took "Candy" to the hospital. The next day, he took her into his empty home "until the girl gets back on her feet." She never left, and he never once questioned it. Of course, that's Hank for you.

"Food is on the table!" Hank called out. "Get it while it's still sizzling! First and final notice!" He'd given up pork for his heart years prior, but still cooked thick, fatty bacon every morning, just as his girl liked.

Candy entered in her coveralls and welder's goggles. She reached into the pantry for ketchup for Hank, Tabasco sauce for herself, and poured two cups of coffee from a French Press.

Candy became everything to Hank, the child he and Marci could never have. She saw him much the same, as evident from the goggles she wore daily, a gift from their first Christmas together. I so envy their bond.

"You always gotta wear those to the table?" Hank asked.

"I'll forget 'em if I don't," Candy said, as if they weren't her most cherished possession.

"Leave them at the shop."

"Did that once. Someone borrowed 'em and POOF... they disappeared. Remember?"

"You got 'em back, didn't you?"

"Sure, after nearly breaking Ruben's arm."

Hank smiled, recalling that fight.

Ruben Escuela, their clutch specialist, never dared to cross Hank's adopted daughter again. "So now they're glued to your noggin for life? I think you wear them because you think they make you look cool."

"Sure, Hank, these exude cool alright."

Candy grinned, also remembering the fight.

Ruben denied swiping her precious goggles and took playful pleasure in tormenting her. He stood six feet tall, none of which was brains, and saw himself as her mischievous big brother, but Candy only saw red. When she strong-armed him in the shop's corner, she'd taken him by surprise from behind, tangling his right arm in a tire iron. After two quick twists of the iron, he gave up the goggles and apologized.

"Don't ever take him from me again!" she yelled with a crack in her voice, snatching back the goggles.

Everyone in the crew understood the verbal slip.

"You don't have to pat down the bacon," Candy said, as the old man pressed paper towels down on the meat. "That's where all the flavor is."

Hank held up the paper towels, now dripping with grease. "Believe me, kiddo, you don't want all this crap running through your heart."

They sat at the table and ate breakfast together like father and daughter, her eggs and bacon beside her pancakes.

"Heard you fightin' with George again last night," she said with a mouthful of eggs.

"Sorry. Did we wake you?"

"Naw, I was still up. Did that neanderthal pay you yet?"

"George Hall is never going to pay me," Hank said with a sigh. "You know that. This is why I never take jobs on the side."

"'Cept you did. Jesus Hank, why do you put up with that asshole? He ripped you off, he bullies you for shit you ain't responsible for, and he does it 'cause he pegs you as weak. You gotta stand up to him."

"I'm too old to care about looking weak," he said. "Only young punks with a chip on their shoulder give a crap about that kinda nonsense."

"That ain't true and you know it."

"You know what is true?" Hank glanced at the front door as if someone might walk in that moment. "If I make any kind of ruckus, Eddie will get involved, and trust me, we don't want that, especially now that Bram's back."

"Ed's brother?" Candy asked. "What about him? From what you've told me, he seems cool."

"Bram has always been fiercely protective of me. I have stories."

Candy perked up, leaned in close as she shoveled pancakes into her mouth. "Stories? Ooooh. Like what?"

"Like... it's not appropriate breakfast conversation."

"Come on, I'm not a kid." Her father laughed, raised an eyebrow. "Just one story. I'm gonna meet this guy, eventually."

Hank nodded and sipped his coffee as he sifted through his many years with the Duque Brothers. "We went out for a drink one time. I brought a tray of beers to our table. A great big fella playing pool backed his cue stick into me. I spilled beer on his suede coat."

"Oh, shit..."

"He and his friends made a big production about it. I offered to buy them a round, but they were immune to my charms. Truth is, they were drunk, pumped up, looking for a fight."

"I'm guessin' they found one," Candy said.

"He sucker punched me, shoved me down. I busted my head open on a chair. Bram ran to me, saw the blood trickle down my face. I swear, I saw fire in his eyes."

"And?"

"And I'm fairly certain that great big fella in the suede coat never walked again."

Outside Hank's two-bedroom home, Castle Street ran for several blocks underneath the dangling power lines of transmission towers, unfeeling giants he'd always blamed for his and his wife's infertility. Seeing them looming above as he stepped out into the morning sun reminded him of Marci. Seeing Candy following close behind reminded him that life worked out fine, and that Marci would have liked seeing him care for a girl much like the one who long lived in their dreams.

They sat in Hank's white 1979 Ford F-150 pickup. Hank took the driver's seat much to the girl's chagrin.

"You ever gonna let me behind the wheel again?" she asked.

"Why? So you can burn the clutch a third time?"

"I fixed it both times, didn't I?"

"Sure, and I paid for the parts." Hank spoke in a mock angry tone. "Thrust bearing, slave cylinder, pressure plate..."

"Yeah, yeah, I know..."

"Two of each, mind you, plus fluids."

"Come on, Hank. How stupid would I have to be to burn it a third time?" Her line of thought halted upon seeing a vintage black Dodge Challenger parked in the next driveway. A large man approached the car with a bucket in hand. He shot the girl a quick glance as he crouched beside his ride...

George Hall, a stocky, middle-aged White man with a graying buzz cut and permanent stone face, waxed the classic muscle car. Rather than work in shorts and a tank top like most, he wore a leather bomber, aviators, and cowboy boots, for he and his car were always on display.

Candy continued to stare at George. He stared back twice in quick turns, as if to fling his contempt at her.

"Look at him," she said, incredulous, "waxing a fresh coat on a dead beast destined for scrap. It's a lost cause."

"It's a beauty," Hank said, eyes forward as he let his truck warm up. With George in his peripheral, it felt like a long, tense five minutes.

"Sure, a beauty that don't run. I guess he thinks he can get laid with it. It's why he's dressed up like a wannabe fighter pilot. Don't change the fact that the car is dead and done."

"A 1971 Dodge Challenger R/T doesn't go to the grave because of a blown engine. He'll rebuild it."

"George don't got the brains to build or rebuild shit," Candy said. "He wants you to do it, Hank, and he wants you to eat the cost."

"I am the one who worked on it."

"But he's the dickhead who blew it up at the track!" Candy couldn't understand how Hank would bow to such a bully. "Now ain't that worse than me glazing a clutch?"

"Twice in a row? I'm not so sure." Hank laughed and started his truck's engine.

"Seriously, though. You're gonna tell him to fuck off, right?"

"No more talk about George Hall."

"Hell, I'll tell him to fuck off for you."

"You gonna tire iron him, too? There's a big difference between Ruben and George."

"But Hank..."

"I said no more talk about him." Hank's firm tone and dead-eyed stare killed the topic. The girl never pushed it once her beloved father figure put his foot down. "And definitely not at the shop, especially now." He shifted into gear and backed out of the driveway.

"Yeah, yeah, not at the shop."

The girl considered telling Bram about the bully next door and wondered what he'd actually do to the man.

38

Intense Dream

Edgardo and Bram sipped a fresh Americano and a Red Eye at The Blume and Plume. A third cup for Hank sat between them on their sidewalk table. Hipsters and college kids on laptops and phones surrounded them. Their youth and ease with technology, along with the ongoing gentrification of the neighborhood, made Bram feel twice his age.

"Diyos, I hardly recognize this old street," Bram said.

"This old street got a facelift."

"I hate facelifts. They're unnatural, never look right."

"A lot can change in ten years, Kuya," Edgardo said. "You get used to it."

"This joint used to be a tattoo parlor, right? Next door was porno video. Now we're sippin' lattes with the cool kids."

"No, you're the cool kids here," a woman said.

The brothers turned to see Monica Torres busing tables nearby. Edgardo smiled upon noticing her, and Bram surely caught her smiling back. She put down her tray and stood between the brothers, wiping her hands on a cloth.

"I see your new employee is gone," Edgardo said.

"Yeah, she didn't work out. I just wish she gave us a heads-up. She got a call, took off her apron, and walked out without a word. Didn't seem to care that we have two weeks' pay waiting for her."

"She left money on the table?" Bram asked. "Ungas, bagito."

"What did he say?" she asked.

"Forgive him," Edgardo said, shooting his brother a stern look. "He's saying she must not have been too bright."

"Actually, she seemed pretty sharp to me, overqualified even, but I guess not. Refill?"

"No, thank you so much."

Bram shook his head and smiled.

"I see you have a new employee, too," Monica said, side-nodding to Bram.

"Me? Nah, I'm not new. I'm his older, wiser, more handsome brother, only with less hair."

"No hair," Edgardo said with a smile, "but you look better bald that I ever could."

"You're Abraham?" the barista asked.

Bram looked at his brother, surprised that anyone in his life outside of family and staff had heard of him.

"Kuya, this is Monica," Edgardo said. "I trust only her with my morning coffee. My day doesn't start until I see her."

"How sweet," she said. "I feel the same way."

"Blame Eddie's OCD," Bram said. "I'm joking. Eddie's told me stories about you, too, Monica."

"And yet you're not running away." She laughed as she picked up her tray of coffee mugs and plates. "Nice to finally meet you, Abraham."

"Just 'Bram.' Nice to meet you."

"Just Bram. I'll be sure to remember that." Monica took her wares inside, taking one last look at the man before she disappeared into the kitchen.

"You always make an impression with the ladies, Kuya."

"It's a gift."

The brothers sipped their coffee as they looked out at Temple Street.

"I never asked if you slept well," Edgardo said.

"Very well. Your guest bed sure beats a prison cot."

"Speaking of which, I had my concerns. I thought maybe you're still adjusting to rejoining the world?"

"No, I slept fine... well, I did have a dream about Tatay, an intense dream."

Other than the quick details at his parents' house, Edgardo realized he'd never told Bram about Otto's slipping mind, how far it had advanced over the past few years. "His confusion at dinner worries you."

"Yes, but I meant Tay from back home."

Edgardo turned to his brother, curious. "Ah, that kind of dream."

Our biological father, Danilo Duque, died when we were little. After he departed, and further after we moved to America, he'd faded from our memories, even mine. Only one picture of him exists, centered on my living room wall. That photo and our dreams is all we now had of the man.

"You were there," Bram said, still caught in his vivid dream. "We were kids again, working in the store."

"Sari-Sari Pamilya Duque." Edgardo pictured their old family general store, a shack on the edge of a canal that offered household goods, tools, and a few shelves of groceries. It always rained in his memories whenever he recalled that time of their lives. "I sometimes wonder, if we go back, will that old store be there?"

"Probably, empty and rotting alongside the canal. No one would dare take it over after what happened."

As Bram sipped his coffee, deep in thought, Edgardo could clearly see he was uneasy. "What's really on your mind, Kuya?"

"You said you've done business with The Panginoon."

Edgardo felt hesitant to follow him. "A few times, yes."

The Panginoon was the largest crime syndicate in the Philippines, expanding to the U.S. by infecting Los Angeles with a flood of Shabu – Filipino meth. From the moment Felix first mentioned them at the noodle shop, I wondered when Bram would question my involvement with such a notorious outfit. I hoped not to share that I'd had eleven exchanges with The Panginoon over six years. Each time we met, I wondered what Bram would think if he knew. His dream of our father, our old family business, must have brought it all back in a cold sweat.

"A few times? Come on, Bata."

"Enough times that I knew not to mention it."

"Pakshet," Bram said, wincing in disbelief. "After what they did?"

"The men I deal with are here in the states. They hadn't even been born when Tatay passed away..."

"When he was *murdered*."

Edgardo looked around to see if anyone had heard his brother's loud correction. All the many ear buds and headphones suggested not. "Should I make it a policy to never do business with anyone remotely connected to someone's death? My clientele list would wither away."

"Not 'someone.' Danilo Duque deserved better. He stood up to them, refused to pay their bantay money, so they took him out."

"Here it comes..."

"Yes, Eddie, here it comes." Bram's mind drifted from his dream to his childhood ordeal. "I was old enough to deal with his death, to help you get through it, and I'll never forget what he did for us."

"You find that honorable?" Edgardo asked. "To challenge The Panginoon?"

"Ain't it honorable to defend your business? Your family?"

Edgardo sat silent, facing his brother's stern glare. "Tay stood alone in front of the largest, most vicious gang in the Philippines and left his wife and children to fend for themselves. When we were living under a bridge in Quirino, washing our school clothes in puddles, did it feel honorable then?"

Bram clinched a fist, but calmed himself. "I mean no disrespect. I've just had too much time to think." He downed his Red Eye, ending their argument. "The coffee is excellent, Eddie, certainly better than the dwarf's sludge."

"Best in town."

"You're right, as always." Empty cup in hand, Bram looked at the passers-by, at the world that had moved on without him. "Do you think it's a good idea to bring me to the garage? TSB are still crawling around."

"It's under control, Kuya."

"This Calixto situation is bad, Eddie, and it ain't goin' away. Does it have to do with that boy from last night?"

"You saw?" Edgardo wondered how much his brother had witnessed in front of their parents' home.

"Christiana told me. Skinny pinoy with a bandana, red Camaro parked down the street."

Edgardo sighed. "That girl's eyes are too big..."

"It's that runt Miguel, isn't it? Did he dare to come make a deal?"

Edgardo looked at him and briefly considered how much he should share. He wanted to be transparent with him, but if Bram knew that "Miguel" had spent years visiting his family's home and knew everything about them all...

"It's under control, Kuya."

39

Stupid Boy

The four bays of Otto's Automotive were backed up three cars each, a typical midweek morning for the busy garage. Candy stood waist-deep in the engine bay of a Ford Mustang, its 351-cubic-inch V8 motor hanging from chains above. This third engine rebuild proved the toughest for her, as the old man had predicted. Still, he felt proud of her fearless approach, her willingness to stumble and fail as she learned his trade, even if she did spit and curse along the way.

"Was the Challenger a bitch like this?" Candy asked, referring to their vulgar next-door neighbor's car.

Hank scanned six clipboards at the nearby counter, trying to keep his customers in order. "Bigger bitch. The higher the horsepower, the tighter the tolerances need to be."

"My first rebuild was a breeze next to this."

"That's because it was an old Jeep. You can wrap your arms around that engine block. It doesn't get much easier than that."

"So you started me on the rookie stuff?" the girl asked as she climbed out of the engine bay. "Muscle cars are advanced shit?"

"Yes, but any engine refurb is advanced work. You're doing good, Candy. Don't be so hard on yourself. You're way better than I was at your age, I can tell you that."

She wiped her hands and joined her father figure. "I ain't being down on myself, I'm jus' thinkin' of fuckin' George's R/T. I mean, how many hours you put into that thing? Like, 45?"

"Try 65." It pained Hank to mutter that number.

"For fuck's sake, Hank, you worked that long and hard on the crate, made the block shine like mirrors, adjusted everything with laser precision, and this ogre blows it up at the track the next morning. That must have fuckin' hurt to see."

"Sure, it did." To her surprise, Hank laughed at the memory. "But he lost to a Chevy Cobalt."

"Sleeper car, right?"

"He didn't know that. The dumb-ass look on his face when that thing blew his doors off was almost worth it."

"Well, I ain't amused," Candy said. "He took 65 hours from your life, didn't pay you shit, and now he wants to take another 65."

"Plus the cost of parts."

"All 'cause he embarrassed himself in front of his club, burned a donut at the finish line until his engine shit itself. Bullshit! He's a fuckin' bully!"

"You're not wrong," the old man said with a sigh.

"Hell no, I ain't! I've been thinking. I say we tell Eddie and Brad... Brant... whatever his name is, his fuckin' demon brother. Assholes like George Hall get away with fuckin' over folks 'cause they let him..."

"Candy!" Hank dropped his clipboard to the counter. He looked around, hoping no one heard her rant or his outburst, and gestured for the girl to lower her voice. "We went over this. We keep this George Hall business to ourselves. How I handle it is my choice. Don't tell the crew, don't tell Eddie, and definitely do not tell Bram. Understand?"

"Sure, Hank." Candy had rarely seen him so serious. "Whatever you say."

"That story I told you? About Bram? It's no tall tale."

"Never doubted it."

"Thank you." Hank took a moment to collect himself. He picked up his clipboard and straightened his collar. "Sorry I raised my voice."

"It's fine. Nice folks can be phony, but when you lose your cool, it's always genuine, you know?"

"That's one way to look at it."

The old man had more to say but silenced himself upon seeing Edgardo and Bram enter the garage, blending in with their coveralls. Hank put down his clipboard and walked up to the older brother.

"My boy!" Hank said with the widest smile. "Look at you! Still a beast! And all dressed up and ready to work!"

"You know I don't know shit 'bout cars, Old Man." Bram laughed. "You're the master mechanic, not me."

"Luckily, Candy and I are here to teach you!"

The two men held each other in a tight embrace, another sight the girl wasn't used to seeing.

Edgardo handed the old man his coffee.

"Second cup of the day," Hank said. "Now, I'll be fully awake."

"You weren't awake all this time?" Edgardo asked.

"He didn't wake up till he saw *him*," Candy said, nodding toward Bram. "So, this is the guy?"

"This is the guy!" Hank said, overjoyed. "Bram, this is my girl, Candy."

Bram looked at her curiously. They shook hands, landing him a palm full of fresh oil. He wiped it on his coveralls.

"Hank's told me stories about you," Candy said.

"That's the second time I've heard that today. I'm not sure if that's a good thing."

"Hey, check out Mr. Popularity here!" Hank couldn't take his beaming eyes off Bram or Candy, his surrogate son and adopted daughter having just met.

Edgardo looked out at the Jeepney food truck on the corner to see that the former cook – an undercover agent with LOCC – was gone, as was the trainee at the coffeehouse.

Hank joined Edgardo, out of earshot of the others. "I see you looking at the food truck. Yeah, that pig packed it up. It's just as well. His palabok was shit."

"Same with the barista at the Bloom," Edgardo said, "and the jogger that used to pass by every morning."

"I guess LOCC pulled all their moles. Makes sense. No point now, right?"

"I doubt they're off my scent."

"Yeah, about that. Felix is waiting in the office."

"Felix is here?" Edgardo felt uneasy, only having met with his assistant at the tiki lounge or the adjacent noodle shop.

"He's got something you need to see."

Edgardo and Bram stepped into the garage's small, windowless office where Felix sat behind his boss's computer. Several windows were tiled across the screen, including video feeds.

Edgardo nodded to Bram to shut the door before turning to his assistant. "I have to admit, it's unnerving to see you here, Felix."

"My apologies, Amo, but this couldn't wait."

The young man kept scouring files, video logs, until he found the moment he wanted. He expanded a video to full screen, showing night footage of the exterior of Edgardo's warehouse in Sylmar.

"I thought everything was handled?" Edgardo asked.

"On our end, yes," Felix said. "Joey and I went to your house, moved the bodies to Sylmar as instructed. Phones off."

Bram shook his head in disbelief. "When?"

"Last night, Bram," Edgardo said.

"While we were at Nanay's? When were you gonna tell me?"

Edgardo ignored his brother and turned to Felix. "Continue."

"Once the bodies were in position, we switched on their phones. TSB was on the scene in forty minutes, just as you thought."

"Actually, a lot sooner than I thought. Calixto must have been waiting for their signal."

"Exactly. But there's a new development."

"This is 'under control,' Eddie?" Bram asked.

Edgardo again ignored his brother. "What development?"

Felix replied by standing and swiveling the chair for Edgardo. His boss sat at the computer, put on headphones, and watched the video his assistant had readied. The tense scene from the night before played out, complete with audio.

Calixto arrived at the warehouse with the Wolves in tow...

An SUV of Temple Street Boyz pulled up behind the bikers...

Bakal threatened Mace at gunpoint...

Miguel improvised a cover story involving Christiana...

The group entered the building to find Jorge and Yoy Yoy...

Calixto called The Wagon Wheel bar...
The TSB left Miguel with the Wolves...

"That stupid boy," Edgardo said. "Why the hell did he name Chris? Unacceptable."

"It gets worse, Amo," Felix said.

Edgardo couldn't imagine the grim scenario deepening further until he saw Mace flash a badge at the boy.

"That reckless, impatient fool," Edgardo said. The brash biker took his "loose cannon" character seriously, which made him difficult to predict. "Did they arrest him? My guess is they did not."

"They talked for a while, mostly out of my range, and took him home. Joey and I followed. They dropped him off at the scrapyard. Miguel lives in a travel trailer on the edge of the property."

"Good man," Edgardo said with a sigh. He took off his glasses and placed his palms over his face, exasperated, overwhelmed. His brother rarely saw him at a loss.

"What does this mean?" Bram asked, trying to piece the scene together. "Isn't it good for us that they didn't take the runt in?"

"It's far from good for us." Edgardo stood and walked out of the office, leaving his assistant alone with his confused brother. Bram shrugged at Felix.

"Mason revealed himself," Felix said. "No arrest means they probably flipped Miguel, and if that's true, it means we can no longer trust him."

"If that's true, Mr. Felix, it means we never could."

40

Variant Cover

Lunch break at Eagle Rock High School saw groups of students sitting on the grassy quad, at scattered picnic tables, and underneath trees surrounding the modern three-story administration building. Christiana sat alone at a table, away from her clustered classmates. She cleaned her eyeglasses, sipped a water bottle, and read *Lord of The Flies* in the shade of an ancient oak. Hearing a familiar laugh, the deep guffaw of a boy throwing his weight around, she looked up and saw her brother Carlo hop into a pickup truck bed with his teammates. Together with a few cheerleaders, the football players hollered as the truck roared off campus.

Chris returned to her book but failed to focus.

She pulled out her cell phone and made a call.

"Fisher Associates," a male voice answered. "Attorneys At Law."

"Is this Mr. Fisher?"

From behind his cluttered desk, alone in his office and halfway through a roast beef sandwich, Fish struggled to recognize the high-pitched adolescent voice. He chugged a can of Diet Coke to wash down his lunch, but still spoke with his mouth full.

"Mr. Fisher is in a meeting," he said. "I can forward you to his voice mail..."

"Mr. Fisher, it's Christiana Duque."

"Chris?" Curious, Fish cleared his throat and set down his sandwich. He spoke formally, as if Edgardo might be listening on the other end. "Miss Duque, what an honor. How can I help you?"

"First, is this going to be, like, confidential?"

"I'm not your attorney."

Chris silenced herself for a moment as a group of students walked by. "But you're my dad's attorney."

"Attorney-client privilege doesn't extend to family. You'd have to be my client, separate from your pop."

"Then I'm your new client," the girl said firmly.

"You'd have to pay me first, not to mention permission from your parents."

"My mom and dad don't know I'm calling, if that's what you're afraid of."

"I'm not afraid of them. I'm afraid of breaking the law."

"We can't just talk in confidence? You know, like a consultation?"

Fish considered politely ending the call and contacting Edgardo, but the urgency in the girl's voice grabbed him. "Look, Chris, just tell me what's on your mind. You don't have to divulge every dirty little detail."

"Umm... okay."

But she did have to reveal dirty details.

That was the point of the call.

Christiana wanted to finally ask about the spreadsheets she'd stumbled upon during the disk recovery of the laptop Fish had given her years before. She intended to present her theory that her father – with Fish's help – had long been involved in ongoing illegal activities, but hearing the lawyer's voice, his friendly tone, made her reconsider.

"Chris?" Fish asked. "What is it?"

The girl hadn't thought about the consequences of revealing her knowledge of the deleted files. She wanted answers, but now realized she'd be opening a can of worms that would forever change her relationship with her father. The spreadsheets were a curiosity before, something she could explain with a stretch of her imagination, but in light of recent events they started to make sense. With Fish now on the phone, she was one question away from learning the truth, but froze in hesitation.

"You still there, Chris?" Fish asked.

She decided she wanted to remain in the dark a little longer, to remain her father's innocent daughter, for she didn't want to hear Fish admit that Edgardo Rigo Duque was a gangster or a drug dealer or a thief, or maybe all of the above.

"It's about my mom's TV show," she finally said, switching gears.

"Hmm, television." Fish said. "Show business. Sticky stuff. The Gourmet Travel Network, or their parent company, Gourmet Foodie Snob Influencers or whatever they call themselves, they probably have a platoon of ivy-league general counsel on permanent retainer. Why call me?"

"She doesn't need a lawyer, Mr. Fisher. She's having problems with her producers. Like, one guy."

Fish held the phone with his shoulder while flipping through a copy of *Hollywood Producers Directory*. "Who's her Executive Producer? Someone with the network?"

"No. Gary something. Gold Award Media Entertainment."

"G.A.M.E. Clever." He looked up the name in the index and turned to the company's page. "Gary Goldsmit. Sounds familiar…"

"That's the guy. He has no interest in heritage and culture. He wants to whitewash the show."

"Burgers and dogs?"

"Exactly. I'm afraid it could hurt my mom's reputation."

"Does she feel this way?" Fish asked.

"Yes, but she's trapped, you know? I know my mom. She acts tough and in charge, but these people don't care about what she wants."

"So, what can I do?"

"You used to be a producer, right?" Chris asked." Can you work something out? Like maybe you can sign on as a co-producer?"

"Whoa, cool your jets, kiddo. It doesn't work like that. And this is really something for her agent."

"Her agent sucks." Chris noticed a boy in a hoodie leaning against a tree a short distance away. He looked out over the quad but occasionally glanced her way. "My mom does all the work, and he swoops in and grabs his ten percent."

"Sucks or not, that's pretty much how most agents work."

"Isn't there anything you can do?" she asked.

"Maybe. I met Goldsmit a few times, years ago." Against his instincts, before he could think things through, Fish agreed to help. "I'll look into it, kiddo, see if I can come up with something, approach him from a different angle. In the end, it's always about money. Simple as that."

"Thanks, Mr. Fisher. I really appreciate it. And please, like, don't tell my dad."

"Ah, is that what all the attorney-client privilege talk was about?"

"Pleeeease…"

"Okay, okay, no need to beg, but I can't make any promises."

"I get it. Thanks, Mr. Fisher."

"Thank me when I actually turn up something."

Fish hung up first. Chris pocketed her phone, unsure about keeping her father's secrets but satisfied that she may have helped her mother. She opened her novel and returned to the island of warring, marooned boys. A page later, she spotted the hooded teen in the corner of her eye, now leaned against a closer tree. He looked familiar, so she waved him over.

Miguel Hortiz looked around and emerged from the shade of his tree with an awkward wave. "Remember me?"

"Miguel, right?" Chris asked. As the boy approached her in the bright sunlight, she finally recognized her old friend. "Maria?" She looked at him with new eyes, stunned. "That was you with my dad?"

"Sorry for lurking like a creep." He flinched a crooked smile. "And it's 'Miguel' now."

"Holy shit! I thought I'd never see you again!"

"Yeah, I wanted to say sorry for that, too."

Christiana tossed down her book, jumped to her feet, and wrapped her arms around him, nearly picking him up off the ground.

* * *

Across the street, several cars down, Bakal Diaz sat at the wheel of his boss's Cadillac. The black sedan blended in with the line of cars along the curb opposite the school lot, and the tinted windows kept him obscured. He watched the teenagers' reunion through the 100mm zoom lens of a camera resting on the dashboard.

Minutes after leaving the foothill warehouse the night before, Bakal was tasked with following Miguel for a day. The boy's recollection of events, about visiting a crush in Eagle Rock, seemed to button up the holes in his story, but Calixto couldn't shake the nagging feeling that he was missing something. Washing and detailing The Duke's car, then driving to suburbia to show it off, wouldn't take six hours, especially considering how the girl rebuffed his advances. Miguel's phone battery was supposedly dead the entire time, aligning with Yoy Yoy's and Jorge's absence. The last piece that didn't quite fit was Mace's defense of the boy, the notion that the bikers wanted that nervous skinny kid to do a dead drop for them even though his trust was in question.

Bakal started that day by watching Miguel's travel trailer through stacks of cars at the scrapyard, Jorge's red Camaro parked beside it. He figured the mission was pointless, that his boss was being paranoid, until he followed the boy to a taco truck in Burbank where Mace and two other Wolves met him for breakfast burritos. Bakal watched them from afar for 30 minutes.

Next, he tailed the teenager to comic book shop in Glendale. Miguel entered with a tall stack of comics to sell. After a ten minutes of waiting at the back of a parking lot, Bakal saw him emerge with a single comic book in a thin paper bag. It must have been quite a trade.

By noon, Miguel was at Eagle Rock High School, leaning against a tree in the quad until the students broke for lunch. Bakal expected him to sling dope to some jocks, maybe unload that comic book to some rich nerdy kid. Instead, the boy stalked a bookish girl in glasses until he gathered the nerve to approach her.

It was one of several scenarios that Calixto predicted.

At her reading spot, Chris hugged Miguel tight, afraid of letting him go. "Last time I saw you was..."

"Last night?" he said.

"Yeah, but, like, I was gonna say when your dad passed away. Where have you been?"

"On my own."

"Did your mom kick you out?" Chris asked.

"She kicked herself out."

"I'm so sorry, Maria... umm... Miguel."

"It's fine. I'm a survivor."

"Are you back? Like, back in school?"

"Nah, school's out for me," Miguel said.

"You sure? It's not too late. Like, I can tutor you, help you catch up."

"I'm sure, Chris. Thanks. Eagle Rock High has seen the last of me."

She realized what that meant. "You're gonna disappear again."

"Thought about it," he said, "but your dad convinced me to stick it out."

"He always liked you."

"Lucky me." Miguel caught the attitude in his voice. "I mean, I know he can be tough."

"Sure, but he can also be a sweetheart... most days. Hey, time for a double selfie!" Before Miguel could protest, Chris whipped out her phone, posed beside him, and snapped a photo of their faces pressed against each other.

It was the first moment of genuine love Miguel had felt in years. This girl wanted nothing from him. She didn't judge him, wasn't trying to use him, wasn't pressuring him to do something he had a bad feeling about. Christiana Duque simply felt overjoyed to see her childhood friend again.

She looked at the photo and shared it with him. "Look at us! I'm still a dork, but you look so cool."

"Thanks."

"I had to take it, you know, like, in case you decide to disappear again."

Miguel ignored the shift in tone. "How is everyone? Is Carlo still the big jock? Still giving you shit?" He recalled how cruel Carlo's teasing could be, whether it be smaller kids at school or his own kid sister.

"No, we get along fine nowadays because he's pissed off at my dad more than anyone. But, like, he's pumped now that our uncle is back in town."

"Tito Bram?"

Chris looked surprised. "I didn't think you ever met him."

"We met." Miguel could still see Bram's fiery eyes inches from his own, still felt him clutch his throat when he pinned him against Edgardo's back fence. "Big, angry bald guy, right?"

"Yep! That's him! I guess you met everyone in my family at some point. Wait till you see him now. Like, he's really mellowed out since we were kids. Hard to imagine, I know."

"I'm done with this place, Chris, but I don't want to be done with you. I miss going to your house every day, eating empanadas, hiking up to the Hollywood Sign, listening to Justin Bieber."

"We'd watch MTV for hours, drink Cherry Coke, play Sequence, read comics."

"Speaking of, I got this for you." Miguel unzipped his hoodie and reached in for the bagged comic book.

Christiana slid a pristine comic book from the bag, revealing two heroes on speeder bikes fighting battle droids, the action-packed cover of the rare title *Star Wars: The Clone Wars No. 1.*

"Clone Wars 1?" she said in awe. "No way!"

"The variant cover," Miguel said proudly, "and Ahsoka's first appearance."

"It looks brand new!" Chris was touched. Ahsoka Tano was their favorite Star Wars character. "How much did this cost?"

"Not much. Don't worry about it."

"Come on." She looked at the original price on the cover. "I know it wasn't $2.99."

Miguel laughed. "No, it hasn't been that price since 2008, and I said don't worry about it." He'd spent $1,200 on the mint-condition comic, money from trading his entire collection plus a wad of cash Edgardo slipped him the night before. Miguel found it fitting to spend it all on the man's daughter – his best and only friend – as if it would somehow bring back a sense of normalcy to them both.

Chris hugged him again before carefully flipping through the perfect pages. "This is insane! Thank you Maria... I mean, thank you Miguel. Sorry..."

"No sorrys," he said. "I mean, it took *me* some getting used to." How he loved seeing her smile.

While watching the two youths' tender moment from his car, Bakal called Calixto. "I think I got something, boss."

"The Wolves?" Calixto asked knowingly.

"You were right. They met with Miguel earlier, spent a half-hour with him at a taco truck. I couldn't make out what they were saying though."

"We know it wasn't about the carnitas. Where you at now?"

"High school in Eagle Rock. He's with some girl."

"That nice girl with the good grades?"

"Looks that way. Plain-looking pinay, glasses, books. I got pictures."

"That won't do me no good," Calixto said. "I need a name."

"What for?" Bakal asked, confused. "She's nobody."

"I got a feeling she'll be somebody when you get a name."

"Man, I can't exactly walk up to them, you know? There's people everywhere, and Miguel will leg it when he sees me."

"Forget the boy," Calixto said. "Let him scamper off. What I need is that girl's name. Use that clever brain of yours, Bakal."

"What's the obsession, boss? Who do you think she is?"

Calixto hung up, leaving Bakal to think of some way to identify the young girl before lunch was over and the students retreated to their classrooms. He didn't want to wait until the school day ended hours later, when 2,000 kids would pour out of the building to awaiting buses and parents.

He found his answer when he spotted a red-headed girl in a cheerleader's outfit roaming the quad with a clipboard. She'd approached several students, making her way to the isolated picnic table.

* * *

"Remember when I asked my mom to make me an Ahsoka costume for Halloween?" Chris asked.

"She made me an Ezra costume," Miguel said with a smile.

"That's right! She had to watch the show to get ideas, spent a week on... oh my God! My mom is going to flip when I tell her you're back!"

"Let's take it easy with me being back." Miguel found it difficult to continue. "Will she be... are *you* okay with me being a guy?"

Chris stopped herself from a quick response. She slid the comic back in the bag and looked at her old friend with pleading eyes. "Why would you ask me that? I don't care if you're a girl or a boy or... like, friendship isn't about gender, right?"

"There's something else. But this is classified information here."

Chris pinched her lips with her fingers and made a *shushhh* sound. "Tupperware."

"Tupperware." Miguel smiled as he remembered their childhood pact. They placed their deepest secrets and sisterhood bond within a small, discarded orange Tupperware bowl from Divinia's kitchen, still sealed and resting under Chris's bed.

"So, what's this 'something else' then?" she asked.

"I've been running with a gang. The Temple Street Boyz."

"Oh wow..."

"But I've been trying to get out, Chris. You know, start over? Maybe your dad can help with that?"

"What can he do?"

"I dunno, give me a job? I work for him sometimes, but I need something regular. Maybe there's an opening in one of his businesses? Some way I can be useful?"

"That's it?" she asked. "You want a job?"

What Miguel actually wanted was The Duke's protection. After enduring the near-death horror of Calixto's interrogation, he felt lost and vulnerable. He knew he couldn't run and that the gangster would soon piece together the truth. The Duke might not find him useful anymore, but a renewed connection to Chris might guarantee his safety.

"Any kind of work," he said. "I'm kinda afraid to ask him."

"I don't blame you. He can be intimidating."

"Yeah."

She has no clue, he thought.

"I'll talk to him," she said. "He's putty in my hands."

"Cool, but look, don't mention the thing about the gang. That ain't me no more."

Chris pinched her lips again. "Tupperware." *Shushhh.*

Miguel pinched his lips as well. "Tupperware."

As they looked into each other's eyes, confirming their sacred vow, the red-headed girl ran up to them with a clipboard in hand...

Jenny Passante was a 16-year-old White girl in a green-and-white cheer uniform and wide smile over clear contempt. Miguel immediately knew her type, the rich, popular girl who would have never spoken to them if she didn't need something. In Miguel's eyes, the rest of the world was populated with Jenny Passantes.

"Hi guys!" Jenny said in her bubbly voice. She held up the clipboard. "Sign our petition? We're trying to get the school mascot changed from the 'Eagles' to the 'Dragons.'"

"But... it's Eagle Rock High School," Miguel said.

"Exactly! Too obvious! Dragons are hot right now, you know, with *Game of Thrones* and all that."

Christiana frowned at Jenny's rude interruption. The two girls had been academic rivals since first coming to the school three years before, the only difference being the cheerleader's popularity. Jenny was used to getting all the boys' attention. With Miguel there, Chris saw her sudden presence as jealousy.

"Later, Jenny," she said flatly.

"Come on, Christine, it'll take five seconds." Jenny had mistakenly called her 'Christine' since they were Freshmen. "Just print your name and address, and sign it, that's all."

"Gotta admit, 'Dragons' does sound cooler," Miguel said.

"See, he gets it." Jenny flashed her winning smile at him.

Chris reluctantly scribbled her name and address, followed by her signature, if only to get rid of her. Jenny snaked the clipboard back.

"See?" Jenny said. "That was easy! What about you, guy?"

"I'm not a student."

"Oh, I see. Dating college men, Christine?"

"Goodbye, Jenny," Chris said.

Jenny shrugged and wandered off, smiling over her shoulder at Miguel.

"She seems nice," he said.

"She's a lot of things, but 'nice' ain't one of them."

"Ah, got it." The boy returned to his request. "Thanks again for talking to your dad for me. I'm done playing gangster. I just want a normal life again."

"Of course," Chris said. "I'm sure he'll figure out something. And don't worry about that gang. Consider them a distant memory."

* * *

The school bell rang a few minutes later, prompting the students to gather their things and return to class. Chris gave Miguel one more hug before she ran inside and he drove off.

During their goodbye, Bakal had been eyeing Jenny from the moment she left them. He counted the three signatures she obtained after getting Chris's.

As Jenny headed back to the school's front doors, he quickly got out of his car and jogged up to her. "Excuse me, what's everyone signing up for?" he asked in his most cheerful tone as he reached her.

Thinking he was a parent, she turned to him and pulled the petition from her backpack. Before she could launch her pitch, he snatched the clipboard from her hand and scrutinized the names.

"Umm, we want to change our mascot," she said, startled.

Bakal ignored her, focused on the entry fourth from last.

His boss was right again.

He handed her the clipboard, shook his head, and walked away. Jenny thought the man was rude but soon forgot him as she entered the school.

Returning to his car, Bakal quickly took a napkin from the glove box and jotted down the words he'd committed to memory.

"Hello, Miss Christiana Duque of Beachwood Canyon Drive."

41

Time to Wake Up

Edgardo leaned back in his shop's office chair, having just finished rewatching the disturbing surveillance video Felix brought to his attention. He took off his headphones, allowing the sounds of the busy garage to fade in through the shut door.

Bram had rewatched the footage as well, standing over his brother's shoulder. He didn't need audio to understand what he'd just witnessed. As Felix pointed out, Mace likely turned Miguel as an informant or even an operative.

"That little runt again," Bram said. "Miguel. He's all over the place. I thought you said he was an asset now, Eddie?"

"He's under control," Edgardo said.

"Yes, but under whose control?"

"Everything happened the way it was supposed to."

"Except for the bikers!" Bram said. "How can you be so calm? How much worse is this shit gonna get?"

"We knew they'd be back in the picture, just not so soon."

Felix pulled his thumb drive from the computer. "The problem is that they never left the picture, Amo. Maybe they never will."

"Vultures don't leave the carcass," Bram said. "They just circle for more."

"Correct," Edgardo said in realization. He looked to his men as he reassessed his strategy, like a pro poker player who just took an unexpected bad beat. "A warehouse full of goods, a safe full of cash, my primary contacts. It's not enough. Fact is, the Wolves can't leave, no matter what I give them. They simply returned to lingering on the edge as Bram said, waiting for their next window."

Edgardo wrote something on a yellow Post-It note and handed it to Felix. "Dig up anything you can about these two. Work with Fish if you need to."

"Yes, Amo."

Bram opened the door for Felix, whipping it wide as if Calixto, Mace, or his entire biker gang might be standing on the other side. Something occurred to him. He looked down at the vents along the office's baseboards and up at the single skylight of the windowless room. He quickly shut the door again. "Mr. Felix, any chance these Wolves or anybody else got eyes or ears on us?"

"Doubtful. We sweep every property regularly."

"How regularly?"

"Weekly."

"Putang ina... sweep every day, starting today."

Felix felt unsure about the command. He looked to Edgardo.

"Bram is Head of Security now," his boss said. "Make it happen."

"Yes, Amo." Felix opened the door to leave, but Edgardo tapped his arm for a final word.

"Felix, I can see why you rushed this video to me, and I appreciate your urgency..."

"But it could have waited until we met later," Felix said, completing his boss's thought.

"Correct." Edgardo eyed Hank who was now waiting by the open door. "This kind of business doesn't belong at the garage, especially now."

Felix nodded and left. The brothers followed him out into an empty bay, something Hank needed to address.

"We got a problem," the old man said.

"I can see," Edgardo said. "Ricky's late with the van again."

"The van is late, sure, but unfortunately, Ricky is right on time."

Hank nodded toward the front of the bay, where Ricky Wash stumbled just outside. He looked drunk, laughing to himself, muttering to no one. To Edgardo's dismay, he started to attract attention from the patrons.

Bram clinched his fists. "Does *this* kind of business belong at the garage, Bata?"

"Go back to my office. I'll bring him in."

After two minutes of coaxing a wandering Ricky with talk of donuts and coffee, Edgardo took him behind the building, out of sight of the patrons and staff. He stood Ricky against a wall and sprayed his face with a hose.

"Fuck, man!" Ricky said. "What's with the brutality?"

"This isn't brutality, Ricky. This is me trying to reach you. I need you alert." Edgardo kept spraying the man, drenching him until he became more coherent. "Time to wake up, Ricky."

"Okay! Fuck! Turn that shit off! I'm awake!"

"Good, because brutality is waiting for you in my office."

Bram shoved Ricky Wash down into the office's lone chair. Edgardo shut the door and joined his brother in standing over the soaked, confused man. In the privacy of the small room, the concern for Ricky's wellbeing and the promise of snacks were replaced by furious, incredulous expressions.

"What the hell is wrong with you?" Edgardo asked. "Where's the van?"

Ricky tried to hide his fear with nervous little laughs. He looked up at Bram. "Man, who's this guy?"

Bram clutched the top of Ricky's head. "I'm the guy who's gonna slam your skull into a brick wall if you don't answer him quick."

Ricky looked through Bram's fingers at Edgardo. "You're asking what's wrong with me? What's wrong is that I'm royally fucked! As for the van, well, you're fucked, too!" He snickered under his breath, mostly from drunken nerve rather than bravado.

"What's he talking about, Eddie?"

Edgardo played out a few scenarios in his mind. "Waldo's upset that I turned away his trucks the last couple of days."

"Yep," Ricky said with a crooked grin.

"And he heard rumors, didn't he?"

"Yep. Rumors that you got fucked by the feds. And he thinks I'm part of your shit, since it was only *my* trucks that you told to fuck off."

"How many trucks does this Waldo punyeta have?" Bram asked.

"A lot, man, like more than a dozen."

"Sixteen daily," Edgardo said. "Twenty by the last week of the month, an extra two every three months, rotated every ten days."

Ricky looked shocked. "Shit, how the hell you know..."

"We're asking the questions," Bram said, tightening his grip on the man's scalp. "And you will speak to my brother like a man, not some ungas buwisit junkie you share a pipe with."

"Yo, I don't know what all that shit means, but..."

My brother.

Ricky instantly realized who this hulking man was, and his fear reached a new height. Having served three months in Lancaster, he'd heard many stories about The Duke's infamous, caged brother, now apparently freed. The startling realization that Ang Makina now had him in a locked room sobered Ricky fast, killing his defiant, awkward laughter.

"Look man, I'm sorry, I don't mean no disrespect... it's just... you gotta help me, man. They said go home, don't need me today. Tomorrow, who knows? We're talking 'bout Mr. Waldo. Maybe I'll be found face-down, ass-up in a ditch."

"Maybe that's exactly where you belong," Bram said.

"Unacceptable." Edgardo nodded for Bram to release his grip from the man's head. "I won't let my brother hurt you, Ricky, and I'll speak to Waldo personally, smooth things out, get you back to work."

"I appreciate it... Mr. Duke... sir." Ricky felt relieved but confused, with one brother looking out for him while the other stood ready to pound him into the wall. It played out like a deranged version of *Good Cop, Bad Cop*, except the Bad Cop here wasn't acting. "Look, Waldo's really pissed. I ain't seen him, I mean, no one's seen him, but I heard he's fuckin' pissed."

"I'll take care of it. In the meantime, head somewhere safe. Don't go home for a while."

"Thank you, Mr. Duke. Sir." Ricky calmed himself, sat up in his chair, and took a slow breath. "Is any of that shit 'bout you true? I mean, I don't think so, but..."

"Maybe. Be specific, Ricky."

Ricky glanced at Bram before carefully replying. "Did the feds really raid your warehouse? Leave you flat busted?"

"Do we look busted to you?" Bram asked.

Edgardo gestured for Bram to let Ricky speak. He suddenly didn't seem so drunk anymore.

"You're Abraham, right?" Ricky asked, even though he clearly already knew. "Abraham Duque? You called him 'brother.' Man, I thought you was still inside."

Edgardo noted the odd question. He shook his head at Bram not to answer. "Don't worry about him, Ricky. He calls everyone 'brother.' Continue."

"I heard about The Nines, something 'bout their guns getting taken by the cops? I mean, what do you know about that?"

Edgardo whispered something to his brother. Ricky didn't know what to think as Bram promptly left the room.

"This is very helpful, Ricky," Edgardo said. "What else is being said about me?"

"That you ain't got no juice no more, that The Duke is done."

"Do rumors also say I'm an informant gone rogue?"

"Yep. Exactly. You're a rat's been thrown overboard is what they're sayin'. Is that... is that what's goin' on?"

Bram returned with Candy, who held a long, thin device, like a car antenna, along with Hank's paper coffee cup. She shut the door behind her.

Edgardo crouched to speak with Ricky eye-to-eye in his chair. "Ricky, what we have here is a misunderstanding. None of those rumors are true."

"Yeah, sure, that's what I figured."

Without warning, Bram grabbed Ricky from the chair and locked him in a bear hug, his forearm covering the young man's mouth. Candy quickly wanded him with her device, pausing near his belly. She nodded to Edgardo and handed him the coffee cup before walking out.

Keeping his arm against Ricky's mouth, Bram pulled up the man's shirt to reveal a small wired mic taped to his torso, just above his navel. Edgardo ripped it off. Ricky froze in terror. That small piece of metal felt like it was burning his skin all morning. Now, its absence felt like a gaping hole.

"I'll explain everything, Ricky," Edgardo said, clear and calm, the mic dangling from his hand. "But now's not a good time. I have customers backed up. The Jeepney's parked a few blocks south. Meet me there in half an hour. Lunch is on me."

"See ya, Ricky," Bram said, his arms still wrapped tight around the man.

Edgardo unlocked the door, opened it, and slammed it shut again, turning its deadbolt in place. Still restrained and muffled, Ricky felt confused by the little act until Edgardo dropped the mic into the coffee. Bram released him, stared at him like a demon. "Finally, it's me, you, and the brick wall..."

Ricky turned to Edgardo. "You said you wouldn't let him hurt me!"

"I guess we're both liars."

Bram threw Ricky to the cinderblock wall behind them and pressed the driver's face against it.

"Nah, man! Don't do it!"

Bram leaned in close and spoke into Ricky's ear. "You know how in the movies when a man's skull splits open and his brain pushes out? Doctor shoves it back in, sews it up? Hollywood bullshit."

"Wh... What?"

"The brain is under a lot of pressure in the skull. Out in the air, it expands like baked bread, can't put it back."

"Yo, what the fuck are you saying?" Ricky felt piss running down his pant leg.

"I'm still going to speak with Waldo," Edgardo said, "but I'm afraid I'm rescinding my offer to get you back in his good graces. Or mine."

"Rats with no loyalty don't deserve favors," Bram said through clinched teeth. He grabbed Ricky by his dreadlocks, pulled his head back, and prepared to thrust it to the wall...

"Wait, man! I ain't the only one!"

Edgardo placed his hand atop Bram's shoulder, halting him. This was the news he feared. "Explain."

"Waldo wires all his drivers!"

"Has he always done this?"

"Naw, just right now, 'cause of all your rumors and shit! He don't know what's what no more!"

"That makes two of us," Bram said with a grunt.

"What did I say about not dropping the ball with me, Ricky?"

"I can't drop it none with Waldo neither!" Ricky said, ready to burst into tears. "He got tabs on my boy! He's only six! Just got his first bike!"

Edgardo took in the unexpected turn in Ricky's words and tone. "What's his name? Your boy?"

"Richie. Junior... please, Mr. Duke, don't... his momma's strung out all the time. I'm all he's got!"

"You just shattered our trust," Edgardo said, unsure. "I don't know if I believe you."

"We can get Mr. Felix to check his story," Bram said in a moment of mercy.

"No, he'll be too busy sweeping every day, remember? We need to end this here and now."

"So, let's end it."

Bram pressed Ricky's face to the cinderblock wall again. Ricky trembled as he chose his words carefully. "Listen, I ain't in no position to screw you like it ain't no thing. Mr. Duke, you don't know what it's like when the man holds your kid over you. That's the only reason I dared to strap on that fuckin' wire, I swear."

Edgardo believed him, realizing the man's plight. He glanced at his brother. "That's why you got drunk before coming here. Liquid courage."

"Stupid, I know! But get me ten bibles and I'll swear on 'em!"

Edgardo thought for a moment, saw the dread on Ricky's face. He gestured for Bram to release him, making him gasp for breath as if he'd been drowning.

Edgardo straightened Ricky's torn shirt and handed him the coffee cup with the doused mic floating in it. "Put this thing back on. I'm gonna give you a new shirt. They're gonna ask why the feed got cut off. Tell them you spilled coffee on yourself. Understand?" Ricky nodded. "If you hear from him before I do, tell Mr. Waldo to expect me shortly."

"No one goes to see him," Ricky said. "I hear he don't see visitors no more, like months now."

"He'll see me."

Bram unlocked and opened the door. Ricky eyed the exit, still unsure, as if it might be another cruel ruse. Edgardo opened his desk drawer and pulled out a T-shirt. He poured coffee on its front and rubbed it in.

"After you put this on," Edgardo said, "I want you to remember that wall, how cold and hard it felt on your face. I hope this means no more games from you, for both our sakes."

Bram stepped up to Ricky, their faces inches apart. He spoke with a menacing whisper. "My brother's much more compassionate that I am. He believes in second chances. But you only get one warning from me, punyeta, and that was it."

Ricky nodded, never taking his eyes off Bram's. He wanted to say thank you, sir, yes sir, never again, but was too scared to speak another word. He put on the coffee-stained T-shirt, white with a red logo: "Otto's Automotive – You'll Always Drive Away Happy."

42

All Hands on Deck

Edgardo and Bram walked several blocks south down Temple Street to the Jeepney. The colorful food truck had moved from the corner near the garage to its second spot of the day, alongside a municipal office building. With sparse signage, Bram wondered what took place within those walls supposedly on behalf of the city. He told his brother it likely contained covert operations like LOCC, DEA-LA, and likely several more without official designations. Edgardo knew the old two-story structure simply housed payroll processing for police, firefighters, and public transit, but didn't bother explaining its nature, for Bram could have been right.

Hank had proposed that a late lunch might help the brothers consider their growing predicament in the aftermath of their tense confrontation with Ricky and the revelations that spilled forth from his quivering lips. Ricky himself was supposed to meet them there, or so went their cover story.

Despite what Ricky Wash may have thought, I had no intention of harming him or his family. I knew Ricky wasn't the problem so much as the unwitting harbinger of dark times ahead. Mr. Waldo used people the way I used Post-Its: valuable for the moment but disposable from the start. Unlike the old gun runner, I saw no one "below the line" in organized crime as expendable. If anything, they often turned out to be one's greatest asset.

"You sure you don't want me to take care of him?" Bram asked.

"To make up for sparing Miguel?"

"Admit it, Bata. You aren't so hot-headed about the runt being spared."

"I admit it."

Just as Calixto used Miguel – and just as I used the boy after – Mr. Waldo used Ricky Wash to test the waters. He knew I'd discover the microphone, though I admit I should have caught scent of it the moment I saw him toddling in a front of the shop in a half-drunk, half-fake haze of defiance. With or without the live audio feed, Waldo waited for one of three outcomes. First, if we had killed Wash, it would have confirmed the rumors of my compromise with the authorities. Second, if we had simply let him go with a warning, denying the gossip, Waldo might think there could be more to the story. Therein lay my hope.

The third and least likely scenario, the one Waldo was most keen to hear, was my sparing Ricky only to recruit him as an informant, like a pyramid scheme for rats. Unacceptable. Anyone working for me always has a choice. I had yet to cross that line.

A block from the food truck, Edgardo's cell phone rang. The name that appeared on its screen shouldn't have surprised him.

Sadly, I was so busy trying to outwit Waldo that I blinded myself to another player and another bold move.

"Pakshet," Edgardo muttered as he glanced at the name.

"You're starting to sound like me," Bram said. "Who is it?"

"Someone else who's likely heard the swirling rumors." Ensuring that he was out of earshot of the passers-by, Edgardo stopped to take the call, nodding for his brother to go on without him.

"Good afternoon, Rom," Edgardo said in Tagalog.

Rommel Basilio, Founder of the HK-9, sat in the backseat of his sedan, tinted windows all around. A laptop rested on the seat beside him. He smoked a Fortune cigarette while he studied the laptop screen. "Such a lovely day, Duque." Rom also spoke in his native Tagalog, his preferred language for business. "I'm surprised you answered your phone."

"Why is that?"

"I hear your business is bust, that you're wanted on all sides."

"Since when do you believe such nonsense?"

"I don't waste time with nonsense," Rom said, taking a puff of his cigarette. "I look into anything from my trusted birds."

"Is that why you called? To speak to a busted businessman?"

"So, it's true?"

Edgardo watched Bram from afar as he ordered lunch at the Jeepney food truck. "You've done your due diligence. You tell me."

"At first, I thought it can't be true. Surely, no one can flip The Duke. But then I remembered how I had to come crawling back to Waldo for guns because our deal with the Wolf gagos was sold to the pigs, a deal you put together. That's all hearsay, but I figured, if I can get raided, anyone can."

"Anyone meaning me?" Edgardo asked.

"I spoke with Waldo. He says you cancelled three trucks this week. Looks bad. Looks like you've been compromised."

"Lies don't suit you, Rom."

"You're saying I'm a liar?" Rom asked, his Tagalog quicker and more pronounced with his tense tone.

"I'm saying a man of your status and respect has no need to lie. So why now? We both know you didn't speak with Waldo. The man hasn't taken calls or seen visitors in months."

"You're right. I misspoke. I talked with his manager."

"That explains the confusion," Edgardo said. "Whoever he is, the manager is misinformed. I confess, I've had run-ins with cops lately, but nothing I couldn't handle. You know how it is. You've had to duck and weave with them before."

"I'm doing so now, dodging, retreating, regrouping. It goes with the territory. I'm just wondering if you're one punch I need to dodge."

"I shouldn't have to utter the phrase, Rom, but I'm not working with LAPD or LOCC or anyone else. You have my word."

"Did they clean you out, Duque?" Rom asked bluntly. "You might not have kissed their boots... yet... but have they bent you over?"

"They took a piece from me, sure, just like they took a piece from you in that raid. Consider it breakage."

"So the rumors about you are all bullshit?"

"Rommel, if I listened to every fleeting rumor about the HK-9, I'd wonder about you in my nightly dreams, but I don't. I trust you can handle your business."

"What about the rumor that you're getting in bed with the Mexicans?"

"That's a news flash to me."

"Let me lay it all out," Rom said. "There's talk about you walking away from our relationship, doing business only with LB-13."

"You insult me. Unacceptable." In the distance, Edgardo saw Bram take two boxed lunches to one of the stone picnic tables by the Jeepney. "Frankly, I'm tiring of these rumors about me, aren't you?"

"I'm sick of them, too, but there's so many, I can't keep track of them all."

"Then allow me to let lay it all out. There's the absurd rumor where I'm an informant for LOCC, the unthinkable notion that they raided me dry and left me penniless, and now you're telling me there's chatter about me working with the LB-13 to overthrow you. Did I leave anything out? A flying elephant, perhaps?"

"Don't forget the one where you're at war with the TSB. Apparently, Calixto Cervantes wants your head in a sack."

"That's nothing new," Edgardo said. "He's always wanted that. He thinks it'll give him an invitation to your kingdom."

Rom considered Edgardo's words.

They weren't enough.

"It's all too much, Duque. Too much. Your house is clearly in disarray. Consider our partnership closed."

"Then why call me just before I sit down to lunch? Why not just let me rot on my diseased vine?"

"After all our years together," Rom said, "I figured I owed you a phone call, a last goodbye."

"This makes you the one walking away from our relationship," Edgardo said. "I'll respect your decision."

"As I knew you would."

"So tell me, my former business partner, why shouldn't I meet with the Mexicans now?" Edgardo instantly regretted the threat but knew it made no difference at that point. He saw Bram holding up two sandwiches from his table, beckoning his brother to hang up and join him.

"Do yourself a favor," Rom said. "Get yourself an Adobo Banh Mi and a Sarsi root beer. Trust me on this."

Rom hung up. Edgardo felt alarmed upon hearing the familiar advice, word-for-word from his talk with Ricky at their first meeting. The hidden wire must have stretched back weeks, perhaps months.

It led to Rom, not Waldo.

Edgardo turned toward the distant food truck in time to see a van race toward the Jeepney, its side door sliding open to reveal two men with assault rifles.

"Bram!"

Bullets rained down on the customers sitting at tables. Edgardo ran to his brother as the hailstorm peppered the Jeepney, the tables, the customers.

Bram upturned his stone table for cover...

Edgardo pulled out his pistol and opened fire on the van...

He reached the shot-up Jeepney as the assassins raced away from the gruesome scene.

Seeing my brother ducked down as guns blazed all around, my world fell apart around me. The world moved in a slow blur as I raced to Abraham. If he had died, my last few threads of courage, decency, and humanity would have died with him. I already felt them being pulled away.

Edgardo dove to the pavement and slid to his brother, who lay flat on the cement. "Kuya! You hurt?? Kuya!" He looked out at the many customers shot, bleeding, screaming.

I should have seen it coming. Rom heard me invite Ricky to lunch 30 minutes before, enough time to put together a drive-by. Like a blind fool, I unknowingly set myself up. Bram, Ricky, and myself were to be handled in one move.

The Jeepney often changed corners, but parked in front of the garage most days. When I looked at those broken and bloody people around us, all I could think was that it could've been Hank and Candy and the crew. The thought made me nauseous. Unacceptable. I can't lose anyone else.

Surprised to find no casualties, the brothers tended to the wounded as they screamed for help while the cook called the police in a panic. Bram checked his brother for blood. His own health an afterthought, he patted their arms, legs, and chests, confirming to his relief that neither of them were harmed.

"Those fuckin' TSB buwisits!" Bram said, spitting out his words in a fury. "They're gonna pay for their little street war!"

"It's not just the TSB, Kuya. It's worse."

Lynn Harrod

Distant sirens blared as Edgardo and Bram hurried down back alleys until they reached Corazon, the tiki lounge closed at that early afternoon hour. Edgardo locked the door and crouched under one of the front windows.

Felix stood high on a ladder, decorating the room with little Christmas trees hanging upside down from the ceiling. Joey prepped the bar but stopped upon sensing the brothers' fear. He called out to Edgardo at the window.

"Somethin' goin' on?" Joey asked.

Edgardo quickly shut the blinds. "We're closed for the day."

"Hold up a sec..."

"Get the shotguns."

Upon hearing that, Joey and Felix dropped their menial tasks and readied two shotguns from behind the bar. Edgardo gestured for everyone to meet at a central table.

"What's out there, Amo?" Felix asked.

"Six police sedans, two ambulances, and a fire truck. Forensics and press will follow. Average media response time is six-point..."

"Fuck the statistics, Eddie!" Bram said. He turned to Joey and Felix. "Rommel Basilio has declared war. His Nines just tried to take out me and Eddie, down the street."

Stunned, Joey and Felix looked to Edgardo for confirmation.

"Rom and possibly Calixto," their boss said. "Hard to say."

"HK-9 and Temple Street?" Felix asked.

"Since when do those two get in bed together?" Joey asked.

"They know I have cabinets of intel on them, and now, thanks to the Wolves, they think I'm an informant."

"After all this time, why?"

"Fish was right," Edgardo said. "Rom blames me for the raid."

"And now he's buying into this rat business," Bram said.

"It all makes sense, and whether Calixto actually believes any of it, this is the opportunity he's always wanted."

"That fuckin' weasel." Joey pieced it together. "Two birds with one stone. He gets rid of you while chumming up to Rom."

"Correct."

"What happened just now?" Felix asked as he peeked through the blinds at the racing police cars. "The cops are all over something."

"Drive-by," Bram said. "They shot up the Jeepney."

"The Jeepney?"

"Not at the garage," Edgardo quickly said. He'd spotted the horror in Joey's and Felix's eyes, their fear of the worst. "Over at city payroll, eight blocks away."

"Anyone hurt?" Felix asked.

"Lots of folks," Bram said. "Old women. Kids."

"How bad is it? Are you guys okay?"

"Seven injured, but no criticals," Edgardo said. "Everybody's breathing."

"Shit."

"We're okay."

"You really think Rom is part of this?" Joey asked his boss. "I mean, it still don't make sense to me."

"Rom wired Ricky Wash," Edgardo said. "He knew where I'd be, called me moments before the attack."

"What for?"

"To gloat, to distract me when his men drove up."

"I thought just the Temple Street fucks was after you?"

"From what I know, Joey, everyone is after me right now."

"After *us*, Eddie," Bram said. "The cops and The Nines ain't just lookin' for you."

Edgardo stepped behind the bar. He singled out the Wild Turkey and downed a long pull of whiskey from the bottle before entering the back room.

Bram looked down in shame, not from his brother's need for a drink, but from his own actions to date that brought Edgardo to it. "It's my fault, this TSB-Nines bullshit."

"What do you mean?" Felix asked, afraid of the answer. "You just got out. How could any of this possibly be your..."

"I killed two of Calixto's men. Let one go."

"The two in Amo's backyard? That was you?"

"Puchanggala, it's all my fault," Bram said, ready to unravel. "All the shit my brother's dealin' with now... they shoulda never set me free."

"Kuya!" Edgardo said. "Now's not the time!"

"Nay was right. I'm bad luck wherever I go."

Joey and Felix sat on the tile floor, speechless. Edgardo returned from the bar with his arms full of ammo boxes. He laid them out on the table. "It's not on you, Kuya. The puta Wolf Pack threatened to spread rumors about me, and they were true to their word."

"Hold up, what rumors?" Joey said.

Felix finally caught up. "Rumors that Amo is broke, desperate, and flipped to the feds."

"They were a lot more specific than that," Edgardo said. "They convinced Rom that I'm lining up with the Mexicans against him."

"Calixto likely added that detail," Felix said. "The Wolves had no reason to throw in another player."

"Agreed."

Joey stared into space, stunned. "Fuck me. Everybody thinks we're rats?"

"Just me, Joey."

"There ain't no 'just you,' Eddie!" For the first time in their working friendship, Joey The Rose seemed angry and frustrated with his boss. "Bram's right, if you so much as fart in the wind, everyone assumes we're on board!"

"No one's thinking that..."

"*Everybody's* thinking that!" Joey's mind spun as he played out their dilemma. "So what's the plan? We just sit here and wait for an onslaught? I mean, those cops ain't gonna be dickin' 'round out there long! I'm surprised they ain't stormin' in here right now!"

"Does Rom know Corazon is yours?" Felix asked.

"Unknown," Edgardo said, "but the Wolves do, so assume everyone does. I expect a warrant within the hour."

"Jesus Christ," Joey said. "This bar could be our fuckin' tomb."

Bram placed his gun on the table as if it were now useless and grabbed Edgardo's hands. "You're the smart brother, Eddie. It's like you told me this morning, fists and guns don't matter, right? You *think* your way out of fights. It's kept you alive all these years when I couldn't be with you. Just tell us what to do."

Felix and Joey silently agreed, deferring to their boss's decision.

My loyal men looked at me like I had an imaginary button that could summon the Hand of God to rewind and delete the days leading to that moment, like I had the answers to everything. How wrong they were.

Edgardo pulled out his Glock 42 and looked at it for a moment, as if trying to decide if it meant anything now. He pocketed a box of ammo and looked his sorrowful brother in the eyes while considering his options. "We continue as planned."

The men looked confused.

The plan seemed dead in the water.

"What are you saying?" Bram finally asked.

"I must see Mr. Waldo."

Edgardo's trusted friends looked at each other, unsure about the strategy. Bram shook his head.

"No. Not that, Bata. Think of something else."

"Mr. Waldo doesn't see visitors anymore, Amo," Felix said. "You'll be gunned down before you pass his gate."

"I have a feeling I won't," Edgardo said.

"And where the hell'd you get that feeling?" Joey asked. "You know I don't normally question your instincts, Ed, but that old factory is a death trap. Even The Nines know better than to go near that fucked up place. Waldo has more reach, more guns, and more trained soldiers than anyone."

"I'm aware."

"We're not talkin' gangbanger punks. They're straight-up mercs."

"Mercenaries?" Bram asked.

"Their captains are ex-military," Felix clarified. "They train daily. Waldo runs them like an actual infantry unit."

"Pakshet." Bram took a deep breath. "This keeps getting better."

Edgardo understood their concern but gestured for everyone to calm down. "Waldo isn't as impulsive or blood thirsty as Rommel or Calixto. He's business first, violence last. Like me. I'm positive he's the one person not involved in this mess."

"He's waiting out the mess," Felix said, realizing. "He wants distance."

"Correct."

"Another reason to avoid his shithole factory," Joey said.

Bram took his brother by the arm to plead with him. "You're actually going to trust that man? After everything Ricky said? With two gangs hunting you down? All we have is us four! We don't have an army! Remember?"

"No, we don't." Edgardo pocketed his gun and headed for the door. "But as Felix pointed out, Waldo does."

"Is that your plan? To flip Waldo?"

"Correct."

"Pakshet!"

"So, we're to stay put at the bar?" Felix asked. "Amo..."

"Fuck the bar," Joey said, "and fuck this Custer's Last Stand bullshit. We're coming with you. All hands on deck!"

"Unacceptable," Edgardo said. "If his men see us all walking up, guns in hand like the OK Corral, he'll keep the gate locked and just open fire from the wall. Death trap. If I go alone, I'd be seen as less of a threat, and I might have a chance to clear the air."

"I agree with Joey," Felix said. "We all go."

"Unacceptable!"

"Listen to reason, Eddie," Bram said.

"All hands on deck," Edgardo said, repeating Joey's words. He realized that the big man was right, just not in the way he thought. Edgardo opened the door an inch but paused, thinking ahead for a moment. "There's no telling how far my life's been blown open. Bram, I need you to watch the house, keep Divinia and the kids safe. Call Chris and Carlo. If they're at friends' houses, tell them to stay there. Make up a story. You follow?"

Bram didn't like this course of action. "I follow."

"I agree with you, big man," Edgardo said to Joey. "Fuck the bar. Let the cops raid it. All they'll find is wine and whiskey and a few registered guns. I need you to go to the garage, watch over Hank and the crew. Don't raise any alarms."

Joey nodded, resenting their new situation.

"Felix, I need you in Eagle Rock. Keep watch on my mother's house. Nice and quiet." His assistant seemed hesitant. "I need you to swear to me."

"My honor always, Amo."

"Good man." Edgardo looked at all three men as if it might be the last time. "Keep a low profile. Keep your phones ready. We might be preparing for nothing, but we won't be caught off-guard."

"Bata, how long's it been since you even seen Waldo?" Bram asked.

"Nine years."

"Puchanggala!"

"This is the only move we have, and if I play it right, it's our best move. You need to trust me, Bram." He turned to the others. "All of you need to trust me."

Bram, Joey, and Felix looked at each other, unable to argue any further. Having no other choice, they nodded to their boss.

Edgardo took a breath and exited the bar, leaving his trusted crew to their appointed tasks.

43

Family is All

Bram arrived at Divinia's house in the Hollywood Hills, an affluent neighborhood he hadn't visited in a decade. Two sedans were parked in the driveway, but there was no sign of Christiana's Beetle. As his brother mentioned, one or both of his kids might be away, likely with school friends. It would make his job easier. The gangs would have no way of reaching them.

He knocked on the door and waited for an uncomfortable minute before, to his great surprise, his mother appeared. She wore a flowery apron and acted as if she lived there.

"Bam Bam," Reyna said, "you actually remembered your family?"

"Nay?" Bram said. "You're here?"

"Why not? I have just as much right to be here as you. My son and daughter-in-law built this house. My grandchildren were raised here."

"I just thought..." Bram questioned his mother's about-face, her jealous hatred of Divinia now faded, but let it go considering more pressing matters. "Where are the kids? Where's Div?"

"Mama, who's at the door?" Divinia asked as she emerged from the kitchen, a smeared apron wrapped around her waist.

"The Bug is gone," Bram said, referring to his niece's VW Beetle. "Where're the kids?"

"Carlo's up in his room. Chris is out with a friend."

Bram stepped inside and locked the door. He stopped himself from peeking out through the curtains, not wanting to alarm everyone. Though he hid his fear well, Divinia noticed the change on his face. His usual scowl, furrowed brow, and amused smirk were replaced by a blank expression, one of tense waiting.

"Why are you worried about the kids?" Divinia asked. It was the first time she'd seen him since his release. "Bram, what's going on?"

Bram glanced at his mother. On his way there, his only thought was to protect the family. Words didn't occur to him, how he'd break the news that they were all at the center of a gang war. To his knowledge, none of them knew anything about The Duke.

"We're in trouble," he said, cushioning his news with softer language. "Family meeting. Have everyone gather in the basement."

"We're testing recipes for Divinia's new book!" Reyna said, offended. "We're not going into some musty, damp basement."

"Our basement was refurbished, Mama," Divinia said.

"And we already know what you're going to say, Bam Bam. Looks like you're the one who's behind."

"You know?" Bram asked. His mind raced from the drive-by shooting to his smug mother standing in front of him, from his brother walking into uncertain death across town to the unmarked van he'd spotted parked on the street. "Wait, what exactly do you know?"

"Your father is recovering, even if you and your brother weren't around for support."

"Tatay? What happened?"

"Hmmph. And here I thought you knew so much."

"Mama, please," Divinia said. "Bram, Otto had a stroke. He's at Huntington now. Doctors said it was 'ministroke,' just a short blockage. He's going to be okay."

"That's why Nanay is here?"

"We're all going to see him," Reyna said, "but right now, Divinia has asked for my help with her book. We have work to do."

"We need to stay here," Bram said. "It's just until Eddie calls."

Divinia gestured for Reyna to return to the bubbling pots in the kitchen before turning to her brother-in-law. "Okay, Bram, now what exactly do *you* know?"

"First, call Christiana. Tell her to stay at her friend's house." Without realizing it, he went to the front window and closed the curtains, taking a quick peek outside.

That van was still there, parked across the street, four houses down.

"No, first tell me what 'trouble' we're all in. Did Eddie piss off the wrong customer again?" Corazon Lounge had its share of wealthy, powerful patrons who'd made jackasses of themselves with too many Rum Runners followed by Edgardo's harsh ejection. "That man never had a knack for customer service."

"No..."

"Another one of Fish's thug clients is out looking for him?" The attorney used to specialize in representing low-rent criminals who sometimes blamed him for time spent incarcerated. "Maybe an ex-boyfriend of his newest secretary?"

Lynn Harrod

"Listen to me!"

Bram hated to be the one to tell her.

It should have been Eddie.

"Div, have you heard of a man folks call 'The Duke'?"

"The Duke of what? Lancaster?" Divinia laughed, relieved, thinking it was some two-bit shylock out for payment from Bram. Her impressionable son had boasted of his uncle's famous games behind bars, poker and dice with murderers and thieves. "Is this about some gambling debt? Whatever it is, Eddie and I will settle it..."

"Eddie is The Duke."

Divinia didn't know what he meant, but the weight of his tone told her it was a disturbing secret that had been buried deep. "What Duke? What are you talking about?"

"He's based in HiFi. Surely, you've heard of him. He's a broker for criminals, a supplier, a concierge. He's a go-between for gangs."

Divinia's heart sank for she long suspected that her ex was wrapped up in affairs beyond his garage and bar, the kind that demanded late-night meetings and last-minute weekend business trips, the kind that undermined and ultimately ended their marriage. Even if she was unfamiliar with the name, she had indeed heard of The Duke of Temple Street. Every business owner in the district knew about the mysterious man who smuggled goods and washed money in and out of Historic Filipinotown, the man who ended small-time extortion, replacing it with handshake deals and an uneasy peace.

She immediately realized that peace had been broken.

"What gangs?" she asked. "You mean street gangs in East L.A.? The Mexican cartel? The mafia? Stick-up men in masks? Who?"

"All of the above, Div."

"How..." She felt ready to faint, and he prepared to catch her. "Why?"

"He did it for me," Bram said in shame. The quiver in his voice startled her. "After we left The Bay, you got him clean and straight, but I got him back into The Life. Me. The worst part is that I didn't even know it."

After failing to prove himself to Divinia, to shake his bloody past loose in hopes of a proper life, it must have killed my brother to describe my criminal career – our criminal careers – past and present. I can only imagine how my ex-wife took the news that she'd married and had children with a demon.

44

The Titan Job

Nineteen years prior, after Otto Harrison retired, sold his L.A. auto shop to Hank, and moved his family north to California's Bay Area, Abraham went by the name "Ang Makina" (The Machine), a notorious enforcer for Ang Mga Demonyo Boyz. Known locally as "SF Demonyo" (The San Francisco Demons), the rising pan-Asian street gang was based in The San Francisco Panhandle, a narrow strip of Golden Gate Park northwest of the Mission District. At 31, Bram was one of the gang's oldest members still active on the streets and was widely considered a founder.

I never would have predicted that Bram would be the one to tell Divinia about The Duke, about his own last night as a free man, and the colossal fuck-up that resulted in his prison term and my new life. At least she heard it from family. The tabloids are always heartless.

Edgardo was 26 and working for a small capital investment firm, a job Bram saw as unworthy of his little brother's gifts.

"You either bleed and sweat for your dream," Bram often said, "or you bleed and sweat for someone else's."

"Like you?" Edgardo said. "Is it your vision or Niko's that guides the Demonyo?"

"We're talking about you, Eddie, not me or Niko. No matter how much I hustle, I'll never have your brains."

"But you do, Kuya. You have my brain at your command whenever you wish."

As touched as he felt by Edgardo's loyalty, Bram winced at the thought of his brother taking orders from anyone, even himself, and he recoiled at his reckless willingness to assist the gang. Bram admired Eddie for his gifts, his ethics, and his steadfast determination to never bend or break his rules, and though Bram knew he could benefit from a genius's counsel, he refused to allow him entry into his underworld. To even discuss gang business with Edgardo would be to soil his pure soul, to cage his unlimited potential, perhaps literally. Someone had to break the "Duque Curse" that started in the Philippines and followed them across the Pacific, the long reach of criminal corruption that ruined men in their family for generations.

Eddie had to be the one to break that curse, for if even a man of his vast intellect couldn't shake the dark spirits looming over their family, all hope would be lost.

"Don't mention Niko again," Bram said. "I work for him and I'm loyal, but I don't speak his name, not at home and not with you. Understand?"

"Understood," Edgardo said.

Niko Vazquez served as the true founding leader of SF Demonyo. With the rank of Pangalawa (Second), he took over for his older cousin Juan Pablo Vazquez, ranked Una (First), an iron-fisted alley tyrant who often chose violence until the day he was locked up for life. To make his incarcerated cousin proud, Niko put together risky, elaborate heists to supplement the gang's street corner drug trade, jobs that usually centered on Bram, ranked Panglima (Fifth), the one-man army, Ang Makina.

Long before Bram was my guard dog, he served the duplicitous Niko for eight years, the thought of which sickens me even now. While I started a family and career in Los Angeles, my brother climbed the ladder in San Francisco, which felt more like descending deeper into a pit.

Just before The Titan Job – I was 34, Bram was 39 – I was transferred to an office in nearby Daly City to develop and test a new system model for my firm. The three-month assignment brought me back into my brother's life. I treasured every day with him, for as each heist grew more risky than the last, I feared Bram's time with the gang was heading to a sudden end. My instincts unfortunately proved correct, even if it didn't unfold as I'd thought.

The last ambitious job Niko Vazquez delegated to Bram in those early Bay Area days was the robbery of a computer shop in nearby Fremont, an affluent Filipino community. Tech Titan was a small, suburban storefront with high-end laptops and plasma monitors ripe for the taking. The heist comprised a cargo van outfitted with heavy-duty bull bars, perfect for ramming the front glass wall in a quick smash-and-grab, a crude strategy that had served The Demonyo well.

Edgardo caught wind of the operation and strongly advised Bram against it. "This job isn't as simple as Niko would have you believe. He's playing you."

"I've led a bum rush before," Bram said, recalling jobs in San Francisco's Jewelry District. "I can handle a little computer shop on a sleepy street. It's just business. Nobody's playin' nobody."

"That's what The Mark always thinks." Edgardo had no choice but to reveal his weeks of legwork. "Don't let the simple window display fool you, most of Tech Titan's clients are commercial contracts. The bulk of their inventory is corporate-grade servers, 200 metal shoeboxes worth ten-grand a pop, far more than any MP3 player or laptop."

"Two mill?" Bram said, shocked at the projected take, more than his last ten jobs put together. "Bata... how do you know..."

"Their front door is fortified by three bollards, cast concrete reinforced with bundled iron-core rebars, each the width of an oak tree. Even at 100 miles per hour, your van would be stopped cold, crumpled like tinfoil. If you somehow survived impact, you'd catch the attention of their PrimeSafe 505-A security system, and police response in Fremont averages 2.4 minutes."

Bram didn't question his brother. His stomach churned, for Niko had assigned him an impossible task, painting it as a routine robbery. If Bram somehow succeeded, it would prove a windfall for the gang, but if he failed, he'd be taken out of the equation with no one left in the gang to challenge Vazquez's rank.

"Niko doesn't want me out," Bram said, unsure. "All he cares about is dollars."

"He lives in the shadow of his brother, while your reputation stretches farther than his. Your men look up to you, and the kapitans defer to your judgement. Tell me I'm wrong." Bram

Lynn Harrod

couldn't argue with Edgardo's logic, having felt the pangs of contempt from his superior many times. "Niko sees you taking over one day. He's playing the game five moves ahead, Kuya."

"That's why the jobs have been tougher each time," Bram said, putting together his brother's logic.

"Correct. But with this Titan job, whether you win or lose, he wins."

"What makes you so sure that's his M.O.?"

"That's what I would do."

"He's not you, Eddie. No one is."

"No, he's certainly not me. If I were Pangalawa of the Demonyo, I would respect you. I would never throw you to the pigs."

Bram felt the pressure of his gang against the dire warning of his loyal, brilliant brother. "What can I do? I can't refuse him. He'd come for Nanay."

"He would, but I'm not saying we should refuse him. I'm saying we play it smart."

"We?" Bram said. "This is not a 'we' situation."

"Any situation that may end in my brother's death or lockup is a 'we' situation."

"Eddie, you're here for three months of office work..."

"It would normally take three months," Edgardo said, "but I finished it in two weeks."

"Of course you did."

"The rest of my time here is my own, and I intend to help you."

"I suppose you have a plan?" Bram asked. "One where we 'play it smart'?"

"I do... but I must be with you for it to work."

"Nope. No way, Eddie. Niko won't allow civilians."

"I won't be a civilian," Edgardo said. "My brother is Panglima, after all."

* * *

On a rainy winter night, Edgardo joined his brother in the basement of a tenement on Oak Street in the Lower Haight district of San Francisco, a few blocks down from the end of the Panhandle. Niko Vazquez and five of his top kapitans gathered to add Edgardo to their ranks, something Bram still hadn't fully accepted despite the lengthy vetting they just endured.

Joining "Pamilya Demonyo," the name of the gang during any rites of initiation, required more than a respected older brother's vouching. Edgardo had three nights, three tests, before any decisions were made. He met Niko, got drunk with him, and faced three of the gang's fiercest fighters, in that order.

Upon their first meeting in a field near Candlestick Park, Niko grilled Edgardo with questions about his background, his ambitions, and his curious desire to become a Demon. Bram worried that his younger brother's sterling education and clean record would exclude him from consideration, but the exchange proved to be a two-way interview. For every question Niko lobbed, Edgardo gauged the man's reaction, his choice of words, and the lines on his face. By the sixth question, Edgardo knew the man inside-out and knew exactly what he wanted to hear. He spit out responses like "Fuck my smug, White boss and his ungas kigol" and "I hope my parents see me in the news," placating the gang leader's contempt for authority and bitter regret about blood relations. If the two had been playing heads-up poker, Edgardo would have won 10 hands out of 10.

For the second night, they met in an alley off Market Street, crossing into the territory of two rival gangs. They drank cheap beer and tequila as they discussed their favorite football teams, their female conquests, and their run-ins with the city's task force, the Central Bay Gang Impact team. Underneath the drunken conversation and horseplay, Edgardo knew the true premise of the evening. Given enough alcohol, a man's loose lips would reveal all.

Edgardo had been tasked with bringing two large bottles of Don Julio tequila to the alley. The first bottle was an authentic 40% abv spirit offered as a gift for Niko, as mandated by the gang's laws. The second bottle was for Edgardo to drink to the bottom. To keep his wits, he created a convincing non-alcoholic concoction of agave juice, vinegar, bitters, and powdered dill. After chugging three beers to offer an authentic, tipsy slurring of words, he drank his fake tequila for the rest of the night. Passing that test proved as easy that the first.

On the third night, the gang gathered in the shadows near Fort Point under the Golden Gate Bridge for the "Tumalon," the violent final rite. Edgardo fought three men, each chosen by his respective Kapitan. Though he could have dispatched them quickly, he didn't want to appear so swift as to attract undue attention. The idea was to portray himself as having potential without posing a threat to Vazquez, a delicate balance Bram deemed necessary to further assuage his boss's ego.

After emerging as the winner, Edgardo's wounds were tended to while he was branded with a Philippine black eagle tattoo spanning his upper back, one that matched his brother's. Bram couldn't stand to look during the hour needed to burn his straight-laced little brother's flesh.

With the passing of each rite, Bram started to think it was a terrible idea, but Edgardo assured him it was only for the Titan job. His career in crime would begin and end there.

Passing the three tests brought the Duque Brothers to one last tradition at the Oak Street tenement on that rainy night. Known as

"Seremonya ng Pamilya Demonyo" – referred to simply as "The Ceremony" – it served as an induction of three fledgling candidates who'd proven themselves. Niko opened a bottle of Baguio strawberry wine and poured a single glass. He and each of his kapitans and totoys (new boys) pricked their fingers with a pin and added a single drop of blood into the wine. They took turns sipping the wine and swearing loyalty to Ang Mga Demonyo, to their race, and to their parents, in that order.

Though Edgardo now wore the mark of the gang across his back, Bram knew he wasn't regarded in the same light as the old vets. Despite all the talk of family, if any heat came from the cops, the totoys were seen as the weak links to take the fall.

The fifth night was the Tech Titan job, considered Edgardo's first contribution to his new family, all that effort just to accompany his brother on what would have been a doomed mission.

"I don't like this, Bata," Bram said as he drove his van, now plastered with the PrimeSafe Security logo, to the loading dock of the computer store in the wee hours of the night. Guided by his brother, he was careful to keep the van out of the dock's security camera's radius. "I still think my crew should be here."

"They'd only be a liability," Edgardo said. "The idea is to keep everyone alive and out of prison. This is a job for two men, not a flock of pumped-up trigger-happy boys out to prove themselves. It's too late to question me now."

"I would never question you. I trust you, Eddie, but you'll have to forgive me for feeling uneasy."

"I understand. You're used to being Niko's hammer, but tonight we must be precise scalpels. I can't let him take you away from me. Unacceptable."

"That's funny," Bram said. "After what I witnessed this week, I feel like he's taken you from me."

Edgardo ignored the sentiment and checked the time on his watch. "Two minutes."

"Promise me this is the only time you follow me down this road."

"Only if you promise to leave the road."

"After tonight, Bata, I swear it."

"Good man."

Bram finally realized his brother's true motive. Edgardo wasn't there merely to assure a successful heist. He became a Demon to save Bram's life and push him out of the gang.

"Take this." Bram handed his brother a Glock 17 pistol. "Just in case."

"We won't need it."

"We may not need to fire it, Bata, but you always come heavy on a job. Just the sight of it could save your life."

With no time to argue, Edgardo pocketed the pistol.

At 2:00 a.m. on the dot, they watched a security guard drive up, scan a QR code atop the storefront's door frame, and promptly leave.

"So much for state-of-the-art security," Bram said.

"The system bears the bulk of the burden," Edgardo said. "The minimum-wage rental guards are just window dressing."

"If you say so." Bram's heart continued to race.

The brothers stepped out of the van dressed in PrimeSafe uniforms, a guise to prevent onlookers from questioning their presence.

With caps covering their eyes from the overhead camera, Edgardo approached the door's keypad and punched in the eight-digit passcode, having watched an assistant manager use it from afar the day before. The man didn't bother covering the keys, something he'd done countless times before without incident. Bram expected hacking, code breaking, and laughed at how a simple pair of binoculars was all that was needed. The code would grant them entry, but exiting later would trigger the alarm, so their departure had to be final.

Once inside, Edgardo donned red-tinted glasses and pulled two teal-and-yellow Fisher-Price periscopes from his backpack. The glasses allowed him to see the intrusion laser guarding the storeroom entrance. The toy periscopes, used with precise geometry, allowed him to reflect the beam across the lobby floor, away from the lone door whose simple deadbolt proved an easy picking.

Over the next half-hour, the brothers carried servers to the rear door, stacking them five high. The task proved tougher than they had thought. Besides being heavy, the units were delicate and hard to manhandle. Soon, they had fifty of the metal boxes – roughly $250,000 in equipment – a fourth of the projected haul.

If Bram and I had left with the first 50 servers, it would have been a fitting parting gift for Bram to leave the gang. It should have been a win for all, but three factors stood in our way: Niko was promised 200 units, Bram opened the rear door early, and my intricate plan had a vital flaw.

What Edgardo failed to account for was the human element, the outlying variable that always added unforeseen risk. That element revealed itself as a second graveyard shift guard, new on the job, arriving 20 minutes early in order to meet his girlfriend later at an all-night rave.

With the alarm klaxon blaring now that the rear door was open again, the young guard, 22-year-old David Solis, caught Bram carrying a stack of servers across the loading dock. Solis hadn't seen their uniforms in the dark, and it likely wouldn't have mattered, as he raised his pistol and radio at the same time. With a gun pointed at his face, Bram forgot their cover story, their scripted response if anyone came snooping.

"We're behind schedule to upgrade the system."

"Management wants the system online again by morning."

"We're responding to a 459 false alarm."

Instead, Abraham Duque, the "hammer" of SF Demonyo, dropped the servers and lunged for the guard's gun.

Inside, Edgardo heard the crash of the gear hitting the pavement. He ran out in time to see Bram and Solis grappling for the pistol.

Bram's cap had fallen off.

The guard wrestled the weapon under his brother's chin.

In a reflex move, Edgardo raised his Glock 17 and fired at the young guard, striking his rib cage, sending him tumbling down the loading dock's concrete steps.

The brothers stood frozen for a moment. Edgardo had never taken a life, and Bram had never imagined it happening. Instead, he saw them both hunted down and locked up.

"Unacceptable," Bram said under his breath.

He looked up and saw the lone camera above the dock. His brother stood outside of its circle, but it had captured Bram and the guard.

Bram ran to his brother and snaked the gun from his trembling hand. "Take the van to Niko. Tell him I got nipped."

"What? No..."

"He'll trust that I keep quiet. He doesn't trust you yet."

"He put the eagle on my back..."

"It just means you earn for him," Bram said. "It don't mean trust!"

As Edgardo stood, lost in his thoughts and actions, Bram quickly loaded the last of the servers into the van and slammed the rear doors.

"Go now, Bata!"

"We can both beat this!"

"Take the gear to Niko! I gotta face the cops."

"Why?"

"If this man dies, it will be a murder rap!" Bram said as he wiped Edgardo's fingerprints off the gun with his sleeve, replacing them with his own.

Of course, Bram wanted to save the guard. David Solis wasn't a hardened criminal, a member of a rival gang. He was a civilian, and whether or not it meant saving them from a prison sentence, the fierce enforcer of SF Demonyo couldn't live with what he deemed an innocent life lost, especially if its fallout might wrap around Eddie.

Worse, he didn't want Edgardo to live with the fact that he'd murdered someone, a young guard who only wanted to meet his girlfriend.

"This is the only way, Bata. It's too late to question *me* now."

As ordered, Edgardo nodded to the new plan. Careful to keep out of the camera's sight, he entered the van and drove it to Niko on Oak Street, as planned.

The gang leader was pleased with the bounty, and only slightly disturbed to hear of Bram's capture.

45

Full of Wolves

"I don't understand," Divinia said, having just heard an abridged version of that fateful night's events. "This Niko person got a quarter-million in goods."

"Yes, but he saw it as being denied the full two million," Bram said. "I was put away in debt to him, and Edgardo spent years making good on the promise. He had to, because my loved ones were his."

The details still didn't add up for her. "Why didn't he just pay back the Demonyo over time? We were doing well."

"My debt involved more than money. There were relationships tied to that job."

"Other gangs," she said, putting it together.

"Eddie did whatever he needed to do."

"So he became 'The Duke'."

"Eddie didn't make up that tanga name, the gangs did. He just used it as a calling card." Bram hated the blank stare across her face. "Div, I understand if this is a lot to take in. He only told me the day I got out."

As dread sunk in, Divinia pulled out her cell phone and called her daughter, only to get her voice mail: *"The voice mailbox of the person you are calling is full and is not currently accepting messages..."* Divinia hung up and nearly threw her phone to the floor. "Dammit, girl!"

While she tried calling again in vain, Bram looked out the front window at the van down the street. He called his brother.

"Eddie? Where you at?"

"I'm nearly at Waldo's," Edgardo said. "Is my family safe?"

"I'm with them. Nanay is here, too." Bram thought of mentioning Otto's hospital stay but didn't want to add more logs to the wildfire burning in his brother's mind as he prepared to risk his life with the gun runner.

"Good man," Edgardo said, assuming his parents were together. "You stay with them. I'll leave it up to you if you want to tell the old man. He knows about me, but keep Nay in the dark."

"There's someone else here, too."

Edgardo feared the worst, imagining an SUV full of Temple Street Boyz invading his family's home. "Who's there, Bram?"

"Not sure. A van's on the street, unmarked, no windows, been there this whole time."

Edgardo pictured the van outside his family's house. He knew the kinds of cars the different outfits used.

TSB drove muscle cars and SUVs...

HK-9 drove luxury sedans...

LB-13 drove trucks and lowriders...

"Call Felix. Have him run the plate."

"What good will that do?" Bram asked.

"If it's not hot, it's likely full of Wolves."

* * *

C.B. sat inside the surveillance van, back in his MC leathers and patches. He felt alarmed at having just heard Bram's half of the brothers' conversation through the microphone hidden in the jade plant.

"Were we just made?" one of his agents asked.

"Too soon to tell," C.B. said. "We have no way of knowing if he can..."

BOOM! BOOM! BOOM!

Before he could finish his thought, a loud pounding on the side of the van jolted them all silent. They remained frozen, but the pounding continued.

BOOM! BOOM! BOOM!

"Either you open this tin can or I do!" Bram yelled outside.

C.B. recognized the distinct voice. To his agents' dismay, he slid open the side door, exposing his operation to Abraham Duque.

"So, my brother was right," Bram said, in awe of the elaborate display. "How long you got eyes on the house?"

"This night only."

"Bushet! You got ears in there, too? Or is it 'too soon to tell?'"

"What do you want?"

"I want you to shut up and listen." Bram handed his cell phone to the confused drug enforcement agent.

Defeated, C.B. shut his eyes and held the phone to his face. "I assume this is Eddie?"

*When Bram described the van outside my family's home,
I instantly knew who sat within. It took some convincing
on my part to keep my brother from from lashing out at
the lurking agents. I didn't want him back behind bars,
but more importantly at that moment, I needed Cyrus
Bernard's help, perhaps more than he needed mine,
though I certainly wouldn't show my hand. Instead, I
had to establish dominance with a seasoned drug
enforcement special agent in the span of a five-minute
phone call.*

"Mr. Bernard," Edgardo said on the other end. "People I care about call me Eddie. I prefer that you call me Mr. Duque with the same grain of respect you showed me at the prison."

"What can I do for you, Mr. Duque?"

"How's my family?"

"They're fine. Your brother can testify to that."

"They may not be fine long," Edgardo said. "There's a war going on, a war you and your keystone cops started."

"So I've heard."

"Then you've heard about the food truck?"

Even having been engrossed with Divinia's house, C.B. had indeed been made aware of the drive-by shooting only moments before. "Yes, I was told just now, and I'm sorry."

"Did you bother to play this out when you sketched it on the whiteboard in your fake biker clubhouse? Were my family's lives included in your PowerPoint?"

"I can assure you we didn't factor in..."

"I told you, my wife and children know nothing of our business."

"I'm glad you finally see it as *our* business... Mr. Duque."

"You made that abundantly clear," Edgardo said. "It feels fitting now, the way you laid it all out inside a prison."

"What's not abundantly clear is how you've managed to stay in operation after our little raid. My guess is you had facilities we haven't yet discovered."

"Let's stay on topic, Mr. Bernard. A minute ago, you asked what you can do for me. Protect my family. You're already in position. My brother described your van. Standard protocol for an eleven-foot survey-and-research vehicle is three field agents, so I assume you have two Wolves sitting beside you. One of them is monitoring my wife while the other is keeping tabs on the HK-9."

"Not the TSB?" C.B. asked. "You sure about that?"

"Calixto Cervantes is too small of a fish for you. His capture would be a blip on your resume, but Rommel Basilio, head of one of the largest outfits in Los Angeles, now that's a catch worthy of a promotion."

"Interesting. And how the hell would I manage that?"

"Obviously, you tapped poor Ricky Washington, had him bugged whenever he checked in with Rom. The man is so desperate, he's destined to wear ten wires to his own funeral."

"Is that so?" C.B. asked, feeling his control slipping away.

"Just like you tapped Miguel Hortiz at my warehouse, just like you considered tapping Carlo while he was in custody. You wisely concluded that flipping my son, a minor, was too risky, too far of a long shot. My son may have resented me at the time, but you figured he'd be loyal after I sprung him from lockup..."

"That's enough." C.B. didn't bother denying Edgardo's detailed, almost clairvoyant deduction. "Like I said, your family is safe."

"And they must stay safe, Mr. Bernard. If one of them gets so much as a paper cut, I blow this whole thing wide open."

"Would you really? I find that hard to believe."

"Of course you would," Edgardo said. "When you look at me, you don't see a family man protecting his home. When you look at my brother, you don't see an ex-con trying to go straight. All you see are criminals in quicksand, but in my world, a wanted man is a trusted man. When you have nothing left to lose, men take you for your word."

"There's always something else to lose," C.B. said in an ominous tone. "Make no mistake, you two *are* criminals sinking in the sand. That's how your rivals see it. Exposing me won't change that."

"Well, the way this criminal sees it, my life is blown up, quite literally. Why not yours as well?"

C.B. followed the path Edgardo threatened. If he spread word of the Wolves' true nature, whether or not all the gangs bought the story, it would mean disbanding his team and flushing years of covert work down the drain. Every one of his leads would shrivel away. They'd either start again from zero or simply fold, handing the Duke files to another ambitious, less experienced agent. "Hold your fire. We want the same thing, Mr. Duque."

"Yes, we do. I simply wanted to remind you of that. Think of the old saying, 'Be careful what you wish for.' You wanted us to have a symbiotic relationship, and so you've got it, in sickness and in health. If I go down in flames, your Wolves burn with me."

C.B. caught the firm context in Edgardo's voice.

You work for me, now.

"Your family will remain safe," C.B. said. "I promise."

"And what is that worth? The promise of a failed cop."

"Good question." With no other options, C.B. folded his poker game, gave up the pointless bluff, and took off his many masks. "Maybe I am a failed cop. I'm also a family man, like you. I have a boy, about Carlo's age. Marshall. Friends call him 'Mars.' We haven't spoken in over a year. My wife, Linda, stopped calling to see if I'm coming home for dinner long ago. She says I'm a bigamist, you see. My second wife is my work, my second family is the pack. We're still married but, like Marshall, Linda gave up on us. But I'm sure you already ran a background on me."

"I did," Edgardo said. "The hour we first met."

"You're wrong in thinking I don't see all that in you. If a man with nothing left to lose is a trusted man, you can rest assured that your family will be safe with me."

"Good man." Edgardo knew that C.B.'s moment of vulnerability was merely a tactic, but he heard the timbre of truth in his tone.

"Now that we see eye-to-eye, Mr. Duque, tell me, what are you going to do?"

C.B. waited in silence before realizing Edgardo had hung up the call. He returned the cell phone to Bram who hadn't heard his brother's side of the conversation, but didn't need to. The veteran agent's fallen expression told him everything.

"Somehow, you managed to play my brother once," Bram said, "but no one makes him a fool a second time."

"I believe you."

Before Bram could pocket his phone, he felt it vibrate a second before it rang.

He looked at the screen.

It showed "Joey The Rose."

46

Meeting Mr. Waldo

A light rain pattered the windshield of Edgardo's copper BMW i8 coupe, his second favorite car behind the Mercedes SLK which now belonged to Calixto Cervantes, a sacrifice to protect Miguel. Having just ended his call with C.B., Edgardo continued to drive south down the winding freeway through Los Angeles with both urgency and awe. He'd always loved the city on nights like this, an overcast sky over an evening shower.

Part of my strict self-discipline is to recognize the peace and beauty around me, no matter how dire the situation. It keeps me grounded, calm, and most importantly, in control of my chaos – my plight, the strategies circling in my mind, my crippling OCD, and the fierce urge to pound a magnum of Kentucky bourbon to drown it all.

Lynn Harrod

The rain dissipated as Edgardo exited the freeway and entered an industrial district, a few blocks from his destination. It felt oddly predestined.

Waldo's Ice Cream Company was based in Rancho Dominguez, California, 45 minutes south of my domain. The vast structure first served as a Wonder bread factory, then a snack assembly line for 7-Eleven, and finally a Mexican ice cream factory before the West Coast's biggest gun runner bought the foreclosed property. Since the facility was already outfitted for ice cream manufacture – complete with a fleet of refrigerated trucks – it made sense to open a frozen treat business as both a laundering front and a distribution network for black-market weapons.

The large industrial building sat among vacant warehouses and shuttered factories facing the 710 Freeway and Los Angeles River. As desolate as the area felt during daylight hours, approaching the sprawling property at night after a brief downpour felt like being on an alien world. The air felt thick and muggy. The sky swirled with dark clouds, the sounds of the city proper had faded into the distance, and the dirt parking lot devolved into a muddy field.

The lot surrounding the factory on three sides could accommodate 500 cars, but I saw none that night. This meant that Waldo's crew hid their numbers by parking within the tall, red brick walls of the compound. The recent rain helped with their subterfuge, having washed away any tire tracks. I had no way of knowing how many of his soldiers waited inside.

Using a 12-inch night vision scope, Edgardo looked up through his sunroof and saw two men in military fatigues, armed with rifles, standing atop the wall. Though the monochromatic, low-resolution view made it hard to tell their race, he assumed they were Black, like all of Waldo's men. The way they flanked the wooden main gate from above gave the scene a medieval feel.

He drove his i8 onto the muddy lot, the sleek hybrid car's whisper-quiet engine helping to hide his arrival. He didn't want Waldo to know he was approaching. Instead, he wanted the old man to know the precise moment he was there.

Edgardo stepped out of his car and tramped across the thick mud to the looming gate and stood almost invisible in the darkness for nearly a minute before the guards overhead noticed him. He'd hoped to hear voices upon their discovery of him, to better gauge their numbers, but the piercing whine of the opening gate covered any mad scrambling taking place behind the wall.

When the gate came to a rest, the mechanical whining stopped, and Edgardo stood in silence as two Black men emerged, one tall and lean, the other short and stocky. Like the guards high on the wall, they wore army gear and held their rifles ready as they approached their curious visitor on an uninvitingly dark, drenched night. Upon closer view of his stone face through the rain, they smiled at each other as if amused by the lone Asian man in the three-piece suit standing in the muck.

Despite their smug grins, these trained, armed men were cautious, afraid. I may have feared being outnumbered and overwhelmed, but they were scared simply because they were unfamiliar with me, a serious man who knew them well, having read their criminal records six years prior. Due diligence is always the best weapon.

"You selling' somethin', Money?" Reggie Simms asked, eyeing Edgardo's custom suit. The short, 28-year-old bulldog grinned at their visitor's expressionless face. "Motherfucka' looks like he's a salesman or a preacha' man."

"Nuh-uh, boy looks more business than all that." Charlie Wood, the taller of the two guards and oldest of his crew at 40 years, wore a tactical vest over a long-sleeve shirt, a contrast to his associate's simple fatigues. No doubt, he'd held high rank after his eight years with the outfit. He loomed over Edgardo and gave him a long, stern look as if trying to read his mind. "He ax'd you a question, Money. What you want here?"

"I need to speak with Mr. Waldo," Edgardo said firmly.

"You shit outta luck then, my man, 'cause he ain't seeing no one, ain't gonna today, ain't gonna tomorrow..."

"I assure you, he'll want to see me."

Charlie laughed. He glanced at Reggie who held his amused grin. "Oh, he gonna see you, huh? You special? How you figure?"

"He's a businessman, as am I."

"You make me laugh, Money!" Charlie said. "It's been a minute since anyone's put a smile on my face. I mean, you's business, he's business... shit, we all business here, aren't we?"

"Aren't we?" Edgardo said, mimicking him. "Or ain't we?"

Reggie Simms was a young thug in training, beginning and end of assessment, but the more Charlie Wood spoke, the more his inner-city gangster "accent" slipped. Proper grammar and an inquisitive approach poked through street slang and attitude, betrayed his forced street talk. I knew Wood was smarter than he presented himself. His record even revealed some college, just 30 units shy of a B.A. Good. It would save time.

"To answer your question," Edgardo said, "Mr. Waldo will see me because I'm The Duke."

As predicted, Charlie Wood knew the name. His cocky expression dropped as he raised his rifle and nodded to his oblivious comrade to do the same. "And I'm Captain Kangaroo."

"I am who I say, and I say let me in."

"And I say you ain't seein' nobody!" Charlie seemed nervous, much to his associate's confusion. "I say you got five seconds to walk back to your Beemer and drive off in one piece!" He spoke into his collar radio to his men on the wall. "Anyone or anything else out there?"

"Nothing," a voice said on the com. "He's alone."

"The Duke?" Reggie asked, his gun still locked onto their visitor. "Charlie, you gonna tell me who the hell is this guy?"

Simms was clearly too green or too stupid to know me, which likely meant he also had no grasp of who he'd been working for. I hoped for more rookies like him on the other side of the wall. That kind of ignorance always helps.

"Five seconds, Money!" Charlie said. "One!"

Edgardo slid his hand onto his belt buckle and imagined the scene unfolding, his countdown aligned with Wood's...

One: Disarm Wood. Strike with a kick to the neck.
Two: Smash Simms's temple with the butt of Wood's rifle.
Three: Dagger against Woods's neck. Use him as a shield.
Four: Gain control. Enter the property with Wood.
Five: Hope there aren't more than three other guards.

Edgardo moved in a flash...

All in one swift motion, he slapped Charlie's rifle upward, setting it off – BLAM! BLAM! – as it swung away... threw a high kick to the back of Charlie's neck and grabbed his rifle... turned and slammed the butt of the rifle to Reggie's head... spun around, dropped the gun... pressed his dagger to Charlie's throat, clutching him as a human shield.

With Charlie subdued in seconds, Edgardo turned to Reggie and kicked his rifle away, both firearms now in the mud behind him. Unarmed, with his partner's life in jeopardy, Reggie raised his palms and backed into the property.

"You're Charlie, right?" Edgardo asked his captive knowingly, dagger to his neck. "Charlie Wood?"

"Yes," Charlie said in a defeated tone, unnerved by how the man knew his name. "Charlie Wood."

"Listen carefully, Charlie Wood. The tip of an extremely sharp blade is resting on the intersection of your brachiocephalic vein and your left external jugular. Our movements must match like ballroom dancers. Understand?"

"Understood." Charlie struggled to remain frozen, calm, his trembling jaw betraying him.

"If you so much as hiccup, Charlie Wood, I'll make a long, deep lateral slice, and not even the world's preeminent thoracic surgeon could save you from the esophageal perforation. Understand all that?"

"Understood."

"Good man. Looks like you paid attention during your 90 units of pre-med at Northridge College."

Charlie felt nauseous. Never had the towering man been so completely dominated. He felt the blade against his neck and imagined it easily slicing through his flesh. It somehow felt far less frightening than the man who spoke like an encyclopedia and knew every minute detail of his life.

Edgardo held his captive tight and advanced into the property. By the time they passed through the open gate, Reggie had fled, likely gathering his comrades.

To Edgardo's dismay, six more Black men armed with rifles faced him in a semi-circle. They stood their ground, careful not to provoke the intruder.

"No one needs to die!" Edgardo called out. "I just need to speak with Waldo! If I die, I promise some you will join me! Unacceptable! This is strictly business!"

"Listen to him!" Charlie said, his voice muffled by the blade's side pressed against his throat. He knew the man could back up his wild threat, even if it meant they'd both end up dead. But his crew, who'd been behind the wall, hadn't seen Edgardo's movements a moment ago, and to Charlie's horror, they didn't back down. "Hold your fire!"

"Take it easy, boys." The calm female voice came from a middle-aged White woman behind the guards. "Like our guest said, this is business." She walked between them, into the middle of the conflict. The guards lowered their weapons, and Edgardo lowered his as he released Charlie.

"Good evening, madam. My name is Edgardo Duque. You must be the voice of logic and reason here."

"Someone must be." Melinda Emery, a 55-year-old with curly, shoulder-length gray-streaked hair, wore a blue pantsuit and black block-heel pumps. She walked up to her guest, sizing him up. "Search him. Bring him to my office."

Melinda entered the massive building as if returning from an evening stroll. Edgardo quickly sheathed his dagger and raised his hands, allowing Charlie to frisk him, failing to find the hidden blade.

"You think you know me, Money?" Charlie asked, nervous, as he frisked him thoroughly. "My name? My schoolin'?"

"You will call me Mr. Duque," Edgardo said during his frisk. "I know all about you, Mr. Charles Benjamin Wood, Junior, and the sooner you know all about me, the better for us both."

* * *

With guns at rest, Charlie and three of his men escorted Edgardo through the facility, past loading docks with fleets of identical ice cream trucks, down peeling hallways, deep into the old factory. They reached an open set of ornate double doors.

"This is you... Mr. Duque."

Edgardo stepped inside with Charlie close behind.

The office was immense, extravagant, pristine, as if belonging to a Beverly Hills high-rise, a contrast to the old factory's crumbling hallways and exterior.

Mr. Waldo's office was exactly as I remembered, every polished detail intact. The only thing missing was Waldo himself. This woman apparently took his place. Whoever she was, I had a feeling she wouldn't sway easily.

"Am I also to call you Mr. Duque?" she said. "Like you told poor Charlie?'

"Correct."

She sat behind a grand mahogany desk surrounded by tall Art Deco murals, Cathedral windows, and shelves of bric-à-brac. She spoke with a tone of confidence and authority.

"First, I need assurances," Melinda said. "How do I know you're really Duque?"

"Who else could I possibly be?"

"What a naive question. Sure, you handled my men the way The Duke might, but you could be a highly trained agent for LOCC. I've had run-ins with those rowdy boys recently."

"My sympathies." Edgardo noted how Charlie remained by the door as he sat on a leather lounge chair in front of Waldo's desk, now Melinda's. "I had my own confrontation with them last week."

"Either they're getting smarter or we're getting sloppier, Mr. Duque, if that is who you are."

"You have me at a disadvantage. I came to see Mr. Waldo, yet here I sit with a stranger."

"Melinda," she said. "Melinda Emery. I'm Walter's Operations Manager. Now, back to those assurances."

Walter, Edgardo noted.

"I could list our last five transactions if that would ease your mind," he said.

"It wouldn't. Any feds watching closely could tell me that, and they're always watching closely. I can practically feel them on the back of my neck from the moment I wake up. Speaking of waking up, care for an Irish Coffee? I find it's a nice pick-me-up in the evening."

Edgardo nodded. Melinda swiveled her chair to a small espresso machine behind her.

"Coffee, Charlie?" she asked her guard across the room. "You deserve one after that little scare out there."

"No, thank you, ma'am."

She poured two coffees and gently topped them with whiskey and an inch of cold cream. Perfection. She slid one across the desk to Edgardo.

"So you claim to be The Duke. I confess, I've long been interested in meeting you. So far, you definitely fit the description."

Edgardo sipped his coffee, the whiskey a welcome respite. "And I confess, I still don't know who you are, other than the 'Operations Manager.'"

"Let's not forget, I'm also the 'voice of logic and reason.' Is it true you're a genius?"

"Lately, I'm not so sure."

"Yes, I've heard. Still, Walter says you have an unmatched intellect. That's high praise coming from him." Melinda glanced at her man by the door. "The dozen guards you encountered on your way here. Pick one. Describe him head-to-toe."

"I saw only ten men," Edgardo said. "Two out front, six in the yard, two on the wall, four fewer than my last visit nine years ago. I could describe each of them, but what would that prove? LOCC agents are trained to observe and remember such details."

"But not like The Duke. Something to eat? I have a Chilean sea bass that's perfect for two."

"The coffee is enough. I'm eager to speak to 'Walter.'"

"I know. All this messy gossip about you being raided dry, going rouge, working for the feds. It must be exhausting."

"Damage control always is," Edgardo said. "I imagine it's exhausting for us both. I sit at the center of a web Walter helped weave, and now that web is falling apart. I must see him."

Melinda sipped her coffee, still unsure about her guest. "I'm afraid that's impossible. He just left to catch the last flight to Miami. Big meeting. He's expected there at eight o'clock tomorrow morning. He likes to arrive early, gives him time to prepare. So, for better or worse, you have me to deal with. I'm authorized to handle any adjustments to our arrangement."

"Then I consider myself lucky."

"If you believe in luck, you're gonna need it, Mr. Duque."

"As Walter always says."

"You mentioned you last met him nine years ago," Melinda said.

"Correct."

"Surely, The Duke can do better than that. What time of year did you meet? What month?"

"It was Friday, May 4, 2012. We were scheduled for two o'clock, but he was on a phone call about acquiring five new trucks, speaking with someone named Tom. We shook hands at seven after."

"Maybe you are Duque. I ask because I wanted to know if you met Walter before or after my time. I'm curious. What do you know about me? Now that we've had coffee together."

Wherever Mr. Waldo was, he'd prepared his assistant well. He surely listed ways to identify me, questions to separate me from a garden variety drug enforcement agent. I was happy to oblige.

"Nothing much. I know your name, what you look like, and your scent."

"My scent?" she said with a laugh. "Are you a friendly bloodhound or a wild wolf?"

"I'm just a businessman."

"So humble. And what is my scent, exactly?"

"Nina Ricci, L'air Du Temps."

Melinda offered a grin. "You are Duque. I heard you were like a carnival mentalist with your little mind tricks."

"I don't need tricks," Edgardo said.

"You'd have me believe you can identify a woman's perfume just like that? Did you go to Sak's, smell hundreds of bottles, and commit them all to memory?"

"No. I deduced the fragrance." He sniffed the air, her scent still strong. "Carnations, roses, peaches, cloves, jasmine, over a musky base of sandalwood and cedar."

"And you know that formula how?" she asked.

"I read it once in a magazine ad, in my dentist's waiting room."

Melinda laughed at what she assumed was a parlor trick. "L'air Du Temps is a vintage perfume. I've had that bottle for 30 years. There are no magazine ads for it."

"There were when I was nine."

Melinda sat in silence, taken aback by Edgardo's deduction. She remembered his brief exchange with Charlie. "Walter always said you're feared for your intelligence. I didn't know what he meant until now."

"Deducing your perfume is meaningless. What matters is that I can detect a lie when I hear it."

"I'm a liar? How do you know?"

"I know Walter never goes to meetings. People come to him. I know the last flight from LAX to Miami leaves at 11:45 p.m. American Airlines, as of Monday, anyway. That would land him in Miami at 7:45 a.m., far too thin a margin for his supposed 8:00 a.m. meeting. I also know there was a light rain earlier, yet there were no fresh tire tracks in the mud leading away from here when I circled the property. So yes, Melinda, you're a liar. The question is, why?"

Melinda found herself again caught unaware by his uncanny observations. "Doesn't matter. I'm fully authorized to..."

"So you've said. But I'll only speak to Walter."

"I hate repeating myself, but I told you that's impossible. It seems we're at an impasse, Mr. Duque."

Edgardo finished his coffee and slid the cup back to Melinda. "I'm his go-between for six L.A. gangs which I estimate accounts for 70 Percent of his operation. He'll want to meet with me, and he'll be angry if he doesn't, as would I."

"I see." Edgardo's tone came across as a threat. Melinda flipped up a cover on her desk phone and placed her finger on a button. "You'd be angry? What would happen if I pressed this button to summon my men and have you killed?"

"I'd be dead, along with 70 Percent of your operation. Unacceptable."

"Indeed."

"There's an Armenian outfit that's been waiting for the chance to run guns through me. Perhaps I should revisit their proposal. That's no one's first choice, of course."

Melinda leaned forward, offended by the ultimatum. "Maybe you aren't The Duke after all. You call me a liar, tell me you're angry, and threaten to do business with our competitors. None of those are reasons to let you walk out of here alive." She nodded to Charlie, who walked across the room toward Edgardo, gun ready.

"I also have a button," Edgardo said.

Charlie hesitated. He looked to his boss.

"My brother's finger is on it now."

Edgardo walked up to an Art Deco mural of families in a park, children lined up at an ice cream vendor. A large stained-glass clock was mounted atop the mural.

"You have sixteen active trucks, twenty at this time of the month. They're on rotation, which means they've all been to my garage. You may have planted a wire on your drivers, but I've planted fuel-air thermobaric bombs under each truck."

"Now who's the liar?" Melinda said. "The science lingo is a nice touch. I imagine it usually rattles folks. It sure shook up Charlie."

"Forgive the way I talk. You can take the boy out of school, but you can't take the school out of the boy." Edgardo looked up at the enormous clock. "Let me put it another way. If I don't emerge from this factory in 22 minutes, my brother presses the button, the bombs go off, and your fleet of trucks, wherever they may be, will explode and burn intensely for half an hour, given their volatile cargo. I assure you, I am walking out of here alive."

Melinda leaned back in her chair, her stone expression failing to hide her apprehension. Charlie remained in the middle of the room, holding his gun ready, unsure.

"You're bluffing," she said. "The desperation of a marked man. Such a catastrophe would spill over onto your own operation."

"It wouldn't concern me since I'd be dead. So I say again, and I also hate repeating myself, I'll only speak with Walter."

"I see." Out of options, Melinda had a tough decision to make. After a moment to think, to read her guest's face, she rose from her chair and walked around to the front of her desk. "Well, now that we've gotten to know each other better, let's go see him."

47

Storm's Coming Down

At the end of another business day, with sunset approaching, Joey Gallo parked his Honda Gold Wing motorcycle in front of Otto's Automotive, in the space normally taken by the Jeepney food truck. Knowing that the familiar truck now sat riddled with bullet holes while its cooks and patrons recovered in the hospital sent a shiver through him. He'd always considered the small pink-and-white truck beyond the circle of their business dealings like an unspoken neutral zone. Until that day, he'd only seen criminals out for each other. He never signed up for innocent bystanders, especially those he knew well.

The scene at the shop appeared normal, with three cars jacked up and being worked on, while two were next in line. The crew usually tried to get as many cars out as possible before locking up for the day, finishing their work shortly after dark, but Joey's news would disrupt their routine.

"Big man?" Hank emerged from the first bay, clipboard in hand, surprised by his visitor. He'd never seen Joey away from his bar just as no one saw him away from his garage, a mandate from Edgardo. Until that moment, the two men had only met at social gatherings. "Something wrong with the Gold Wing?" He hoped for a simple "yes," though Joey's stern face said otherwise.

"Bike's fine."

"I figured. One thing I always loved about Honda bikes is their reliability. Just turn the key and go..."

"We got problems," Joey said, interrupting his friend. "I need you to close the shop and head home."

"Come on, Joey, we're backed up here! Is this coming from Eddie?" Hank realized the folly of his question. "Of course, this is coming from Eddie. I love the man, but he doesn't know what it's like to belly up to a transmission for six hours. Our customers deserve our time."

"Hank, no offense, but fuck the customers and get your ass home now. Tell 'em it's a family emergency. Better yet, tell 'em the power went out. Whatever. We gotta go."

"I'll tell the two folks waiting their turn to come back tomorrow, but I'm not leaving until the current jobs are done. That's two oil changes and buttoning up a rear diff. Those folks need to drive home in something. Gimme a half-hour, tops."

Joey felt nervous about the plan. "A lot can happen in a half-hour, Old Man, especially when it's a half-hour heading into night."

"Well, it's a good thing I got Joey The Rose here, isn't it?"

Joey pulled Hank close, kept his voice low. "The pink truck was hit by a drive-by."

Hank remembered seeing cop cars racing down Temple Street. He feared the worst, and Joey could see the dread dawn on him.

"Ed and Bram survived," Joey said, "but this shit just started. The shop could be next."

"Where's Eddie?" Hank finally felt the fear cut into his calm. He worried more about Edgardo's well being than his own, knowing what he might do to contain the chaos. "Where's Bram?"

"Bram went to Div's house. Ed is on his way to Waldo's. Do you get what I'm saying?"

Hank nodded in shock. He clutched his clipboard with shaking hands and looked around the neighborhood as he digested the news. Before he could start his string of apologies to the customers, a lowered, primered pickup pulled up.

"I'll get rid of him," Joey said, his eyes on the Black man behind the wheel.

"No, I don't think we want to shoo him away just yet." Hank recognized the driver and guided his lowrider truck into an empty bay. The mere sight of him made Hank grip his clipboard white-knuckle tight.

Ricky Wash stepped out of the matte black pickup, wearing a hood and sunglasses, an odd choice given the hour.

"We weren't expecting a load today," Hank said.

"Do you see a fuckin' ice cream truck?" Ricky asked. "And I ain't here for no tune-up."

Joey's expression begged an introduction.

"Big man, this is Ricky Washington," Hank said.

"The fuckin' rat with the fuckin' wire," Joey said, turning to Ricky. "Yeah, I heard all 'bout Ricky Washington."

"That's history, Joey," the old man said. "Eddie and Bram straightened it out. Ricky delivers Tuesdays and Thursdays."

"For Waldo." Joey knew that the gun runner's crew comprised hardened Black men.

"Not for no one," Ricky said. "I'm out. Me and my son are takin' off, and you should, too."

Hank spotted a Black pre-teen boy in the front seat of the pickup, blissfully engrossed in his iPhone video game. "Is that Richard?"

"Junior."

"Good lookin' kid. Must take after his mother." Hank waved and smiled at the boy. He pulled Ricky aside as if the man hadn't been roughed up by the Duque Brothers earlier in the office ten feet away. "Eddie is meeting with your boss tonight. I'm sure he'll smooth this whole thing out..."

"You don't get it." Ricky looked over his shoulder before continuing, something he'd done all day. "I'm out. Gonna be on the freeway in a minute. HK-9 is out gunnin' for The Duke, for you, maybe Waldo next, maybe me. Storm's comin' down, man."

"What makes you say that?" Hank asked. He wondered how one of Waldo's low-level drivers could possibly know a rival gang's plans. "Are you stating a fact or just spitballin'?"

Ricky looked around again, nervous that the brothers would return at any moment.

"Hank asked you a question." Joey stood between Ricky and his son, his large frame keeping the kid from witnessing their tense exchange. "Talk. Now."

"That wire you ripped off my chest? I didn't wear it for Waldo."

"What the hell are you talking about..."

"He wore it for Rommel," Hank said. He felt flushed, his face and chest burning from the grim realization. "Well, shit..."

Ricky blurted out the rest as fast as he could get the words out.

"I was wired by Waldo just for a day, that day we met. It's something he does with all his new drivers. But The Nines pulled me over, wanded me, and caught it. Shit luck, I thought I was a dead man. Instead, Rom gave me five-grand and the promise that Junior would live to see high school if I bugged you guys. That's the truth, all of it, I swear on my mom's grave."

"Why not tell Eddie earlier?"

"You crazy?" Ricky said. "After what his psycho brother did to me? Man, I made sure they wasn't nowhere around when I came back here. I don't plan on seeing them again."

"Hold up, what the fuck does all this mean?" Joey asked.

"It means Rommel Basilio heard our private chat." Hank suddenly felt overwhelmed. "Godammit, he heard me tell the boys to go have a late lunch at the truck..." He quickly waved Candy over and gave her a quiet order. "Go to the breaker box, shut off all the power. Do it now."

"What the fuck?" she said. "I'm in the middle of a teardown. That F-150 is laid out in pieces."

"Please do as I say." Hank kept his head low with a fake smile on his face as he spoke to her. "Day's almost done anyway."

"But I ain't almost done..."

"Shut it down, Candy. Everything stops. Tell everybody we lost power and we need to close until it's resolved."

"This is nuts, Hank. You know I'm gonna be fuckin' lost if I gotta pick this shit up tomorrow."

"I'll explain later," Hank said, eyeing the giant man before them, "as soon as it's explained to me."

Candy noticed Joey impatiently pacing in front of an unnerved Ricky Wash. "What's their deal?"

"Breaker box. Now. Please."

Picking up that something was terribly wrong, she nodded and went to the office to shut down the garage's power. She then told the customers and crew that business was done for the day, blaming the power outage on a brownout.

"Why'd you come here, Ricky Washington?" Joey asked.

"Don't you listen?" Ricky felt his stomach churning. "I already told you why! HK-9 is out in force!"

"Got that, but why not just run? And don't tell me you wanted to warn us to clear your conscience 'cause we both know you ain't that guy."

"Fuck that," Ricky said. "I just don't want your boss coming after me. I figure if I tell you everything..."

"So warning us about shit we already know and showing up with your cute kid in the car, you think that clears you of all the shit you pulled?"

"That's enough, Joey," Hank said. "He was threatened, he's sorry, and he won't be a problem anymore." He turned to Ricky. "Did I get all that right?"

"Sure enough."

"Look, son, you might have Waldo or Rom or even the cops after you, but consider our business closed."

"For reals tho?" Ricky asked. "I worry about The Duke and his bro more than the rest."

"We're too busy covering our own asses to worry about yours," Joey said, "so fuck off while you can."

"Joey may be blunt," Hank said with a sigh, "but he's right. You have my word. Good enough?"

Ricky nodded. He'd rather have heard it from Edgardo, but Hank's tone told him The Duke wouldn't hunt him down.

"Goodbye, Ricky, and good luck."

As the customers left, with Ricky and his son close behind, Joey wanted to call Edgardo, but remembered his strict instruction to defer to Bram for now. He pulled him up on his cell phone.

"Yeah," Bram said on the other end.

"Shop's closing down. Ricky came by to say Rom is out for you."

"How kind of him to tell us something we already knew."

"He had you guys bugged at the garage," Joey said. "Shit's gettin' hot. Who knows what else he heard?"

"Pakshet," Bram said in a tired breath.

"What do you want me to do?"

"Take Hank home. Watch over him and his girl."

"Will do."

"One more thing, Joey."

"What's that?"

"I need you to believe that Eddie is going to fix this."

Joey could hear the worry in Bram's voice, a timid tone he'd never heard from the fierce enforcer before. "Sounds like *you* need to believe it, Big Brother."

"I just need you to have faith."

"What choice do I have?" Joey asked.

"Right. As for me, I'll believe it when I see it."

At Divinia's house, Bram hung up the call with Joey. He turned to C.B., now sitting in the shadows on the front porch. Though his cover was blown with the Duques, he didn't want snooping rivals to see him out of character.

"Who was that?" C.B. asked.

"What do you care?"

"If you want my help, I need to know what you know and who you know. You might've been talking with a turncoat just now."

"Joey's no fuckin' rat."

"Joey." C.B. skimmed through the known names in Edgardo's circle, practically seeing the file tabs in his mind. "Joey Gallo. The bartender. You trust him to guard your friends?"

"He's been guarding my brother for ten years," Bram said, "something I shoulda been doing."

"It needs to be said that anyone you think you know could turn out to be someone else."

"You, of all people, don't need to tell me that," Bram said with a grunt. "What do you know about The Nines' movements?"

"They're cleaning house," C.B. said. "Their crew is split up. Not sure where they're going."

"I know a couple of spots."

"My men are coming here, if that eases your mind."

"You always played that you Wolves were a hundred strong," Bram said. "I hope you fight the same way."

"One call from me and LOCC, SWAT, and the LAPD will be on the front lawn," C.B. said. "I can have an actual hundred here if needed, but only here."

"Good enough."

C.B. understood the context. "You telling me you got somewhere else to be?"

"I got some house cleaning of my own to do."

48

Hail Mary

Christiana sat on the patio of the Blume and Plume looking up at strings of overhead Christmas lights as they flickered on with the setting sun. She sipped a cappuccino in one hand while checking her phone in the other. Miguel had asked to meet her there but hadn't returned her texts for a half-hour. When he finally showed up, he looked as if he hadn't slept in days. In fact, she felt sure he wore the same clothes from their last time together in front of her school, a baggy hoodie over carpenter jeans and forest green Converse sneaks.

Her worry fell away when she saw his blank expression form an apologetic smirk. She smiled as he sat beside her.

"You're late," Chris said.

"My bad."

"And you look like dog shit."

"Nice to see you, too."

They laughed together, the combined sound as familiar in that moment as in their days hiding from Carlo inside his bedroom closet. They looked at each other, their exchanged glance an echo of the times they disrupted Mrs. Rankin's sixth-grade classroom with dirty jokes murmured under Algebra lessons. Theirs was the kind of friendship that resumed without pause after years apart, even after their lives had diverged to extremes.

"Remember when I used to tell you that?" Chris asked. "You'd come into class late, of course, wearing a wrinkled shirt or stained sweats, your hair a hot mess. I'd say you look like dog shit, and you'd say..."

"But I smell like cat piss."

"Oh, my God! That's right! Your mom had like nine cats!"

"Ten. I'd wake up with them curled up all over me, and if I forgot to clean the litter box the night before, two of them would piss in my bed, usually Mariah and Alanis."

Chris laughed so hard that coffee nearly came shooting out of her nose. "Do you remember all their names?"

"Of course. Mariah, Alanis, Celine, Britney, Whitney, Christina, Gwen, Jojo, Nelly, and Tupac."

"Tupac! The one boy!"

"Tomcat Tupac." Miguel smiled at the memory. "He was so screwed. The girls gave him shit all the time."

Christiana's memory of those cats opened a door in her mind to countless other adolescent afternoons and nights. She missed that chapter in their lives, the innocence of that age when their biggest problems were making it to school on time, finding the right shoes for their Barbies' new dresses, and getting new cleats for soccer tryouts. Chris liked their younger selves and missed them in much the same way one would miss old friends who'd switched schools or moved out of town.

"Weird to think those cats are gone, huh?" she said.

"But we're still here."

"Yeah, we are."

The hard turn in tone ended the nostalgic small talk, bringing them back to the purpose of their meeting. As much as Chris just wanted to catch up with her former girlfriend, Miguel mentioned on the phone that he had "news to share." She assumed the news was the city he'd planned to move to, a new job he'd just landed, or maybe a mutual friend he'd recently run into. She imagined their meeting over coffee as the beginning of their renewed friendship, reconnecting to their silly, carefree, childhood personas.

How wrong she was.

"Thanks for coming," Miguel said, suddenly almost business-like. "I wanted to talk about your dad."

"My dad?"

Across the street, three storefronts down, Mace sat at the wheel of a primered 4x4 truck. He watched the teens in his rearview mirror, listening through headphones and a hidden mic, as his new informant worked the Duque girl. He could see how it pained the boy to be there, to manipulate his old friend, but a deal's a deal.

Stop mumbling and speak up, Mace thought.

"I told you I worked for him," Miguel said to his friend, "but that's not exactly true."

Come on kid, just get the goods and get out. Time's tickin' fast.

"What are you talking about?" Chris asked.

"It's gang shit. I don't know how to say this... fuck..."

"What's my dad gotta do with your gang? Is he in trouble?"

"I think so..."

"Is this because of my stupid brother? I thought that was all done, just a misunderstanding?"

Chris hoped that some fallout from Carlo's brief trouble was the bad news Miguel wanted to meet about, but she knew better.

Her suspicions about her father were about to be confirmed.

"No, nothing about Carlo," the boy said. "Your dad's business... it sometimes crosses into TSB shit."

"What business? Maria, just spit it out."

"Miguel."

"What... oh, sorry..."

"Nah, fuck, I'm sorry, I know this shit is new to you..."

Miguel caught himself cursing more, something he did whenever he felt scared. "Where does he store his imports?" He asked the rehearsed question, given to him by Mace moments before, in a flat tone. "Here in the city?"

"He works on Temple Street," Chris said, alarmed. "Near Rosemont. Why?"

"I don't mean the garage or the bar. I'm talking about like a warehouse or some shit.... Look, Chris, there's something you gotta know..."

"Miguel, you're scaring me."

Mace gripped the steering wheel, leaned forward, and turned up the volume on his headphones.

Don't tell her, boy.

Stick to the script and keep her out of this.

"Chris... your dad is The Duke." The words fell out of Miguel's mouth before he could think of anything else to say. "He works with the gangs, like all the gangs. Him and his brother."

Goddammit.

Mace stepped out of the truck.

"Tito Bram?" Chris asked. "He just barely got out of prison."

"Do you know of any other place your dad might have storage? It's important. I'm kinda fucked if I don't find out."

Christiana realized the situation. Miguel was being pressured to steal from her dad – "The Duke" – and he hoped to learn something from her that would seal the deal. It hurt her heart and hammered home the fact that those two little girls that made root beer floats with Pop Rocks and fawned over boy bands were long gone.

She now missed their childhood selves the same way one would miss friends who'd died tragically young.

"I know nothing about my dad's business," she said, "but even if I did, I'm not gonna help some gang steal from him."

"We don't call it stealing," said a man in a leather vest, torn jeans, and army boots. She'd seen the scary biker step out of a 4x4 and approach the coffee shop from down the street, the remorse on his face betraying his fierce appearance. "We call it confiscating."

"Who's this?" Chris asked, scared.

"Ain't got no clue," Miguel lied, returning to his 'street' attitude and voice. He shot Mace a look like he was about to blow their rehearsed assignment. "You want money or something? How 'bout you get lost for five bucks?"

"Forget it, kid," the biker said flatly. "You were moving too slow... and you told her."

"Told her what?" Miguel laughed. "What the fuck are you..."

"I said give it up. Mission is FUBAR."

"You crazy, man. What the hell does that even mean?"

"Fucked up beyond all recognition," Christiana said, picking up on the biker's tone. "Military slang. Soldiers talk like that."

"She's right," Mace said, "'cause now we're on damage control."

"Yo, what the fuck, Mace?" Miguel said in a low voice, glancing at five nearby patrons on the patio. "Man, there's people here."

"Don't worry, kid, they're my people." Mace sighed, turned to Christiana. "I picked a public place so you'd feel safe, but I stacked the deck with my associates to be sure."

Despite his gentle tone, Chris didn't believe the intimidating stranger. The other patrons included a table of college students, a businessman in a suit, and a woman in a jogging outfit. "We both know these aren't your 'people.'"

"Not no more, they ain't." Mace pointed both hands at the others. "You guys are burnt. Standby and wait for my call."

Instantly, the coffee shop customers picked up their laptops, purses, and briefcase, and silently left the patio, walking away down Temple Street in different directions. Chris could see on Miguel's face that even he didn't know the extent of the sting.

Mace sat down at the table, his loose cannon persona put away. "This was a long shot, Miss Duque, but we had to try."

"Miguel, he isn't part of your gang... is he?" Chris asked.

"Hell no, he's with another gang."

"Hell no, I'm a cop," Mace said, quietly revealing his badge to her under the table. "ASAC Tim Mason, drug enforcement. Miguel is right, your dad goes by the alias 'The Duke' and is involved in a number of gang-related activities throughout Southern California. His repair shop and bar are fronts."

His words landed like red hot embers atop her head. Of all the possible explanations that had run through her mind over the past two years, this was the one scenario she dreaded.

"I don't believe you," she said, overwhelmed. "This is crazy!"

"I'd hoped Miguel could get something from you, friend to friend, but he doesn't exactly have training for this. Like I said, long shot."

"I don't know what you guys are talking about!" Chris felt light-headed, on the verge of tears. "My dad is a genius! Why would he stoop to... it doesn't make sense... Miguel..?"

"Don't blame Miguel. He just got sucked into this. It's got nothing to do with him. It does, however, have everything to do with your father and every other outfit in the Eastern Los Angeles Area."

Chris's mind sought family for comfort, and it occurred to her she'd been ignoring her cell phone for the past hour, choosing to focus her thoughts on her reunion with Miguel. She pulled up her silenced phone and saw a dozen texts and voice mails from her mother and uncle. They'd been desperately trying to warn her, and she ignored them for what she thought was a walk down Memory Lane with an old friend.

"Text them you're okay," Mace said. "Tell them you're with the cops. Nothing more."

"Why? What's going on?"

"Do as I say." Mace looked at his watch. "NOW."

Chris's thumbs typed so fast that half her words were a mess. Mace grabbed the phone from her and looked at the message.

IM OK IM WIH THG POLUCE SOMTHNG ABOUT DUK

"That'll work," Mace said, sending off the text. "Back to business. We need information about your father's operations, his storage buildings, anything you can tell us, and we need it yesterday." He held up his phone. "My people are listening."

Christiana questioned the strange man in leather and assumed he was trying to corner her just as he had Miguel. "Who are you, really? Why should I tell you anything?"

"I told you, I'm ASAC Tim Mason."

"What does that even mean..."

"Assistant Special Agent in Charge of LOCC, a state drug enforcement task force. The Duke of Temple Street is a person of interest. So is Miguel. Unfortunately, so are you."

"I want to call my mom..."

"I'll call her for you." Mace spoke like a concerned neighbor, but could tell the girl wasn't ready to believe it. "I'll even take you to her. But first, if there's anything you can..."

"I said no!" Chris felt a panic attack coming, a familiar feeling from the wake of her parents' divorce. "I don't know anything! I didn't even know about any Duke until you just sprang it on me." The situation felt like a bucket of cold water thrown in her face. She caught the despair in Miguel's eyes and knew he was in over his head, just as she was sucked into this, as Mace had said.

"You're a bright girl," the biker said in a comforting tone meant to deescalate the tension. "We saw your grades, your AP classes, your wall of awards. Physics and Calculus are like 'Chutes and Ladders' to you. Unlike your MVP jock brother, it's clear you take after dear ol' dad. That means you knew, or you had your suspicions. Right?"

Chris refused to confirm his reading of her. "Why are you pinning any of this on Miguel? On me?"

"Because time's running out," Mace said calmly, "because we don't know where your father is, and because we could be compromised at any moment. You must believe me when I say we're trying to protect you all. We can reassign your family if it comes to that..."

"Reassign?"

"She don't know nothin'," Miguel said. "How many times she gotta say it? It's over, man, enough with the interrogation bullshit."

Mace sighed. The boy was right.

"Okay, kid. Interrogation over." Guilt hit him hard as he saw the lost expressions on the two teenagers' faces. This Hail Mary was a bad idea. He should've listened to C.B. and cut Miguel Hortiz loose at the foothills warehouse rather than force him to become an informant. "But we aren't done just yet. I'm taking you both to a safehouse for the duration..."

"You ain't taking us nowhere!" Miguel said, rising to his feet.

Before Mace could say another word, a Cadillac SUV pulled up with a screech of its tires. Four Filipino gangsters stepped out and opened the rear doors.

They're early, Mace thought, his fears realized.

Miguel fought panic, recognizing the men as TSB. "Godammit, fuckin' Calixto..."

"Be glad they aren't Nines," Mace said under his breath. Out of time, he quickly tucked his and Chris's phones into a napkin box on the table. "You left it at home," he told the girl.

"What? No..."

"You left it at home." Mace looked over his shoulder at the TSB approaching. He leaned forward in his chair and whispered to her. "I know you're scared, Miss Duque. I know you wanna run and call for help. But if you wanna keep your family safe, you gotta follow my lead, understand?"

Chris looked to Miguel, who nodded.

She also nodded, scared, unsure.

Mace pushed the phones deep into the napkin box, out of sight. He feared the TSB would force them to unlock the devices, that recent text messages might blow their cover. Worse, they might have used the girl's phone to lure Edgardo into a trap.

"Let's go," one gangster ordered as the group walked up.

Mace turned to the four men, his arms outstretched, as he slipped back into character. "Hey, what the fuck happened to half an hour? Calixto didn't teach you how to tell time?" He spoke to the gangsters in his bellowing, defiant tone. "Grab a cappuccino or something, 'cause we ain't done here, boys."

"Yes, you are," one of them said. "Calixto wants you back. All of you."

"Fine, but the girl don't know shit. She ain't no use to us..."

"ALL of you."

"Okay, sure, whatever the man said, amigo."

Two of the men frisked the trio. They took Mace's gun and Miguel's phone and waited for the others. "Phones," their lead man demanded.

"I left mine at home," Christiana said, unsure.

"Mine's in the truck," Mace said. He wanted to signal for backup on the truck's radio and retrieve his other gun from the glove box. "Just a sec. Let me go get it."

"Leave it. Let's go."

"I'm parked right there..."

"LEAVE IT. Bring her."

"No need to get snippy, compadre." Mace grabbed Chris by the arm and pulled her up from her chair, spilling her coffee. The girl still wasn't sure if she could trust him, but had no choice. Miguel's compliance assured her, as nervous as he may have looked.

While everyone piled into the SUV, Mace looked across the patio at Monica Torres, Edgardo's favorite barista, who had just witnessed the entire scene from inside the coffee shop.

As the SUV sped away, Special Agent Torres pulled out her cell phone.

She quickly called her superior.

49

Summoning His Mentor

Unlike Joey The Rose, who barged into Otto's Automotive and ordered everyone out, Felix chose a stealth approach with his assigned guard duty on Magnolia Street in Eagle Rock. Straddling his motorbike at the start of the suburban cul-de-sac, hidden in the shadows behind tall bushes, he kept his eyes on the picturesque home of Lola Reyna and Lolo Otto, known within his files simply as "The Harrison House." He kept his left hand on his cell phone and his right hand on his pocketed pistol, careful to remain in darkness as he always did.

With no social security number, no tax records, and a wallet full of fake identification, Felix was a ghost on the grid. Only a handful of people knew he existed, and those who did couldn't prove it. Even Edgardo couldn't be sure if "Felix Ramirez" was actually the man's true name, given that he had four active aliases when they first met.

* * *

Six years prior, Edgardo saved Felix from one of the city's largest stings on illegal imports. Known as "Operation No-Vacancy," the raid was a collaboration of the combined forces of the Los Angeles Port Authority, the LAPD, and DEA-LA. The name came from the timing of the massive joint sting, a rare one-hour window when all 270 berths of the port's harbored ships were loaded bow-to-stern with cargo. Every vessel was boarded and searched while their destined warehouses were put on lockdown. By day's end, they were each assigned one of three classifications: "Lawful," "Unlawful," or "Suspect."

During that fateful week, Felix co-owned four large warehouses, each adjoining its own dock. His partner at the time was Bakal Diaz, a petty thief who hadn't yet joined the Temple Street Boyz as an enforcer, known as a "bill collector" at the time.

At the start of the day-long raid, Felix sacrificed Docks 17, 23, and 49, filled with stolen electronics, haute couture fashions, and fine jewelry, respectively. Their loss proved a brutal hit financially, but their fictitious owners "Allen Papillon," "Salvador Vega," and "Ricardo Belmont" were nowhere to be found.

Instead, Felix sweated over Dock 118, its warehouse full of liquor bottles containing opioids, shabu (Filipino meth), and other illegal narcotics. He normally avoided trafficking drugs, but he'd been cornered into a deal by The Panginoon, one of the largest and most dangerous outfits in the Philippines. To Felix, Dock 118 stood as a powder keg set to blow up his life, and Operation No-Vacancy couldn't have come at a worse time. To have such a vast amount of drugs confiscated and scrutinized would have resulted in an arrest ending all nine lives of the hacker-thief regardless of his chosen name.

Feds looking for five-star contraband eventually give up the ghost when they merely find a room full of hot TVs, but they burn the midnight oil eternal upon seizing pallets of meth, heroin, and fentanyl. Well aware of the ramifications pressing down on him, Felix stood ready to risk The Panginoon's wrath and literally burn it all to the ground, fleeing the scene in a dingy docked in the Venice canals.

The fire was averted, for one of the confidential clients attached to Dock 118 was Edgardo Duque, a recognized and respected local business owner, having just won the Small Community Business of the Year award with his wife, the celebrity TV chef Divinia Duque. With his business clout and Fish's acrobatic legal expertise, Edgardo claimed the entire warehouse for his lounge and its proposed expansion, effectively placing it on the "lawful" list pending a delayed inspection.

With the liability now on Edgardo, Felix could have pinned the warehouse's contents entirely on him. The agents knew that The Panginoon – the likely point of origin – was outside their jurisdiction with numerous fronts covering for them, so they were itching to tie the narcotics to a local bust. Instead, Felix used prepared fake records to protect Edgardo, keeping the heat on himself. The risky, selfless decision cemented their relationship.

To Felix's surprise, Edgardo then took the preventative measure of "discovering" the hidden drugs himself and reporting them to the joint task force. He vouched for Felix, who pleaded ignorance to the found substances and was charged with the relatively minor offense of distributing alcohol without a license while unknowingly harboring narcotics through neglect and insufficient inspections. A staged break-in and doctored records further supported the notion that a foreign third party was responsible and that neither man knew that their imports had been compromised.

All Edgardo asked of the young man in return was a vow to never traffic hard narcotics again, whatever the circumstance. He had no problem with booze and weed, but he put his foot down at epidemic drugs, blaming them for society's decline and the corruption of its youth. Felix had no problem with the demand, having felt he was becoming more corrupt himself, his morals twisted from the overseas deals.

After Fish reduced a two-year prison sentence to six months plus probation, "Felix Ramirez" repaid both Edgardo's loss and aid by joining his side business as a steadfast, loyal assistant, keeping the last alias used as a reminder of his careless brush with the feds.

His former partner, Bakal Diaz, had no faith in the justice system, even when tilted in his favor. Distrusting Edgardo's helping hand, he rejected any jail time, reduced or not. Instead, Bakal fled, and has looked over his shoulder ever since. He eventually found a home with the TSB, but always placed the bitter blame squarely on his former partner, as if Felix had sentenced him to a life on the run.

In contrast, Felix felt reborn from the experience. Being proficient in security systems, hacking, and sourcing virtually any goods and services, from firearms to forgery, he could obtain anything for Edgardo. His connection to the city's thousands of security cameras – a simple agreement with operators on his payroll – proved invaluable time and again. The ability to reset or "wipe" any camera, public or private, helped keep Edgardo and himself off the radar, rendering The Duke another ghost, pulling strings that most didn't even know existed.

Their subsequent friendship surprised even Edgardo, for the young man never had a mentor, and The Duke never had a criminal "nephew" to depend on when things got hot, which they often did. In time, Felix's loyalty proved unbreakable. He admired Edgardo, referring to him by the formal title "Amo" (Tagalog for "boss"), and soon knew every detail of the man's parallel lives.

* * *

Watching over Lola Reyna's house as the sun set behind the San Gabriel mountains made Felix uneasy. With two gangs, possibly three, out in force for The Duke's traitorous head, violence seemed inevitable. Though Felix was a practiced marksman, he rarely needed to fire at a living soul and had yet to take a life. He knew that night on Magnolia Street would test him.

Using his parabolic microphone from afar, Felix heard no sound coming from the Harrison House. After 20 minutes, he felt sure no one was home. A call from Bram confirmed it.

"Mr. Felix?" Bram said on the phone.

"I'm here."

"My mother is with me at Divinia's house."

"I figured. What about your father?"

"He's in the hospital. Stroke."

"I'm so sorry, Bram..."

"Don't be. He's a tough old goat, and he's in excellent hands." Bram tried to convince himself that Otto's health issues were a simple aside. "Keep it classified for now. Eddie's got enough on his mind. He should hear it from me, anyway."

"Understood."

"You heard from my brother?"

"Not a word," Felix said. "I was tempted to call him, but he made it clear that you're my contact now."

"Right. Leave Eddie to his business. If you're a religious man, maybe pray for him to come out of that impiyerno snake pit alive."

"Should I head to Waldo's? I haven't staked out that factory in years. Could give us some valuable intel."

Bram considered the idea. "I appreciate the gusto, Mr. Felix, but no. We can't risk them thinking Eddie's staging some kind of offense. They spot you, they'll assume there's fifteen of you in the woods."

"Agreed. Where do you want me, then..." Felix's line of thought trailed as he spotted an SUV enter the cul-de-sac, slowly making its way down, likely casing the neighborhood on its way to the target house on the end. "Bram, our guests just arrived."

"Pakshet. Who?"

"TSB."

"You sure?"

"Dead sure. I can see their kapitan." Felix watched three men step out of their SUV under a streetlight.

"Listen to me carefully," Bram said. "I don't know to what end you serve my brother, but right now, you serve me."

"Understood."

"And right now, I want you to take out your trombone case and kill that punyeta buwisit the second his big bald head is in range."

"No bald heads here."

"Who's the kapitan?" Bram asked.

The man Felix identified from several houses away wasn't Calixto Cervantes, as Bram has assumed. It was Bakal Diaz, his old partner, armed with a *panabas*, a long-handled curved blade with a forked tip. The unique weapon was the prize of his boss's martial arts collection, and he was told to finish the job in a 'spectacle of blood,' so that night it was meant for the Harrisons.

Over the years, Bakal had issued three contracts on Felix, all turning up dead ends. Felix knew their beef would only come to a close with one of them in the ground and that it now had to be that day. It felt like fate.

"Gotta go," Felix said.

"What are you gonna do?"

"Gonna play my trombone."

Bakal stood at the front door of the Harrison House with blade in hand. Two of his associates, Joselito and Agustin, flanked him in the flower beds. In contrast to Bakal's determination, his men looked unsure, more accustomed to back-alley brawls than suburban home invasions to end in murder. Bakal peeked through the small window in the front door and fiddled with the lock.

Felix let his pistol drop into his jacket pocket as he reached behind him, into his bike's saddle bags. Without taking his eyes off Bakal, he blindly assembled his bullpup rifle, its scope already attached and zeroed, a round already resting in its chamber. "Sniper rifles" are normally never folded or in pieces for better concealment, but his was a custom mod with only the extended barrel, mag, and suppressor needing to be fitted. In 20 seconds, he had the weapon ready with his former partner's head in its crosshairs.

A moment of hesitation cost Felix his window as the three gangsters walked around the garage and into the backyard. He knew he might waver at the moment of truth, having never killed a man, but he had to push on. He stepped off his bike, walked

Lynn Harrod

across lawns to hide the sound of his footsteps, and swore to himself that he wouldn't waste his next chance.

He hopped a gate on the opposite side of the Harrison House and crept toward the backyard where he heard someone break a window, a muffled sound likely done with a jacket or shirt wrapped around an arm. As he imagined, when he turned the corner, he saw Joselito bust a small pane of glass in the rear door, his jacket bundled around his fist. All three men had their backs turned to Felix and his suppressed bullpup, another perfect opportunity to knock out a leg from Calixto's forces.

Still, Felix hesitated. As if he were split into two men, he was surprised to find himself frozen, and shocked to hear himself speak.

"Bakal," Felix called out. The three men slowly turned around. It took them a moment to spot Felix, standing in the dark against the back fence. Once they did, his powerful custom rifle stood out as if five feet long.

"Felix?" Bakal said, still peering into the dark. He finally saw his old partner's eyes. "Ah yes, Felix, or whatever your name is today."

"Step away from the door."

"Nah, we're good." Bakal looked at his men, gestured for them to remain on the back porch. "You know how to use that thing?"

"I can nail the bridge of your nose from 600 meters, and I'm standing 10 steps from you."

"So why don't you?" Bakal's bold stance was clearly not shared by his nervous companions who knew nothing about the armed man in the dark. "You got us dead bang. Why not pull the trigger? Because you're not a killer, totoy. Because you're scared."

"Because I'd rather kill one than three." Having learned from his mentor, researching every criminal they might encounter on his behalf, Felix pointed his weapon at the man to Bakal's right.

"Joselito Vazquez. 20 years old. You were a journeyman apprentice for three years before being sucked into The Life by Calixto."

"Don't listen to him," Bakal said. "He thinks he knows so much, but he's more full of shit than anyone. Believe me, I know."

Felix didn't relent. "Consider this your second chance, Joselito Vazquez, because the TSB won't be around much longer. You don't want The Duke's army hunting you down."

"The Duke's army?" Bakal said with a laugh.

"Our civilized talk stops now if you don't drop that blade."

Bakal nodded, dropped his vicious blade, and hovered his hand over the pistol tucked into the front of his pants. Felix whipped his rifle at his groin and gestured for all weapons to be tossed on the ground. Bakal slowly pulled out the pistol and threw it to Felix's feet without incident.

Felix failed to see that his old partner had another tucked in his back pocket.

"What now?" Joselito asked, still hearing the offer in his mind.

"Put your real skills to work," Felix said. "I'll find you, get you ten-grand toward getting back to building things instead of destroying them. A couple more years, you'll be a card-carrying journeyman. That's the respect you really want."

"How generous," Bakal said. "What a guy. Do you fools really believe this shit?"

"Between you and me, I think they know who to trust."

"Trust? You left me to die on the docks!"

Bakal's words went unheard as Joselito stepped away from his kapitan, knelt down, and placed his gun on the porch step.

Bakal grunted in frustration, but didn't move.

"Agustin Abayon," Felix said to the other man, this time keeping his barrel aimed at Bakal. "You've been around a little longer. 24 years old, running with Temple Street right out of high school. Impressive. Most don't live that long."

"Shut the fuck up!" Bakal barked.

"On weekends, you help your sister Alma with her catering business. You even bought her an old truck and a pizza oven. We both know she deserves your hard work more than Calixto. Drop your piece and walk away."

"You do that," Bakal said, staring into Agustin's soul, "and all your 'hard work' will be done!"

"You don't have to listen to his bushet," Felix said. "The only one here who's done is Bakal."

"You got ten G's for him, too?"

"I will tomorrow. Ten large in cash can go a long way toward fixing that truck's transmission. I know it skips gears, cost Alma a sweet gig at City Hall two weeks ago."

"How you know so much?" Agustin asked in awe.

"I know where you have lunch," Felix said, fully summoning The Duke. "I know what you order, what gas pills you take afterward, and I know you'd rather be cooking with your family instead of hanging around a dump all day. Most of all, I know you've never been asked to take someone out, not until tonight. So I ask you the question I asked Joselito: what kind of future do you want?"

Agustin nodded. He'd heard enough. Fearful of the man beside him more than the man with the rifle across the back lawn, he reached into his back pocket, pulled out his gun, and tossed it to Felix's feet. For good measure, he kicked Joselito's gun off the porch step, closer to Felix.

"Good man. Now go. Both of you. You hear gunshots, don't come running back, or the next one will be yours. You'll get your money in the morning."

As if the back porch was on shaky ground, Joselito and Agustin carefully made their way down the steps and back around the house to the front, leaving Felix alone with their kapitan.

"Your turn," Felix said. "Either your gun on the ground, or you."

"Look down. You got my fuckin' gun."

"You'd have me believe that Bakal Diaz only carries one gun? Back in our day, you always had a .38 tucked at the top of your ass."

"Back in our day," the gangster muttered with a laugh. "Fuckin' priceless. Ain't been no baby side piece on me in years. Only boys carry toys."

Bakal's mind flooded with rage. He wanted to rush his old partner, to rip the rifle from his hands and cave in his skull with it, but something in Felix's voice told him the threat was no bluff. He chose to stall instead, to distract, to wait until the man who had him point blank eventually dropped his guard. A couple of seconds was all he needed to determine their fates.

"Why make the deals first?" Bakal asked. "Why not just blast me in the back and then make your offers? I still think it's because you don't have it in you to pull the trigger. It's the only reason I'm still on my feet."

"Wrong again, as always," Felix said. "It would have been hard to sell them any deal with your blood on their shoes."

"Makes sense." Bakal's mind turned. His old partner was clearly afraid, hesitant, but he'd been gathering his courage. "How'd you get out? The raid at the docks. I always wondered how you weaseled your way outta there. I figured you either died in that warehouse or were rotting in a cell. Imagine my surprise when rumors swirled about you runnin' around as The Duke's dog."

"Only dog here is you, Bakal. Calixto tells you to rough up an old woman running a laundromat, you do it. He tells you to kill a kid for slinging dope on Alvarado Street, you do it. Yes master, yes master."

"Fuck you. Duke tells you to kill me, you do it. No ten-grand is coming my way, so don't act like no saint 'cause we ain't so different, me and you."

"Everything I do, I make the choice," Felix said. "I do things for him even before being asked. I'm his partner, not his lackey."

Bakal laughed. He stepped forward, off the back porch, toward the rifle pointed at him. His discarded blade now rested at his feet. "You can't fuck with me, Felix. Duke's shit don't smell any sweeter than Calixto's or Rom's or Nino's. You're the most brainwashed mutt of all, you just tell yourself you ain't."

Bakal's bravado faded when he saw Felix's face shift as a gear turned in his mind.

"I'm sorry I left you at the docks," Felix said. "I'm sorry shit went down between us the way it did. And I'm sorry all the hits you put out on me went nowhere."

"The night ain't over just yet." Bakal looked down at the long, serrated blade.

"Yes, it is," Felix said, a trace of remorse in his eyes. "After all these years, it's about time the night ended. And for the record, The Duke never asked me to kill you. You're nothing to him. This is about us. Maybe now we'll both get a little peace."

"Peace? Your amo is the only one who gives a shit about that, now that him and his people are Most Wanted."

"Like I said, I'm sorry, Bakal."

Still staring the blade below, in one swift motion, Bakal whipped the .38 tucked behind him toward Felix.

BLAM!

Bakal pointed his gun at Felix but didn't have the strength to pull the trigger as he fell flat to the pavement with a hole in his chest.

Felix walked up to him, pressed the long barrel of his suppressed bullpup to his forehead...

BLAM!

Lynn Harrod

50

A Devil's Deal

With Charlie Wood keeping his distance at the rear, Edgardo followed Melinda Emery away from her office and down a long, decrepit corridor, deeper into the old factory. Like the entry hall, this part of the property looked as if it was barely functional. Most of the ceiling lights were out. Portions of the roof had collapsed. The few intact floor tiles were surrounded by patches of concrete.

The depths of Waldo's ice cream factory brought my old HiFi noodle shop to mind. For nearly ten years, I kept that shop in a state of arrested decay to maintain the appearance of a shuttered storefront, the kind that's normally overlooked by the public and dismissed by curious cops. It's where I met with Felix for daily business and where I kept a small cache of weapons, documents, and clean cash.

Melinda led him to a large steel door. Its rusted hinges and stains didn't fool him. Rubbing the surface with his fingertips, he could tell the difference between iron oxide and mixed tempera paint.

Walking through Waldo's compound, I could see that he clearly used the same camouflage, a simulation of decades of rot. Melinda's immaculate office, with its espresso machine, antiques, and commissioned art mounted on pristine walls was normally sealed and likely the only room in the factory that didn't look like an industrial ruin. I'd most assuredly been sitting in Waldo's office, and there was only one conclusion as to why the man himself wasn't in his grand room, the same reason he stopped taking meetings months prior. I'd hoped to be proven wrong.

Melinda unlocked the massive door and turned to her guard. "Wait here, Charlie. We won't be long."

"Yes, ma'am."

She opened the door just enough to allow Edgardo and herself entry. As Edgardo expected, she shut it behind them, for even the head of their security likely didn't know what lay within.

Edgardo walked into another large, refurbished room. Not lavishly appointed like the office, this space resembled a modest bedroom suite. On the far end of the room, a four-poster bed draped with sheer ivory curtains was flanked by medical support machines covered in opaque plastic. Through the curtains, he could see the shape of a man resting in bed.

"What's wrong with him?" Edgardo asked as he peered through the translucent fabric.

Melinda took Edgardo's arm, kept him from parting the curtains. "He's in recovery from back surgery. Tennis injury."

"I sympathize. I once pulled my lower back playing pickleball."

"The Duke plays pickleball?" she said. "I find that both charming and hilarious."

"My point is that it took me weeks to work through it, during which I literally worked."

"All business all the time. Isn't that your famous mantra?" Melinda kept her voice low. "You're also younger and in better shape."

"An injury from playing ball can't stop the money flow. You know that. If I dared to call in sick this long, business would suffer. Relationships would fall apart."

"That's because you didn't have me," she said with a coy grin. "No offense to your brother." She checked her boss's machines, satisfied by their numbers.

"He stays out of the game long enough, men from the wrong crowd will come calling."

"You see, that's the difference between you two. Walter is the *overlord* of the wrong crowd." Melinda guided Edgardo to the foot of the bed, still cloaked by the curtains, and gestured for him to stay put. "Give me a moment. He may be asleep, and he absolutely hates being woken up, by me or anyone else."

She pulled aside the curtains and approached the old man in the bed. "Walter. There's a Mr. Duque here to see you. Walter, I apologize. Are you up for a visitor?"

After waiting a moment, Edgardo defied her request and stepped through the curtains, finally seeing the man he'd been eager to meet.

Walter "Waldo" Robinson, a 66-year-old Black man with a frayed gray afro and white pajamas, lay asleep in the bed. An open book rested in his right hand, *Things Fall Apart* by Chinua Achebe.

"He's knocked out," Melinda said. "He always falls asleep reading. And before you ask, we are not waking him up."

"No, we certainly aren't."

"Really? And here, I expected resistance."

"We won't wake Walter because we can't," Edgardo said. "The man is in a coma."

Melinda laughed as she poured a glass of water from a pitcher on the bedside table, as if preparing it for when Walter woke up. It took all her focus to keep her hand from shaking. "Your mentalist routine is getting absurd, Duque. I told you, I'll have none of your mind tricks."

"And I told you, I don't need tricks. When I met with Walter nine years ago, we had Irish Coffee, just as you and I did. Must be tradition."

"Indeed. Given our business, you'd think it'd be hot fudge sundaes." She caught herself raising her voice.

"I remember. He held his cup with his right hand."

"Well done. Walter is right-handed, just like 85 Percent of the population."

Edgardo nodded to the sleeping man. "But his book is in his right hand."

Melinda looked at the hardback novel in her boss's grip. "Forgive me, but I don't follow you. A right-handed man holds something in his right hand, and that grabs your attention?"

"You also picked up your coffee cup with your right hand."

"Guilty. I'm a Righty, like him."

"Like 85 Percent of the population." Edgardo picked up a paperback from a stack near the bed. He handed it to Melinda. "Turn to Page 20. Humor me."

"Another mind game?" Melinda shook her head as if this were pointless. She took the paperback from him and held it in her *left* hand while flipping pages with her right. She paused, realizing Edgardo had caught her in yet another lie.

"There's no head trauma that I can see," he said. "Given his age, I'm guessing he had a stroke. How long has he been out?"

Melinda spoke in a low, defeated tone. "Six months."

"He's your husband, isn't he?"

She stopped herself from spitting out a quick, defensive response. Edgardo had figured out the ruse, as she feared he would.

"All that from how he held the book?" she asked, no longer bothering to keep her voice down. "That one little detail?"

"It's never just one detail," Edgardo said. "That machine you checked is a VNS."

"A what?"

"A Vagus Nerve Stimulation unit. An AspireSR 106. My father was hooked up to the 105 twenty years ago, so I'm familiar with the series."

"Of course you are." Melinda kept her stone face even as her mind reeled from his startling memory. "So that was the tip-off? The machine? What makes you think he's my husband?"

"You call him 'Walter.' Not even I knew his real name until today. And back in your office, you prepared Irish Coffee, his favorite drink, with the care of a Chinese tea ceremony. The preparation, the glassware, the taste, it all reminds you of him."

"Every time," she whispered, turning away her welling eyes. She put down the paperback and wrangled her mixed emotions, addressing her guest with an angry passion. "Thirty-five years ago, my husband came here from Nigeria with nothing and immediately started building his empire. He spent decades becoming the foremost supplier of ground guns on the West

Coast. He's respected and feared by clients, competitors, and the politicians in his pocket. His brain and brawn held California together while you were still watching Saturday morning cartoons and skimming magazines in your dentist's office."

"Mr. Waldo is a great man," Edgardo said, down-shifting his tone from confrontation. "No one disputes that."

"They would if they saw him... like this." Melinda's tough talk gave way to pleading. "If his rivals knew his wife ran everything in his name..."

"Do his men know?"

"His men are like family. Most would follow him into a fire. But I haven't let them step foot in this room. I don't have the heart or the stomach for it."

"Who does know?"

"Charlie, I'm pretty sure. He's the smart one of the bunch."

"And now me."

"Yes," Melinda said with a hollow dread. "And now you." She leaned over her husband and kissed him tenderly on the forehead before stepping out through the curtains, back toward the door. Edgardo followed.

"Despite what you may think, Melinda, I'm your husband's ally. I'd like to think he's mine as well."

"Walter always said you were a man of discretion, a man of your word."

"Your secret won't leave this room," Edgardo said. He headed for the door.

"He also said you were a shrewd businessman. Surely, there's a price for your silence? Your reason for coming here?"

"You owe me a favor. Nothing more."

"What favor?"

"That's to be decided." Edgardo opened the door and spotted Charlie Wood standing in the hall. Realizing the woman hadn't moved from her spot, Edgardo turned to her, felt her piercing stare.

"Forgive me for being cynical," Melinda said. "If word gets out about my husband, any one of his competitors could walk in here and take whatever they wanted. Our trucks. Our home. Even some of our men. His secret must be kept intact until he recovers, and he WILL recover. He's far too strong to let this be the end."

"On that, we agree."

"I ask you the price for your silence and you have the audacity to say 'you owe me' as if you'd simply paid for my lunch? Do you expect me to believe that?"

"I expect you to believe whatever I choose to say." Edgardo left the open door and walked back toward her, returning her dead stare. "Now you must forgive me, Melinda. We just met, so perhaps I should be more clear. You're in debt to me a favor. I may call upon you tomorrow, next week, perhaps next year, but I intend to collect. If you knew me half as well as Walter does, you'd know that a debt to me is a high price to pay."

Charlie sensed the rising tension. He stepped into the room, blocking Edgardo's exit.

"Let him go, Charlie," Melinda said.

"Ma'am?"

"Politely escort our guest to his car. Once he leaves, tell everyone The Duke is off-limits. In truth, he's under our protection."

"Yes, ma'am."

"He knows."

"He knows what, ma'am?"

Melinda gave him a blank stare. "You know, too, Charlie."

Charlie looked at his boss across the bedroom, then into the eyes of the serious man before him. "Yes, ma'am." He lowered his rifle and moved aside for their guest to leave.

Edgardo looked at the waiting hall but turned to the head guard. "You have ten men here tonight, plus another sixteen. Is that right?"

Charlie looked to Melinda as he nodded. "Yeah, 26 in all."

"And another 30 on call?"

"That's right." Charlie knew his boss would never disclose their numbers. Edgardo's accurate deduction was uncanny, ominous.

"Until you call in that favor, Mr. Duque," Melinda said, "what shall we do in the meantime?"

"In the meantime, business as usual."

"All business all the time?" She forced a smile, having no choice but to trust the man.

"You will continue to protect your operation which now means you will protect mine."

Melinda nodded, his words landing like a heavy weight. With her continuing business at stake, with Edgardo's knowledge of her husband's condition, she understood the context just as others had before her.

You work for me now.

"I expect the trucks to resume tomorrow," Edgardo said. "I want to see Ricky Wash on time, clean and sober."

"Ricky's flown the coop," Melinda said, "or doesn't the omniscient Duke know that?"

"Ricky Washington's last move is the open road, but he's actually holed up with his son at his cousin's house. My man spotted his car there last night. Look up Roger Fuller in Burbank. Offer Ricky his old route with assurances, as you say. Assurances from the both of us."

"Of course." Melinda didn't understand the point of Edgardo's odd request but felt she had no choice but to comply... for now. "I'll try, anyway."

Edgardo walked past Charlie, out of the room. Charlie shut the door and followed him, as ordered.

Melinda returned to Walter in his bed. As she pressed a cold compress to his forehead, she could only hope that her agreement with The Duke didn't end up a devil's deal.

51

Last Cup of Tsokolate

Divinia prepared five cups of tsokolate (Philippine hot cocoa) and brought them on a wooden tray into the living room where Carlo and Lola Reyna sat on the couch. Seeing where her son was positioned, she quickly set the drinks on the coffee table and grabbed his arm.

"Move away from there," she said.

"Nay, what's going on?" the boy asked. "Where did Tito Bram go?"

"Stay away from the windows." She took him by the arm and guided him to a chair near the fireplace.

"Your scaring him!" Reyna said.

"We're all scared. Bram said to keep away from the windows."

"Since when do you listen to him? And why are you so paranoid?"

"Reyna..."

"And why did you make so many drinks?"

"For Bram and the others, when they come back."

Divinia lied. She knew it could be hours before she saw the rest of her family again.

She also knew they might not all return.

Lola Reyna saw the vacant eyes of her daughter-in-law and took in the silence of the house. Her fierce narcissism was muted by the shared dread. She looked at her grandson curled in his chair as she sipped her tsokolate.

"It's good," Reyna said.

"Good?" Divinia said, confused.

"The tsokolate. It's just right, better than mine."

"Thank you, Reyna."

The old woman's uncharacteristically kind gesture, the first in many years, didn't comfort Divinia. Instead, it came across as last words, further stamping their peril into her mind. Knowing about Edgardo's second world, how it was now flooding their sheltered life, both she and her mother-in-law faced an unknown danger together, huddled in her house while her ex-husband and his brute of a brother confronted it somewhere in the depths of the city. With her daughter unaccounted for, Divinia had to put them out of her mind.

"Text your sister again," she told Carlo.

"I just did."

"Well, do it again! I want to know where..."

BLAM! BLAM! BLAM! BLAM! BLAM!

In a storm of thunder and debris, a shard of glass sliced Divinia's cheek as the front windows shattered in a barrage of gunfire. She grabbed Carlo and Reyna and pulled them to the floor, covering their bodies with her own as the deafening siege ripped her living room apart. Picture frames flew off the walls.

Couch pillows exploded in clouds of cotton. Carlo's many trophies fell in pieces.

Divinia opened her mouth to scream, but no sound could be heard in the unending assault. She heard more guns joining the frenzy and imagined a hundred gangsters outside blasting her home without mercy, intent on annihilating anyone and anything inside.

When the storm ended, the house was thrown into a silence more gripping than the chaos of the attack. At any moment, men would bust down the front door, find them cowering on the carpet, and finish their mission.

"I love you, Carlo," Divinia whispered, eyes shut tight.

"I love you all," Reyna said, her eyes wide, body shaking.

Carlo eyed the back door, past the kitchen. "We need to get the fuck outta..."

BOOM!

The boy's words were cut off by the sound of the splintered front door being kicked in, hanging awkwardly to the side, as a man holding an assault rifle stepped into the room.

"Charles?" Divinia said in shock, looking at the charming man from the lounge, now dressed in biker leathers and holding a menacing weapon. With him were three armed men in military ballistic gear. The were all draped with large "LOCC" signage stuck to their backs to identify them in the crossfire.

Divinia's mind was a blur.

"You all okay?" C.B. asked. "Nobody's shot?" The three on the floor remained frozen in shock, but seemingly unharmed. "Medic's on the way. You can get up now, if you're able."

Divinia was the first to sit up. She reached over and patted down her loved ones for wounds. "I think... I think we're good."

"What the fuck is happening?" Carlo yelled.

"It's over, that's all you need to know," C.B. said.

"The fuck it is!"

"Carlo!" Reyna said.

"Where's my father? Where's Tito Bram?"

Divinia walked up to C.B. "Who the hell are you? I know it's not 'Charles.'"

"Charles was my grandfather, ma'am." His face had a look of apology for having deceived her. "I'm SAC Cyrus Bernard..."

"No more lies! SAC?"

"Special Agent in Charge," Carlo said in wonder. "He's FBI."

"You're smarter than you look, kid, but I'm not federal. I'm with a county task force." He pointed to the letters across one of his men's vests. "Your uncle asked me to watch the house while he's away. His instincts proved correct. I wouldn't go out on the front lawn right now if I were you."

"What or who is out there?" Divinia asked.

"Members of the HK-9. They've been dealt with."

"Dead?"

"Yes, ma'am."

C.B.'s men searched the house and secured the property as EMTs arrived to tend to the civilians. He took Divinia aside, not sure where to begin. He noted the deep slash across the cheek, the blood dripping down her neck. "Let's get that stitched up..."

"You're out for my husband, aren't you?"

"We were, but today there're others to worry about."

"That's why you were at Corazon," she said, piecing things together. "Our conversation was just a cover. You were looking for him."

"No, ma'am. I really was looking for you. That was no lie."

"But everything else was."

"Had to be," C.B. said, "and I'm truly sorry for that. But know that the lies are done. Everything from here on out is the truth."

"How could I possibly believe you?" Divinia looked at her destroyed living room, at her mother-in-law being examined by a medic. She wanted to bash her fists into his chest. "How could I possibly believe anyone?"

"We can talk about the ethics of covert deception tactics later. Right now, we need to get you to safety."

"My husband!" Lola Reyna said from the kitchen where an EMT was examining her. "Otto!"

"We have men at the hospital, ma'am. He's safe in his recovery room."

"And where is *my* husband?" Divinia asked. "Why are they doing this?"

C.B. picked up the last cup of tsokolate from the coffee table, the only one not obliterated in the melee. He took a sip, pausing in thought. The calculated mundane gesture and calm demeanor somehow helped ease Divinia. "I can't tell you exactly where he is or what he's doing because I simply don't now, but from what I do know about him, it should all be over soon."

"What do we do until then?"

C.B. remembered something he heard Bram say on the phone earlier. "If you've ever prayed before, Divinia, pray for him now."

52

Another Kind of War

Joey The Rose straddled his motorcycle, motor running, parked in the early-evening shadows across the street from Hank Brighton's house. The street was quiet, with no signs of cops or gangsters on the suburban block. Candy sat behind him, her legs hot from the bike's engine, barely able to keep from jumping off and running to her front door. She took off the helmet Joey had lent her and stared at Hank's pickup truck in the driveway, having arrived ten minutes before them. The garage door stood open in front of it.

"Why the hell did you make me come with you!" she yelled over the rumble of the idling bike. "This thing's barely big enough for you!"

"Hank's orders!" he yelled back.

"And why are we still out here? Hank's alone in there!"

"Ed's orders! We stay back! Gotta scope out the neighborhood before moving in!"

"Nobody's..." Frustrated, Candy reached over Joey's arm and shut off the loud bike. "Nobody's coming here, dumbass."

"Then why the hurry?"

"Because he's alone, scared." Candy imagined the old man worrying about her, about their safety. "Nobody's coming, Joey."

"We sit tight until we know for sure." Joey hoped she was right. "Bram's on his way. We need to regroup with him before we do anything stupid."

"You really think someone out for Ed's business gives a shit about an old man who fixes cars for him?"

"We're past just business at this point. They wanna bend and break him any way they can. That means his people could get caught up in this shit."

"More reason to head inside." Candy clutched the car door handle. "Can't imagine Ed bending over for no one."

"I don't think they can imagine that either. That's the scary part."

Candy looked at her house as if she had night vision and could see through walls, her imagination poking at her. "Dammit, Joey..."

"Hank's fine. He's tougher than you think. Besides, you said no one was coming, dumbass, remember? We stay here until we hear word."

Candy waited to hear a gunshot, clatter, or scream, but found the peaceful scene even more unnerving. She pulled her leg over the bike, got to her feet, and shoved the helmet into Joey's lap. "The word is 'fuck that shit.' I'll leave the sitting tight to you, Joey."

"Hold on, if we..."

She didn't hear the rest of the big man's warning as she walked across the street toward her home. She almost hoped someone would spot her, try to tangle with her, for her hand gripped a canister of pepper spray tucked in her jacket pocket. How satisfying it would have been to melt the face of some fool who dared mess with her father figure.

Joey muttered a curse as he got off his Honda and jogged behind her, trying to catch her before she reached the front door.

"Thought you were staying back?" she asked, still heading toward her house. "Ed would be disappointed if he knew you disobeyed orders."

"He'd also be disappointed if you died."

Standing on her front lawn, Candy turned to confront him as he reached her. "Jesus, you're dramatic, you know that?"

Joey looked around to ensure that no one was watching. He clicked on his phone's flashlight and pulled up his right sleeve, exposing a long scar that stretched down his forearm. "See that? Know how I got that?" Candy shook her head. "I did a pickup once, at a nice, quiet house like your house, on a nice, quiet street like this street. They said to just walk in and take the package. Front door was rigged with a pipe bomb."

Candy traced the long scar with her finger. "No shit?" she said under her breath. "And you're still breathing?"

"Blast was weak, not enough to kill me, but it turned my arm into taco meat. Eddie blames himself even though it was my fuck-up. Dramatic enough for you?"

"But Hank..."

"He's always gone inside through the garage. Shit, I don't live with him and even I know that."

She glanced over her shoulder at the front door, then down to his scar. "What are the odds of that happening to you twice?"

"Not zero," Joey said. "So maybe take it easy with the Rambo approach."

Joey led her into the open garage, a space that served as Hank's home workshop. Industrial equipment for woodworking and machining metal made it feel like a labyrinth, with a single lamp hung over a drill press lighting their path.

"Taco meat, huh?" Candy said with a laugh. "From now on, I'm calling you Sloppy Joe."

Joey gestured for her to shut up, listening as he crept across the garage. He pointed his phone light to the floor, covered in years of aluminum shavings and sawdust. A trail of footprints led from Hank's truck, between the machines, to the door that led inside.

"So?" she asked.

"One set of footprints," he said. "Just Hank's."

"So he is alone, just like I fuckin' said."

"Yeah, except now we're not just fuckin' guessing." He opened the door and entered first, with Candy following close behind.

Hank sat at his kitchen table sipping a "Bilog Breeze," a simple drink comprising a can of Sprite with a shot of Gin Bilog added. He recalled the day, three decades earlier, when Bram made one for his beloved "Tito Hank" while celebrating his 21st birthday.

> *I cannot sufficiently explain the relationship between my brother and Hank. Growing up around our father's shop – first in San Francisco, later in Los Angeles – I'd always regarded Hank as an uncle, but Bram saw him as a kindred spirit. In turn, I believe Hank saw Bram as the son he and Marceline never had, just as he now saw Candy as his daughter. Divinia credits the Nightingale Effect, concluding that Hank saw them as broken souls to shelter under his wing. I think the lonely old man simply had a lot of love to give.*

Hank sipped his drink, took a small wooden box down from a tall shelf, and wiped the years of dust from its top. His fingers trembled as he steeled himself to open it, but the lid felt as if it were glued down. He shook his head and laughed at his hesitation before taking another swig of his Breeze.

While helping our father in the shop, Bram worked closely with Hank. They must've repaired and rebuilt five hundred cars together. The work was good for my brother. It calmed him, gave him a sense of purpose and pride, to service rather than destroy.

Fridays meant Happy Hour, and the "Bilog Breeze" became their favorite shared drink, if only for the ceremony behind it. According to Bram, it must be mixed in the soda can and could only be made with genuine Ginebra San Miguel's gin. Most important of all, it had to be shared with a close friend or relative.

Sitting scared and alone in his house, waiting for a call from the brothers, Hank ignored the last prerequisite, making a Breeze only for himself. He broke his adopted nephew's tradition based on the superstition they created together, the notion that the Philippine drink brought out a man's courage. With his nephews running headlong into a city-wide gang war, the old man felt helpless and in need of all the spirit and mettle he could muster, the kind of bravery he depended on in Vietnam long ago.

Hank stared down at the decorative wooden box where his morning breakfast normally sat. The box hinge squeaked as he opened it to gaze upon his old 9mm pistol, a Walther P38 he bought in his youth from an Oakland pawn shop shortly before he moved to Los Angeles. He'd bought it for protection against the hoods that harassed small businesses in The Bay, but never felt the need to brandish it in his new life working for Otto Harrison, then later for the man's stepson. He figured he'd left all the trouble behind him.

The Latino and Asian gangs around Historic Filipinotown were all small-time when Hank first arrived in SoCal. They mostly locked horns with each other while ignoring my father's shop, run by harmless old putis. What little drama that unfolded was handled by Bram and myself, but with all the heat on me now, Hank realized what we all came to discover, that a man's pistol is never truly retired. He'd merely been waiting for trouble to catch up to him.

Hank looked up at a framed photo of his wedding, hung on the wall next to his war medals. The photo was so clear, it could have been taken that week: a bride and groom surrounded by friends and family. It felt like those joyous times happened to another man in another life. The memory brought a tear to his eye, but seemed tainted when he picked up the gun.

"I may finally have to use this, Marceline," he said to his late wife. "If it was just me in this house, I'd wait it out, but it's not just me no more. I have to protect our little girl."

"I can protect myself," Candy said, as she and Joey entered the kitchen from the garage. Touched by Hank's words, she choked back her feelings. "And I ain't little no more."

"Of course not." Startled, Hank wiped away the tear. He quickly placed the pistol back in its box, shut the lid, and turned away. "I don't doubt you."

"I never took you for a cowboy, Hank," Joey said, opening the box for a peek. "A gun ain't like a camera, where you just point and shoot."

"You don't think I know that?"

"Since when have you ever used a piece?"

"I used them plenty in the service, son!" Hank remained sitting, facing away from the big man. "You think I've been under a car my whole life? I know you and Eddie get mixed up with vermin every day, but I was knee deep in the shit! You think some street punks can compare to a jungle full of VC? Or PAVN?"

"That was a long time ago." Joey had forgotten Hank's former life as a soldier in the jungles of Vietnam and felt foolish for questioning him. He'd never heard the sweet old man raise his voice, ferocious, barking like a drill sergeant, and realized that "a long time ago" can seem like yesterday to a veteran. "I'm sorry Hank. I only meant that a gun at your head is a gun at your head, here or there or wherever, that's all..."

"Wherever?" Hank's voice deepened as his rage reached a boil. "I've had guns trained on me more times than you've wiped your ass! Guns, shells, mines, grenades, from all sides in pitch black darkness and pounding rain, 9,000 miles from home, and you say wherever?"

"Easy, Hank," Candy said, having never seen her father's trauma surface before.

The old man could smell the burning trees, see the moonlight shine off the spent ammo at his feet. "I burrowed deep into the mud to stay alive only to climb out and bury my brothers-in-arms piled taller than even you, big man! And now I may have to bury more! Wherever??"

"I meant no disrespect," Joey said, careful. "You're here now, Hank. You ain't there no more."

"I'm here now."

"That's right, here with me and Candy."

The wall of flames faded, and his wife's flowery wallpaper returned. Having vented it all out, the old man suddenly felt like a heel. He took a breath and shut the box. "No disrespect from me either, Big Man. Forgive me for being jumpy. It's been... a day."

"Still is," Joey said. "I wasn't in the mud with you, can't imagine what it was like over there, but we're in another kind of war now, and I don't wanna bury nobody, neither."

Hank nodded and placed a hand on Joey's shoulder, still facing away slightly from him and the girl as if trying not to show the hopelessness and fear on his face.

"Enough of this touchy-feely bullshit," Candy said, fighting back her own welling emotions. "Now that we're all chummy again, have any of those goons come by?"

"Nah, they don't even know I exist," Hank said, tired. "They're too busy with the brothers. Any word from Eddie?"

"Not yet," Joey said, "but let's all keep our phones ready."

"Coffee?" Candy asked. She needed an everyday task to distance them from her father figure's moment of heartbreak, to grab some semblance of normalcy and control. "I could use a boost of caffeine."

"Make mine a Grande," Joey said. "Lotsa cream and sugar."

"No Jameson?" Hank asked.

"Gotta keep a clear head."

"Good man, as the boss always says."

"Well, I hope the boss calls soon. I normally don't worry about Ed, but him and Bram being out there has got me thinking."

"Don't think too much," Candy said. "You'll hurt yourself."

Joey ignored the jab as he secured the house while Candy filled a kettle with water and set it on the stove. She poured ground coffee into a French press and waited for the boil. From the corner of her eye, she saw Hank – still facing the wall – press his

Lynn Harrod

soda can against his left cheek. She spun around in an instant, turned his head, and saw that the left side of his face was swollen red.

"You said the gangsters didn't come? What the hell, Hank?"

"Simmer down, girl." Hank pulled her hands from his tender face. "It wasn't no gangsters."

"Then who the fuck tattooed you?"

Joey heard the commotion and ran back into the kitchen. Hank gestured for them to calm down.

"I said it wasn't no gangsters." A story about slipping on an ice cube and falling against the kitchen counter formed in his mind, but Candy's fierce stare killed it the idea. He never could lie to her. "It was George."

"That fuckin' gorilla!" she said, clutching the pepper spray in her pocket. "I knew that dumbass had no guts! He wouldn't have tried nothing if I were here!"

"That's one helluva shiner," Joey said, shocked, as if he could see Hank's discolored face getting worse before his eyes. He knelt down beside his friend and took a closer look. "Who is George, and what did he do to you?"

"George Hall," Candy said. "Great big motherfucker, lives next door. He's had it in for Hank for a long time."

Joey looked out the window at George Hall's house. He could hear several men talking, laughing. Loud music kicked on, the start of a party. "What happened, Hank?"

"We had words. Things got hot."

"So, he fuckin' smacked you in the face?" Candy asked.

Hank nodded.

"Wasn't just a smack." Joey said. He noticed little pools of blood soaked into Hank's clothes, on his left pant leg and lower back. The old man's rage, his memories of war and feeling helpless, suddenly made sense. "He hit you a few times, didn't he? And not with his fists."

At that point, Hank didn't bother trying to spin it. "He used a wrench."

"That son of a bitch!" the girl said.

"I'm sore all over," the old man said, "but I've had worse. I'll be okay, Candy."

"And I'm gonna march over there and rip his fuckin' balls off!"

"Whoa, let's take a moment to breathe. We're in no position to make waves right now."

"Bullshit!"

"When this all blows over, and Eddie's given the All Clear, maybe then we can straighten things out with George."

"I'll go straighten him out right now," Joey said, fuming. "I'm a great big motherfucker, too. Which house is his?"

"Next to our garage," Candy said, eager to shove her pepper spray into George's eyes. She knelt and pulled up Hank's pant leg, saw his bloody laceration. "I say we go over there and teach him some manners..."

"Settle down!" Hank said firmly. He rose to his feet, dizzy, losing balance for a moment, a sight that broke the young girl's heart. "Listen to me! George ain't alone! He's got his buddies over there right now, a pack of roided up gym bros, so no one is gonna do nothing, understand? We wait for Eddie's call and that's that!"

"Hank..."

"I said listen! We seem to be off the gangs' radar right now."

"And the cops," Joey said.

"That's right. The last thing we need is to cause a scene. The brothers are out there fighting for their lives in a goddamn war zone. Attracting attention could get them killed." Candy and Joey didn't seem convinced. Their bodies swayed as if ready for a fight. "I need to hear you say 'Yes, Hank,' and I need you to mean it."

Lynn Harrod

"You got it, Hank," Candy said, relenting.

"Sure thing," Joey said. "I intend to cause a 'scene' with this George Hall bastard soon enough, but you're right, we gotta sit tight for now. That was the plan."

"That's *still* the plan," Hank said, "and whatever you do, whatever happens, for Crissakes, do NOT tell Bram about this. I mean never! Is that clear?"

The kettle whistled as it reached a boil.

Hank saw that Candy's eyes were fixed on the living room behind him. His stomach fell out as he turned to see Bram standing there. The loud music had covered the sound of their front door opening.

"Bram, how long have you..." Hank silenced himself, didn't know what to say to his nephew, for Bram's wide eyes and clinched fists told them he'd heard every word.

53

The Right Question

George Hall stood in the middle of his dining room holding a bottle of Coors Light, his fifth since coming home with his friends an hour before. The tall, stocky man grinned as he walked around his new pool table, allowing the sides of his leather overcoat to brush against its oak trim. His long-time drinking buddies, Artie Guzman, Ryan Toreno, and Jimbo Perkins, had just finished assembling it for their leader and set their beers down for celebratory tequila shots at the corner wet bar. Together in the same room, they looked like a pack of bulldogs standing upright, donned in denim and leather.

"Oh, we're gonna use the hell out of this," George said to the smiles of his group. "Friday night, we shoot some pool, get fucked up, bring in some strippers..."

"One for each of us this time," Jimbo said. "Three ain't enough. I ain't sharin' again."

"What're you fuckin' moaning about? You had your turn with that Mexican chica. What was that bitch's name? Rosalinda?"

"Yeah, but she was all spent by then. Girl had no enthusiasm left after suffering with you."

George's eyes narrowed as if dared to a duel. "What do you expect? Maybe after having a real man, she could barely stand the sight of your dried up gummy worm."

The group laughed, though Jimbo was not amused. "Or maybe she took a whiff of your dog-ass cologne, and it just drained the life out of her."

"You got it backward, Jimbo. Bitch drained me." George laughed so hard he almost shot beer out his nose. "Least with me, there was something to drain! You need to remember your little blue vitamins!"

Jimbo dismissed the mockery with a wave of his middle finger. "I mean it, one for each of us. Either that, or I get first pick this time."

"I tell you what," George said as he poured four more shots of tequila. "We'll get the same three bitches, plus we'll have them send a fresh, oiled up fag just for you."

George, Ryan, and Artie howled with laughter and shot their tequila, while Jimbo shook his head and downed his. He gave up on the slam war with his leader.

"Sloppy seconds is what you get for always being late," Ryan said. "Always late, just like today."

"Fucker gets here in time to enjoy the pool table," Artie said. "Didn't get here sooner to help haul it in and set it up... and deal with that... other thing."

"I bolted the legs on, didn't I?" Jimbo said.

"Oh yeah, real hard work."

"Gimme a break. I had shit to do."

"You always got shit to do," George said. "That's why you're always late, and that's why you get the exhausted leftover bitch, jus' saying."

"Fuckin' forget it," Jimbo muttered. His friends were already five or six beers ahead of him, and he felt the pressure to catch up quickly or risk being the butt of their jokes for the rest of the evening. He stepped behind the corner wet bar and cracked open a beer. Being late to the party, he didn't know where the bloody crescent wrench on the bar came from. "What's with that?"

"You ain't the only one who had shit to do," George said. "We had a talk with my so-called mechanic."

"That old dude next door?"

Hank had come home an hour before while George was 'supervising' Ryan and Artie bringing in the new pool table. George saw fear in Hank's face when he arrived, and it inspired him to use that fear to 'settle' their dispute.

The wrench they used for the table laid within reach.

"You shoulda seen George shove him around," Ryan said as he chalked a pool cue. "Just when he got his balance back, George kicked him down again, like five times in a row. Guy was shaking, pissin' himself."

"His daughter didn't say nothin'?"

"She wasn't home," George said, "not that it matters."

"What'd he do?" Jimbo was familiar with Hank and Candy and actually liked them. He'd brought his Camaro to the shop many times over the years.

"He stuck a used up turbo in the Charger," George said, "even though I paid for a new one. It ended up blowing the engine on me at the track."

"That don't make sense," Jimbo said, knowing it wasn't true.

"And yet that's what happened."

"How the fuck does a bad turbo... so what'd you do to him?"

"You saw the wrench!" George said with a laugh. "Clocked him in the face. Got him good in the leg, too!"

"And the back!" Ryan said.

"Old man fucked around and found out!" Artie said.

Jimbo imagined George, Ryan, and Artie before he arrived, confronting Hank in his home, taunting and pushing him around before their argument ended with several swings of the heavy tool. "You don't think that's a little harsh? I mean, the guy's a senior citizen."

"Fuckin' hell, Jimbo!" George said. "If I knew you were sucking his dick, I would have gone easy. But hey, maybe I should have hit him in the mouth! No teeth makes for better head!"

Jimbo sipped his beer, didn't share in the wild drunken laugher of his pack. It was one of those moments where he questioned his place in this circle of toxic friends.

George saw the disapproval in Jimbo's eyes. He picked up the bloody wrench, held it upright like a scepter. "Look, think of it as a preventative thing, conditioning, like training a mutt. From now on, all I gotta do it hold this fuckin' wrench, and the old fart won't give me shit. Wouldn't have meant nothin' before, but it sure as shit will now."

"I guess," Jimbo said, "but don't be surprised if Candy comes over here with a vengeance. I wouldn't fuck with her."

"Candy? You know her name?"

"I'm serious."

"Let the bitch come! You think I can't handle her?" George faced the front door, holding the wrench like a weapon. "In fact, I hope she comes over. Maybe you can have her sloppy seconds..."

BOOM!

All four men turned to the front door as Bram kicked it down with the anger and force of a mob.

"George Hall!" Bram shouted.

"Who the fuck are you?" George asked from the other side of the pool table. He'd never seen the short, bald, muscular man before.

"Wrong question!"

Bram ran toward the group. In one swift movement, he slugged Artie in the gut, clutched him by the hair, and slammed his head to the pool table's oak railing three times, sending blood spatter across the green felt.

He spun around and thrust his foot into Ryan's knee, snapping it back, before punching him in the square in the chest, making him vomit his tequila. An upward kick broke the man's jaw.

"George Hall!" Bram shouted again.

"You wanna fight?" George screamed. He ran behind the wet bar and threw open the drawers. "You come here for a fight?"

"Wrong question!"

Bram sprinted toward Jimbo, who held up his hands, dropping his beer bottle.

"I had nothin' to do with it!" Jimbo said, quickly figuring out why the demonic man was there. "I jus' got here!"

"Where is it?" Bram asked. He grabbed Jimbo's arm, raised it up, and spun it down around his back, threatening to break it at the shoulder. "Where is it??"

"Wh-where's what?"

"The wrench!"

Their arms intertwined, Bram bent his elbow and twisted Jimbo's arm to where it nearly burst from its socket. With three solid jabs to the face, Jimbo was out, limp in Bram's arms.

George breathed heavily as he rummaged frantically through the wet bar until he found his gun. He grabbed it from its drawer and blindly fired...

BLAM! BLAM! BLAM!

...hitting oak and brass and glassware as Bram overturned the entire bar and tossed it aside, removing the only barrier between them. George was now cornered, unprotected, and more frightened than he'd ever felt in his life.

"You want... money??"

"Wrong question again! You're as stupid as they say!"

George raised the gun, but Bram slapped it from his hand and snaked it from the air. He shoved the barrel into George's neck, pressing so hard that the man couldn't breathe.

"The right question is, am I here for Hank? The answer is yes!"

Though Bram stood half the size of these men, he was ten times their menace, something George instantly knew from the moment he exploded into his home.

"Where's the wrench?" Bram demanded.

George tried to spit out an apology, a plea for his life, but his voice was muffled by the gun barrel that nearly collapsed his windpipe. He knew words wouldn't have made any difference anyway, and he pointed with his watery, terrified eyes to the wrench at his feet.

Bram released George and picked up the heavy tool with a firm grip. He stared at the large, wheezing man shoved against the corner, looked him up and down as if deciding what to do with him.

"I got carried away," George said in his horse voice, trying to catch his breath. He looked past Bram at his friends sprawled across the room, beaten, broken, bloody. "We had an argument! I got carried away!"

"Maybe I'll get carried away!"

"I'm sorry!" George trembled, felt his motor functions failing.

"I should strike you in the face like you did to Hank, but that would likely kill you, and he made me promise to spare your life."

"Th-thank you..."

"It's not me you should thank!" Bram yelled.

"Thank you... Hank!"

"That's right, thank you Hank! Thank you Hank! He's the only reason you and your jackals are still alive."

"Th-thank you H-Hank!"

"I'm taking your car."

"My car?" George felt his bowels release.

"No. *My* car."

"Your car!"

"That's right," Bram said, his eyes aflame. "That shiny pimped Dodge out there? My car."

"Yes! Take it!"

"And I'm not going to kill you with this wrench upside your head. That was my promise."

"Thank you... Hank!"

"Good. You may be stupid, but you learn." Bram was to leave George with a dire warning, but the image of the old man being beaten by a group of men laughing with glee set his blood boiling. "I promised, not the head.... but that leaves the rest of your body."

"Wait... no...!"

The next minute felt like a lifetime.

Bram beat George's body with the bloody crescent wrench, each strike coming down like a sledgehammer. He shattered George's knees, elbows, ribs, legs, every bone below his neck. He crushed his feet and hands, landed blow after blow against the man's back until the massive bruises seeped blood. The pain was so overwhelming that George could only whimper.

When Bram finally tossed the wrench aside, he stood over the mutilated body of George Hall and took a moment to gather himself, for he knew he could easily continue without pause until the man was reduced to a hulking pile of gristle.

"I promised not to kill you," Bram said, "and I keep my promises. But if you ever so much as look in Hank's direction, it'll be you, me, and the wrench again." George nodded and moaned in agony, unable to move even a finger. "If you see Hank or Candy anywhere in this world, you run and hide, and if you ever see me, just close your eyes."

Bram turned to leave, but his rage fell to shame when he saw Joey and Candy at the open door. They'd watched the brutal scene unfold, but were too scared to intervene.

* * *

With his friends watching in silence, Bram tried to start the Charger sitting in George's driveway, but it wouldn't turn over. He slammed his fists to the steering wheel in frustration.

"Where you hurrying off to?" Joey asked, breaking the awkward silence.

"To look for Eddie! But not in this glossy piece of shit."

"Dude blew out the engine at the weekend track," Candy said. "That's why he fucked with Hank."

Bram looked up at the girl and shook his head. "That tangina kigol targeted Hank because he's a kind old man who doesn't fight back. The car was just an excuse. I know his type well." Before breaking down George's door moments earlier, Bram had crouched below his front window and heard the last minute of the group's vulgar boasting. "They enjoyed beating Hank, like twisted boys tormenting a puppy."

Bram got out of the slick race car and headed back to Hank's house, his friends close behind. They saw blood drip from Bram's shirt, but assumed it belonged to one of the men sprawled across the floor next door.

Upon entering the house, Joey saw Hank down the hall, asleep in bed with an ice pack on his cheek. Candy went to shut his door.

"Fuck, Bram," Joey said in a low voice. "You really drove over the cliff with those guys."

"It's the one and only message these kinds of men understand," Bram said from the bathroom as he searched the medicine cabinet. He picked out several cotton squares and a bottle of alcohol. He tended to a wound on his torso, keeping it out of Joey's sight. "They won't harm Hank ever again."

"No, I don't think they will."

"I don't think they'll fuck with anyone again," Candy said when she returned, still in shock, the image of their broken bodies burned into her mind.

She knew that the Duque Brothers were notorious, especially Bram, who was known for his monstrous wrath. She'd heard all the stories, how Bram seemingly had no fear, but now she knew he also had no mercy. From her life on the street before entering Hank's life, she'd known about the violence that SoCal's gangs were capable of, the same men the brothers dealt with every day. All of it was dwarfed by the savage display she'd just witnessed in George Hall's den.

Candy feared the man washing up in her bathroom, but also felt relief knowing how highly he regarded her adopted father. Abraham Duque may have been a demon, but he was *their* demon, and in a sense, he was like her half-brother.

"Candy?" Hank called from the bedroom in a sleepy voice. "You guys back? You okay?"

As she left to tend to him, Bram's cell phone rang.

He picked it up and recognized C.B.'s voice.

"Abraham?" the agent asked. "Abraham, talk to me."

"You talk to me," Bram said with a grunt. "My family?"

"There was a hit on the house, like Ed figured, but we handled it. Everyone's fine."

Bram shut his eyes tight. He hated how the special agent called his brother "Ed" as if they were friends, but felt thankful that he hadn't left his loved ones to die. "Christiana?"

"Still missing," C.B. said. "We haven't heard from her. One of my men found her for a moment, but now he's missing as well."

Bram could feel his rage building, swirling with equal regret and despair. "Eddie?"

"I had a man tracking him, but he lost the trail. I think Ed made him and shook him off."

"Which way was my brother headed?"

"From the direction he was driving, my guess is the scrapyard. What do you want us to do?"

"Stay with my family."

"Now hold on a minute..." C.B. didn't want his Wolves seen in gang territory during this war, for it risked blowing their cover, but he felt compelled to help Edgardo in what seemed to be a suicide mission. "I can send three men..."

"No," Bram said firmly. "I'll go. You won't want to be near that shithole anyway, not with your badges and your rules."

"Fuck the rules, Bram. What are you going to do?"

"Eddie needs me."

"I asked you a simple question," C.B. said with authority. "What are you going to do?"

Bram hung up and took Hank's truck keys from a wall hook. Without a word, he headed for the front door but was stopped by his giant friend, blocking his path.

"Who was that?" Joey had overheard bits of C.B.'s side of the phone call.

Bram ignored him. The big man looked down at Bram's ripped shirt, to his exposed abdomen, to a four-inch square of cotton now taped to his right oblique.

George had managed to shoot Bram during their scrap. A small circle of blood now seeped through the patch.

"How bad is that?" Joey asked, glancing down at the wound.

"I'm still alive." Bram glared at his friend. "Now move."

"Bullet still in your gut?"

"Joey, I need to go…"

"What you need is a doctor, brother…"

"Manahimik ka!" Bram knew Joey meant well, but only saw him as an obstacle at that moment. "I need to go, and I need you to stay here with them."

"Don't worry, I ain't goin' nowhere." Joey could hear Candy comforting Hank in the bedroom and felt for them. He imagined the HK-9 dropping by at any moment, just as they did at Divinia's home. "Maybe you shouldn't go either, huh? The Nines might come in force, and I won't be enough to face 'em."

Bram relaxed his stance, looked Joey in the eyes. "My brother speaks highly of you, told me many stories. From what I hear, you're worth ten of those punyetas. I trust you."

"That means a lot, really, but whoever that was on the other end of that call… I heard him say he can send Ed some help…"

"That whoever was the cop who fucked over Eddie and locked up Carlo."

"He also saved Div and the kids," Joey said.

"Look at you, big man with the big ears. You really do hear everything goin' on."

"Look, maybe let the cops help Ed for once. They owe him."

"My brother doesn't need a cop right now," Bram said. "He needs his loyal dog."

54

Ringside Seats

Edgardo pulled up to the entrance of Galvez Salvage and Scrap, a tall, open gate that led to a winding dirt path through stacks of wrecked cars, big rigs, and mountains of household junk. Sunset approached as he stepped out of his BMW and looked around through a pair of binoculars. The property looked deserted, but he knew it wasn't, not on a night like this.

The few times I had to enter the TSB's yard, the gate had always been chained and locked with one or two men leaning against it, usually smoking, drinking, eyes alert. It served as more of a flex than any real security. Calixto wanted his visitors to get the impression that his scrap pile was actually a fortress and that the gangster sitting atop it was a king on his throne. That night, the kingdom's gate stood open, unattended, inviting.

"Got eyes on them?" Edgardo said into his two-way earpiece.

"A few," Felix responded from his vantage point. "Five men armed with handguns. No sign of Calixto."

"He's here. He fancies himself a warlord, but he's not the type to join the frontline. He'd stay back at base and wait for word."

"Maybe," Felix said. "You might know how he thinks, but that doesn't make him predictable."

"Agreed. As we've said, he may just be a junkyard rat, but he's a smart junkyard rat. That's why he's suddenly so ambitious."

"It won't end the way he wants, Amo."

"However it ends, it must end tonight."

Calixto managed an alliance between the TSB and the HK-9, which explained the joint raid across town. It made sense, considering that they were two sides of the same peso, two Filipino gangs that saw me as a traitor and blamed me for their setbacks. There were no reports of other gangs involved in the attacks. I had to act before that changed.

"Still nothing from the Mexicans or Koreans?" Edgardo asked.

"My sources say they're not even aware of the war, not yet, anyway. Looks like it's just the two pinoys out for you."

Calixto may have convinced Rommel Basilio to join him, but he clearly failed with Mr. Waldo and, of course, The Wolf Pack MC. This concerned me because Calixto would want at least two other outfits backing him. Either he got the LB-13 or the AFA on board without my knowledge, or maybe he did poach one of Waldo's or C.B.'s men. I'd know soon enough.

"C.B. says one of his men is M.I.A."

"Mason," Felix said over their two-way com. "He was last spotted in HiFi, at your coffee shop. He left his truck behind, got into a van with some men... and a girl."

"Christiana?"

"Not sure."

Alarmed, Edgardo quickly checked his phone. He saw a blue dot on a GPS map that placed Chris at the Bloom and Plume. It offered no comfort. "Take care with your aim. She could be here."

"Yes, Amo."

Regardless of who was waiting for me in that scrapyard, I felt certain that my daughter waited with them. It was reason to tread lightly, but also reason enough to strike the final nail in Calixto's coffin when given the chance.

"Eyes inside?"

"Barely," Felix said. "I can't see too far into the main building. I'm gonna circle around, see if I can peek into the others..."

"No. I'm heading in. Proceed to Position Two."

"Yes, Amo. Nearly there."

"Good man."

Edgardo returned to his car, started the hybrid engine, and drove further into the scrapyard. He expected an ambush as he rounded each bend, but when he reached the central cluster of warehouses – his "stolen" Mercedes parked between them – he knew Calixto would certainly not be predictable. The man clearly had something else in mind.

* * *

Calixto Cervantes sat in one of several office chairs in the corner of his largest warehouse, hidden behind stacks of stolen electronics and power tools. He cut and lit a cigar as he watched Edgardo on his iPad. His well-dressed visitor stood alone at the scrapyard's entrance next to his car, the sun falling behind him. He was looking around as if waiting for someone else to arrive.

"Turn around, Duque," Calixto muttered. He wanted to see if Edgardo was talking to someone, but the man kept his back to the gate's camera the whole time. "Putang ina mo! He knows I got him in my sights."

"My dad is smarter than you," Christiana said, hoping to take the gangster's eyes away from the monitor. She sat in another office chair beside Miguel. Mace and two other men stood behind them. "Whatever deal you plan to make, he's going to come out on top."

"Deal?" Calixto laughed. He rose to his feet and circled his guests. "Is that what we're doing here? Making a deal?" He turned to Mace, who grinned at the notion. "Tell this girl about our deal with her smart tatay, Mason."

Mace spun the girl around in her office chair, knelt down, and looked her in the eye. "The only deal being made tonight is your tah-tay's life for yours. How smart is that?"

Chris looked at the floor and stifled a tear. She felt betrayed. Worse, she felt stupid. At the coffee shop, Mace told her what she needed to hear in order to get her to come with him without incident. That's probably how he got Miguel, too, or so she hoped.

"Good news is that it'll all be over soon," the biker said.

"Over for you, anyway."

"Quiet now," Calixto said. "He'll be here in a moment. Man, this is gonna be good."

"What are we doing?" Miguel asked.

"We? So, you're TSB again?"

"When was I not?"

"Oh, I dunno, maybe when Mason took you under his wing at Duque's storage in the hills? How about when you brought me his Benz and pretended that everything went according to plan?"

"I didn't pretend nothing!" Miguel said. "The car's here, ain't it?"

"Cal, what the fuck are you goin' on about?" Mace asked.

"Come on, Mason, you expect me to believe that when I left you alone with my boy in the foothills in the middle of the night that you wouldn't take advantage?"

Mace had to think fast. There's was no point in denying it. Hopefully, the gangster hadn't uncovered his identity. "I got him to work with us, sure, but last I checked, you and me was working together."

"You work for me," Calixto said to both Mace and Miguel. "Ain't no 'together.' Whatever you had Miguelito do for you, I allowed it to happen. You need to remember who's who and what's what, especially in the next 20 minutes."

"However you want to put it, compadre."

Calixto took a long pull of his cigar and stood over Miguel, frozen in his office chair. He exhaled as he spoke. "What did you do for the Wolves?"

Don't fuck this up kid, Mace thought.

"Two drops is all," the teenager said.

"Where?"

"Lincoln Heights."

"Why you?"

"We burned that bridge last year," Mace said, hoping to take over the cover story. "We needed someone who..."

"I was talking to my boy." Calixto kept his eyes on Miguel. "Continue."

"They couldn't be seen by the Mexicans," Miguel said, the words pouring out as he came up with them. "They had some beef."

"There's a hundred Wolves in the pack." Calixto turned to Mace. "You're telling me none of them could have made those drops? All you desert putis may look the same, but did you really think the LB-13 would have recognized every single one of you?"

"Rule Number One is we never take off our colors," Mace said, following the boy's story. "They'd make us in a second."

"I dunno. Still smells funny."

"They needed TSB to represent," Miguel quickly added. "They couldn't send a kano in leather out there."

"I'm getting fuckin' sick of the innuendos, Cal," Mace said, leaning into his defiant character. "We work for you, right? So we got Miguel to do a couple of drops. Don't sweat it, you'll get your cut. Everybody wins."

"Now that I've uncovered it, sure, you bet your ass I get a piece." Calixto rolled the story around in his head, his eyes fixed on Miguel. The boy could almost feel the dice landing in the gangster's mind. "C.B. knows you flipped him?" he asked the biker.

Mace dreaded the word "flipped," for it was usually used when cops turned someone informant. He still wasn't sure if his fake biker gang had been made. "Alpha knows everything I know. I don't think I could hide something from C.B. if I tried."

"Alpha! I love the wolf lingo!" Calixto took a puff of his cigar. "So, where is the old man? This is a big night! I'd think he'd want to be here, but I don't see him. In fact, I don't see any of you Wolves, 'cept you." He walked up to Mace, blew smoke in his face. "And I know ain't none hiding up in the shadows like before. I checked. Tell me the truth, you gone rogue, Mason? You jockeying for your Alpha's seat? You seem like the type. Not sure if I can trust that type."

"Hold your fire, amigo," Mace said. "If you gotta know, he's working a deal with the Armenians in Glendale. They're probably drunk off their asses on brandy rit 'bout now."

"Getting drunk with the Armenian Lords! Ambitious! The AL don't usually work with outsiders."

"Working with outsiders is our speciality," Mace said. "It's why you and me became such good friends."

"Call him," Calixto said. "I want to ask him how good that Ararat brandy is."

"I would, but I left my phone in my truck. You can blame your boys for that."

Calixto looked at his men, the same men that nabbed them at the coffee shop. One of them nodded that Mace spoke the truth. "Maybe I'll call him?"

"He won't pick up, not in the middle of wining and dining the AL. Would you?"

Calixto took a moment to read the biker's perfect stone face. "Hustlers gotta hustle, am I right?"

"And the game goes on."

"Shit, the game ends tonight, kaputol. Lucky you, you're gonna have ringside seats." He looked at his tablet and saw Edgardo's car pull up to their building. "Here we go."

As Calixto walked away, Mace exhaled in relief.

The biker assessed his plight. He'd disobeyed his boss, deviated from their plan, and now stood alone and unarmed, surrounded by Temple Street Boyz in their lair. Two teenagers' lives were in his hands, kids scared out of their minds as an ambush was about to be sprung.

He recalled his boss's odd admiration of The Duke, how he could supposedly emerge from impossible situations with only his keen mind. Whereas Mace had always doubted Edgardo before, believing his reputation to be overblown and unearned, he now hoped that the legend was real, for there could be no other way they'd all make it out alive.

55

Kings in a Corner

Edgardo drove up to the main warehouse. He spotted the living room set in the mud, with cracked leather couches and ratty chairs surrounding a fire pit. He knew it served as the gang's nightly gathering spot, a place for booze and drugs and business out in the open with no place to hide. Another flex.

"Position Two," Felix said over their two-way com. He felt worried when his boss didn't respond, but he knew second position meant radio silence. It had long been their standard procedure, though this was no standard meeting.

Edgardo remained behind the wheel of his car with the engine running as he scanned the scene. The absence of any Temple Street Boyz told him they were surely in their second position as well. With the sun now gone, the area was lit only by the rising moon and the fire pit between the couches. He shifted into Park and pondered the situation.

I've met with Calixto Cervantes enough times to see his thoughts unfold in real time. I could usually gauge his decisions before he reached them. He would never abandon his property, for he'd consider it cowardice, and his men weren't bold enough to stand out in the open during a war. They were likely sheltered in one of the three warehouses, waiting for me or the cops or another gang to make a move. If the other players were where I assumed them to be, they were watching and waiting for me to take my turn.

Edgardo stepped out of his car and slammed the door. He waited to see if someone had heard it. When no one came running, it further confirmed what he was dealing with.

No doubt, there were two or three guns trained on me, not including Felix's. That I was still alive revealed Calixto's hubris – he wanted to be the one to kill me. He instructed his men not to fire until he gave them a signal, a simple gesture after he'd had time to relish what he believed were my last minutes alive. All I had to do was deduce the signal, to spot his tell.

Edgardo walked into the living room set and sat down on a sofa with the same ease of sitting in his own home. The coffee table next to the fire pit held several bottles of booze and a set of fine glassware. He took the role of a guest and poured himself a double bourbon, his first in many days, as he readied himself for the host. He savored the woodsy spirit, rolling it across his tongue, for he knew that sip of Kentucky rye might prove to be his last if he misread his cards. Out of reflex, he slid his hand into his coat pocket. Despite his uncanny memory, he felt startled to find it empty.

For a moment, I forgot that I deliberately left my gun in the Beemer. How unlike me. I got out of my car with open, empty hands as a peaceful gesture and because I knew it would've been pointless to walk up armed. Considering the fact that I was still breathing, they didn't intend to rush in for the kill. They figured I'd do that. Instead, I would force them to show themselves, to frisk me, to ensure that I was helpless in my final moments.

After waiting ten minutes for others to arrive, a lull in the night meant to further disarm him, Edgardo saw Calixto emerge from his largest warehouse with four men in tow. They held handguns, just as Felix had reported, but Calixto held only his cigar, yet another flex to show his dominance, his control of the situation. Edgardo knew it also served as a facade of predicability, a misdirection.

I had to assume that as I became familiar with Calixto over the years, he also became familiar with me. If this scene had played out a year prior, I'd have projected an 85 Percent chance of survival. By the end of my slow bourbon on that cold leather sofa, I took it down to 55.

"The Duke, here in my yard!" Calixto said with a wide smile. "What an honor!"

"You really mean that?" Edgardo asked. "Or do you greet all visitors with such charm?"

"Both. I always mean what I say, and I'm always charming." Calixto walked up to Edgardo, still relaxed on the sofa. He nodded to one of his men to frisk his guest and showed no surprise to find him unarmed. "I may despise you, Duque. I may even want you six feet in the dirt, but I can still acknowledge the honor of having you here. I imagine Lee Harvey Oswald and John Wilkes Booth both stood in awe before they pulled the trigger."

"You know your history."

"I'm not the idyota you think me to be."

"And I may despise you," Edgardo said, "I may even want you six feet under as well, but not once have I thought you to be anyone's idyota."

"You hear that, boys? That's mutual respect! Pay attention and you might learn something." The gangster took a pull from his cigar, taking a moment to enjoy the smoke swirling in his mouth as he loomed over his guest. "Thank you for coming. I know you don't normally do house calls. I mean, the last time you were here for business, my brother still ran this place."

"That was a long time ago."

"Feels like another life. Smoke?" Calixto pulled a small leather case from his jacket and slid out three cigars. "La Perla de Luzon, Tabacalera, and Arturo Fuente."

"No, thank you so much. This fine bourbon is all I need."

"Good stuff, isn't it? Smooth, well-balanced, notes of vanilla, caramel, and just a hint of spice." Calixto set his cigar case on the coffee table, as if his guest might change his mind.

"Regardless of whatever else is said between us, you have good taste in tobacco and spirits." Edgardo nodded at his Mercedes parked a few yards away. "You also have good taste in cars. I see you still have my SLK. Couldn't bring yourself to chop it up?"

"My SLK, you mean," Calixto said. "How could I chop my favorite trophy? It's a simple yet elegant ride for a simple yet elegant man like you. Not as flashy as that plug-in Beemer you rolled up in, but still a sweet machine. I'm so glad you gave it to Miguel to bring to me."

"I gave it to him?"

"The boy denies it, of course, but really, Duque, don't insult my intelligence. My men failed to boost it twice. You would have me believe that little Miguelito somehow managed it all by himself?"

"Your men failed once, not twice."

"Yes, the tunnel incident. You let them go. How honorable. But what about the next day at your home? Only Miguel walked away from that, probably pissing himself trying to keep your master plan secret."

"If I had a master plan," Edgardo said, "I wouldn't be sitting here helpless in front of you."

"Helpless?" Calixto smirked. "You may be unarmed and outnumbered, Duque, but you're never helpless, are you? What every other hepe, kapitan, and sundalo fail to understand is how that big brain of yours is a weapon."

"But you alone understand it?"

"Oh yes. You used it to kill my men and compromise my boy."

"Interesting theory," Edgardo said.

"No, what's interesting was that little show-and-tell in Sylmar."

"Explain."

"If I must." Calixto relit his cigar. "I was supposed to believe that Yoy Yoy and Jorge were caught breaking into your warehouse in the middle of the night and were killed there. That was the 'show' part. Simple."

"Too simple for you, obviously," Edgardo said. "So what did that 'tell' you?"

"My cousin and Jorge were killed somewhere else, probably your house. You brought their bodies to the warehouse, dropped them on the floor, and gave Miguel that fuckin' mahina story to follow. Your mistake? You forgot to set the scene. Sloppy work."

Edgardo instantly realized his error.

"Their phones were off for hours," Calixto continued, "but were suddenly on again that night. Miguel's phone, however, was on all day, despite what he says, and it placed him at your nanay's house on Magnolia Street. More?"

"Please."

"Up at the warehouse, I saw no sign of struggle, no bullet holes, not even a scuff mark on the cement. Either you weren't smart enough to think of those details, which I doubt, or you figured I wasn't smart enough to notice. Growing up, I was a big fan of *Columbo*. I sense when little details don't add up. They keep me awake at night. Speaking of Columbo, you sure you don't want a cigar?"

Edgardo shook his head as he contained his nerves. "I drink, I don't smoke." He offered no further response to Calixto's point-by-point dismantling of his diversion.

Satisfied, Calixto leaned back against his couch, took a drag from his cigar, and exhaled a long trail of smoke. "Enough bullshit pleasantries. This is the part of every detective story when we lay out our cards, when we give up playing games and stop underestimating each other."

"Agreed."

"So, what brings you to my yard? Truth."

"You tell me," Edgardo said. "You're the warlord here."

"Aren't we all?"

"Perhaps, but you're the warlord who started the war."

Calixto laughed, cigar smoke drifting from his nostrils. His men merely smiled. "You hear that, boys? He says I started the war. You know, I always saw The Duke as a cold, hard, no-nonsense man, yet here you are with a sense of humor."

"Explain."

Edgardo's quick one-word responses were meant to keep Calixto talking, and the arrogant gangster was happy to indulge. Every moment gave Edgardo more clues and more time to think.

"How about a story?" Calixto sat on the couch across from Edgardo, the fire pit and coffee table between them. He took another pull from his cigar as he began. "Once upon a time, there was a small family carving out its own piece of the city. Corner by corner, block by block, the family expanded its operation. Then one day, a shrewd businessman came along and took a juicy cut of everything. The family sold a van full of TVs, the businessman took 50 Trinitrons. The family moved a truck full of damo, the businessman took 20 bricks. And so on and so on. One day..."

"You paint me as a thief. Ironic."

"ONE DAY, the family decided to stand up for what's right, to claim their full share of their hard work. The shrewd businessman didn't like that. Did he propose one of his famous deals that benefits everybody? No. Instead, he turned coat and worked with the cops to reclaim his chunk of the loot, even if he never did shit to earn it. The family fought back, of course, but the shrewd businessman visited the family one night with the audacity to accuse them of starting the war. You with me so far?"

"I'm with you." Edgardo said. "It seems we both have a sense of humor." He poured another bourbon, offering one to Calixto. The gangster waved it away.

"How would you end our story, Duque?"

"We're telling different stories," Edgardo said.

"In that case, don't think of it simply as two men telling two tales. Think of it as a chess game. Some look at chess as a battle of two armies, but I like to think it's two opposing stories fighting for a happy ending, for there can be only one."

"This is no chess game, Calixto."

"Ah, but it is! We've been playing it for weeks! Yoy Yoy was my Bishop. Jorge was my Knight. They tried to take you in that tunnel, but you ended up taking them both. Again, don't insult my intelligence by denying it. And I haven't seen Bakal, my other Bishop, so I can only assume you took him as well. Brilliant moves across the board."

"They weren't clever chess moves," Edgardo said. "You left me no choice but to defend myself."

"I even tried to take your lovely Queen... well, Rom tried... but I just learned that his gambit failed. The feds, men who unknowingly serve as your Pawns, defended her corner. Last I heard, she was alive with a bunch of dead Nines fertilizing her flower beds."

"I thought we dispensed with bullshit pleasantries?"

Calixto revealed a gun. He placed it on the coffee table beside the cigars. "Humor me, just a bit longer."

Calixto felt he had complete control of our shared story, our "chess game," and maybe he did. He had me cornered, wanted to enjoy his win for as long as possible before folding the board, so I endured his gloating. My hands were tied until I knew Chris was safe. Until then, any move I made would fail.

My chance for survival had dropped to 35 Percent.

"Where's my daughter?"

"Christiana! Your Rook! Yes, I took that piece a little while ago. Strangely enough, one of your Pawns helped. I took him days ago."

Calixto pointed to one of his men who then signaled toward the large warehouse. Mace and Chris emerged from the metal building, the biker clutching the teenage girl by the arm. Edgardo could barely make out their faces in the firelight but could see his daughter had been crying.

"Tay?" the girl said, confused, scared.

"Don't worry, Chris, we're working it out," Edgardo said to his daughter. He turned back to his host. "You win, Calixto. You outsmarted me."

"Did I?" Calixto asked. "Say that again, this time with *feeling*."

"You win. Game over. Take all my 'Pawns,' make them yours, I don't care. Take my money, my territory. Take it all. Just let her go."

"Game over?" Calixto nearly salivated as his guest begged for his child's life. It felt surreal to hear The Duke completely surrender, a succulent feeling he couldn't get enough of, even as everything he'd ever wanted was laid before him. "The game is over when I say it's over. You see, we're still playing. Our pieces are still in action." He looked back at the girl, her desperate eyes locked onto her father's.

"But a King doesn't want a Rook," Edgardo said. "The point of the game is to capture the other King. Here I am."

"Ah, there it is," Calixto said with a wide, sinister smile through cigar smoke. "Finally! The Duke of Temple Street acknowledges that he and I are the two Kings of HiFi! The Lords of Los Angeles! How sweet words can be. The problem with releasing her is... that's not how I play. I don't just want the King. No, I want all his pieces. For example, as we sat here just now, drinking bourbon, smoking stogies, I captured one of your Knights."

Calixto pointed to another of his men. From behind a stack of crushed cars, Felix was brought out, beaten bloody. They tossed him to the mud near the Mercedes.

The girl shrieked. Mace grabbed her by the shoulder, tried to shake her back to her senses. "Take a breath, kid. Your dad's working it out."

Edgardo fought the savage anger building in his mind, fueled by both his hatred of the gangster and the three pours of bourbon swirling around his brain.

"If this ain't checkmate," Calixto said, "I don't know what is."

With my man in the shadows brought out into the light, our chance for survival had dropped to 20 Percent. All I could do was hope for an outlier I hadn't anticipated. Until then, I was cornered. I had to flip the script.

"Enough chess!" Edgardo said, dead-staring Calixto. "I've already resigned and offered you everything I have. Tell me exactly what you want, and it's yours."

"I've been asking myself that all day." Calixto eyed the gun on the table between them. "First, I want you to stop begging. It's pitiful and ruins the moment. Second, I just want me and you, two Kings in a corner. All that's left is for one to overturn the other. Rookies or grandmasters, the game always boils down to that last move."

Edgardo looked at Mace, seemingly in Calixto's grip. He assumed it was a ruse, that the undercover agent hadn't been corrupted and was just waiting for the right moment, as he was. There was no other hope.

A slight nod from the biker – and the faint sound of a familiar car in the distance – told him that the game wasn't over just yet.

Edgardo's stone face betrayed nothing.

"My men tell me they've never seen no one fight like you," Calixto said. "They say The Duke strikes like a cobra." He leaned forward. "So many stories. I want to judge for myself."

This was it.

This was the moment Calixto had long fantasized about, King versus King with everything on the line. The two men faced each other, the gun sitting on the coffee table an equal distance between them.

"I'm tired of this game," Edgardo said. "I've been at it far too long. It bores me. I told you we're telling different stories. How about I tell you mine? An old fable."

"Fable?" Calixto laughed as if his guest were merely stalling the inevitable. A moment ago, he was begging for his daughter's life. Now he wanted to tell a futile story.

"Fables are my favorite stories," Edgardo said. "Know why?"

"They end with a lesson." Calixto saw this brief diversion as a way to further savor the moment. "Sure, Duque. Let's have another one. Perhaps I'll finally learn my lesson."

"A shoal of piranhas lived in an underwater cave in a river near the coast. None of the river's fish dared go near, for they knew they'd be devoured."

"Oh, I like this fable so far," Calixto said with a grin, puffing his cigar. "A 'shoal' of piranhas. Please, go on."

"One day, the piranhas saw a big, blue fish swim upriver from the ocean. They waited for it to enter their cave for it would be a feast for the ages. But when the big fish swam into their lair, they were shocked to discover the reality of their situation."

Edgardo heard the familiar truck engine coming closer, and he saw that Calixto was too enraptured in the moment to notice. As the gangster looked down to relight his cigar, Edgardo shot a glance at Mace and Felix.

"The big blue fish was a shark, right?" Calixto said. "And the piranhas never saw it coming? The lesson is that they weren't ready?"

"Maybe, maybe not." Edgardo slid his hand over his belt buckle. "Point is, by the time you have a shark in your cave, feeling ready doesn't matter."

Calixto stared at the gun between them. "The problem with your story is that the shark isn't the big blue fish who wandered into the cave. The shark isn't the famous genius, the man with the legend to live up to, the fool outnumbered seven-to-one."

Seven-to-one, Edgardo noted.

"No, Duque. The shark in any story, the apex predator in any situation, is the man holding the gun."

As we both eyed the pistol on the coffee table, I knew Calixto had long dreamed of that finale, a Wild West showdown to see who's fast and who's dead. If I so much as twitched a finger, he'd make his move, but he wouldn't bother reaching for the gun. Even with the scenario tilted to his favor, with guards and hostages and a home field advantage, Calixto Cervantes, as I understood him, would never offer his opponent a fair fight in the end. I had to keep stoking his fire.

"I told you that I never found you to be a fool," Edgardo said, "but I admit, you're smarter than I thought."

Calixto grimaced at the back-handed compliment. "And you're not the infallible mastermind everyone thinks you are."

"Worrying about what everyone thinks is your obsession, Calixto, not mine. It's what's held you back, kept you small-time on the street corners and in the shadows of a scrap heap. It's why Kalaw Cervantes is still known as the founder of the TSB, the man who built up the gang from nothing, and why you're seen as the little brother who merely put on his boots."

Calixto saw red. "Your mind tricks are pointless, Duque."

"As I always tell people, I don't need mind tricks. It's clear that you want everyone to think that you're smart and powerful, mataas na klase, just like Kalaw, just like Rommel Basilio and his limos and tailored suits. Personally, I find it all meaningless. The only thing that matters to me at any moment is what I think right now."

"So confident, so all-knowing." Calixto flicked his cigar into the mud. "Then make your move, Duque. We're all waiting."

I certainly sounded bold, but even as I arrogantly told my fable of the shark and the piranhas, even as I admonished Calixto and listed his weaknesses and insecurities, my odds of surviving the night hadn't improved. The war of wits was over. Men were about to die. As he said, they were all waiting for me, and I was about to risk everything.

The next minute played out in Edgardo's mind, a risky sequence that involved an unnerving number of factors and players...

One: I throw my dagger at Calixto, disorient him.
Two: Mace takes out the two men near Christiana.
Three: Felix kills the man standing over him.
Four: Bram arrives.
Five: I kill Calixto.

Despite his dare to Edgardo, of all the men in that scrapyard, on edge and anxiously watching each other, it was Calixto who made the first move. He pulled a hidden second gun from his jacket, triggering the events of that final minute...

Edgardo slid the dagger from his belt buckle and flung it across the table at the gangster, the blade plunging into his ribs.

Mace threw the girl to the ground and grabbed the man to his left. As they grappled for the gun, it fired into Mace's left arm. He elbowed the gangster to the face, snatched the weapon, and pointed it at the man to his right.

Felix, still kneeling in the mud, grabbed the leg of the man beside him and pulled him down. After a brief struggle, he took the man's pistol and peppered his legs, sending him down hard.

Bram burst onto the scene in Hank's old truck, its engine roaring as he ran over two other men.

Calixto struggled to raise his gun with the dagger burning in his gut, but Edgardo leapt over the coffee table, yanked his dagger from the Calixto's belly, and thrust it deep into his neck.

The last TSB guard standing watched in horror from the main warehouse. He wisely ran, but Miguel – who had been cowering in the building – tackled him, holding him down long enough for Bram to take over. To the teen's horror, the former enforcer granted the man no mercy, using his firearm to end his life with three quick bursts.

Seven-to-one.

Edgardo looked down at Calixto clutching his neck spewing blood. Seeing that his daughter was distracted by Mace and the men near them, Edgardo quickly pulled his dagger from Calixto's neck and shoved it in twice more. The two men locked eyes as the self-appointed warlord fell limp, his gaze frozen in shock as the life drained from his face. The last thing he saw were The Duke's eyes staring down at him like a demon.

Years of conflict, intense rivalry, and bitter jealousy came to a sudden end. The power structure of organized crime in Los Angeles had shifted, for as Calixto Cervantes died in that scrapyard, so too did the Temple Street Boyz.

Bram rose from the mud near the warehouse and glared at the four surviving men. "Bata! You alive? Eddie?" To his relief, his brother raised his hand. "What do you want me to do with these punyetas?"

Edgardo's first impulse was to execute every TSB on the spot, but as he stood atop the coffee table to survey the grim scene, his heart sank when he saw the shock and confusion on his daughter's face.

"Tatay?" she said, disoriented.

Edgardo ran to Chris and picked her up off the ground. "Batang Babae," he said as his child cried into his shoulder. They held each other in a tight embrace, still reeling in the wake of the violence. He looked down at a guard curled in agony at their feet, the man Mace had wounded.

"What now?" Mace said, catching his stare. The girl looked at the biker with fresh eyes as he wrapped his arm wound tight with his belt. "Duque? You still with us? We got four still breathing."

I was eight again, a frightened boy standing on the edge of a canal in the Tondo District of Manila, watching my father's body floating face-down after The Panginoon shot him behind our store. My mother turned our faces away.

I was nineteen again, quietly stitching my brother's leg in the kitchen at 3AM after a brawl with The Demonyo in the Mission District of San Francisco. Otto watched from the hallway, as we all hoped the injury wasn't permanent.

"Eddie, we need a decision!" Bram said.

"What's wrong with him?" Miguel asked.

They were both unnerved by the man's thousand-yard stare.

I was 35 again, catching my reflection in a puddle after snapping the neck of an LB-13 goon in the Watts District of L.A., the first time I was forced to take a life.

In my panic attack in that scrapyard, as I held Christiana, I realized it was never the violence that shook me. It was the feeling that my soul was being chipped away, and the fear that my family would no longer recognize me. In my hubris, I thought I could keep my family in the dark, but after the murders Chris had just witnessed, I feared that we also murdered her innocence, her feeling of safety, and her faith in me.

"Let them go," Edgardo said, unsure.

Bram looked at his brother in confusion. Hearing his niece's nervous, heavy breathing, he quickly understood the order. "You heard him!" Bram shouted at the others. "You're alive because my brother wishes it!"

Now unarmed, Calixto's men stood frozen, terrified.

Still clutching his child, Edgardo looked to his brother to take over. Seeing Chris tremble in her father's arms, Bram respected his wishes.

"You still have your lives!" Bram called out. "My brother has spoken..." Without warning, he collapsed to the mud, light-headed, and pressed his palm against his wound.

"Aw shit," Mace muttered.

"Tito!" Christiana said. Edgardo kept her from running to him, not wanting her to see the extent of his injury.

"Okay lang, magpahinga ka." Bram dismissed their concern with a scoff, but his grimace spoke otherwise. He wanted to stay strong for the girl, but he knew he would soon succumb to George Hall's lingering gunshot without medical attention.

"What'd he say?" Mace asked quietly, not quite nailing the Tagalog.

"He says he's fine," Edgardo said. "He lies."

"I can get a doc over here, get my guys to clean up this mess..."

"Unacceptable. Keep them away."

"Are you for real?" the biker said. "The man's bleeding out!"

"I said no!"

"So what then?"

Everyone stood in silent shock, rooted to the spot, particularly the remaining guards.

Felix saw both brothers in a bind and took control, just as he did at the Magnolia house. "If you men are still in town tomorrow, we'll find you," he said in an assuring tone. "There's work if you want it. Unlike Calixto, we pay what's right."

Without consulting his boss, Felix offered the same mercy and redemption he granted Bakal's men, knowing they were simply foot soldiers, not power-hungry madmen like their dead chief. He gave Edgardo a look of apology and hoped for approval.

A simple nod allowed it.

"Leave now," Felix said. "Drive your man to the hospital before his legs are gone."

Confused and unsure, the remaining TSB hurried to help their comrade to an SUV in the warehouse. They would have agreed to anything in that moment.

One of them, Paulo Nastor, opened the driver's door but paused, suspicious, as if the vehicle would be riddled with bullets the moment it started down the trail. He stared at Felix, knowing the young man wasn't the decision-maker of the group.

Mace tightened the belt on his arm wound and walked up to the driver. "I'd listen to the man if I was you, amigo."

"And tell them what?" Paulo asked. "When we roll up to the hospital, what am I supposed to say?"

"Fuck if I know. Use your head. Tell 'em you were fucking' around shootin' cans on a fence when your buddy got shot. Tell 'em you were drunk. Say it was a gang thing. Whatever. Otherwise, homeboy's gonna bleed out, and you're gonna have to dig a hole."

With no other choice, Paulo started the engine as his men carried their injured brother and piled into the SUV. The Duque Brothers watched them leave, waiting for the sound of their engine to fade from their ears.

Edgardo took Chris to his BMW and put her in the passenger seat. He knelt beside the girl and rubbed her back, comforting her in the aftermath of the carnage. "I'm sorry you had to see all that. But it's okay now. Everything's going to be okay."

"What about Nay?" she asked, nervous. "And Carlo? He said... he said they were gonna..."

"The cops are protecting them. We're going to see them now. I know this is a lot to ask after everything that's happened, but do you trust me?"

Christiana nodded. Despite all she'd seen, despite learning about her father's second life, her faith in him had never wavered. She still looked to him as the head of their family, a brilliant, caring man she could depend on. "I trust you, Tay."

"That's my good girl. Now give me a few minutes and we'll leave. Okay?" Chris nodded again, grateful to be in the relative quiet of her father's car. Though she still shook with fear, she knew her dad was back in control. Maybe that's all she needed.

Edgardo shut the door and walked away from the car, out of her earshot. He joined his men near the living room set.

"How'd you know how it'd play out?" Mace asked.

"I didn't."

"What do you mean you didn't? We was all on a fuckin' tightrope just now! Me and your boys, we could've made the wrong move at the wrong time, zigged when we shoulda zagged..."

"You could have, but you didn't." Edgardo said.

"You're telling me you rolled the dice on us?"

Edgardo took a moment. "If I had to gamble my life on any group of men, it would be you."

Mace laughed. "Come on, C.B. and I have been studying The Duke for years. You and your brother had this night all planned out, right? Every minute thought out?"

"No," Edgardo said. "I didn't even know he was coming until a minute ago, when I heard his engine."

"Sorry I was late, Bata," Bram said, wincing in pain. "I had other fires to put out."

"So did I," Felix said.

"My parents' house?" Edgardo asked.

"There was a confrontation." His assistant had difficulty wording his update. "Bakal Diaz. He won't be a problem anymore."

"Explain."

Bram realized Felix's hesitation. "Your man finally had to play his trombone."

I knew what Bram meant, and I felt ashamed for pushing Felix to elaborate. After years of living as a nameless, invisible man, my young assistant had to put someone down for the first time. I also knew of his history with Bakal, how it festered into hate over the years, and how his death would haunt Felix for the rest of his life. His loyalty was always clear, but it was unquestionable now.

"Good man... I'm sorry to have put you in that position."

"It's my job."

"It was certainly *not* your job," Edgardo said, "but I tasked you with it, and I promise never to do it again."

"Hold up," Mace said, incredulous, still trying to figure out Edgardo's seemingly clairvoyant actions. "You didn't know your bro was coming? Cars pass by this place all the time. It's all background noise to me, but you're saying you singled out the sound of his truck?"

Every vehicle has a distinct engine signature. Mace's 2019 Harley Davidson Fat Boy 114, for instance, has a slower cadence and more sustained resonance compared to C.B.'s 2020 Soft Tail. My Mercedes SLK had a refined hum that crescendoed into a more powerful throaty rumble when revved high. The sound of a Hank's 1979 Ford F-150 was consistent across the tach and as familiar to me as a song. I'd heard it every morning and every evening for years. It's always idled a little high, even long after its cold start. I explained it all to Mace as a simple matter of observation and deduction, but it still seemed like magic to him.

"You gotta be fuckin' kidding me."

"We can talk cars later," Bram said to Mace, eyeing the biker's arm wound. "Right now, we need to get you to a hospital."

"You first, amigo. Christ, your belly is swelling up like a giant strawberry." Bram nearly fainted. Mace caught him from falling flat to the ground.

"No... hospitals..." Bram said in a pained exhale.

"No 9-1-1 for me, neither. The Wolves will stitch me up, and I suppose I can get 'em to save your ass, too."

"Thank you, Mr. Mason." Edgardo understood their reluctance. An undercover agent's life would essentially end in the ER of a public hospital, and Bram's injury might bring disturbing questions.

"I hate 'Mr. Mason.' My sergeant calls me that. My stepdad calls me that. Cervantes used it fifty times tonight just to get under my skin. My friends call me Mace."

"Are we friends? Mace?"

"We are for now. Duke."

"Eddie." Edgardo nodded in gratitude. He looked at the belt cinched tightly around the biker's bloody left arm. "How bad is that? Can you drive?"

"Not as bad as his gutshot." Mace helped Bram to his feet. "Don't worry, our doc ain't far. I can get us there, make sure we both survive the night."

"Felix will check in with you in an hour, after he's done here." Edgardo turned to his assistant. "Keep me updated. I'm taking Christiana home."

"Yes, Amo." Felix looked at the bodies sprawled across the surrounding mud. "How do you want it done?"

Mace finally realized why Edgardo didn't want any feds coming to the scrapyard to tend to Bram.

There was dirty work to be done.

"Get the boy to help you," Edgardo told Felix. "Keep them whole, but spread them around." Edgardo eyed the thousands of wrecked cars surrounding them, their trunks awaiting.

"Of course."

"We'll finalize them together another day."

Miguel looked confused, but Felix, Bram, and Mace knew that 'finalizing' a body meant teeth, fingerprints, tattoos, and any other identifying marks were to be plucked, cut, and burned away before their corpses were compacted within the confines of a dead sedan.

"And Felix... thank you for being here."

"My honor always, Amo."

"Get the boy to help?" Miguel asked with dread. "Me?"

Bram limped to Miguel, placed both hands on his shoulders. "You wanted to be a gangster, right?"

"I did." Miguel looked at the bloody aftermath, his eyes landing on his childhood friend sitting traumatized in her father's car. With her lost stare, she looked the way he felt. "Not no more."

"Well, you're gonna be one just a little longer." Bram pointed at Felix, who was already dragging a body through the mud. "Ain't nothing more stone-cold gangster than what you're 'bout to do, barako. Think you got another hour in you?"

"I can do another hour." It felt surreal for Miguel to be comforted by the monster who once stood ready to murder him in Edgardo's backyard.

As Felix and Miguel faced the morbid task before them, Edgardo sat behind the wheel of his BMW and drove his daughter home, with Mace and Bram close behind in Hank's old truck.

Lynn Harrod

56

Home Again

Christiana tumbled out of her father's car and ran across the lawn to the porch, straight into Divinia's arms. Mother and daughter held each other as if it were the first time in years, for a few hours ago, they both feared they'd never see each other again. Carlo stood beside them, too tough to join their embrace, but not so tough as to fight back tears. Divinia summoned him with a wave, and he walked into them with his head down, burying his sobs in his mother's shoulder.

Edgardo and Bram remained standing by the car in the driveway.

The girl still didn't entirely trust Mace and insisted at the last minute on making sure her uncle's wound was tended to before coming home. She wanted Carlo to see him alive and well and didn't want to answer questions with morbid uncertainty. To her surprise, the biker was true to his word. She and her father waited in his car behind an abandoned bodega while C.B.'s associate, Benjamin "Preacher" Prendergrast, worked on Bram inside the covert safe house. He extracted the bullet from his ribs, cleaned and stitched the wound, and injected a powerful antibiotic. Bram's next stop would be the "recovery room" of the old shop for a couple of days, but not before showing his smiling face at Divinia's house.

"That biker did a decent job," Bram said, rubbing the bandage wrapped around his torso.

"The man knew what he was doing," Edgardo said.

"Remind me to buy him a beer when this is all over."

LOCC Special Agent Benjamin Prendergrast spent three years in the Level II trauma ward of Cedars-Sinai Medical Center before C.B. recruited him for The Wolf Pack. He had nightly experience dealing with injuries far worse than my brother's gunshot or Mason's arm. Though the words weren't spoken, Prendergrast and the rest of his Wolves saved my brother's life with care and discretion, a debt I can never repay. They wanted to keep Bram for monitoring prior to release, and I agreed, but my daughter and brother both insisted on delaying that order for one hour. Seeing my family huddled together on the porch, glancing over at us in the driveway, I finally understood.

"Why aren't you in that group hug?" Bram asked. The scene made him emotional, filled him with both love and regret.

"I wanted to give them a minute," Edgardo said in his usual stoic tone. "They need each other, need to feel safe and whole, before I step in and explain the way things will be."

"You don't need to explain nothing right now, Bata."

"Yes, I do, now while everything's still fresh in their minds. They may not listen later. Carlo hates me. Chris fears me. Divinia blames me. They're all correct."

"Incorrect," Bram said. He shot his brother an incredulous look. "You know, now that I think about it, Calixto might've had a point."

Edgardo turned to him, curious. "Explain."

Bram nodded his chin to the three-fourths of a family on the porch, holding each other tight, crying together. "Sometimes, Bata, you ain't so smart."

"I'm not ignorant, Kuya." Edgardo found the words difficult. "I'm just afraid."

"Now you explain. Afraid of what?"

"I'm afraid of ruining the moment, as I ruined our family. That includes them, your injury, your time in prison, Tatay's health, Hank and Candy, the boy I mindlessly used like a puppet..."

"Pakshet," Bram said, frustrated with his brother's overthinking. "Maybe you are 'spectrum' like some say. Pull your head out of your self-pitying ass and take a look around. So I got hit. Ain't the first time. I got more lives than a hundred cats. So I spent a dime in prison. I'm here now and I ain't goin' nowhere. Tay's recovering in the hospital, and we both know that tough old goat will outlive you and me."

Edgardo laughed. "Most likely."

"Hank and his girl are fine, I saw to it myself. That runt, Miguel, he's gettin' outta The Life, starting over fresh, and we're gonna keep eyes on him, make sure he doesn't fuck it up again. As for Div and the kids? They're right over there, Bata."

"In a house full of bullet holes."

"So what?" Bram said. "Holes can be patched, the holes in the walls, the hole in my gut. Me and this house and everyone living in it, we're all still standing. You gotta stop thinking and analyzing and replaying what's happened for one fuckin' minute and open your eyes to what's in front of you."

"I'm afraid of that, too. I'm afraid to stop thinking."

"I know." Bram felt for his little brother. "You've always been this way, always gotta be working things out ten moves ahead. It's how *you* feel safe and whole."

"So you do understand," Edgardo said, relieved that at least one person in this world truly knew him.

"But that's The Duke talking, the fixer, the grand strategist. What those three hugging on the porch need right now is Eddie Duque, the father in this family. You follow?"

Edgardo nodded and took a reluctant step toward the house.

"And don't worry," Bram said. "If anyone rolls up, I got you covered." He revealed a pistol tucked into his jeans.

"Good man."

Edgardo walked onto the porch and looked into his family's watery eyes. He expected Christiana, maybe even Carlo, to reach out for him, but it was Divinia who broke the group hug and threw her arms around him.

"Thank you," she whispered into his ear.

"I don't deserve any thanks."

"You brought our baby back, kept us safe. Charles explained everything."

"Charles?"

"C.B.," Divinia said. "I think that's what they call him. He's still inside."

"He's right here." C.B. emerged from the house through the open front door. His men had swept the property while he called in a status update from the living room. As he spoke to his superiors, he couldn't help but overhear the tender reunion outside. "Good to have you back, Duque. The premises are secure, the lines are clean."

Edgardo released his ex and took his kids in each arm. "What exactly did 'Charles' explain?"

"It's okay, Tay," Carlo said. "He told us a lot of it is still classified stuff."

"Really? Well, I'd still like to hear it."

"And I'd be happy to lay it all out again," C.B. said.

The Special Agent explained for the second time that night how Edgardo had been working with Los Angeles Organized Crime Crackdown (LOCC) and the Drug Enforcement Agency of Los Angeles (DEA-LA) in the biggest ongoing series of drug stings in California history. He used his genius, his extensive business contacts, and his former life as a Bay Area gangster to investigate, infiltrate, and ultimately bring down the heads of several crime families – the feared Filipino street gang known as the "Temple Street Boyz" (TSB), the elusive African-American gun running outfit (collectively known as "Mr. Waldo"), the drug-dealing desert bikers ("The Wolf Pack MC"), and the suit-and-tie pan-Asian mob called "Mga Hari sa Kalle 9" or "The Nines" (HK-9).

In the endless war on drugs, the authorities realized that they needed an inside man without a badge. "The Duke of Temple Street" was a character that Edgardo and the authorities came up with together, a legendary fixer who formed ties with every criminal outfit in the Greater Los Angeles area.

C.B. took full responsibility for allowing the Duque Family to get roped into the massive undercover operation, starting with Carlo and the trumped-up charges against him that led to his night in jail. The breadcrumb trail leading to the boy's arrest was orchestrated by the TSB in an attempt to blackmail Edgardo. C.B. unwittingly fell for it at first and didn't realize it was a frame-up until after Carlo was detained.

Of course, none of it was true.

Edgardo simply nodded at C.B.'s outrageous story. He felt guilty about helping the agent feed the grand lie about The Duke's origins, but one look at his mesmerized son cemented it.

"Why didn't you tell us?" the boy asked in admiration. "I guess you couldn't."

"He did it for HiFi, for the city," C.B. said. "He did it for you."

Carlo now saw his father as a superspy, a man who risked his livelihood – and his very life – to help the feds in their ongoing war. It explained everything to him, all those nights his dad couldn't be there for sports awards or family dinners or science fairs. In the boy's eyes, Edgardo was no longer a cold, negligent parent. He was now a hero.

Christiana had a slightly different view, having seen her father as a cunning and brutal killer when cornered. Despite what Edgardo thought in the scrapyard, the girl had witnessed with open eyes the bloody end of Calixto Cervantes by his hand, the rampage her Tito Bram executed with startling efficiency, and the frightening lengths her friend Miguel would endure to survive. Seeing Carlo's renewed love for their father, she kept her knowledge buried inside, just as she had kept her suspicions to herself for years. She concluded he did what he had to do in order to protect them, but that he wasn't the James Bond type her brother had painted in his mind.

Divinia knew better than either of her children. Bram had privately confessed to the Titan Job, a heist that landed him in prison and resulted in the crippling injury of a security guard. It planted the seeds for The Duke in order to repay his debt to Niko Vazquez, head of SF Demonyo. But even if Bram hadn't confided in her, she'd observed and overheard the unabridged, unedited truth from C.B. and his men throughout the tense evening, no hidden mic needed.

Her ex-husband continued using his underworld persona many years after the debt to Vazquez was paid, building his reputation and empire through seemingly impossible exchanges with the city's most dangerous criminals. She wondered if he was trapped in that role, if a mob had threatened him were he to ever walk away from "The Life," as Bram called it. She also wondered if he did it simply for the challenge and thrill, to fully utilize his genius in a way the legal business world didn't offer.

Despite the dangers of his second life, Divinia felt grateful for having such a man fighting for her family. Though she could never forgive him for entangling them in his escalating troubles, she didn't want to shatter the image her children now had, a man who places family before business even when facing the end. Divinia had to accept, for better or worse, that he was the man they needed now.

She may have felt different had she witnessed the scrapyard carnage while her daughter cried and cowered in the middle of it all.

"What's the next move, Tay?" Carlo said, still held in his father's right arm. "You going after the rest?"

"The rest?" Edgardo asked.

"You know, the other gangs."

"What do you know about other gangs, boy?" Bram asked as he limped up to the porch.

"You know, Tito. The Mexicans, the Koreans, all the drugs on the streets."

"Don't forget the Armenians."

"Them, too," Carlo said. "You got business with all of them, right?"

Before Edgardo could think of an extension of the grand cover story, C.B. stepped in. "Your father and I need to discuss that. You folks settle in. My men will stick around for a few days, make sure the coast is clear, so don't be afraid if you see one of us lurking around the neighborhood. It's just a precaution."

"Standard procedure," Carlo said with pride.

"The boy gets it."

"I suppose I get it, too," Divinia said, eyeing her ex.

"But that can wait until tomorrow," Edgardo said.

"Very well." C.B. waved to his men to head out, and Edgardo and Bram started to leave with them.

"Eddie," Divinia said, pushing the words out. "Maybe it would be better if you stay the night. You and Bram."

"Is that what you want?" Edgardo asked, surprised.

"It's... I think the kids would feel safer."

Edgardo looked at the house, past the bullet holes, to the home he once helped build with his ex-wife and the family they had raised together. "Agreed."

"Not me," Bram said, patting his wound over the shirt the Wolves gave him. "I need to get this boo-boo looked at."

"Doctor Prendergrast's orders," Chris said knowingly.

"Your dad knows where to reach me."

Edgardo and his family went into the house together as Bram and C.B. left the property, while two agents quietly remained in a van across the street.

57

Forthright

After three days in the Wolves' care, Bram joined his brother for a meeting. Though he was still in recovery, taking pills and having his wound redressed every few hours, he was well enough to attend the in-person update.

With a bottle of Baguio strawberry wine on the table between them, Edgardo sat beside him, across from C.B. and Mace, in his shuttered noodle shop on Temple Street. The morning sun streamed in through holes in the thin sun-worn paper that covered the windows. As always, business began when Felix brought five glasses to the table and poured everyone three fingers of wine.

As the Duque Brothers sat stone-faced, C.B took the first sip. "Good stuff. Never had wine from the Philippines before, even when I was working over there. Didn't even know they made wine."

"I prefer the rum myself," Mace said. "Tanduay rum's better than any of that Pirates of the Caribbean shit, but this strawberry Boones suits me just fine."

"Baguio," Bram said, correcting him in a curt tone. "It's just cheap table wine." What he actually wanted to say was, "Let's get on with it."

As strange as it felt to be at a table with the Wolves again, this time in one of my own businesses, it also made sense. I owed them for Bram's life and for the cover story with my family. Perhaps more importantly, we had common enemies despite our different goals. Not only were our paths likely to cross again, they seemed destined to align. Like my brother, I also wanted to forgo the pleasantries, but I didn't want to spoil relations before they began. It's simply bad business. Regardless of whatever leverage the bikers had on me, I had no choice but to view our sit-down as just another meeting.

"That was quite a story you came up with," he said to C.B. "though I'm not sure my ex bought it."

"She's too sharp to believe it, but also sharp enough to go with it. For the kids."

"Just know that I appreciated it."

"After landing your son behind bars, it was the least I could do."

"Is that an apology?" Edgardo asked.

"It's as close as you're gonna get to one," the Special Agent said. "Like you, I did what I had to do, but I regret wrangling a youth into it. Looking back, I'm sure there was a better way."

"If it helps, it was my idea," Mace said. "C.B. was against it."

"It doesn't help at all," Bram said, curt. "Visiting Carlo in the joint, that day will burn in my brain forever."

"It will burn within him, as well," Edgardo said.

"He wasn't mixed in with Gen Pop," Mace said, referring to the detention center's General Population block. "We made sure the kid had his own private cell. I hope that at least..."

"Again, that doesn't help at all," Bram said, "because 'the kid' shoulda never been anywhere near that impiyerno in the first place."

"You're right," C.B. said, "and Mace is right, I was dead against that plan. But I'm the lead on this team. I gave the green light, so that's on me. Despite the autonomy Mace enjoys, nothing happens without my say-so. I'm sure you understand how that works, Ed."

"It remains the one thing we have in common."

"That's only because we haven't gotten to know each other yet. There's only so much to learn from reading each other's files."

"So, what now?" Bram asked, impatient. "That's why we're meeting, right? We're patting each other's backs here, but the war ain't exactly over."

C.B. sighed before pushing forward with his proposal. "What now is that I'm going to lay out a future neither of us wants, but it's not like we have a lot of options."

"Proceed," Edgardo said, bracing for the worst.

"Ed, I got a mountain of dirt on you both, more than even you know. It's enough to put you away for a long time. You made a lot of my men, but not all. I have eyes behind all the eyes you spotted."

"The girl at the coffeehouse."

"Yes. Monica Torres. She'd been watching you long before I came on board. Top of her class in Quantico."

"*Second* of her class," Mace said with a grin.

"Behind you, I assume," Edgardo said. "She's good. She actually had me convinced that she found our conversations about clothes and coffee interesting... for a while."

"I also had a custodian at your kids' high school," C.B. said, "and a production assistant at your wife's studio. I figure we might as well be forthright at this point."

"Why pull back the rest of the curtain now?"

"We're getting to know each other, remember? And like I said, I have enough to put you and Bram away today, but given the circumstances, I'd still rather work with you than against you. I think I proved that last night."

"If we're discussing a business relationship, let's lay all our cards on the table, as you put it before." Edgardo finally took his first sip of the business wine, ready to deal. "Turning Bram and myself in would essentially end The Wolf Pack MC, end the years of legwork and the web of connections you've made. The 'circumstances' are not just the gangs at war or my family in danger, but also the existence of your task force. The city would start over with a new team, without you and your hand-picked agents. At your age, it would also likely be the end of your career."

"A future neither of us wants."

"Indeed. Knowing you, I don't believe you're ready to retire to cocktails on a sunny beach just yet."

"If you really knew me," C.B. said with a laugh, "if you knew all the work I've put in, all the sacrifices I've made, you'd realize that tropical escapes have never once crossed my mind. I'll retire when someone takes me out of the game with a double-tap to the temple. The Wolf Pack intends to make it all the way down this rocky road, not pull over and hand it to a team of first-year agents. What I'm saying is that we can navigate this road together. It's a win-win."

"A win-win with the Sword of Damocles hanging over me," Edgardo said.

"My friend, you hung that sword yourself long ago. It's the story of every crime lord I've ever dealt with. I'm just adapting to the situation, and I implore you to do the same."

"Pakshet," Bram muttered. "You want to keep us under your thumb, control our business."

"Pakshet to your business," Mace said. The brothers looked confused. "Pretty sure I fucked that up, but you get what I'm saying."

"What Mace means is that your business is not our top priority," C.B. said. "To be honest, it never was. My superiors may care about the go-betweens, about every featured and walk-on player, but I'm hunting big game. I want the predators that rip this city apart, not the clever fox that scavenges their carcasses."

"We're a means to an end," Edgardo said.

"If you can live with that, I can promise that your day-to-day operations will not be interfered with, assuming there's no bloody warpath involved. I just need help, the kind that only you can provide. I guess what I'm proposing is that you become the hero... the antihero... that your children think you are."

The two brothers looked at each other, their expressions in reluctant agreement.

"Let's say we're in this together," Bram said. "I ask again, what now?"

"That's up to Ed."

"Unacceptable," Edgardo said. "I need to know that your cover is still intact. No one saw you at my wife's house defending my family?"

"I thought she was your ex-wife?" C.B. asked with a grin.

"Answer my question."

"Oh, plenty of guys saw us," Mace said as he poured another finger of wine. "Plenty of dead guys."

"You're absolutely sure no one got out?"

"I had men blocking both ends of the street," C.B. said. "Before we left that night, we searched every yard front and back, found every body, gun, and cartridge. No one got out."

"What about the neighbors?" Bram asked. "Did they call the cops?"

"Six households reported the shooting. I had a scenario prepared regarding a late-night drug raid gone wrong but didn't have to use it. We got lucky."

"Lucky how?"

"They heard it but didn't see anything because the trees blocked their view. And the insides of Divinia's house may still look like hell, but we got the front looking mostly normal by daybreak."

"I wouldn't say 'mostly normal,' more like 'a little shot up.'"

"That was the idea, Kuya," Edgardo said. His brother looked confused.

"Ed's right," C.B. said. "We intentionally left some prominent bullet holes and one broken window. We had to."

"Did those details support your story?"

"What story?" Bram asked.

"Joyride drive-by, amigo," Mace said with a smile. "A few other homes and businesses down the block got some fresh holes in them as well. I made sure of that. Nothing serious. You know how punk kids can be."

"Puchanggala, that's your story?" Bram asked with a laugh. "Punk kids? People really believe that shit? When The Nines came for us, it sounded like World War III!"

"In my experience, folks don't need a detailed, feasible explanation," C.B. said. "Conspiracy theories begin with people who feel unheard, ignored. Psychology 101. Lookie-loos and busy-bodies just need *any* story to make them feel informed, and we happily gave them one. To be sure, my men asked around, and our informants have since confirmed that word on the street is some rowdy boys horsing around with guns shot up your street as they raced by... and we were never there."

"You worry too much, big guy," Mace said to Bram with a sip of his wine. "Cover-ups are our craft, and we're good at our craft, better than you were with the warehouse, anyway."

Bram sighed, trying to keep up. "Okay, so Div's neighbors won't be a problem. I got that. But what about everybody else? How do you explain a bunch of missing Nines? Rom sent them to my sister-in-law's house!"

"They never made it. As we speak, their bodies are being found in an alley in Koreatown. The AFA will take the heat. Sad to report yet another gang-related alley war."

"Why pin this on the Koreans?"

"Simple geography, Kuya," Edgardo said, surmising the agents' fiction. "It actually makes sense."

The Wolves truly were masters at cover stories, and C.B.'s latest tall tale bordered on brilliance. The Asian Family Assassins held territory in Koreatown, on route from Rom's compound to Divinia's house, and they famously had long-standing beef with HK-9, an unresolved conflict involving opium. Of course, no one in the AFA would be identified or arrested, and they wouldn't bother contesting the accusation. If anything, the "alley war" would bolster their standing with the other gangs. A stack of dead Nines with not a single AFA casualty would become legend. C.B. was actually doing them a favor.

"It's a perfect cover," C.B. said, "but regardless of what anyone else thinks, the story will make sense to Basilio."

"It's *almost* perfect," Edgardo said. "The problem is that Rommel is smarter than you realize."

"No, Ed. You were smarter than we realized. Calixto Cervantes was smarter than we realized. But Rommel Basilio is exactly the man we figured. With all the clues we planted, including timed text messages, he won't stop to analyze the scene like you would. He'll simply want payback, and with him that means blood."

"Dugo para sa dugo," Bram said, recalling the HK-9 mantra.

"Perhaps *you're* smarter than I realized," Edgardo said to C.B., seeing the logic in the plan. "That sounds like Rom."

"How can we be sure, Bata? You've always told me you can't think ten steps ahead unless you know your opponent."

Edgardo pondered his brother's question, which lined up with his next move. "I'll find out tomorrow."

"Tomorrow?"

"I'm going to meet with Rom."

"I don't recommend that," C.B. said.

Bram nodded. "We'll meet him together, Bata."

"I definitely don't recommend *that*."

"After everything we discussed," Edgardo said, "you still fear that my personal grievance with Rommel will cloud my judgement?"

"I do," C.B. said. "Convince me otherwise."

"For the second time, gentlemen, you have me in a corner. I know that my business, my freedom, and my family's safety hinge upon my ongoing relationship with The Nines. Thus, my hands are tied, so there will be no revenge from me, not now, anyway."

C.B. took a moment to read Edgardo's stone face. The veteran agent was one of the few men alive still able to sense if there were ulterior motives in his eyes. "I believe you, Ed." He poured some wine into Bram's glass. "It's your suddenly silent partner here I'm worried about."

"If Eddie says Rommel is off limits, so be it," Bram said.

"You, I do *not* believe. That's the rub."

"Putang ina mo! I don't care what you believe! Eddie needs me there! But I get that we don't want any more eyes on us, that we must keep a low profile. It's as simple as that."

"What about George Hall?" Mace asked.

"Who?" Bram said as he scratched the side of his head.

"Goddamn, we gotta play poker some time! Your tell is like a neon sign! George Hall? You know, that guy you took apart on Castle Street? Come on, amigo, we're way past playing dumb."

Bram shrugged at Edgardo.

"Eddie, in case you never met the guy, this is George Hall." Mace held up a disturbing photo of the man shortly after being admitted to the hospital following Bram's vicious attack. "Four of his ribs, his sternum, and his right femur. Those are the only bones in his body *still intact* after 'Ang Makina' was done with him. He'll be in the ICU for the next six months, drinking his supper through a straw." Mace turned to Bram. "He's the fucker who shot you, isn't he?"

Bram shook his head. "It was one of Calixto's men..."

"Nahhh, don't give me that shit. You showed up at the scrapyard with that gutshot. I remember, and I'll bet you a million dollars Eddie remembers, too."

"Of course, he does," C.B. said. "He'd remember if Bram showed up with one shoelace an inch shorter than the other."

"Your point being?" Edgardo asked.

"We fear he'll do far worse to Rom if he got the chance, and I wouldn't blame him if he did. The man doesn't deserve to breathe the same air as you after what he attempted, but it doesn't change the fact that we need him alive and running his outfit. Surely, you understand our concern?"

"Understood." Edgardo knew about George and Hank, and the extreme measures Bram took, but considered the matter handled. He failed to consider how it might factor into his dealings with the feds. "Are you certain it was Bram? We had more important matters. Did Mr. Hall drop his name?"

"You know he didn't," C.B. said flatly, "and neither did his three buddies who were rushed to the ER. At this point, I don't think any force on Earth could compel those men to utter even the first syllable of your brother's name. But Hall lives next door to Hank Brighton, who was treated for similar blunt force trauma the same day. It didn't take us long to put two and two together."

Edgardo considered everything C.B. laid out. The incident with George Hall was yet another log on the fire in the ongoing case against him and Bram. "You are indeed smarter than I realized."

"Yeah, I get that a lot."

"I assure you, any personal vendetta my brother and I may harbor is shelved and will not interfere with our arrangement..."

"Okay, enough." C.B. silenced him with a wave of his hand. "Go ahead and meet with Basilio if you still feel the need, but Bram stays behind. I'll say it one more time so it's all clear, he must remain alive. ALIVE, Ed. Full stop. Your calm voice doesn't fool me. I know you want to bury the man in a closed casket, and I'd feel the same, but without him, we lose the HK-9, which means we lose all their connections. The idea is to use one big fish to catch a basket full of others. Understand?"

"Understood."

"And I wanna be extra clear," Mace said, "those connections he mentioned, The Nines' daily business, are the only things keeping you boys out of prison. Forgive me for being blunt."

"Blunt, I can handle," Edgardo said. "Blunt is the only time you're being transparent. All that being said, I still plan to meet with him."

"What for?" Bram asked. "They just said he's untouchable." He saw no point in facing Rom without the intention of killing him.

"I'll confront Rommel, ask a few questions, and after he's done spitting and fuming, I'm going to rewrite the rules."

58

Rough Business

The old airfield came into view as Edgardo drove his Mercedes off the desert road and onto the cracked pavement of the runway. He knew every square foot of that property, every patch of rust on the corrugated steel walls and oil stain on the cement, but something changed that late morning. The time of day and the business at hand made the silent airfield seem like unexplored territory, an unnerving feeling that kept him on edge.

I'd been to Anders Butler Airfield seven times before, with each visit starting at dusk and ending in the black of night as Felix watched me from the dunes through his rifle's scope. Though my hidden assistant awaited in a new position – trip wires surrounding him this time – that day's visit felt different, the kind of different that turned the page to a new chapter in my life.

Edgardo looked in his rearview and saw a dot in the distance. He wondered if it was the same dot he saw half an hour before.

The sun hung directly overhead while a panel van tailed me from the city. Looking back at it from a red light in Downtown, I identified it as a 1994 Chevrolet Grumman. I could hear it idling rough with a distinct cadence and sputter, which told me its diesel engine had a misfiring cylinder. This explained why it followed from a mile behind... that and the weight of its passengers. But on that desolate road, there was little chance the driver would lose sight of me.

The last time Edgardo drove across the desert, his brother sat beside him. He pictured him staring out the window at the vast land, his eyes wide with visions of a new life, a new freedom.

I wished Bram was with me. He'd never accompanied me to the airfield, probably didn't even know it existed, but his absence was still felt. To his chagrin, I insisted that he comply with the Wolves' wishes and spend more time in their recovery room before joining me in the field.

Of course, my true concern was his need for justice. The Wolves were correct to assume that whatever George Hall endured for harming Hank, Rommel would receive a hundredfold after gunning for us and our family. I promised Bram that he'd be my right hand again the moment his health fully returned, and that Rommel would get his comeuppance one day when the time was right. He didn't agree, of course, but he didn't protest.

At the end of the runway stood the lone hangar where Rommel Basilio, Nino Timbol, and three other HK-9 awaited. Edgardo parked to the side of the hangar entrance as before, ensuring an unobstructed line of sight for his camouflaged sharpshooter in the distant sands. He noted the other cars parked nearby.

2023 Lexus LS-F Sport, Rommel's personal car driven by Nino. 2023 Lexus GX, a large black SUV that brought his personal guards. Knowing that Rommel preferred to travel only with his driver, the SUV likely brought three or four men, possibly bringing their total to six. Of course, I had requested that we limit our numbers to three per party and that they respect my usual rules against coming armed, but based on recent events, I knew those requests would be ignored. As such, I chose to ignore my rules as well.

Edgardo stepped out of his car, pulled a duffle bag from the trunk, and walked into the hangar, fully exposed in the middle of the 50-foot entryway.

"Rommel," he said as he walked to the center of the space. "It's good to see you again."

"I admit, I almost didn't come," Rommel said, curious at Edgardo's almost pleasant demeanor. Nino stood beside him. His other men stood behind them where a plane would normally be stored. "When Nino handed me my phone this morning, I was startled to see your name on it."

"What he means is that we assumed our business relationship had ended," Nino said.

"And what *you* mean is that you assumed my *life* had ended," Edgardo said in a stern tone. "My life and the lives of my family."

"Yes, that is exactly what he meant." Rommel spoke in an apologetic tone. "To be honest, I'm surprised any of us are still alive with all the territory pissing going on right now. Ours is a rough business, and it's all business all the time, as it must be. You once told me that."

"I remember." Edgardo nodded, his eyes fixed on Rom's.

"Do you?"

"It was a Friday evening, February 6, 2015. I've spoken those words many times since, 'all business all the time,' but lately, it makes me wonder."

"I had no doubt that you remembered the day, but I didn't think you remembered the lesson. Listen to your words. You say you wonder." Rom sensed the wrath rising within Edgardo, just under his skin. "In our business, everyone is forced to make the tough decisions under fire. It's regrettable, but something I had to accept long ago. I thought you'd understand."

"I do, and that's the only reason it's good to see you, for it's good to see anyone and anything, given what I've been through this past week."

"What *we've* been through, Duque. You aren't the only one forced to live with a target on his back."

"That target moves week-to-week in our line of work, and this past week has undeniably been my spotlight."

"No doubt," Rom said. "Yet you come alone." He looked over at his three guards. "Bold decision. Some might say foolish."

Edgardo heard another car pull up. "I may be bold, Rom, but I'm no fool."

The panel van that followed him from HiFi parked near the hangar entrance, sputtering to a stop. The blocky white vehicle was adorned with a mural of colorful flowers and stars, a stark contrast to both the desert location and the point of the meeting. To The Nines, it was an ominous sight. Even before they read the blocky words above its windows, they knew who that van belonged to.

Rom kept his stone face as he eyed the colorful vehicle. "You brought treats to celebrate? A gesture of goodwill, perhaps?"

"You know what I brought."

As if on cue, Charlie Wood and five other heavily armed Black men – Mr. Waldo's security – emerged from the boxy van. They entered the hangar in full tactical gear and casually took positions along the north and south walls, essentially flanking Rom's men in the middle.

"I see the old négro sent his simios for his cut," Rommel said.

"Incorrect," Edgardo said. "He makes no such claim."

"Ah, then it's 2-to-1." Rommel noted how he and his Nines were outnumbered. He didn't count himself, Nino, or Edgardo among the gun hands, considering them strictly businessmen. "You speak on his behalf, so I assume you work for the nognóg gun runner now. 'Waldo,' yes? You're with him now?"

"Incorrect."

"How I love the way you speak!" Rommel laughed. "So straightforward, without feeling. But, of course, I am correct. First, it was me, then it was the Wolves. Now it's the négros. The Duke latches on to whoever he must in order to survive, like a leech in a swamp. As I said, we make the tough decisions when we're cornered. I can respect that."

"I'm not with Mr. Waldo," Edgardo said. "Mr. Waldo is with me. The real question is... are *you* with me?"

"Watch your tone, Duque." Rommel put away his calm, measured words and took a defensive stance. "I come out here to a last-minute meeting in the tangina desert and see guns all around me. Not the best way to start a deal."

"I walk into rooms full of guns trained on me all the time," Edgardo said. "You get used to it. But whether or not this is a business deal remains to be seen. I'm going to update you on our situation, and you're going to listen closely, for your response will dictate how this meeting ends."

Rommel barely contained his boiling rage. "Now you speak to me in front of my men like you're ten feet tall. I told you to watch your tone. I find it disturbing."

"And I find yours intriguing," Edgardo said. "What should disturb you is that many people were hurt when you shot up a food truck in an attempt on my life. What should keep you up at night is that my brother, Abraham Duque, survived your ambush, knows your face, and now waits for my word."

"Threats?" He mockingly looked around the hangar. "I don't see any big brother here."

"What should occupy your busy mind is that two carloads of your men were sent to my home but were killed by the Koreans. Seems the AFA has declared war on you. Instead, you obsess over my tone. Again, it makes me wonder."

"Smells like a load of bullshit to me," Charlie said, his loud, deep voice startling the room. "The man tells lies as easily as I take a piss."

Rommel stepped back from his anger. "I concede to the hit on the food truck, but I only wanted to send a message. If I wanted you and your brother dead, you would be, but that's something we can sort out later. Right now, I'm confused about any men being sent to your home or any involvement of the AFA. I know nothing about it, so you can wonder all you want."

"Smells like more bullshit," Charlie said.

"I intercepted their texts, Rom." Edgardo held up his phone for all to see, revealing a message thread that C.B.'s men modified. "They were on their way to my family in the Hollywood Hills, and they came heavy, but they made a pit stop in Koreatown." He took a moment to read the false messages. "It seems your ambitious men had a side hustle selling opium, an arrangement not everyone in the Asian Family Assassins had signed off on. Like you, they tend to stick with their own."

"Opium?" Rom looked genuinely surprised. "I had no knowledge of that either."

"But I do, and that's what matters here."

Rom shook his head, confused. He looked to Nino, who offered no explanation, no spin. "I feel like we're dancing around the reason we're really here. How I hate these games you play."

"No games," Edgardo said. "I wanted to meet to tell you that the TSB is done. So is the DEA mole who worked for them. And since dead men don't do business, whatever arrangement you had with that crew, you now have with me."

"You're telling me you took out... you're saying one of the Temple Street Boyz is a rat?"

"*Was.* Don't you keep up with the news?"

Rommel looked at Nino for confirmation. He checked his phone and simply nodded to his boss.

That morning, C.B. had leaked to the press that former TSB underboss Gabriel "Yoy Yoy" Aquino was an informant who died from police crossfire in a drug bust.

"He's gone?"

"They're all gone."

"Now I smell bullshit." Rommel smiled. "Calixto's cousin was a rat? Whoever may be dead or alive, I think you're bluffing, Duque. Knowing you, I'm certain of it."

Edgardo read the old man's face, his facade of control slipping. "And I'm certain that's not what you think."

"No? What about Calixto? What does he think?"

"As of last night, what Calixto Cervantes thinks about anything no longer matters."

Rommel laughed at the implication. "You sure about that? I must've heard rumors about his death ten times over the past year alone. The man is like a cockroach."

"I'm quite sure," Edgardo said coldly. "I killed him."

The HK-9 were clearly shaken by the news, though their boss kept his poker face. He'd long pegged Edgardo as a negotiator, a paper pusher who moved money around. The idea that he murdered a gang chief in cold blood seemed absurd. "What about his five kapitans?" Rommel shot a glance at Nino.

Edgardo walked up to Rommel with one hand held up, five fingers spread. "Yoy Yoy Aquino. Jorge Vega. Bakal Diaz. Joselito Vazquez. Agustin Abayon. Their business with you is done."

"Anyone else?" Rommel asked, amused by the notion.

"Eight biker basura," Edgardo said, as if The Wolf Pack MC were an afterthought. "Two DEA agents and a few others from outlying gangs. You once suggested that I get my house in order, and I took your advice to heart. It's been a busy week."

"Busy trying to stay alive, you mean." Rommel found it difficult to stay in control, to remain flippant against Edgardo's monotone, macabe update. He looked around at Waldo's men and singled out Charlie Wood. "You, big man. Am I to believe that you work for Duque now?"

"Mr. Waldo's entire force works for The Duke," Charlie said in his booming voice. "I suggest you stop talkin' and start listenin'."

Rommel looked about the room, eyes wide, as if everyone had lost their minds. "I've never been so disrespected! This is not how business is done!" He walked up to Edgardo, their faces inches apart. "If you want to work with me, to take over the TSB's trade, you'll need to sweeten the deal!"

"Unacceptable." Edgardo's stone face was unnerving.

"Kigola ka! That's what you do, right? You use that big brain to put together a sweet deal to appease me? The Duke always brokers business that benefit all parties..."

First Rule of Exchange: Avoid escalation unless necessary. When it is necessary, it's either all them or it's all me.

Rommel's rant was cut short as Edgardo clutched the old man's throat and forced him down to the cement floor. The Nines readied their guns but were quickly halted by Waldo's men moving in with rifles raised.

"Your men were sent to kill my family!" Edgardo yelled. "My wife and children! My brother! The days of fair, sweet deals are over!"

"What... is this...?" Rommel barely got the words out with his windpipe nearly crushed.

"Let me absolutely clear with you." Edgardo knelt down and pressed his forehead against Rommel's, his threats pouring out in a fiery whisper. "This is not negotiation or meaningless disrespect. This is me threatening to kill you here in this hangar. But it won't end with you or your six kapitans. Think of your wife Rosalina in Long Beach, and your sons Alejandro and Aldo at UCLA."

"You're bluffing... and you know nothing..."

"Whether or not I involve them, there are four ways I could end you, Rom."

"Only four?" Rom coughed a laugh, feigning amusement to save face in front of his men.

"Four methods of my choosing. I could press my thumb against your trachea right now. It would collapse like puff pastry thanks your prolonged intubation six years ago. I could force feed you onions, which you're deadly allergic to, let your blood pressure plummet in anaphylactic shock. Maybe I'll bury you in a trunk and allow your claustrophobia to consume you before you die of suffocation or heat stroke. I could always stick you in a closet with a brown recluse, let your arachnophobia swell before the little guy's hemolytic and cytotoxic enzymes rip your veins apart."

"You... you're crazy..." Rommel's words were cut short as Edgardo tightened his grip on the man's throat.

"And you're a man of many weaknesses and fears. I know each of them intimately and keep them close to my chest, like bullets in a bandolier with your name engraved. Blink twice if you finally understand the situation."

Rommel Basilio looked into Edgardo's eyes, all pretense of control evaporated. The mobster didn't wade in fear so much as drown in abject terror of the man who now literally held his life in his hand. After digesting the many threats, he gulped a breath of air and distinctly blinked twice.

Edgardo released Rommel, letting him fall to the cold cement of the hangar floor, and backed away to take in the sad spectacle of the broken man.

Charlie Wood stood astonished at the detailed threat. As instructed an hour before, he followed up with his own. He shoved the barrel of his rifle against Nino's temple. "Duque, how many you want done to send a message?"

"Message is clear!" Nino said, bracing for a bullet. "We understand! We all understand!"

Edgardo shook his head and helped Rommel to his feet. "I was clear when I first walked in, our ongoing business depends on you. Your response will dictate how this meeting ends."

"Yes," Rommel said in a coughing fit. "Yes, I agree... with your terms."

Second Rule of Exchange: Always sweep away your footprints.

"The scrapyard is burnt," Edgardo said. "The feds are all over it, so all goods that Calixto handled now go through me. I moved the inventory last week. The airfield is burnt as well. Once we leave this hangar, we'll never see it again." Edgardo nodded to Charlie, who raised a hand to his men. Waldo's security took the guns from the three Nines.

"You've got some balls, Duque," Rommel said, "but you have your deal."

"Waldo is with me, the Armenians will be soon, and I'll have ties to the Mexicans by the weekend, just as you have. It's in both of our interests that we keep the trade going, for continuing business is far better than an ongoing war. Better to prosper together in the city than die alone in the desert."

"That seems to be the case," Rommel said, the fire returning to his eyes. "But add 'for now' to every sentence you just spoke."

"You may know my real name and where my family is, but I know everything about you, Rommel Emiliano Basilio. I know where you live, where you conduct business, how you like your morning cup of Kapeng Barako with two spoons of muscovado."

"I get it." Rommel straightened his tie and pulled down his vest and jacket. "You're thorough, I'll give you that."

"I'm thorough when I clean my kitchen. I'm thorough while weeding my garden. The word you're looking for is 'obsessed.' I'm obsessed with the tanga kigol and his goons who tried to kill me and mine. Tell me you get that."

Rommel nodded, finally catching his breath.

Nino nodded as well.

It was as close to a confession as they'd offer.

Lynn Harrod

"Good. It should go without saying that any attempt at retaliation, any move against me or my family, will be met with force, all the force I can summon. I will come down on you with an endless storm, and if I were to die, the storm would avenge me."

"No need to worry, Duque. You made your point. Business is business, you have my word."

"Unacceptable. Your word means nothing to me. Just remember that I have your lives in my hand. Let it be your guiding light."

Third Rule of Exchange: Remember everyone and everything because the man you didn't notice, the detail you missed, those are what kill you.

Edgardo turned to Nino. "I have a file on you as well, Nino Timbol." He looked at the other Nines. "Jacob Gomez. Gabriel Rodriguez. I have files on all of you, on all your fallen brothers. Forget everything your ungas boss told you about me and remember my words."

"We'll remember," Nino said, waiting for a bullet to the head. "We'll all remember."

Per my arrangement with The Wolves, I'd promised to keep Rommel alive. However, to keep business under control, I had to reinvent The Duke as even more ruthless and violent than him, with an army more feared than his own. My plan appeared to be working, but Rom's eyes kept repeating his sleeved threat, "for now."

"As before, remain here for ten minutes. *Ten* minutes."
Rom nodded with a sigh.

Nino held up ten fingers.

Satisfied, Edgardo walked out of the hangar and into the afternoon sun. Once out of earshot of the others, he spoke through his earpiece. "You heard all that?"

"I heard," Felix said over their two-way com. Even he seemed startled after witnessing his boss's flame. "You went pretty hard on them."

"It's the only language these men understand."

Edgardo sat in his car and took a deep breath. "As always, avoid the roads. Cut across the desert to Palmdale. Give them ten minutes, then head out."

"What if they leave at nine minutes?"

Edgardo thought for a moment as he started his car and drove away from the airfield. "Warning shot."

"You sure?"

"Shoot the floor near their feet. They'll wait. We clear on that?"

"Warning shot. Understood." Felix exhaled slowly before accepting his orders. "My honor always, Amo."

Whenever doing business at a remote outskirt like the airfield, I always told whoever I'd met to wait 10 minutes before heading back to the city, and I always had Felix remain to enforce it through his scope. The idea was to give me time on the road before anyone could tail me home. Felix would add that it also served as a show of force and control. I usually told him to shoot anyone who tried to follow me, but that day I felt the pressures of change. My family now lived in both halves of my world, and I endeavored to be more, a forgiving businessman perceived as a merciless gangster. Felix may have had his misgivings, but C.B. said it perfectly when he told me to "become the hero... the antihero... that your children

think you are." I admit only on these pages: the old agent
actually inspired me.

"Amo?" After a few minutes on the desert road, Felix's voice
came through again. With Edgardo's earpiece shut off and resting
in the glove box, the young man spoke through the car's sound
system. "Are you still on?"

"I'm here. Is something wrong?"

"No, the men are still waiting in the hanger. Rom isn't even on
his phone."

"No cigarette?" Edgardo asked. "No earbuds?"

"They're still in Nino's pocket, as you predicted. Amo, I'm still
not sure why that's important."

"Just know that it is, Felix. Where's Rom's phone?"

"Nino has that, too."

Perfect.

The arrogant man makes his assistant carry everything.

"Amo, he's just standing there burning time, and I can tell on
his face, he hasn't swallowed the deal yet."

"Understandable. It'll take him some time."

"If he gives it time." Felix heard the doubt in his own voice and
shook his head in regret. "I have a question."

"Go ahead."

"If things get too hot, are we really going to involve his family?"

"No," Edgardo said with a shameful sigh, remembering his vile
threats. "We're not going to torture him, either. That's not who
we are, but I must play the part now, and they must believe it."

"Hell, I believed it," Felix said. "I guess the game has changed."

"Indeed. From this day on, it's not enough that The Duke is
respected. He must be feared."

"And if Rom is smart enough... or foolish enough... to call your
bluff? What if he still wants your head on a spike?"

"There's a Plan B," Edgardo said, "but right now, let's just go home."

"Hopefully, I'll never need to know the details of Plan B," Felix said, "though I'm pretty sure I know what the 'B' stands for."

* * *

As instructed, Rommel waited the full ten minutes before walking to his car. Nino ran ahead of him to get the car running and the air conditioner cold. The three unarmed guards returned to their SUV where they found their unloaded weapons laid on the hood. None of them heard Felix take down his perimeter and motor away across the dunes.

Rom sat silent as they headed down the cracked, narrow road, alone in the backseat of his sedan. From the driver's seat, Nino occasionally glanced back at his boss, offering his ear, but the man was lost in his thoughts. Despite The Duke's long, aggressive stance in the hangar, despite all his threats, his frightening details of their lives, Nino knew Rommel Basilio still planned to kill Edgardo Duque.

Lynn Harrod

59

Panabas

Listening to jazz on his earbuds, Rommel paced across the grand foyer of his house as two men swept every room for hidden surveillance, a weekly ritual that began after an unexpected raid six years before. The Tudor Revival mansion sat on the north end of Hancock Park, an affluent neighborhood in the Wilshire area of Los Angeles. Palm, magnolia, and sycamore trees lined Highland Avenue, their shadows stretching across the property as the late-afternoon sun began to fall.

Nino followed the men around to ensure that every window, bookcase, and piece of furniture was scanned thoroughly. His boss had new plans and wanted to map them out immediately. Two more men guarded the front and back entrances, with another at the gate.

"How much longer?" Rom asked Nino as he passed one of the bug hunters. He pulled out an earbud. "It's been more than 20 minutes!"

"All that's left is your study."

"You should have started there! 18 rooms and you choose the one room I need for last?"

"We swept it first, sir," Nino said, "but I want it done again because it's the most likely room..."

"So do it." Rommel grunted with frustration but silently agreed with his assistant's request for a second scan of his study, a place he often referred to as his "war room." They once missed a microphone, embedded in the wooden floor underneath a rug, but luckily caught it with a second pass of the wands.

He walked in a circle, vintage jazz blasting in his ears, as he looked up at the wide, winding staircase encircling a high chandelier. The walls were ivory with gold crown molding, adorned with impressionist art. The surreal landscapes and idyllic scenes normally comforted him, but at that moment he thought only of The Duke as he eagerly waited for the all-clear of his study.

The bug hunters folded their wands – mobile nonlinear junction detectors – satisfied that the house was secure. They nodded to Nino who gestured for them to quickly return to their posts at the front and rear doors.

"Cut them loose," Rom said, interrupting Nino's unspoken order.

"I thought we might want extra men outside."

"No need. Duque made his move when he put his foot down today, thinks he's got me by the betlog. Tell those men they can go home."

"Opo, sir." Nino dismissed the two men, leaving three remaining to guard the property. He followed his boss into the study and shut the door.

Lynn Harrod

Rommel walked to his desk where his dinner awaited. A platter of chicken adobo, shrimp sinigang, and steamed rice was prepared and placed there by his kasambahay shortly before she left for the day. Nino and the guards had bowls of adobo and rice when they first arrived.

"What are your thoughts?" Rom asked as he pulled the cork from a bottle of Tempranillo. He poured two glasses of the garnet wine before sitting down to eat. "I want to know what you'd advise before I tell you my plans." The ride home from the desert gave him time to think of ways to regain his entitled position in the city, a throne The Duke arrogantly assumed he'd stolen.

Nino sat in front of the desk as his boss slid the second glass of wine to him. He placed his hand on the stem but didn't take a sip until he voiced his concern. "I'm not sure, sir. Perhaps if you tell me what you're thinking first..."

"I don't want your opinion on my opinion, that delicate little dance we always do. No, right now, I want to know what you would do if you were me."

"If I ran the family..." Nino had a quick answer but waited a moment before speaking. He wouldn't dare risk his words coming across as obvious strategy, for his boss would see it as an insult and would brutally dress him down for such an indignity. "If I ran the family, I'd follow Duque's play, see if it brings good business. Maybe it'll work out better with him in place of Calixto. You know I never trusted that junkyard rat."

"Now *that's* the Nino I want and need," Rommel said with a smile and a mouth full of food. "You're so quiet in front of the men, but here, you can't be afraid to speak your mind."

"I say we trade with Duque for three months, see how the numbers pencil out."

"And if they don't pencil out?"

"I trust they will. Duque may have a loud bark, sir, but he's a businessman. At the end of the day, that's what he cares about."

Rommel frowned at his assistant, disappointed. "You're smart, Nino, but not wise. It's not your fault, wisdom comes with age and experience. You're young, you have no wife, no children, and though Rosalina took my boys and moved away to live off my alimony on the beach, I know what it is to be a family man. I can assure you that Duque cares about more than business. That tantrum in the hangar wasn't about money. His little terrorist act, his grabs for power with the Armenians and the Mexicans, none of that was about money. And if the TSB is truly gone, if he personally killed Calixto Cervantes as he said, it certainly wasn't a business decision."

"Then what's it all for?" Nino asked.

"He wants to hurt me," Rom said. "He wants to corner me, control me, as payback for going after his family. I get that, and it's because he's a fellow family man that I can't kneel to his demands."

Alarmed, Nino finally sipped his wine, still struggling to make sense of his boss's words. He knew the man wanted blood, it was only a matter of how and when, but the talk of family confused him. "Now that I've told you my thoughts, sir, what are yours? If we don't trade with Duque, then what?"

"How can you ask me that, Nino? After the way he invaded our lives, threatened us ten different ways?" Rommel shoveled a fork full of adobo into his mouth and spoke with juice dripping down his chin. "He wants to take everyone and everything, so the plan remains, The Duke must die."

Nino Timbol had served as Rommel's assistant and advisor for years. Among his darker duties, he arranged to destroy rival shipments, extort local businesses, and bribe law enforcement, but up until recently had never ordered a hit on anyone. Tasking their men with striking Duque's homes was the first time he'd been involved in planning murder. As scared as he felt at the airfield meeting, he left feeling relieved that the war would end, at least for the time being. Educated, business savvy, and focused on running the family like a fine-tuned machine, Nino was at his best during peacetime. He'd hoped that his boss's old-school bloodlust would be countered by a new-world boost in revenue, that a thriving partnership would cancel any notion of vengeance.

He should have known better.

"Are you sure, sir?" Nino asked. "You actually want to continue this war with The Duke? He's got Mr. Waldo now."

"Waldo?" Rom said with a dismissive grunt. "We won't have to worry about that old nognóg once Duque is dead. Duque, that gorilla he calls his brother, his famous wife, his brats, I want them all worked out." Rom frowned at the feigned confusion on his assistant's face. "Salvaged. Nasawi, Nino."

"Why involve his women and children? They're not in the game any more than yours."

"His boy is. He was arrested for a killing a judge's son."

"Carlo Duque?" Nino asked, not sure if "his boy" referred to Edgardo's biological son or perhaps a trusted associate like himself. "Seventeen years old? Him?"

"His blood-born son, whatever he's called."

Nino shook his head. "No, I looked into the kid. He gets good grades, keeps out of real trouble, and that business with the judge's son was just a rumor."

Rommel looked at Nino with pity, as if his naiveté was adorable. "Good grades can be bought, childhood visits to the principal's office are trivial, but rumors of murder don't float around without some truth to them. Whatever happened, whether he pulled the trigger or was just an accomplice, that boy's in a gang, just like his father and uncle. Duque covered it up well, but let's face the truth. If we only kill the brothers, his son will take over their operation and come after us."

"How can you possibly know that?" Nino asked.

"I know, because that's what I did."

Decades before The Nines existed, Rommel Basilio followed his father Andres "Dre" Basilio into the "O.G. Pinoys Locos," a small Filipino gang based in Boyle Heights, east of the Los Angeles river. During a brawl with a group of Mexicans over a trunk full of Damo, Dre was killed, and young Rommel vowed revenge. He took his father's *panabas* – a long-handled curved blade with a forked tip – and thrust it into the stomach of Ricardo Bagani, his father's killer.

Ricardo was 19.

Rommel was 16.

His mother moved their family to Historic Filipinotown, but his reputation followed. Rom soon joined the "Mga Hari sa Kalle 3" and reformed the gang with his brothers and new friends into the HK-9. Before the suits and sedans, their legacy was painted with blood.

Nino knew his boss's brutal past and feared that their family's dark history was about to repeat itself. The war with The Duke would only be the beginning.

Rommel finished his meal, pushed the plate away, and poured another glass of Tempranillo. "Tomorrow, I want you to gather the kapitans. This time, we forget Duque's houses. We'll hit his family where they work, where they go to school, where they eat breakfast. His old man is in the hospital. The morning he's released, we'll be waiting in the parking lot."

"This is too much, sir," Nino said. "There's no need to wage war. We already made that move, and he's letting it go, giving us a second chance."

Rommel winced at the notion that Duque *gave* him anything. "The man who grants second chances is in control. The man who's eager to take that chance is a fool."

Rom often worded his thoughts like the lesson of a fable, as if tutoring Nino about the ways of the weary world, something his assistant found patronizing.

"You may be right, sir, but I still think it would be wise to see how business plays out first."

"Wise?" Rom laughed. "Remember what we said about wisdom? I told you, Duque cares about more than just money, and so do I. But let's say you're right, let's focus on business for a moment. If word gets out that I got down on my knees for him, others will expect the same."

"Negotiation and compromise are not the same as kneeling."

"Negotiation is a showy way of begging to stay in the game, and compromise is a pretentious way of saying you've weakened yourself. Your problem, Nino, is that your college professors taught you that money is power, but that's only true for the billionaire putis and the politicians who were born into it. In our business, where men start from nothing and rise up from the dirt, power comes from what you're willing to do to get that money. Power comes from striking first and striking hard, from doing what the other man couldn't imagine himself doing."

Nino quashed the urge to argue with his boss, to counter his little lessons, for he knew there was no turning him around. Once Rommel Basilio decided someone's fate, having second thoughts would make him appear hesitant and indecisive. It came from yet another of his fables.

"Opo, sir. I'll call the kapitans tonight, arrange a meet."

"Call them tomorrow." Rom sipped his wine, satisfied with both the vintage and the fact that Nino finally stopped questioning him. No matter how morbid the task, his assistant's clawing conscience always relented. "Tonight, I want you to put together a list of addresses and times. We need to know when and where to hit The Duke."

"I'll draw up a plan."

As Nino left his boss to enjoy his traditional digestif – a newly-opened bottle of Tiffon XO Cognac – Rommel stopped him for a final word. "Before you hand out that plan to the kapitans, I want it known that Duque is to be killed last. He needs to see what his arrogance has brought."

Nino nodded. As he left to compile the list, his boss took off his jacket and hung it on a coat rack in the nearby corner. He took a Fortune cigarette from his desk drawer, held his highball glass to the light, and swirled a finger of cognac. With each sip, he imagined The Duke and his loved ones being plucked from his beloved Temple Street like overgrown sidewalk weeds before that bottle was finished.

60

Plan B

Four hours and three pours later, Rommel awoke in his study, the bottle of Tiffon XO still opened before him. His hands smelled of cognac and tobacco, a copy of *The Los Angeles Times* spread out across his desk. Philippine jazz played from a speaker built into the bookshelf behind him. He often fell asleep from that nightly routine of booze and smoke and music, a ritual that started after his puta wife and ingrate sons left him, his life, and his massive house "built from blood money" for a new start in Long Beach.

He rubbed his blurry eyes, and as his vision came into focus, he saw Nino in the chair in front of his desk, another part of his evening routine. The young man usually had papers fanned out on his lap, the next day of business outlined and ready for approval, but he now sat empty-handed as if he's simply been waiting for his boss to wake up.

"Give me a moment," Rom said, his head still fuzzy. He pulled a bottle of water from his desk drawer. "Make a pot of coffee and we'll finish our business."

"Skip the coffee," said a man sitting in a far corner. "We finish this now."

Rommel sipped his water as he peered across the room. His pulse raced when he saw Abraham Duque on a leather bench, a sword resting across his lap. The hulking man wore a simple black T-shirt and jeans over combat boots, the same outfit he'd seen him wear a decade prior. Though seeing Bram in his home was akin to a visit from the grim reaper, Rom relied on his voice of authority and old-school instincts to keep control.

"Nino," he bellowed. "What the hell happened?"

"Don't speak to him," Bram said. "You speak to me."

"You dare tell me what to do? In my house?"

"I dare. Do you know who I am?"

"Of course, I know." Rom tried not to stare at the sword. "I make it my business to know everyone, just like your brother."

"Good. That'll make things go faster. None of us want me here any longer than necessary."

Rommel looked through the windows and out the open door to the grand foyer, expecting to see one of his guards. He hid his apprehension well when he saw no one.

"Your sundalos are still here," Bram said, "but don't bother calling out for them." He didn't explain why the guards weren't a factor, but Rommel knew.

"They're dead?"

"Dead to you."

"I see. You bought them. What's the market price for a man's broken loyalty nowadays?"

"To tell you the truth, I haven't decided what to do with them yet... or you."

Rommel ignored the indirect threat. He found Bram's hesitation curious. "Cognac? Wine? No, you don't seem like the type."

"What type am I?" Bram asked, running his fingers along his sword.

"*That* type," Rom said, eyeing the blade. He cleared his throat and poured himself another finger of cognac. He'd had his fill of the spirit but wanted to give the impression of calm and control. "You didn't come to the hangar. I was certain you'd be there."

"Oh, I wanted to be there, to put a bullet through your heart, but my brother was determined to set things right with you. He wanted to continue business between men, so he left me behind. He figured I'd ruin any chance of peace."

"Was he right?"

"You should know by now, my brother is always right." Bram stood and walked across the room to Rommel's suit jacket, still resting on a coat rack near his desk. "You rejected his proposal."

"Proposal?" Rom scoffed as Bram manhandled his jacket. "Is that what you call it? He grabs me by the throat, tells me how I'm to run my family, and that's a proposal? But I rejected nothing because he gave me no choice."

"Pakshet." Bram rummaged through Rom's jacket's pockets. "He gave you a choice. You could comply with his wishes or you could die."

Rommel grew angry at his own building fear. "If you had been there, you'd know that I agreed to his outrageous demands. Call him! Ask him yourself!" He turned to his assistant. "Nino, tell this tangina gago that we struck a deal!"

Nino remained silent.

He could barely look at his boss.

Bram's fingertips felt something tucked inside a pocket of Rom's jacket. He pulled out a thin device the size and shape of a quarter. "Your men swept the hangar, as they always do, and they swept every room of your house just before you drank yourself to sleep like a mahina mánginginom. But they didn't wave their magic wands over you." He tossed the small device onto Rommel's desk. It spun for a moment before coming to a rest, like a coin in a game of chance.

"What is this?" Rom asked, failing to hide his nerves. "A good luck charm?"

He knew exactly what it was.

He realized Edgardo had planted it on him when he dramatically grabbed him in the hangar.

"You bugged me?" he asked with a laugh. "Quite a risky move for The Duke. Stupid move. I could've found this at any time."

"Nope, not risky at all." Bram unfolded a Post-It note and read it. "My brother's met with you... 22 times..."

"And?"

"He said in all those years you've never once reached into your suit pockets. Nino holds everything for you. Your schedule, your cigars, phone, earbuds, even your wallet. You treat him like a walking purse."

"Your brother is... observant." Rom looked at his assistant who still sat silent, his face flat. "But it's still risky because it insults me." He picked up the coin mic and examined it for a moment before tossing it back onto his desk as if it meant nothing. "Bugs are for overly ambitious cops and baboy feds, not men like us."

"Is that what you told Ricky Wash?"

Rommel laughed. "Ricky is nobody. I saw it as bug on a bug. To stick one in my suit is a personal affront. What happened to honor among businessmen?"

"If you ever had any honor, you abandoned it long ago." Bram pulled out his phone and pressed a button. Rom's voice emerged from its tiny speaker...

"This time, we forget Duque's houses. We'll hit his family where they work, where they go to school, where they eat breakfast. His old man is in the hospital. The morning he's released, we'll be waiting in the parking lot."

Rommel had no words, his braggadocio gone.

"You told Nino you wanted my family worked out," Bram said. "Salvaged. Nasawi."

"It was a possibility! That's all! In the event that your brother didn't keep his end of the deal!"

Bram ignored Rom's spin and slid his finger across the device, advancing the recording...

"Before you hand out that plan to the kapitans, I want it known that Duque is to be killed last. He needs to see what his arrogance has brought."

To Rom's horror, Bram held up his sword, the familiar long-handled curved blade with a forked tip.

"What do you think you're doing with that thing?"

"This thing is a panabas," Bram said, "a vicious blade from back home. Don't you recognize it? It's part of your legend, isn't it? You famously used one as a kid." Bram spun the blade as if to gauge its weight and balance. He traced its edge with his eyes and caught the two frightened men in its reflection. "Bakal Diaz brought this one to my nanay's house, but my brother knows the kind of man he was."

"Was?"

"Bakal was a simpleton with no loyalty, a thug who'd kill for whoever paid him, whether it be Calixto... or you."

"Ridiculous!" Rommel said. "He was a Temple Street rat! Not one of mine!"

"The way my brother figured, a simpleton wouldn't have a fine hand-crafted sword like this, and he definitely wouldn't bother using one on a job. A simpleton would keep things simple, right?

He'd just shoot up a house from the street and drive away. No, the only reason a man like that would bother with a special blade is if you sent him on a special job, to send a message. My brother knows how men think, and he has a way of explaining things to me that make sense. He figured this panabas had to be yours, had to be the same one that killed Ricardo Bagani."

"Then why am I still alive, detective?" Rommel rose to his feet, forcing himself to stand up to the enforcer. "Why is Nino still sitting there breathing? You see, I also know how men think, and I know the kind of man *you* are. You are not your brother, with his mind tricks and intimidation tactics. You're don't talk, you act. By the time a man sees Abraham Duque coming for him, he's already dead. Isn't that part of *your* legend?"

"You're right."

"Of course, I'm right! With all your bugo sword spinning, all your talk talk talk, you came here for a reason, so let's cut the tangina bushet and get to it!"

Bram looked at a wall clock: 8:55. "You have five minutes to work it out."

"Work what out?" Rom huffed at the sight of the blade.

"Mga Hari sa Kalle 9. The Nine Street Kings." Bram checked the Post-It note again. "Five are dead, two were put away for life, one was locked up and killed his first night inside. That just leaves you, Rommel Andres Basilio, the last of the founders."

"What's your point?"

"Who'll take over when you're gone?" Bram asked.

"Who says I'm going anywhere? And what concern is it of yours who's next in line..."

"I'll take over," Nino said, breaking his silence. He finally looked his boss in the eye. "I'll run the family and honor the deal."

Rommel looked ready to explode, but Bram pointed the sword at his face, gesturing for him to sit down. As Rom returned to his chair, he looked at the stern stares and realized what transpired while he was asleep. His three house guards were apprehended, likely by the same men who accompanied Duque to the hangar – Waldo's men. Nino was then offered a revised proposal, one where he'd become the new ruler of the HK-9.

What Rom didn't know was how quickly his assistant and guards accepted the situation, choosing to live with the new business arrangement rather than die for a cutthroat gangster eager to throw them headlong into a bloody war. No persuasion or "intimidation tactics" were needed. Edgardo and Bram had heard the entirety of the conversation between Rommel and Nino over the bottle of Tempranillo four hours earlier. They knew Nino could be reasoned with and that his boss deserved his fate.

"So, this is what it's come to?" Rommel asked, a tear contrasting his angry eyes. "After all of The Duke's lofty speeches of business, it comes down to this?"

"This is Plan B," Bram said. "I am Plan B. My brother tried to reason with you, tried to corner you, but he failed to do things his way. Now, we do it my way."

"Putang ina mo! Your way? Ang Makina?"

With fury in his eyes, Bram stabbed the panabas into the center of the desk, silencing Rom. It took all of his nerve to keep from slicing the man's throat with a swipe of the sword. "That's right. They call me Ang Makina. Ang Halimaw. Kamao ng Demonyo. I've killed smaller men for smaller reasons, and I must live with that. But here, now, my way spares women and children, yours, ours, anyone not in the game, as Nino tried to tell you. My way helps keep the peace, men earning on both sides. My way avoids war. So, who's the monster here?"

"Men earning on both sides," Rom said. "That's the key, isn't it? I see now, I was wrong about Duque. Forget family, forget wives and sons and daughters, it really is just about money." Rommel's uneasy expression betrayed his defiance.

Bram slid his finger across his phone, played the recording again.

"...hit his family where they work, where they go to school, where they eat breakfast. His old man is in the hospital..."

Bram stopped the playback and tossed his phone on the desk next to the coin mic, the devices taunting his prey.

"I spent ten years inside," Bram said. "I wanted to leave Ang Makina in that desert impiyerno, to never pick up a gun again, to stop sleeping with a knife under my pillow, always looking over my shoulder. But I see now that men like you won't let that happen. You were right about one thing. Normally, by the time someone sees me coming, they're already dead. Sometimes it happens before they even know I'm in the room. Tonight, you would have fallen asleep with that cognac and never woken up, because I normally don't talk to the man I've come to kill, certainly not a man like you. You may think you're the master of this house, but like Bakal, you're just a dog with no loyalty. You demand blood after any slight. You send your sundalos out heavy the moment you sense a loss of control, but now you must control me."

"Is that even possible?" Rommel forced a laugh. "I bet not even The Duke can control Ang Makina. I bet Mr. Genius doesn't even know what you think you're doing here."

"How many ways can a man be wrong in one night?" Bram stared at his host. "You asked me why you and Nino are still alive, but you already know the answer. You still live only because my brother wishes it." He looked at the wall clock again: 8:59. "Out of respect for him, you have one minute to convince me to spare you."

Rommel Basilio knew this could be the end, but he also knew to cower and beg for his life would change nothing, for he heard his own damning words on the recording echo in his mind. All he could do was make his final stand, even if it might be his last words.

"While you were rotting in prison, I built this empire from a rusted warehouse like Calixto's to the biggest operation in the city. We rake more money in a month than The Duke has ever seen in all his precious spreadsheets put together. Mga Hari sa Kalle 9 has earned respect, a legacy connected to every outfit in the state. Ships from the Philippines, trucks from Mexico, leads from cops in our pocket, they keep coming every week, all for HK-9. I made it happen. You kill me, you kill all of that. Unacceptable, as your brother would say."

Bram looked torn, unsure of what Edgardo would want.

Nino looked uncertain, afraid of the outcome whether his boss lived or not.

Rom glanced at his assistant, still firmly in his seat. "Nino? He won't be the boss. He'll be your puppet and everyone will know it. Word will spread like a fire, and that 'desert impiyerno' you fled will catch up to you." He saw the indecision in Bram's eyes. Feeling empowered, he rose to his feet again, standing face-to-face with him. "That brings us to you. Let's be clear, you remain Ang Makina because that's who you are. 'Men like me' didn't chose that life for you. No one did. You chose that path back when you were running night raids for The Demonyo, and you still choose it every day. You call me a dog, but I have no master, while you simply traded Niko Vazquez for Duque. You want me to reconsider his proposal? To keep the cash flowing? To protect women and children? I can do that. I can *choose* that. You see, some men actually can turn around and make the difficult decisions. Now that we're done fluffing our feathers, do we have a deal? You can go back to your brother and tell him that *you* made it happen for a change, and he'll tell you 'good man' which is another way of saying 'good dog,' for isn't that what we all are? Dogs fighting for meat and bones on the street? Yes, we can work together, even if we despise each other. Duque can accept that. I can accept that. Can you?"

Bram looked at the clock on the wall: 9:00.

"I reject your proposal."

He thrust the panabas into Rommel's stomach, grabbing his shoulder to pull him closer as the blade wedged deeper into his gut. To Nino's horror, Bram pulled the blade up Rom's torso, spilling his innards onto the grand desk. The mob boss's lifeless body fell to the floor, his eyes frozen in a pained expression of shock.

After we heard Rommel's new plans for my family, Bram insisted on confronting him. Of all the promises I made, I had to honor my promise that Bram could personally decide our next move. I did what I could at the hangar, tried to reach Rommel with logic and fear, but it clearly wasn't enough.

Charlie Wood and his men secured Rommel's home while Bram went in alone, armed with only a few notes from me. I urged him to reason with Rom but ultimately granted him the final decision, and I swore that I'd uphold it, even if it risked an uprising. After speaking with Nino and the house guards, I realized the risk was minimal. The HK-9 were sick of Rommel's vendettas. Like all criminals, they simply wanted to earn.

Nino watched as Bram released the panabas, keeping the blade firmly in Rommel's chest. When the enforcer turned to him, Nino stood and put on his best businessman face. "What's next?"

Without a word, Bram retrieved his phone from the desk and called someone.

Nino knew who was on the other end of the line.

"Tell him the deal is done," he said. "Tell him HK-9 will honor the agreement."

"Tell him yourself." Bram held out the phone.

Nino steadied his hand and took it, speaking in his usual calm manner. "Mr. Duque?"

"There's another part of the deal we haven't discussed," Edgardo said. "You must take the credit."

Nino knew that "credit" really meant "blame."

"Why me?" he asked, nervous.

"It's not to contain you, to put you in my corner. You must take the credit to keep control of The Nines. It's how Rommel rose to power, and it's how you will now. His wife and sons have disowned him, so no vengeance will follow, and if word ever got out that we took him out, the legacy and respect that he bragged about will vanish. You must keep it within the family."

The legacy and respect that he bragged about.

Nino realized the coin mic was still active, and that The Duke had been listening all along. It explained why Bram dug the mic out from Rom's suit and tossed it onto the desk. "I understand."

"We had to bend our morals to keep the peace," Edgardo said, "and so will you."

"What about the men who were guarding the house?"

"Don't worry about them. You have to trust when I say they're willing to move forward with you."

Despite the exchange of power, Nino still felt trapped. "They didn't have a choice, did they?"

"As my brother told Rommel, we always have a choice."

The insinuation gripped Nino.

"I understand," the young man said.

"Good man."

Edgardo hung up.

"What's next?" Nino asked, returning the phone to Bram. He didn't know what else to say.

"You're the head of the HK-9," Bram said. "In a way, you always were, so you tell me."

Before Nino could think of a response, Bram walked out of the room, leaving him in his new house with his new title, overwhelmed at what was to come.

61

Showtime

"Eddie, I need you in makeup," Divinia said for the fourth time that morning. "Get your butt in the chair."

"I'm cutting onions for bulalo," Edgardo said, "not walking the runway for Miss Universe."

"On TV, everyone wears makeup, women and men, especially men."

Soundstage "D" at Royal Studios in Burbank was still dressed as a country kitchen, and would remain so through the end of the current lease. Whether the Gourmet Travel Network would renew that lease remained to be seen. The crew of *Masarap Divinia* set lights, positioned cameras, ran sound checks, and readied ingredients for their Christmas episode, the all-important episode that the network decided would ultimately decide the show's fate.

When I was growing up, television shows offered 26 episodes per season. Today's shows average between 10 and 12. GTN ordered a mere eight episodes of Divinia's passion project, a sign that they still weren't entirely sold on the idea of a cooking series dedicated to Philippine cuisine and culture. The debut season's ratings, digested and spit out by the network's algorithm, would dictate Divinia's career path. Of course, she handled the pressure like a pro. I wish I could've said the same for myself.

"I don't wear makeup in public," Edgardo said, eyeing the makeup kit awaiting him, a colorful toolbox on the brightly lit vanity. "I fail to see why I should wear it on television."

"When people see you on the street, it's just a passing glance, and most folks are too distracted to even notice you. But when you're on TV, cooking in their living room, they're staring at your face for a half-hour. You need to look your best."

"They'll also be staring at heads of cabbage and plates of raw meat. I think I'll look just fine by comparison."

"See those things?" Divinia asked, pointing to three manned broadcast video cameras. "They're 4K. Know what that means?"

"It means your show is recorded with a horizontal resolution of 3,840 by 2,160, achieving approximately 8.3 million pixels, four times that of Full HD."

"Wrong, genius. It means the pimples and wrinkles on your face will look like volcanos and ravines. That middle camera is for close-ups. Every time you smile, it'll look like lightning streaking across the Amazon delta."

"The Santa hat you're making me wear will cover most of my hideous flaws." He smirked at her, knowing his argument was weak.

"You're not pulling it over your face, Eddie. Just get in the chair."

Episode Eight was slated to broadcast on Christmas Eve, and it was the first time I celebrated that joyous day with Divinia in years. It felt awkward, but right, as if we were meant to be together, with or without our wedding vows intact. Still, I was glad I wasn't alone.

"Just let them touch you up, Tay," Christiana said. "You'll poke someone's eye out with those crow's feet."

"I like to think of them as wisdom lines," Edgardo said with a smile. "Each wrinkle denotes experience and intelligence."

"Damn, then you really are the smartest guy around," Carlo said. He and his sister snickered and fist-bumped as Edgardo relented and sat in the chair.

"Laugh now, boy, but one day you will look like that," Bram said, holding his nephew in a bear hug. "Think of your father as a walking, talking mirror from the future."

"Pakshet."

"Carlo!" Lola Reyna said. "Language!"

"And if you're lucky, later on you'll look like me!" Otto said.

"This is suddenly depressing," the boy said.

Divinia had ambitious plans for the show. She envisioned weekly guests representing the country's best Filipino restaurants, special segments exploring obscure regional dishes and, most of all, episodes with family members learning a recipe along with her and thousands of other members of their "TV family." Early in her career, Divinia's favorite shows featured famous chefs paired with their heirs: Jacques Pépin preparing Coq au Vin with his daughter Jeanette, Rick Bayless making Oaxacan Black Mole with his daughter Lane Ann, Lidia Bastianich preparing Bucatini con Pancetta with her son Joe, and Gordon

Ramsey showcasing his signature Beef Wellington with his daughter Tilly.

Divinia wanted to go a step further by having each member of her clan – from Carlo to Otto to even Bram – don an apron and serve as the day's sous chef. She saw it as a way to stand out in a world where dozens of food shows were on the air 24 hours a day, and countless internet videos were available at the tap of a screen. She imagined folks tuning in not only to learn a recipe, but to also discover the Philippines and meet her loved ones.

While her mentors usually brought their children into their studio kitchens, she wanted to start with her ex-husband, locally famous as the owner of Ang Corazon Lounge. Edgardo reluctantly agreed, seeing his appearance as a one-time deal. He assumed he'd simply stand beside her while she made bulalo, a rustic soup of beef shanks and vegetables, but was startled and surprisingly nervous to find he'd be doing much of the work. Divinia also tasked him with being the audience surrogate, asking questions about the dish's origins as if he weren't already intimately familiar.

Sitting in the makeup chair, being "touched up" with layers of pancake foundation by veteran Linda Patterson, I stared at myself in the brightly lit mirror. I desperately wanted a slug of bourbon, both to calm my nerves and complete the morning mirror ritual I'd conditioned myself to, but I countered my OCD by glancing at my family smiling at me in the reflection. Knowing how important that shoot was to Divinia and knowing that I'd be on TV with her for the first time, everyone was there for support, even my mother, whose relationship with my ex broke new ground after The Nines' assault. Her constant need for attention was met with a warm welcome by Divinia's well-informed crew. "Div talks about your cooking all the time!" It also helped my mother to know that she'd be a special guest soon enough.

"Don't be scared, Doy," Reyna said. "Divinia will be in charge. You'll be fine."

"Strangely enough, Nay, everyone telling me I'll be fine is what's putting me on edge. You all talk as if I were walking into a storm."

"What's the worst that can happen?" Carlo asked. "Public humiliation? It'll be fine. Hey, remember that time we made halo-halo and you forgot to put the cover on the blender and..."

"See, this is what I'm talking about. No more 'fines,' please."

Cameras were minutes away from rolling, and I wanted to do my best for them, for Divinia's success would be theirs as well, far more than my shadowy empire ever could.

It had been three months since the death of the TSB and the restructuring of the HK-9. C.B.'s cover story held, Nino's appointment as head of his family transitioned without incident, and Mr. Waldo awoke from his coma, just as Melinda had predicted, astonished at the change in landscape that occurred while he slumbered.

Fish walked the set with a clipboard in hand, checking in with Camera and Sound. In addition to now being a co-producer, he unofficially served as the First Assistant Director, something the actual A.D. had to contend with.

"Almost ready to roll," Fish said as he approached the group encircling Edgardo in his makeup chair. He looked up at his friend's reflection. "Looking good, Ed, 20 years younger already."

"Thanks, Fish, I guess."

"You look nervous. Don't be nervous. You'll be fine."

"Another 'fine.' Et tu, Fish?"

"Don't make him look too good, Linda. Folks won't recognize him."

Neither Divinia nor I knew that Chris reached out to Fish to help hammer out the retooling of the show. True to his word, he kept things quiet as he spoke with my wife's manager. Fish may be small in stature, but he has a way of taking over a room, including the ominous boardroom at GTN. It must have been the Holy Grail of PowerPoints.

Shortly after his phone call with Christiana, Fish arranged a meeting at Gold Award Media Entertainment to propose a new style of cooking show that doubled as a travelogue of the Philippines. He bombarded Gary Goldsmit with charts and graphs that illustrated the untapped Filipino-American audience eager for representation. He promised steady ratings and awards of excellence for G.A.M.E., a company that would be known for embracing its diverse viewers. He listed Divinia's mentors – French, Italian, Mexican, and British – and pointed out how they each brought their heritage to American mainstream television, something no Filipino chef had yet achieved. Fish ended his pitch by saying Divinia Duque was ready for the global spotlight. The only question was, were they?

"I just got word from the board," Fish said. "So far, they like what they see, and they're ready to greenlight a second season."

"Don't make bold promises yet," Divinia said. "Let's just focus on today."

"It's never too early to map out Season Two. We got Ed now. Next will be Reyna, then Chris, then Bram..."

"Pakshet," Bram said.

"Don't worry, I'll give you an easy one," Divinia said. "Even kids can wrap lumpia."

"Bram's not worried about the cooking," Edgardo said. "He can run a kitchen like a pro. He's just nervous about looking as good as me."

"I hate cameras, Bata," Bram said.

"Agreed."

"But Tito, you had cameras on you for ten years," Carlo said with a sly grin.

"Too soon, my Mahal Caloy. When you're up to bat, I'll be sure to crack jokes about *your* time inside."

The set's actual First A.D. waved his hand from across the set, signaling that they were ready to roll. Fish nodded to him.

"Showtime," he said. "Button him up, Linda. He's ready for his closeup."

"Knock 'em dead, kid," Otto said.

"No good luck for Divinia?" Edgardo asked.

"Nah, Div's a seasoned professional. You're the train wreck waiting to happen! But don't worry, son, you'll be fine."

"Ah, there it is again."

"Remember to smile," Chris said, "but not too much or your pancake will split like a busted plate."

"You're telling Edgardo Duque *not* to smile?" Carlo said.

"You guys are doing wonders for my confidence."

Wearing elf and Santa hats respectively, Divinia and Edgardo stood at their marks behind an island counter, complete with stovetop, pan, sink, and bowls of beef shanks, corn, and root vegetables. First Camera nodded to the First A.D. He announced "rolling," Sound announced "speed," and Second Assistant Camera held the slate in front of the hosts.

"Magandang umaga!" Divinia said, starting the morning show. "Maligayang pasko! Merry Christmas! I've been looking forward to today for three reasons: beef shanks, ox tail, and my husband, Edgardo, are here! Are we ready to cook?" She looked at him, his hands pressed firmly to the counter.

Husband, Edgardo noted.

"It feels good to take third billing behind shanks and ox tail," he said with a laugh.

"These shanks aren't just any cuts of meat. These were the underrated, unsung heroes of many dinners when I was growing up in Cebu, and after today, they'll be the stars of your table, too."

As the episode progressed, with Edgardo's ex-wife beside him and their family watching from behind the cameras, it felt like the beginning of not just a new chapter, but an entirely new story for them all, and it compelled him to revise his early journal entry to better document The Duke's journey. Unlike Felix, who wanted to forever remain invisible, Edgardo wanted his tale told one day, detailing his circular path – from family man to feared criminal to something in between – if only to the few who would hear it.

After the taping, he sat alone in his dressing room with a pen and notepad. He didn't know exactly where to start his rewrite, but perhaps narrating his life choices so far, with the new perspective he'd recently gained, would help guide him onward to the end of his story.

My name is Edgardo Rigo Duque. I started this journal not to scribble down my life as a Filipino-American, business owner, reformed father, or repentant husband, but to chronicle my work as "The Duke." I made connections, brokered deals, and took my cut, only to be forced into decisions that swallowed my world, my wife, and my children. I regret their involvement, the forced entry of the undercover feds, and my new role-play as their criminal mastermind informant. But regret is a useless emotion. I just have to come to terms with the new job description.

I know now that "All business all the time" is a terrible mantra to live by, especially when balancing my love for family with my work for jealous psychopaths and violent megalomaniacs, but it's the path I'm on for now. It's the path we're all on, for better or worse. More than ever, I must think of those who depend on me, for I can no longer live in the shadow of the man I once was. I must reclaim my life and everyone in it.

Men like Bram and I don't die in bed at a ripe old age, though we'll certainly try. We raise our loved ones, stake our claims, swipe our fortunes, and fade into history.

Unacceptable. I'll take my cut of history, too.

About the Author

Lynn Harrod is an award-winning writer, artist, filmmaker, and educator with over 30 years of experience crafting shorts, essays, and screenplays. His characters often find their worlds spun sideways by a startling revelation.

Lynn was awarded the PRSA Image Award of Excellence and has placed in the Quarterfinals and Semifinals of the Nicholl Fellowship, the Finals of the Nevada Film Office Competition, the Semifinals of the Writers' Network Competition, and twice in the Semifinals of the FadeIn Awards.

Born in Texas, raised in California's San Joaquin Valley, educated and trained in Hollywood, Lynn is a writer and partner with Only Human Productions, where several of his works are in development. When he's not spending time with his wife and daughter, or writing all night on his patio, he's usually having a pint with friends.

www.ingramcontent.com/pod-product-compliance
Lightning Source LLC
Chambersburg PA
CBHW021834010726
47493CB00005B/1396